A Great Kisser

A Great Kisser

DONNA KAUFFMAN

BRAVA

KENSINGTON PUBLISHING CORP.

www.kensingtonbooks.com

BRAVA BOOKS are published by

Kensington Publishing Corp.
119 West 40th Street
New York, NY 10018

All Kensington titles, imprints, and distributed lines are available at special quantity discounts for bulk purchases for sales promotion, premiums, fund-raising, educational, or institutional use.

Special book excerpts or customized printings can also be created to fit specific needs. For details, write or phone the office of the Kensington Special Sales Manager: Kensington Publishing Corp., 119 West 40th Street, New York, NY 10018. Attn. Special Sales Department. Phone: 1-800-221-2647.

ISBN-13: 978-0-7582-3131-4
ISBN-10: 0-7582-3131-8

First Kensington Trade Paperback Printing: November 2009

10 9 8 7 6 5 4 3 2 1

Printed in the United States of America

For Rhonda
My life is better for having you in it.

And a special thanks to Debbie & Jean, the and rest of the Magnificent Minions, Refugees, and New Regulars for making this past year such a fantastic new beginning for me. I couldn't have done it without each and every one of you.

Chapter 1

Jake McKenna was good at fixing planes. Not people. It was easier to rebuild a P-51 Mustang that hadn't been in the air since World War II than it was to endure a single phone call from his baby sister.

Ruby Jean could be an absolute doll—with other people. She didn't confide in other people. She didn't call every other day and cry her heart out with other people. Because somehow, she'd gotten it into her head that the only one who could solve her problems—and he'd never met a person who thought they had so many problems—was her big brother.

"Don't—" he cautioned. But it was too late. "Cry," he added, uselessly. "Ruby Jean, it's not your problem." It rarely was. Ruby Jean made a habit of taking the whole world on her tiny shoulders. Whether the world wanted to be there or not.

"But that's just it, Jake. It *is* my problem!"

"How is entertaining your boss's new stepdaughter suddenly your job? You're his personal assistant, not a cruise director."

"You don't understand, Jake."

And that was Jake's problem. He rarely understood anything where his little sister was concerned. Or, for that matter, women in general. Which was why, at the ripe old age of thirty-three, he was a happy, well-adjusted bachelor. "I'm sure you'll explain it to me." He wiped the sleeve of his ragged sweatshirt across his face, heedless of the grease smear now decorating both sweatshirt and skin, and sat on the overturned oil drum. He stared at the regulator that two straight days of work hadn't come close to fixing, and half listened to everything he never wanted to know about Ruby Jean's crisis du jour, which he had no intention of fixing.

"So, that's why it's so important that you do this. I finally have some room for advancement, Jake, and you know in this town that's not a small thing. I can't let this one little thing screw up my chances."

Personally, Jake didn't see where working for Arlen Thompson, even if he was the mayor of the mountain resort town of Cedar Springs, was a job worth holding on to. He thought the man was a bit of an egocentric who took full advantage of anyone who might help him and not require his help in return, and Jake's softhearted sister, who worked like a dog as his personal assistant, was near the top of that list.

But there wasn't a great deal of commerce in Cedar Springs, Colorado, that wasn't directly related to the ski resort, which was, more or less, the reason for the town's continued existence at this point in its long history. But Ruby Jean didn't ski anymore. Nor, thanks to Swing Thatcher, now the head of the resort ski school and the bastard who broke Ruby Jean's tender heart when they were both in high school, did she want anything to do with anyone who did.

Jake had encouraged her to take her dreams east, at least as far as the front range, and find a job in Denver or one of the suburb cities, where she could build the kind of future she desired. But Ruby Jean was all about family sticking close, and as they were the only family each other had, he supposed he was stuck with her and the drama that accompanied her. Not that he minded. Usually. He loved his sister and would defend her to the death to anyone else. But Jake had no intention of leaving Cedar Springs. He loved the central Rockies. Being surrounded by their snowy peaks did his heart and soul good. If Ruby Jean wanted to be within wailing distance, that was up to her.

Then she was sniffling, and the sniffling was threatening to turn into a full-blown sob, and his attention was pulled back to the drama.

"Just say yes, okay, Jake? I'm only asking for you to show her around a little. That's all."

"Wait, what did you just say? You want me to what?"

There was a long, wavery sigh. "You never listen to anything I say."

He couldn't really argue with her there. "RJ, you know I have a race to prepare for and *Betty Sue* here needs a hell of a lot of work."

"As she always does. I'm just asking one tiny favor."

"The difference is, now I have willing sponsors chomping at the bit, but they're demanding some kind of proof that we have a chance to really compete or they're taking their money elsewhere. And I have to keep the flying school going, or what's left of the roof over my head also goes. So, I really don't have time to do . . . whatever it was you just asked me to do."

"Her name is Lauren Matthews. She's your age."

"Wow, that old, huh?" The way Ruby Jean had said it made the woman sound positively prehistoric. But then, given RJ was eight years younger than him, anyone over thirty was ancient to her anyway.

Ruby Jean sniffled. "I'm just saying you might even have something in common. You could even like each other."

"Don't. I have enough problems at the moment. No matchmaking."

"I'm not, really. I know I promised to stop that, and I have. This really isn't that at all. According to Mayor Thompson, she's a bit of a workaholic—she works on Capitol Hill for a senator, which is so exciting I think, but doesn't leave her with much of a social life. She completely hates the idea that the mayor has married her mother, because, you know, they eloped after barely meeting and all. So, now she's finally coming out here to check him out, and he's all freaked out that he needs to make this great impression on her, probably because of his own political aspirations, and being as he's the mayor, he wants her to see how great Cedar Springs is, and—"

"Okay, okay, take a breath. What political aspirations? He's been mayor forever."

"Oh crap, I wasn't supposed to—just forget I said anything."

Jake was perfectly willing to do that. "I don't want to know."

"So, you'll help me then?"

Jake swore under his breath. "What am I supposed to do? I'm not the mayor's idea of a town ambassador. I can't believe this is his idea."

"Well . . ."

"RJ?" he said, a note of warning in his tone.

"See, there's this other thing that he sort of mentioned, that made me think of you and . . ." She trailed off. And sniffled a little more.

"Ruby Jean McKenna, what have you done now?"

"Don't get mad, okay?"

"Oh, I'm sure I will, just as I'm sure you'll cry huge crocodile tears, and then I'll feel like a schmuck, and then we'll make up because I hate you being mad and sad and upset, and I'll do whatever you ask me to, then you'll do it all over again."

"Good," she said, sounding amazingly better. "Then why don't we just skip over that part and you can just agree to do this one teensy little thing without giving me a hard time."

"Which brings me back to why me? Arlen is not my biggest fan—"

"Because you wouldn't fly that banner for him when he was running for re-election."

"I run a business. I'm bipartisan."

"He was going to pay you."

"So do my students, and I'm not pissing half of them and their families off by flying a banner for one side or the other. Besides, that was two years ago and he managed to get re-elected anyway. As he always does. No one really runs against him, Ruby."

"Well, here's your chance to make it up to him."

Jake clamped his jaw and fought the urge to yell. Or beat the wrench in his hand repeatedly against his forehead. One would have done about as much good as the other. "I don't have anything to make up for. Other than the fact that he's your boss, Arlen Thompson can kiss my ass."

Ruby Jean sighed. "Can we get back to my problem then?"

"Sure."

"Okay, and, remember you promised about not getting mad. So," she hurried on when he just growled, ". . . according to the mayor, he thinks Lauren is just so career driven that she's a little uptight, which is why he thinks she doesn't understand about the whirlwind courtship and elopement between him and her mom. He thinks if she gets out here and, you know, relaxes a little, and finds out how good it can be when you're not working every single minute of the day, that—"

"I get it, I get it. Thompson thinks she's a repressed manhater who needs to get laid so she'll ease up on judging him for having sex with her mother. At least he married her. And did it ever occur to anyone that his stepdaughter might like what she does for a living and is perfectly happy dedicating her life to the pursuit of the happiness it brings her? And did anyone stop to consider that maybe her opinion of Arlen Thompson is right up there with my opinion of the man? And I'm not the least repressed, nor do I need to get laid, which brings me to my other point—"

"Jake, just listen a moment—"

"No, you listen, RJ. I love you, and I love that you like your job and want to stick with it. I'm proud of you, I am, and really happy that you seem to have found your niche. I think Thompson totally takes advantage of you, but you are good at what you do and I support that. But not only am I not the town ambassador, I am definitely not the town gigolo."

"But, you're single, and her age, and I've seen a picture of her and she's not even that bad looking. If you ignore the black-framed glasses. You don't have to, you know, sleep with her, I didn't promise that, I just—"

"You *promised*? What, exactly, did you promise?"

"Well, maybe promise is too strong a word." She rushed on. "I just sort of said that you might be willing to, you know, show her a good time. I didn't elaborate. And the mayor didn't ask me to. But it might be that he kind of has the impression that I meant you'd, you know, take her out. She just needs to understand a little more about romance and—"

"I am not romancing the mayor's stepdaughter. I like his wife. Charlene seems like a very nice woman. I haven't a clue what she sees in Arlen, but she appears to be an upbeat, positive woman, and if that can have any impact on him, then all's the better. But I have no intention—"

"If you like Charlene, then you'll probably like her daughter, right? Just . . . do this for me, will you, Jake? My job is important and this is so important to the mayor that if I can pull this off, I know he'll keep me on staff when he runs for—" She broke off abruptly. Very abruptly.

"When he . . . runs for what, RJ? Is that what this is really about? These 'aspirations'? Does Arlen have plans to try and move to the big pond of state politics? And maybe he could care less what his stepdaughter thinks of him, except that she has contacts in D.C. that might help? Because that sounds a hell of a lot more like the man I know than a guy who just wants his stepdaughter to like him."

"I don't know that. Really, I don't. I only know he wants to make a good impression and it's very important to him. And Charlene is a nervous wreck and I think it's affecting their marriage. Apparently Lauren hasn't spoken to her since shortly after she found out they eloped. That was six months ago now. Just . . . help us all out. Okay? One date, Jake. That's all I'm asking. Just . . . make it a really good one. Okay?"

Jake sighed. Then he swore. "I don't want to get tangled up in this."

"One date is not tangling. It's just a date."

"With your boss's politically connected stepdaughter."

"You can be charming. I know you. Just . . . do something fun."

He sighed again. And swore again. "Daytime date. I'll take her up for a ride. Show her the sights from twelve thousand feet, and make the town and surrounding area look good, which won't be hard because it's the most beautiful place on earth. But I'm not going to preach any propaganda about our esteemed mayor. And I'm not romancing her. Cedar Springs can romance her, but I'm out of this after the plane ride."

Ruby Jean sniffled a little, but when he didn't say anything else, she finally dried up and said, "Okay. That sounds like fun. Make it really fun, though, okay? And don't bash the mayor."

"I'm fine with letting her draw her own conclusions. Deal?"

"Deal," Ruby Jean said, not sounding entirely confident but being smart enough, for once, not to push him further.

"I really need to get back to work. What day is she arriving? How long will she be here?"

"Um . . . twelve thirty."

"Twelve—you mean December thirtieth? It's August, Ruby—"

"I mean twelve thirty, as in her plane lands out in Holden then, and I was kind of hoping you could go pick her up. In one of your planes. Because that's way more impressive then just having her rent a car."

"What might be impressive is her mom and stepdad driving out to Holden to greet her personally."

"They can't. They have that Chamber of Commerce luncheon thing that Charlene is sponsoring for that charity she started, and the mayor is the keynote speaker. So, having you there, to pick her up in a private plane, that's perfect. But that can't be your date! It's not far enough. A thirty-minute hop doesn't count. She needs a bit more . . . time. Okay?"

Jake looked at the clock on the wall. It was ten thirty.

"I love you, Jake. You're the bestest brother in all the world. Thank you a million times over for helping me with this. I owe you so much. And I will make it up to you. Promise. Kisses!" And then she hung up.

Which was a good thing. That way his eardrums were the only ones assaulted by the loud clanging of metal on metal when he threw the wrench and let it bounce off the curved wall of the hangar. "It's a good thing I love you, too," he muttered, then rolled his tool chest closer and turned his attention back to the automatic manifold pressure regulator, which was, up until five seconds ago, the biggest pain in his ass. Now there was competition for that honor. But he didn't have to think about Lauren whatsername for another two hours. And he didn't plan to.

Chapter 2

Lauren Matthews was going to die. Her life was going to end in this tiny little gum-wrapper-size plane, which, given the way it was bouncing around in the air like a Ping Pong ball, was surely going to drop from the sky any second now and burst into flames as it crashed into the side of the nearest mountain peak. Of which there were thousands, so the chance of missing one and miraculously surviving was slim to none.

"Sorry for the turbulence," the senior pilot called back. "Storm coming, but we'll beat it in. Not to worry."

She knew how he'd gotten every one of his gray hairs, too. And did he announce his reassuring tidbits over the intercom? No. He just called out the information over his shoulder. Because she was less than ten feet away. And she was at the back of the plane. In fact, she was the only passenger filling one of the ten available seats. "Not much call for trips past the front range during this time of year," he'd told her when she'd boarded the tiny piece of tin back in Denver. After she'd disembarked off of the very nice, very large, very steady jumbo jet that, once she'd finally made it out to Dulles and found a place to park and made it all the way in to the terminal, then out to the other terminal, had delivered her quite smoothly all the way, nonstop from Washington to Colorado. A pleasant flight. She'd actually gotten some reading in. Now, with less than thirty minutes left in her daylong journey, she was going to die. Figured.

Sure, the pilot had gone on to say that he made the trip west several times a day during peak season. Which translated to ski season, since, other than mining or ranching, that was all they did in the middle of Colorado as far as she could tell. And she assumed the miners and ranchers didn't need to fly anywhere all that often. But with the plane bouncing around like some massive cosmic cat was using it as its personal play toy, batting it this way and that, she wasn't all that reassured by his past success rate.

"How mu-much longer?" she asked, her teeth clacking together as the plane dropped into another air pocket. She had to raise her voice to be heard over the engines. Had she mentioned the engines? The incredibly loud engines?

"We're descending now."

"Just what I was afraid of," she muttered, but looked out the window anyway. Might as well see where she was going to spend her eternal rest. But there was cloud cover now. Thick, dark, gray-black clouds. Swirling all around them. That couldn't be good.

"Ho-how do you know where to la-land?" she called out, fingers digging even more deeply into the already deep indentations on the armrests as they bounce-bounce-bounced along. "How can y-you see?"

"Radar. Don't worry," he said, tossing a quick smile over his shoulder. "I've landed in worse. Much worse." He seemed almost happy about the challenge.

Great, she had the crazy pilot with a death wish. She wasn't entirely sure she wanted to know what "much worse" could consist of, given that, at the moment, her teeth felt like they were cracking from constant impact. A mouth piece would have come in handy, but who knew flying had become a full contact sport?

Just then the plane dropped, then dipped to one side then the other, causing her to rap her head against the window. She added helmet to her new list of must-have carry-on items. "How much longer?"

But the pilot didn't respond. He was too busy flipping switches and talking on his headset to someone on the ground, trying to land the plane. Which should have instilled all kinds of confidence but fell way short.

She was debating on whether to keep her eyes open or shut, when the pilot called back, "Hang on, we're coming in."

"Hang on? To *what?*"

That question was answered a moment later when the wheels touched down, then bounced up, then touched down, then bounced again, jerking her body around like a rag doll strapped to a roller coaster. She grabbed the seat back in front of her with one hand, braced her feet against the bottom of it, gripped the armrest with her other hand, and held on for dear life. Which, in this instance, was not simply a cliché. The plane bounced and jerked for a few hundred more years, then finally stayed on the ground and eventually rolled to a stop.

She wanted to first kiss the pilot, then the ground, but couldn't seem to pry her cold, stiff fingers from the seat and armrest to do anything but stare dazedly and give a silent and quite fervent prayer of thanks.

"Sorry for the rough commute. It's that time of year." He slid a compact umbrella out of a side pocket and handed it back to her. "Here, you'll want this. It's a bit fierce out there."

Now that the droning engine noise had subsided, and her ears had stopped ringing, she identified the new noise she was hearing. It sounded like thunder, but was just the heavy drumming of rain on the body of the airplane. "What are you going to use?"

"I'm fine. Hope you enjoy your stay in Colorado." The pilot grinned and sketched a quick salute as she took the umbrella and gathered her things.

"They'll have your bag in the terminal shortly," he said, shifting to stand long enough to open the mechanism that opened the door, which lowered into its own staircase.

"Okay," she said, rising on shaky legs. "Thanks."

He lifted a hand in a quick wave, then seated himself once again in the cockpit and turned back to his wide panel of instruments. A few seconds later, he was back on the radio checking flight plans, it sounded like. Just another day at the office for him.

Lauren hefted her laptop bag and purse strap over her shoulder, then positioned herself so she could open the umbrella outside the door. The wind almost yanked it from her hands, but she grabbed tightly at the last second, barely keeping herself from making a Mary Poppins exit, smack onto the tarmac. Carefully, she exited down the stairs and headed toward the small building that, she assumed, was the terminal.

It was raining so hard, with the wind whipping even harder, that she didn't even attempt to take a look at her surroundings. Not that she could have seen much anyway, but she'd been looking forward to seeing the Rocky Mountains. All she could do, however, was focus on the wide rivers of water cascading across the paved tarmac as she skipped and hopped her way to the double set of glass doors.

Just as she went to reach for them they swung open for her, and a large male hand snaked out and gripped her elbow. The action startled her into loosening her grip on the umbrella, which was immediately snatched away by the wind and went flying back over her head toward the tarmac. She turned instinctively to see where it went only to get hit with a full swath of rain, which immediately plastered her hair to her head and her clothes to her body, along with fogging up her glasses. She was, for all intents and purposes, blind. She'd never considered herself much of a screamer or a squealer, but she might have done a little of both.

The man holding her elbow tugged her in out of the rain.

"Thank you," she gasped. "I'm so sorry—my umbrella—"

"Marco picked it up," came a very deep voice with a bit of a rough edge to it, like maybe he'd just woken up.

She was still blinking water out of her eyes and he still had a hold on her elbow. Her other hand was clutching her purse and laptop bag to her side in a death grip. Everything was just a blur. "Marco?"

"Ground crew. Here, let me take those."

Her elbow was abruptly released, which sent her a bit off balance, then her bags were suddenly lifted from her shoulder and slipped out of her death grip as if her hands were made from putty, sending her staggering a step in the other direction. Both her feet slipped a little as the smooth soles of her shoes were not made for . . . well, any of this. And then his hands were on her again, both elbows this time, and, and . . . well, the entire last sixty seconds had been so discombobulating, for a person who was never discombobulated, that she didn't know quite what to do. She blinked at him through wet ropes of hair and fogged glasses, arms still akimbo as he wrestled her to a balanced position.

"Bad day?"

It was the dry amusement lacing his tone that gave her the focus she so mercifully needed. She tugged her elbows from his grip, as if all this was suddenly very much his fault, but instead of being the liberating, independence-returning move she was so desperately seeking, the action only served to send her wheeling backward. Which resulted in being caught, once again, even more humiliatingly than before, by his very big, very strong, and very steadying hands.

"Thank you," she managed through gritted teeth. She carefully removed one elbow from his grip, not chancing leaving his steadying powers all at once, and scraped her hair from her forehead and removed her fogged glasses from her face. Finally able to see, she looked up . . . only to be thrown completely off balance all over again. But, this time, her feet were totally flat and stable, on hard, steady ground. "You can let me go now," she managed in a choked whisper.

He was just above average height, probably not even six feet, but given she topped the height chart at five-foot-six, and that was in three-inch heels, he was very tall to her. But it wasn't the height part that commanded the attention. Nor was it really the square jaw, the thick neck, broad shoulders, very nicely muscled arms and chest that were obvious even through the old sweat-shirt and T-shirt he wore. The thick, sun-bleached brown hair might have been a teensy part of it, but mostly it was the piercing blue eyes—truly, they pierced—staring at her from his weathered, deeply tanned face.

Crinkles fanned from the corners of those eyes, and there were grooves bracketing either side of his mouth, but she didn't know if that was from squinting into the sun or smiling a lot. He wasn't smiling now, so it was hard to tell. But he was still holding on to her, and it was that, plus those look-right-through-you eyes, that were keeping her from reclaiming the rest of her much-needed balance.

"I'm—fine. Really. Thank you. Again."

He held her gaze for another seemingly endless moment, then gently let her go. "No worries."

"I, uh, need to rent a car." She was normally calm and cool under fire. It was why Todd had been so impressed and pro-moted her up the ranks of his campaign staff so quickly. It was also why she'd been one of the first ones the senator had hired to his permanent staff when he'd won his bid for office. If he could see her now, he wouldn't even recognize her. She didn't recognize her. Of course, the fact that she probably looked like a drowned cat didn't help matters. "If you could just point me in the right direction—" *I will slink off and pretend we never met.*

"You don't need a car."

She looked up at him again, and though she'd never particu-larly thought of herself as vain, she'd have given large sums for the use of a comb, a tissue, and a handheld mirror. Okay, so a full salon makeover probably wouldn't have hurt at that mo-ment, but her pride wouldn't have minded at least a brief at-tempt at restoration. "Where I'm headed is about two and a half hours from here, and though it's probably not all that far-fetched to think they probably rent horses here, I'm thinking the locals, not to mention the horse, will be a lot safer if I get a nice SUV instead."

His lips quirked a little then, and her pulse actually did this zippy jumpy thing. And it felt kind of good—in a somewhat startling, disconcerting kind of way. However—reality check—she hadn't forgotten that her appearance was highly unlikely to provoke the same reaction in him. Besides, she was not here on vacation. She was here on a very serious mission that had absolutely nothing to do with having a vacation fling of any kind. Not that she was the fling type. Or that men ever flung themselves at her, vacation or otherwise, for her to know. But, still.

"Given the weather, it would probably be as uncomfortable for the horse, but that's not why I said you don't need a ride. You don't need one, because I'm your ride."

God help her, she looked him up and down before she could stop herself. *He* was her ride? If only. She jerked her gaze back to his, thankful to find it just as unreadable as before. "I—I don't know what you mean. Who would send—" She broke off abruptly. Her mother, that's who. Her mother, who, as of six months ago, had turned into a complete and total stranger, running off with a man she'd barely met, moving her entire life across country to the middle of absolute nowhere, all because of some supposed fairy-tale romance Lauren suspected was anything but.

The mother she'd had six months ago would have never dreamed of interfering in her daughter's personal life. Talk about it? Yes. Encourage her to get out and date more? Or at all? All the time. But actually fix her up? No. But her mother today? Lauren had no idea what she might do. Or what her motives might be. Whatever the case, Lauren wasn't having any part of it. "Please tell my mother that I appreciate her concern, but that I'd be more comfortable with my own transportation. I'm sorry if you've wasted your time, truly, I am. And if it's a matter of getting paid, I'll take care of the tab. But, your services won't be needed." *More's the pity.* She tried really hard not to look him over. One last time.

His lips quirked again, as if they shared a private joke. And her pulse did that dippy, slow-down-speed-up thing. Which made no sense since she was pretty sure the joke was her.

"There's no tab. I'm here as a favor."

"Oh. Well . . . I really am sorry you went out of your way. Let me at least pay for your gas."

His smile quirked again. "That won't be necessary."

"Okay, then. If you're sure. Thank you again for your trouble." She picked up her bags from the short row of airport chairs he'd dropped them into and slung them again over her arm. He was still standing there, staring. "Did you . . . need anything else?"

"Well, to be honest, I'd appreciate a ride back to Cedar Springs."

"I beg your pardon?"

"If you wouldn't mind. I'll even drive, if you'd like to get some rest."

She was confused. "I thought you were supposed to drive me back. Why do you need a lift in my car?"

"I flew."

"You . . ." She turned and looked back out through the doors to the small, single runway, then back to him. "You're a pilot?"

He nodded.

She thought about his quirky smile . . . and her offer to pay for his gas. Good thing he hadn't taken her up on that!

"But unless we want to wait out this storm, which isn't supposed to move out until sometime tomorrow, then the best alternative is to drive." His eyes danced a little, crinkling the skin at the corners. "I seem to have left my horse at home." Then he did smile. "He hates to fly."

She laughed before catching herself. "After today, I have to admit, I'm not much of a fan, either."

"You don't like flying?"

"Oh, flying is fine. But being tossed around like your plane is being used as the central piece in a cosmic game of foosball? That I'm not so fond of."

"Ah." He shifted his weight and the penetrating stare was back. "I'm almost afraid to ask, but what, exactly, is foosball?"

"You've never played—seriously?"

"Seriously." And he said it so . . . seriously, it made her laugh again.

"You know, I'm not sure I could explain it. You'll have to look it up sometime."

"I'll do that."

And she suddenly felt foolish again. "Right. So . . . which way to the rental counter?"

He nodded his head toward the one and only counter in the small building. "It's pretty much one-stop shopping here."

"Right." Was she ever going to look less than a complete idiot around this man? And now she was stuck with him, in the close confines of a car for at least a couple of hours, maybe longer given the weather. But what could she do? He'd come all this way as a favor, presumably to her mother or the mayor, and had his offer to escort her rejected—despite the fact that he, apparently, couldn't have escorted her anyway given the raging storm. Still, she could hardly say no to this, too. "How were you planning on getting me to Cedar Springs?"

"My plan was to fly you, but the storm came in faster than predicted. I thought we'd be back before it blew in."

"So . . . we were going to wait it out?"

"I thought it best to let you know I was here, then we'd figure it out from there."

She'd been on the outs with her mother for months now, which was both painful and frustrating as hell, given how close they'd been B.A.—Before Arlen. And if she was being stubborn there, she felt it was well earned. But that was no excuse to take it out on her chauffeur here. He was being a Good Samaritan, doing a favor. Even if, from what she'd determined about their mayor was true, she could have told him he was likely just being used.

"So, we're renting a car anyway. Why didn't you just say so?"

"Because we're not. Wait here," he said.

"I'm perfectly capable of—"

But he'd already taken off. However, instead of going to the counter, he'd headed toward the doors leading back to the tarmac. "Don't rent anything," he called back, then he disappeared through the doors, and though her shortsightedness kept her from seeing clearly, she could make out him ducking down and running over to the big dome-shaped airplane hangar.

She looked at the row of seats and thought about collapsing into one of them—how nice it would be to sit in something that remained steady—but opted for a trip to the bathroom instead. Vanity might not be a driving force in her life, but she was human enough, woman enough, to at least feel the need to assess the severity of the damage and mitigate it as best as possible. After all, it was precisely because she was good at doing exactly those things that she got paid a rather handsome salary. Or had. Surely, if she could avert media probes and spin-doctor live interview slip-ups for her boss, she could do basic repair to her appearance.

One step into the small bathroom and a peek into the mirror after sliding her carefully wiped glasses back on proved that even she might not be up to this particular task. "Wow." Up until three days ago, she had been slated to appear at a charity fund-raiser in October on Halloween. And to think she'd been worried about what she'd wear as a costume. "Zombie, risen from the dead. And—bonus!—you don't even need a rental costume." It was almost a shame she wouldn't be going now.

She turned on the water out of habit, but really, it would take a team of Georgetown's finest hairdressers-to-the-Hill to even make a dent in the mess. She ran a paper towel under the stream anyway and did her best to remove the raccoon-eye mascara streaks. There was nothing she could do about the freckle exposure because her foundation was completely gone. She'd been covering them for years. Once she learned that it was hard enough to be taken seriously as a woman, harder still as a very short woman—especially when she was actually built like one—she'd quickly figured out that looking like the "all American girl next door" only further undermined whatever advantages she might have had left. Katie Couric might be able to pull it off, but not so much with Lauren Matthews as it turned out.

Using a comb from her purse, she managed to make her hair go from drowned cat to merely wet and stringy. "Why am I bothering?" After all, given that neither her mother nor her mother's spouse could be bothered to come to the airport to pick her up, who she was trying to impress, she had no idea.

A vision of the sun-streaked, blue-eyed Marlboro man waiting for her in the airport lobby swam through her mind. Except, he'd already seen her at her Halloween worst, so no point in even going there.

Sighing, she packed up her comb, straightened her damp jacket and slacks as best she could, and marched out of the bathroom, shoulders squared, chin high. Just because she looked like Rocky Mountain roadkill was no reason to act embarrassed.

"Feel better?"

She about half jumped out of her skin as she whirled around to find Rugged Outdoorsman Guy leaning against the wall beside the bathroom door.

She smiled ruefully, and just owned her fate. "As I'm sure you can see, nothing short of a guest appearance on Extreme Makeover is going to improve things much. I'll feel better when I get to Cedar Springs and check into the first room that has a nice, hot shower."

She could have sworn the pupils in his eyes flared a little bit, and her pulse fluttered accordingly. It was probably a trick of the light.

"Your chariot awaits," he said. He swept his hand toward the doors on the opposite side of the terminal from where she'd entered.

All she saw was an aging pickup truck sporting more rust than paint. She craned her neck a little, but . . . that was it. "The . . . truck? You rented that?" She knew she was in the middle of nowhere, but she'd traveled a lot, and even in third world countries, she'd scored better conveyances than that. And it wasn't like she needed anything fancy. But something that wasn't held together with carbon particles a breath away from disintegrating to soot would be a start. She turned back to him with what she hoped was an optimistic smile on her face. "Why don't you let me talk to the rental agent, see what I can do?"

"It's not a rental. Loaner." When she looked confused, he added, "Friend of mine. Works on planes out here."

"Ah." She glanced at it once again. "What about your plane? Won't you be stuck having to drive that all the way back here?" At the risk of insulting him further, she pasted the smile on her face again as she looked back at him. "I hate to put your friend out. I really don't mind paying for a rental." Her gaze went back to the truck, which she feared might not survive the assault of the rain pounding down on it, much less any actual driving. "Besides, I'll need a car once I'm in town."

"I'll be out here again in a few days anyway, so there's no problem. And I'm sure Charlene won't mind you borrowing her car when you need it while you're in town."

Her expression smoothed. "You're a good friend of my mother's?"

"I wouldn't say that, but it's a small town. We know each other. She seems like a nice woman. I like her." He held up his hand to stall her. "I don't want to get in the middle of any family stuff. I'm just here—"

"—doing a favor, I know. And I do appreciate it, I do," she said quite sincerely. "I had already been informed they wouldn't be able to pick me up." She'd gotten an e-mail from Arlen's secretary, in fact, with news of the luncheon and keynote speech.

Of course, regrets had been expressed. Via the secretary. Delivered from his office-of-the-mayor e-mail address. Any contact she'd had was always so . . . official, where Arlen was concerned.

Okay, so the description she'd used at the time was pompous and self-important, but she was trying to be open minded here. Really she was. Maybe she'd spent too much time around blowhard politicians. Just because in all the research she'd done on him he always came across like the kind of man who smiled, kissed babies, and made promises to anyone and everyone, without a sincere bone in his body, the kind of guy who was just looking at every angle to see what was best for himself, not his constituency, didn't mean he was a self-absorbed ass. She could be totally wrong. "But I didn't know they'd sent someone else. I really—I didn't want to put anyone out."

"I'm here, you're here," he said, matter-of-factly, which made her wonder why exactly he was here.

Despite his claims, he really didn't seem any more thrilled than she did. If he wasn't a good friend, then why had he put himself out? It was a five-hour round trip. No small favor. Well, she supposed it wouldn't have been if they'd flown as planned. Maybe it really was just an easy errand that had turned into something more complicated and time consuming because of the storm. She'd wondered if Arlen had pressured him, or called in a favor of some kind, but the man standing in front of her didn't look easily pushed around. And it probably wasn't that big a deal after all. Still . . . she couldn't help but be curious about how they all connected.

"We should get on the road," he said. "It's not going to get any better when the sun goes down."

"No, I'm sure you're right. Sorry, I was just—you know, I'm really not normally this hard to get along with. In fact, back home, at work—which, trust me, is filled with the jaded and cynical—I'm known for my relentless, upbeat optimism." She smiled. "It's a large part of my charm."

His lips quirked, but he politely said nothing. Which made

her feel even worse for not being more gracious in accepting his help.

"It's just—" Where to begin, really? How was she to explain to this complete stranger why she'd come here? What her suspicions were? How things had so badly deteriorated between her and her mom that she was sincerely concerned that something else was going on? Had to be going on. What did she tell a man who, for all she knew, understood more about the situation than she did. Who was she kidding? In such a small town, everyone probably knew more than she did.

But she also knew small towns were a close-knit society, and close-knit societies might gossip to each other about each other, but they held on to their secrets where outsiders were concerned. And despite her connection to the mayor's wife, given their estrangement, she harbored no illusions as to which category she'd fit into. Which was going to make poking around in local affairs that much more challenging.

At least Rugged Outdoors Guy was being hospitable. It was a start. One she should be more grateful for. Not to mention possibly use to her advantage. She wished she knew more about the local politics and where he fit into the hierarchy of it all. But, at the moment, he was the only opening she had, and she should be using it. The rocky plane ride had really thrown her off her game. She needed to get her head in gear right now, not three hours from now after a hot shower and a good meal. Campaigns were lost with that kind of strategy. And she was kidding herself if she didn't think what she was about to mount was exactly that.

A campaign. A campaign designed to free her surprisingly deluded mother by exposing the real Arlen Thompson. And if the rest of the town learned something new about their community leader, well, she had no problem with that, either.

So she went with honesty. Which she still believed was the best policy, even if that concept was oftentimes a foreign one in her day-to-day world. Her former day-to-day world. "Not to get personal, and I'm not dragging you into it, I swear, but this is kind of a tough trip for me. I've put it off too long and that has only made things worse. But now I'm here, and . . ." She glanced out at the pounding rain, then down at her sodden self, then back at him, and smiled, this time quite naturally. "So far, nothing is really going as I thought it would."

His smile threatened to surface again, and she found herself wishing it would. For the campaign, of course. The better connection you made with the locals, the better your chances were when it came time for them to decide who to put their faith in. And the incumbents almost always had the edge.

"Colorado is a pretty optimistic place," he said. "It's hard to be jaded or cynical when you look out at a view like the one we have here. Even with the rain, it's awe inspiring."

Why his comment surprised her, she couldn't have said. Most people lived where they did for a reason. But she hadn't pegged him as the philosophic type. "How long have you lived here?"

"Every day of my life."

"Impressive," she said. "That you don't take it for granted, I mean."

"You can't live here, and look at that, and not be aware of how insignificant your place is in the big picture of things. It keeps the little things in perspective. And yet, at the same time, you can't live here and not know, with absolute certainty, that if such majestic things as those mountains can exist, surely anything a mere human wants to accomplish can be done with a little grit and perseverance."

He pushed away from the wall and grabbed the handle of her suitcase, which she hadn't noticed he'd retrieved for her. In fact, at the moment, all she was noticing was him.

His lips curved more fully under her continued regard, deepening the grooves on either side of his mouth, and the crinkles at the corners of his eyes. "You don't strike me as someone who gives up all that easily."

"No," she said, a little too taken with his easy charm and surprising depth. "No, I don't."

"Why don't we get on the road, so you can tackle what comes next?"

"Yes," she murmured, falling into step beside him, feeling, suddenly, like she might have to scramble to catch up, in more ways than one. "Why don't we."

Chapter 3

S he was nothing like he'd expected.

Not that he'd had any expectations, or given it any thought, really. But he must have formed some opinion, because he'd been surprised when she'd stepped out of the commuter and run across the tarmac.

Given Ruby Jean's description of the workaholic, no-nonsense, no-life, thirty-something, he guessed he'd pictured someone tall, thin, tight-faced, and humorless.

Lauren Matthews wasn't close to matching any of those descriptions. She was short, curvy in all the right places, and her self-deprecating humor had been a welcome surprise. Caught in a downpour, she'd more or less just shrugged it off and dealt with the less-than-flattering consequences. It was probably the freckles that had done him the rest of the way in. The rain had streaked off whatever makeup she'd had on, revealing a surprising scatter of them across her nose and cheeks. Sun kisses, Ruby Jean had called them when she was little. It had been a long time since he'd thought of that. It had made him smile then, and made him want to smile now.

They'd been on the road for a little over an hour now, but the combination of the noise the rain was making, pounding on the roof of Teddy's truck, the repetitive squeak of the windshield wipers, and the loud rumble of the engine had kept conversation to a minimum. He should have been relieved. Ruby Jean was the chatty sibling. He enjoyed his solitude and the peace and quiet that allowed him to do, think, or just be, without distraction. It's why he loved to fly.

But he found himself more curious about his passenger than he'd expected to be. The few times he'd stolen a glance in her direction, or commented on this mountain name or that mountain pass, she'd smiled and nodded, but otherwise she seemed mostly lost in her own thoughts. He remembered what Ruby Jean had said, about the estrangement between mother and daughter. Lauren had been a little prickly when he'd mentioned her mom by name. He imagined her comments about this trip not being a necessarily fun one for her were probably tied to that. He'd also meant what he said about not getting involved, but with nothing better to do than think at the moment, he found himself spending most of the drive thus far thinking about her.

RJ had said their problems started when Charlene had eloped with Arlen. His guess was the daughter didn't approve. Either of the elopement, or of Arlen, he wasn't sure. Jake didn't have an opinion on whirlwind romances, except to know he didn't have them, and therefore really didn't understand why any two people would be in such a rush to get to the altar. If it was right, waiting a few months, or years, certainly wasn't going to change that. And the more a person knew, the better prepared they'd be to make such a monumental decision. At least that's what made sense to him. But he didn't begrudge anyone else rushing. As long as they weren't rushing him.

However, if her problem was with Arlen personally, well . . . Jake couldn't fault her on that. Not that she'd asked, or that he'd offer up the opinion. He'd keep his word to Ruby Jean. Besides, he wanted no part of whatever drama was playing out with Cedar Springs' First Couple. Just because Arlen Thompson had always struck him as the kind of man who held only his own interests as sacred, and would sell his grandmother's pearls if he thought it would help him advance his cause—and anyone was a fool if they thought his cause had anything to do with putting others' needs before his own—didn't mean he couldn't be a good partner or spouse. Jake had a really hard time imagining it, that's all. Not that he cared enough to share that opinion with anyone. He just steered clear and went about taking care of his own business. In fact, Cedar Springs would probably be a lot better off if more folks did the same.

Jake found his gaze sliding over to Lauren. Again. She was staring out the side window, thoughts far away from her immediate company if her pensive expression was anything to judge by. He wondered what she was thinking about, what, specifically, she was worried about, but caught himself before he actually gave in to the urge to ask if there was anything he could do. He had a laundry list of things to think about and worry over. Lauren Matthews was not on that list, nor would she be.

He thought about Ruby Jean's idea that what Lauren needed was a little loosening up. And that she'd thought her older brother would be the perfect guy to do the loosening. If he hadn't been enduring his sister's attempts to match him up with any woman who dared linger long enough for Ruby Jean to discover she was single, he might have been offended by the implication. But Ruby Jean didn't have a mean-spirited bone in her body. In fact, all she'd ever wanted, since the age of thirteen when she'd been very abruptly left with only a big brother to take care of her, was for everyone in her immediate orbit to be content and happy.

And, from the moment he'd hit thirty without a "prospect on the horizon" she'd begun searching in earnest, despite the fact that he'd done everything to assure her that he was perfectly content and happy to remain just as he was.

But, of course, RJ was having none of that. And now she was hell-bent on fixing her boss's marital problems. Jake figured he should be thankful for the distraction, as it meant he'd be spared for the time being. Except now she was dragging him into it, likely hoping to kill two birds with one matrimonial stone.

"I'm really sorry."

"What?" Jake looked over at her. She hadn't spoken in so long, the sudden sound of her voice had caught him off guard. "Why?"

"Oh . . . no, you just—you sighed. And I was apologizing for being the reason you were dragged away from whatever it was you were doing to come and pick me up."

"It wasn't that. My thoughts were . . . elsewhere." *As yours seem to be,* he wanted to say but didn't. "It was probably just as well I stepped out when I did. Another ten minutes and I might have done more harm than good trying to fix that damn manifold regulator."

She smiled. "What's a damn manifold regulator?"

His lips curved, naturally, easily. It felt good. Shouldn't have been so surprising. He'd always thought he was a pretty upbeat person, but just in the short time he'd been around her, he was realizing the smiles must have been a bit fewer and farther between of late than he'd realized. Ruby Jean had complained that he'd been too stressed out lately, but with everything currently on his plate, stress was unavoidable. Still, he hadn't thought it had been getting to him as much as it apparently had. "It's one of many engine parts that keeps my P-51 Mustang in the air."

"Well, then it's probably just as well you did step out. What kind of plane is a P-51? Crop duster or something?"

His smile turned wry. "Or something. They were flown in World War II. I race one."

She turned to face him more fully. "Really. I didn't know people raced airplanes."

A quick glance over at her showed the color was coming back into her cheeks, making her freckles less stark. Her hair had started to dry, and he noticed she had a lot more of it than he'd realized. It hung to her shoulders, almost poker straight, but in a kind of thick, shiny, brown waterfall. He wondered if it felt as silky as it looked.

Flexing his grip on the steering wheel, he looked back to the road. Which was where his mind should be. And not on any part of Ms. Lauren Matthews. Even if he were to entertain any ideas about her, in any way, two things would stop him. One, his baby sister did not need even the slightest bit of encouragement. And, two, Lauren was Arlen's stepdaughter. "Some folks do," he said at length, realizing she was waiting for him to respond.

"Just antique planes, or others?"

"All kinds. Sort of like car racing, there are different types, different sports. It varies country to country. I only race the Mustang. It was a renowned fighter plane. In fact, the car was named after the plane."

"I didn't know that, either. Wow, that's so wild. About the racing, I mean. So it's an international thing?"

He nodded. "The first organized races started back in the twenties in Europe, different form, different planes, of course. Some races were 'get from Point A to Point B the fastest' kind of races and others were through a marked course."

"Is that what you do? The course?" When he nodded, she added, "What kind of course? I mean, obviously it's in the air; how is it marked?"

For someone who had spent the entire time lost in her own thoughts, her sudden interest and chattiness were surprising, but seemingly quite sincere. Perhaps they both could use a detour from their personal musings. And he never minded talking on this particular subject to anyone who was interested. Which wasn't often, unless they were a fellow racer. Or one of his students. Most women of his acquaintance thought it was an interesting hobby, but glazed over if he actually started to get into specifics. He wondered how long it would take before Lauren did the same. "There are what amount to huge pylons that form gates that you actually fly between."

"So, rather low to the ground, then?"

The curve of his smile deepened. "Low and fast."

"Sounds pretty intense."

"It is that. The division I fly in is called the unlimited class."

"Which means?"

Now he grinned as he looked at her. "That we go really fast."

Her gaze caught his and hung there, as if he'd snagged it. But her smile was bright enough to light up her eyes. "A need-for-speed guy."

"Fair description."

"Adrenaline junkie?"

"Plane junkie. Flying junkie. The adrenaline comes free of charge."

She laughed. "How long have you been doing it? How did you get started?"

"My grandfather got me into it when I was little."

Her eyes widened. "How little is little?"

"He raced and I watched. But I knew from very early on that I was going to get up in one myself."

"Do you both race then? That's pretty cool, actually."

"We did. And it was. The best, actually. He died a little over twelve years ago."

"Oh, I'm so sorry."

"I am, too. We all were. Heart attack. He was healthy like an ox, so no one saw it coming. He ran a flight school—we ran it together at that point—and along with that, I inherited the Mustang. It took a long while before I could get her back up in the sky, but for the past five years, we've raced every September. So, I race her for us both. I think he'd be pretty happy with that."

Which was another reason Jake was stressed. He'd finally gotten *Betty Sue* to be a contender, which would have made Patrick McKenna fiercely proud and more than a little smug, as he'd been handed defeat after defeat with a plane he knew could be a champion but simply couldn't afford to fix it up the way he needed to.

But his grandchildren had come first in those days, about whom he was also fiercely proud. He'd taken good care of the two of them, all things considered, which was a lot, given his own wife had passed on only five years before his only son and daughter-in-law—Jake and Ruby Jean's parent's—were taken in a car accident on a snowy mountain pileup. He hadn't the first clue what to do with a heartbroken seven-year-old girl and an angry fifteen-year-old boy. But, in the end, he'd done right by both of them. And it was because of him that, six years later, they'd known how to handle life when he was taken from them, too.

So, Jake would be damned if he lost out now because he couldn't convince his sponsors that *Betty Sue* could be ready come race time. This was his year. Their year. He was going to bring the title home.

"I'm sure he'd be very proud. I think it's great that you're carrying on the tradition. And sorry I've kept you from working on it. I can imagine it takes a lot of your free time. Or is that how you earn a living now?" She held up a quick hand. "Sorry, that's none of my business. I just didn't want to assume you couldn't. Do that. Race planes, I mean. For a living. I know nothing about racing, so for all I know you're the rock star of the circuit, living the high life. I just—I didn't mean to insult you, is all I'm saying." She laughed and he glanced over to see her looking down, shaking her head with a rueful smile on her face. "And to think I'm the one the senator relies on to put words in his mouth when I can't even string mine together for two seconds without sounding like a total flake."

"You write speeches?"

"Sometimes. I write a lot of media statements. I also get coffee, keep track of every Senate and House vote, pick up the dry cleaning, book travel and events, and figure things out like where is the best place to have your Gordon setter personally trained." She grinned. "Toby MacLeroy. In Arlington. In case you ever needed to know."

His lips quirked again. "I'll make a note of it."

"It's a glamorous life. Somehow I managed."

He looked back at the road in time to see the sign for tight curves ahead. And wondered why people didn't come with such easy to interpret warnings. Lauren was throwing curves at him right and left. Seemingly without even trying.

"You were right," she said, after the silence had extended a bit longer. "About the rain." She turned back to the window on her side of the truck. "And the mountains. They are awe inspiring. I've traveled, but never in anything like this. And to think they're right here, in our own country." She laughed. "That sounded kind of idiotic, but—"

"I know what you mean."

"Have you traveled? Do you race in other parts of the country? Or the world?"

"I just do the one race in Reno every fall. With running the school, it takes pretty much the full year to get ready for that."

"Do you have help?"

"A little. Mostly old friends of my grandfather's who come and help out. When the race gets closer, I have friends who come in to help with the final round of prep, testing, that sort of thing, and crew for me during race week."

"It's a lot of work for one race."

"It's a series of races over the course of a week, but yes, just the one event."

"Would you enter more of them if you could?"

He shook his head. "This is pretty much the only one of its kind. It's enough for me. My grandfather also used to do all kinds of exhibitions, county fairs, air shows, that sort of thing, when he could get away. It's a popular sideline for pilots and owners and not a bad way to earn some extra income."

"Do you follow that tradition, too?"

He shook his head. "No time. And, to be honest, not the same inclination he had for that part of the culture. I'd like to travel more, in this country, and out, see more of the world. Been to Canada, down to Mexico, but haven't gotten over to Europe. I'd enjoy that."

"For racing?"

"They have some big events over there, and I wouldn't mind

getting to see them, but mostly I'd go for the history. You've traveled, I take it?"

She nodded. "It's a little bit like your mountains here, how you described them earlier. The more I see of the world, the more it keeps me firmly rooted in my place in it, and how it's both so insignificant and yet profoundly meaningful. If I want it to be."

He slowed a bit as the road wound tightly and steeply down the side of another mountain, then finally glanced over at her as the pickup flattened out across a high meadow, before climbing once again. "Do you want to follow your boss? Into politics I mean."

She looked over at him, and their gazes collided for a moment, then hung here a moment longer. Then she smiled and laughed. "I used to think I could make a difference. I started out as a lawyer, which runs in my family, but they were all very involved in politics, too, and when I got involved working on a campaign, the bug bit."

"Did you run for office?"

"No, I was never really compelled to do that, but I wanted to be vital to those who did, to be involved in the everyday workings of Capitol Hill, be a part of history being made." She laughed again. "Sounds so altruistic and naïve now."

"No, it doesn't. I think it takes exactly that kind of mentality to do what you do. You have to believe, otherwise, why bother?"

Now her smile turned a bit wry, and he found himself easing up on the gas, prolonging the moment when he'd have to keep his gaze tight on the road ahead as they made the next ascent.

"Maybe I've been in Washington too long, but after a while, I started to wonder how anything actually gets accomplished. I spent far more time feeling frustrated and hopeless than I did energized and aggressive. I finally decided that can't be good. For me, or anyone."

"Doesn't sound like it." He reluctantly returned his gaze to the road. "How long are you planning on being out here?" He glanced her way. "I mean, what will the good senator do if he needs to find the best pre-school for his future, unborn children if you're not there to do the research?"

"He already has five children," she said. "And, believe it or not, you're not all that far off on in vitro private pre-school enrollment."

"And here I thought it was a cliché played out in the movies."

She laughed. "Cliché's come to be for a reason."

"A little scary to contemplate, given some of them."

"You have no idea."

They fell into silence again, but now that he had her talking, the silence seemed hollow rather than comforting. "You here for a long weekend? Sounds like you can't be away too long." And why he was suddenly so interested, he had no idea. The reasons for not getting involved hadn't changed. But his feelings about wanting to might be.

She didn't answer right away, so he looked over at her. "You don't have to answer. I was just making conversation."

"I quit," she blurted out.

"What?"

She looked back out through the windshield. "I am no longer the senior staff aide to the gentleman from Virginia."

After a quick look, he returned his gaze to the road. She looked both defensive and a little sick. "I take it this is news you haven't shared with your loved ones."

"With anyone. Other than the senator. And the person he's named as my replacement. The rest of the staff found out today."

"Is that going to be newsworthy?" He glanced over again and smiled. "For all I know, you're the rock star of Capitol Hill."

She smiled back and looked a little less green. "It won't make the papers, if that's what you mean. There is no scandal or anything. And he's not on the forefront of any topical committees or bills at the moment, so I don't think it will be more than a tiny ripple. Natasha will take my place and all will move along."

"Natasha. Is this a good thing?"

Her smile widened. "You're very nice for pretending to care. And it's perfectly fine. She's still hungry."

"And you're not." He said it as more statement than question.

"I want to be. I'm restless. Like I'm treading water and there's a pretty good chance I'm going to drown rather than figure out how to swim and save myself. So, I got out of the pool altogether. For now, anyway."

"Might be the best thing you could do. How does it feel?"

"Scary. A little sad. Mostly because I miss the people on my team. No regrets. But . . . scary just the same."

"Is that all?"

She had folded her arms across her middle. But she rocked forward just a little. "Okay . . . so maybe it's also a little exciting, portentous. It's been a while since I've felt either of those things."

"Then it sounds like you're on the right track. Did you burn bridges? Could you go back if the new pond isn't any better?"

"I don't want to go back. Not now, maybe not ever. I need a fresh challenge." She sounded definite about that.

"Well, then," he said, "sounds like you made the right choice."

"Have you ever done anything like that? Just change course completely?"

"I've had my course changed for me. Circumstances beyond my control. Like you, it's been scary, sad, exhilarating, terrifying, satisfying. And that's any given week," he added dryly.

She smiled and relaxed a little. "I guess it's normal then. In a very abnormal way."

"Guess so." They were less than fifteen minutes from town. And he realized he didn't want their time to be over quite yet. "You have plans?"

"For my future, you mean?"

He glanced at her. "Why don't we start with this weekend."

"Oh," she said, and blushed just a little. "I'm—I have to see my mother. At some point."

"I take it you're not staying with them?"

She shook her head. "Things are a bit . . . strained. I thought it would be best if I had my own place to retreat to until the battle lines were more clearly defined."

"Charlene seemed pretty happy that you were coming."

Now the guarded look came back and Jake cursed inwardly that he'd gone and done the one thing he'd sworn not to. Get involved. "Never mind, none of my business. Where can I drop you?"

"Greater Pine Lodge. I made reservations."

"You chose well. Mabry Johnson runs the place, along with her sister and daughter-in-law. She's a character, but one of the best people you'll meet."

Lauren smiled again and relaxed a little. "Good. Thank you. And thank you again for—"

"If you're not doing anything Sunday, why don't you let me show you the area."

She looked surprised by the offer.

That made two of them. Mostly because he meant it. In fact, he hadn't thought about his favor to his sister in the last hour or so.

"It'll give you a chance to see how spectacular the view really is."

"Is there really that much to see?" She lifted a hand. "There I go again. What I meant was, I understood the town to be quite small."

"I was thinking of giving you a different view." He slowed as they bottomed out from the last descent. Cedar Springs laid sprawled just below them. McKenna Flight School topped the mesa just beyond the opposite end of town. He liked coming into town from this direction, ascending down from Cooper Pass, with Wisternan, the main resort peak, towering over the town nestled at its base, directly to the north, the winding Panlo River, bordering Cedar Springs to the south . . . and McKenna Flight School in the distant west. It made him feel a part of something bigger than himself, but a part nonetheless. A permanent part.

He looked over to see her giving him a speculative look. "Just exactly what view did you have in mind?"

His lips quirked. He liked that she was direct and didn't duck a subject. He was pretty sure when Lauren Matthews wanted to know something, she came out and asked. "I was thinking the view from about twelve thousand feet might be interesting."

She looked both relieved and a little embarrassed, making him wonder exactly what view she'd thought he'd been offering.

"I should be sufficiently recovered from my last plane ride by then," she said. "And I'd actually really like that. But—I need to see what's going on first. I'm not sure—"

"No worries. I don't teach classes on Sunday. I'll just be working on the Mustang." He made it sound like it was nothing, when he was pretty much going to be umbilically attached to the damn thing until the race. Still . . . a few hours spent not tinkering on *Betty Sue* or operating the school wouldn't kill him. "Early afternoon is good, but I'm flexible."

"I might be thankful to be up in the air and out of reach by then."

"It's none of my business, but maybe it won't be that bad. Like I said, it seemed to me your mother was happy you were coming."

"I think we'd both be happy to get past this."

"Well, then . . . ?"

She sighed. "You've lived here your whole life, right?"

"Yep."

"Then I'll just say that it's not my mom I'm really having a problem with. But I don't know a lot about the situation, which is why I'm here."

Jake had promised Ruby Jean not to slam Arlen. Sounded like Lauren was already well on her way to forming her opinion of the man without his help. So all he said, was, "Well then, you'll get to know for yourself, and you can figure it out from there."

She sighed. "I certainly hope so."

She didn't sound all that hopeful, though. Which made Jake wonder exactly what her goal was while she was here. *Not your business, buddy. Not your concern.*

But when he dropped her off at the registration office at the rustic little motel just inside the town limits, it didn't keep him from wondering exactly what she was getting herself into.

Chapter 4

"Okay. Sitting in your room is no longer an option." Lauren fiddled with her cell phone but didn't press the CALL button. The button that would dial her mother's number. She'd been in Cedar Springs for exactly one hour. She was unpacked, showered, and changed, makeup and hair mercifully repaired. All she had to do now was make the call.

Her mother knew she was here. At least, Lauren had to suspect she knew. She hadn't thought to ask her friendly neighborhood pilot if he'd planned on letting her mother know he'd gotten her safely to town. But then, she hadn't thought to ask the man his name, either. Who did that? Who drove with a complete stranger for more than two hours, chatted with him—agreed to see him again—and even went so far as to share her deep, dark, job-quitting secret . . . and didn't get his name?

She couldn't even blame the rocky commuter flight and subsequent storm for scattering her brain. Not really. She might blame Hunky Local Pilot for discombobulating her a little. Okay, a lot. He'd been all rugged good looks and enigmatic personality back in the airport hangar. But once they'd started talking, she'd been surprised at how laid back and easy-going he was. He'd made her forget she looked like airport roadkill, and even took her mind off her immediate future for an hour or two.

Well, she knew Hunky Pilot Guy's name now. There had been a copy of the local phone book in the nightstand drawer by her bed. She'd simply looked up flight schools in the slim Yellow Pages section. There had only been one listed. McKenna's Flight School. Owned and operated by Jake McKenna, or so the modest ad proclaimed.

Jake. It suited him. He might not have been a traditional western cowboy, with boots and spurs and tobacco in his back pocket, but he definitely filled the bill for mountain man outdoorsy type. He fit here, among the soaring peaks and beautiful high meadows. And he raced airplanes. How sexy was that?

"Too damn sexy," she muttered. And she had no real business getting involved with him, in any way. Not that being asked out on a short plane ride around the area was getting overly involved, but it was prolonging their acquaintance. She wasn't sure what, if anything, he had in mind. She assumed, given her bedraggled appearance, and the fact that she hadn't exactly employed the most scintillating conversational skills, that he was still doing a favor for her mother. And, possibly, the mayor. She hadn't missed the fact that he'd politely refrained from saying anything directly about Arlen. He'd claimed he wasn't close to her mother, but that didn't mean anything where the mayor was concerned.

Regardless of why he was asking, or if anyone had put him up to it, Jake struck her as being one of the Good Guys. He might look and sound like a Bad Boy, all crinkling eyes and crooked grins, enough to make her pulse do a little tap dance more than once . . . and, yes, that might have had a tiny bit to do with why she'd accepted his offer. But the offer itself, she was pretty sure, had been issued by the Good Guy, not the Bad Boy.

Which was for the best, really. "Very really," she warned her pouting reflection. She looked away from the mirror as her thoughts turned further inward. Her entire life was upside down at the moment. She, who had always had a Life Plan, a list of goals, and a pretty good idea about how she was going to go about achieving them—usually successfully, mind you, because that was the Matthews-O'Grady way—was currently floundering. No job, no prospects, no real idea of what she wanted to do with herself. All she'd known was that she was done in Washington. And that she couldn't figure out what came next while she was still putting in grueling eighteen-hour days with no time to think.

The other thing she'd known was that she hated what had happened between her and her mother. And Lauren had figured *that* was something she could do something about. At the very least, she needed to make peace with her mother. At best, she hoped to get her normally levelheaded, responsible, and very smart mother to open her eyes and see that maybe she'd had some sort of mini–life crisis or something, but that making a mistake didn't mean she was doomed to live with it forever.

Perhaps they would both figure out what came next, together.

"Yep. That's the better plan. Flirting with Sexy Airplane Racer Man . . . out. Making up with Mom and charting my new future . . . in." She stared at her cell phone. And still didn't push the button. Because pushing that button didn't just mean reuniting with her mother, it also meant meeting her new stepfather. Gah. She couldn't even think of him like that. Hell, she couldn't think of him at all. He was a complete stranger to her. Well, maybe not a complete stranger. She'd done a little—okay, a lot—of digging into his political and personal background over the past six months, which hadn't exactly left her feeling optimistic that her opinion of him was going to miraculously change upon meeting him.

The fact that her mother had refused to even talk to her about any potential problem with her new spouse was what had alarmed Lauren the most. Her mother was not the run-off-to-Vegas type. Far, far from it. But she had. And with a man she'd only just met. Of course her only daughter was going to be concerned, was going to ask questions.

But instead of that leading to any answers, it had led to a stubborn refusal to even consider that anything might be amiss in her happily-ever-after fairy tale. Lauren realized now she should have flown out here immediately, but, as her mother had pointed out, she was a grown woman and fully capable of making up her own mind. And things had deteriorated by then to a point where Lauren felt perhaps a cooling off period would do them both some good.

Well, cooling off time was officially over. Nothing had changed, and nothing was going to change unless she personally did something to change it. She'd done a lot of soul searching. About her job, about her once-close relationship with her mother, her goals, what her role was, both in her own life and in her mother's. Which had, at length, led her to quit her job and book a flight west. She'd figure the rest out. Eventually.

But she couldn't do any of that sitting on a bed in her motel room.

Her finger was hovering over the speed dial button to her mother's cell phone, when a rap on the door made her jump. In her e-mail exchange with Arlen's office, prior to coming out, she hadn't mentioned where she'd booked a room, just that she would be booking one. All she'd gotten in return was the note from Arlen's assistant saying they'd be unable to come pick her up but were looking forward to seeing her. Which she took to mean that they'd be waiting for her to make the first move upon arriving. So . . . who knew she was here, besides—"Jake?"

She might have hopped up off the bed a little too enthusiastically, but she didn't let herself think about that as she took a moment to check herself out in the vanity mirror before answering the door. Not her most excellent, but definitely an improvement over the last time he'd seen her.

So much for her grand plan to avoid meaningless flirtations.

She'd originally thought to stay in the resort hotel, but given her employment situation, despite the healthy nest egg she had squirreled away, that didn't seem like a wise move. So, she had to squint a little to look out of the tiny peephole, the glare of the late afternoon sun behind her visitor's back further stunting her view. But she could see well enough that her smile immediately fell. Not Jake. In fact, she had no idea who the woman was standing on the other side of her door. "Can I help you?" she asked without opening the door.

"It's Melissa, with a message from the mayor's office."

She recognized the name as the secretary who'd sent her the e-mail. She unlocked and opened the door. "Hello."

Melissa was a tall brunette, more wiry than slender, though she was that, too. Lauren had noticed that about a lot of the women she'd seen as they'd rolled into town earlier. Must be good mountain living, she thought. They all looked like distance athletes, with tanned skin and ready smiles. Melissa was no exception.

"Hi, I'm Arlen's personal secretary. We communicated a few days ago?"

"We did. Thanks for the note."

"The mayor and your mother both felt terrible about not being able to come pick you up themselves, but were hoping you wouldn't mind the short flight over with Jake."

Her smile was friendly, but Lauren wondered if, by mentioning him by name, she was putting out feelers to see what the new girl thought about the hunky local pilot. Probably a bit paranoid on Lauren's part, but she had no idea where Jake fit into the small-town-bachelor hierarchy. Or who it might piss off if it were discovered that he'd asked her out.

Okay, so it wasn't a date. It was more like a . . . tour. Still, it could be misinterpreted . . . even by the one invited to go on the tour. She didn't think she was reaching all that far.

"So . . . it was okay?" Melissa said.

Realizing she was standing in the open door, fantasizing about Jake McKenna when she should be worried about saying the right thing to Arlen's secretary, had her snapping to attention. "Yes, I'm fine. Just a little fatigued—long day." She didn't bother to tell her about the storm or the truck ride she'd ended up with versus the intended short plane ride. "I appreciated the gesture, though. How did you know where I was staying?"

"I contacted Jake. I hope you don't mind. He wasn't exactly forthcoming, but—"

"It's okay," Lauren said, not wanting to make this whole thing any more dramatic than necessary. But the little warm spot for Jake grew a bit larger. He'd protected her . . . or tried, at least. That earned a few extra points. "I was just about to contact them, in fact, when you knocked."

Melissa leaned down and lifted a basket that Lauren hadn't noticed was sitting by her feet. "They are still tied up at the charity function. There was an auction afterward and it's dragging on quite a bit longer than expected. So, Arlen asked that I deliver this to you. And your mom asked me to tell you that she was very happy you had arrived and is looking forward to seeing you. They are hoping you'll join them for dinner this evening at the Ragland Gap Steakhouse."

Lauren wondered what Melissa must be thinking about a family who used a secretary to deliver personal messages between its intimate members, but it was more than she could worry about at the moment. She took the basket, which was filled with all kinds of goodies: fruit, food, coffee mug, and even some wild flowers.

"It's kind of a welcome to Cedar Springs. Lots of local products, a little taste of our mountain town."

She was so darn cheerful, it was hard not to like her. In fact, the few people Lauren had actually met since hitting eight thousand plus feet had all been the same. Sunny, warm, sincerely nice, and always helpful. Definitely not typical of her experience living in D.C. Must be the thin air.

"Thank you," she said, and meant it. She had no idea yet, what the dynamic would be between her and Arlen, or even with her mother, much less with the two of them together as a couple, but that wasn't Melissa's problem. "I appreciate it, and appreciate you taking time from your schedule to deliver it personally."

"No problem. It got me out of listening to the mayor's luncheon speech." She leaned a little closer and in a more conspiratorial but still cheerful tone, added, "Which, frankly, doesn't change much, event to event. Neither does the food."

"I guess Chamber of Commerce luncheons are the same across the country," Lauren said. "More than once I swore that if I never saw another over-seasoned chicken breast and limp piece of broccoli, I'd die a happy woman."

Melissa laughed. "Exactly! And I only have to do them a few times a year. You must do them weekly, working for the senator."

Lauren's smile tightened slightly. "One of the perks of the job."

"Well, we're all happy you're in town."

"All?"

"Oh, don't look alarmed or anything. Cedar Springs is small, so we're tight knit. It was pretty big news when the mayor came back from the national mayor's conference in Florida with a new wife! I mean, you can imagine, right? So we were happy to hear you were finally coming to pay us a visit."

"So . . . the whole town knows I'm here?"

"Well . . . yes," Melissa said, but again, with such cheerful goodwill, as if it were impossible for her to comprehend why that could possibly be a bad thing, or even a disconcerting thing, it was hard to hold it against her. "But, don't worry, we may be like one big family, but we're an easy family to get to know, and we always welcome new members with open arms."

Lauren was beginning to miss D.C., where no one spoke to anyone they didn't have reason to, and were generally so distracted by whatever they were doing that they paid no attention to anyone else unless it involved cutting them off on the beltway. "I appreciate that. Thank you."

"So, will dinner work? I'm sorry, it's been great getting the chance to meet you, but I need to get back. If you'd rather just call—but they won't be out of there for at least another hour or so. There were several speeches, with a question-and-answer session that ran really long, then the local schoolchildren were putting on some kind of little production, then the auction, so it's just a never-ending thing, it seems."

"Dinner is fine."

She beamed. "Great. Seven at Ragland's. Enjoy your afternoon!"

Melissa waved and was gone, her long strides carrying her quickly across the parking lot before Lauren thought to ask what the dress code was for the steakhouse. She supposed she could just call the desk and ask. One bonus to being in a small town, everyone would probably know all the local establishments.

She closed the door and leaned against it. Still, it was more than just a little disconcerting, realizing that the whole town knew she was here. And she had a feeling that wasn't an exaggeration. The woman who'd checked her in had commented on it, as well. But Lauren had just assumed she'd made the connection from getting Lauren's information while taking the reservation.

Lauren set the basket on the small dresser, then sank down on the edge of the bed. So. She no longer had to make the call. That, at least, was a relief. But now she had a few hours to kill. She thought about wandering around the town a little, getting to see it through her own eyes first, but now there was this feeling that everyone would be watching her, talking. About what, she didn't know, but still.

Between reconciling things with her mom, and reconciling herself with her unplanned future, she had enough to deal with without wondering what every person who said hello to her might be thinking. She had no idea what the townspeople knew or didn't know, and was having a hard time wrapping her head around the fact that anyone other than her mother and herself might care.

She knew what it was like to live under a microscope, at least in political circles, due to her job. But even then, she was an adjunct to that life. The senator was the one being personally examined. She was just the person in charge of mitigating the effects of it as much as possible.

Restless and unable to think clearly, she got up and rummaged through the basket, finally settling on a little pouch of organic, locally made granola. Crunching on fruits and nuts didn't help much with the thinking process, but it did give her the impetus to get the heck out of her room. She should go rent a car. That was something to do. She wasn't sure how long she was going to stay, but even a day or two required transportation. And she wanted to make sure she had that taken care of before meeting up with her mother and Arlen. She didn't want to run any risk of being dependent on them to get wherever she might want to go.

She started to get the Yellow Pages out again, but decided what she really needed was to get out of the room. Fresh air, even of the thin variety, would be very welcome. Taking the bag of granola and her purse, she left her room and stopped by the front office to ask where she could rent a car. The rain had stopped and the storm clouds had fully moved out of the area. The sky was a deep blue streaked with the palest streams of gold and pink as the sun began its slow, late-summer descent. She loved this time of day. When she'd had time to notice it, anyway. The difference was, out here, the sky seemed endless, and the only thing obstructing her view from seeing forever were the jagged mountain peaks that surrounded her no matter what direction she looked.

Jake was right, they truly were magnificent. And to think, she was already at eight thousand plus feet, and they still soared so much higher. She was thinking about what he said, about being both humbled and inspired by them, and could see where he was coming from. She pushed open the door to the registration desk area and found herself wondering where his flight school was. Right at that moment, he was pretty much the only thing that felt grounded, which . . . how ironic was that?

The desk registrar's name was Debbie, according to her nametag, and was the same person who had checked her in. She was older than Lauren by a decade. Or two. Hard to tell with the Olympian genes these people all seemed to have. Her hair was cropped short, streaked with blond highlights that Lauren was pretty sure she hadn't had to pay for. In her deep blue polo shirt and khaki pants motel uniform, she looked more like a golf pro than a motel manager. She was average height, which meant she still had a handful of inches over Lauren, and greeted her with a sunny, toothy smile. "Good afternoon, Miss Matthews. Settling in okay? What can I do for you?"

What were these people on? And where could she get some?

Lauren wondered if Debbie was the owner's daughter or sister. And if the other two were as naturally caffeinated as Debbie, here. Even with her growing dissatisfaction with her career choice, Lauren had prided herself on maintaining an upbeat, optimistic attitude despite living in a town, and working in a field, that prided itself on grinding the optimism out of a person as early in as possible. But out here, she felt downright crotchety and grinch-like. Apparently she'd been assimilated into her old life more deeply than even she'd realized.

"I was thinking about renting a car."

"Oh, you don't really need one if you're planning to stay in town. We have a free bus system that runs here and out to the resort village. You might enjoy renting a bike, though. That's how most folks get around." She smiled. "Until the snow starts falling, anyway, but that's a few months off yet. Between the bike and the bus, you'd be all set. There's a rack on the front of every bus to put your bike in, if you get somewhere you don't feel like peddling back. And it'll save you some money, too," she added cheerfully.

Lauren paused a moment, wondering if—no, there was no way anyone could know about her job. She was being a little too paranoid. Besides, Jake was the only one she'd told—stupidly, now, she supposed—but Arlen's secretary, Melissa, had said he wasn't wanting to be all that chatty about where he'd dropped her off, which Lauren appreciated. So she would guess he hadn't been in a gossiping mood, either. She hoped. Her sudden lack of both a career and steady income was definitely news she needed to spring herself.

"I'll think about that. But, just in case, where would I rent a car?"

"Well, back at the local airport in Holden is your best bet, but sometimes the resorts will have them brought out and delivered for you. Usually, that's more a seasonal thing, but I'd be happy to ring over there."

"Isn't that more of a service for their guests?" She should have held her ground and gotten a car before leaving the airport.

"Normally, yes, but I'm sure when I tell them you're the mayor's daughter—"

It was on the tip of Lauren's tongue to correct her and say "stepdaughter." But even that left a sour taste in her mouth. And now that she'd been clued in to her quasi-celebrity status in town, the less fodder she provided the better. "That's okay," she interrupted. "Truly. I'm—going to think about it. I appreciate your help."

"I'm sure the mayor would be happy to take care of it for you. I can just ring Melissa, or Ruby Jean and—"

"No, that won't be necessary." It was on the tip of her tongue to ask Debbie a question or twelve about her thoughts on the mayor, but now was not the time. Somehow she didn't think Debbie was as stalwart as Jake when it came to being discreet. Which, admittedly, would be to her advantage in getting some answers, but not so much in keeping Debbie from telling everyone else that Lauren had some questions. "I think I'm just going to set out on foot and see the sights for a bit."

Debbie waved her a cheery good-bye and, once on the sidewalk, Lauren turned and headed into town. Her motel was at the near end of Main Street as you entered Cedar Springs from the highway—if you could call the little two-lane road that. The resort was on the opposite end of town, and even now, in the summer, you could see the trails cut through the soaring pines, all over Mount Wisternan, the massive monolith that served as a spectacular backdrop to the entire village. She'd skied a few times, but only on the East Coast. She tried to imagine the pine green mountain, and the picture postcard town, buried in snow.

One thing was certain to be true, and that was that every

person in Cedar Springs probably looked adorable in their brightly colored fleeces and snow gear.

One of the things she'd argued about with her mother, who'd retired and moved from Richmond, Virginia, to sunny Coral Gables, Florida, eighteen months earlier, was having to abruptly adjust to life in a place where it snowed at least seven months out of every twelve. The average snowfall of Cedar Springs was over a hundred feet each winter. Average. Being raised in the mid-Atlantic, where it occasionally snowed, sometimes even several feet . . . she still couldn't really even imagine a hundred of them.

Her mother had laughingly responded that she'd moved to Colorado, not Siberia. And she'd moved here in February, so it wasn't like she hadn't seen the snow yet. Which, fine. Except her mother had been thriving since the move to a sunnier, consistently warmer climate. She'd bought a little place of her own in a great, waterfront retirement community that Lauren had privately dubbed Camp Seniors. But, kidding aside, it had seemed like a wonderful place to live.

Charlene had been active in several clubs, did volunteer work for a couple of charities, as well as a few other local organizations—and that was a very reduced pace of life for a woman who had been the toast of the hostess circuit in the society and professional realms in the capital city of Richmond. She had gushed to her daughter about all the new friends she was making, while still finding it relatively simple to keep up with many of her old ones, a great number of whom spent time in Florida, as well.

And almost all of whom had also expressed shock over her sudden elopement and subsequent move west.

Charlene had been so happy, so relaxed, so involved. Her friends, new and old, had all echoed Lauren's sentiments in that regard. And then, wham, her mother meets Arlen during some political luncheon hosted by one of her ladies groups in Miami. He was in town for a national gathering of mayors, and before anyone even knew she'd even met the guy, she was running off with him. They were married less than two weeks after meeting each other, and she moved, lock, stock, and lawn flamingos, to Cedar Springs.

Then, to compound matters, her mother had been hurt when Lauren hadn't been over-the-moon excited for her when she'd called with the stunning news. In return, Lauren had been hurt that her mother hadn't even told her what was going on, before going off and doing it. At sixty-three, Charlene O'Grady Matthews was still every bit as sharp, if not sharper, than most of Lauren's thirty-something peer group. So . . . she couldn't reconcile what in the world her mother had been thinking to run off like that, on some spontaneous whim with a guy who was tantamount to a complete stranger.

Her mother had taken offense at that tack. She'd outright refused to talk about her mental state, and whether or not, perhaps, they should be concerned about such an abrupt departure from her normal behavior. Yeah, that whole conversation hadn't gone over well. At all.

Which was when Lauren had started digging into Arlen's history. Her mother might not know him, but Lauren planned to know everything she could find out on the guy. Being that he was a public official, and applying her personal contacts, there had been a fair amount to sort through despite his position being in such a small town. He was from San Francisco originally, and had made a run to be his party's pick for governor many years back, early on in his political career—too early, it seemed, as he hadn't won their support.

He'd ended up marrying one of his aides and settled with her in her hometown of Cedar Springs, running for the far less prestigious position of mayor, which he'd won handily with the support of his new wife's family, who carried enormous clout in the area. It was a position he'd held ever since. Lauren hadn't been all that thrilled with the rest of what she'd turned up. His first wife died shortly thereafter in a car accident. Drinking was rumored to play a role in the tragedy, as was a turbulent marriage. He remarried and divorced shortly afterward. Then remained single and focused his energy on trying to grow Cedar Springs into the next Aspen or Telluride, despite less than enthusiastic local support. In fact, from what she'd learned, Arlen Thompson was mostly all about Arlen Thompson . . . and thought everyone else should be, too.

What she couldn't figure out is why they kept electing the guy, but that wasn't her problem. Her mother marrying him was.

But try to caution her mother that she might not be fully aware of some pertinent information about who she'd married . . . and all Lauren had gotten was a chilly blast in the ear about daring to dig as she had, about not trusting her mother's judgment, and, well, that had just been the launch pad. It had swiftly devolved from there, until Lauren didn't even recognize either one of them during even the briefest phone conversation.

She mourned the loss of both a parental bond and the one true friendship she'd always counted on. Not only because it kept her from being a part of her mother's new life, but also removed the one voice of reason she could count on when she really needed help. Like deciding whether or not to ditch the career she'd worked so hard for.

She'd really tried to see it from her mother's point of view, but that hadn't stopped her from worrying. Or from continuing to dig. She'd finally had to face the fact that the only way her mother couldn't avoid the topic was if she was standing right in front of her. They had to talk about this . . . aberration. So, she wasn't entirely sure just how "excited" her mother really was to see her, but she hoped that they could get past their seeming inability to get through even the most rationally approached conversation about this, and move on to some kind of common ground. Or, at least, a peaceful détente.

She really hoped she'd feel better after meeting Arlen, seeing them together. Her gut, and her reams of research, however, were telling her otherwise. What in the world did her smart, intellectual, witty, and wise mother see in this guy?

"Open-minded," she reminded herself. She'd promised herself she'd do her best, despite her predisposed opinions. Blame it on her workplace of the past eight years. An environment her mother also knew quite well, as both the daughter of James O'Grady, a well-known lawyer and eventual appellate court judge, and widow of Daniel Matthews, a very respected trial attorney, who'd also been Lauren's dad. She just couldn't fathom what had made her mom, who'd been courted plenty over the last sixteen years since her father had passed away, and by some pretty distinguished men . . . fall for this one?

Yep. Apparently she had a little more work to do on her whole "unbiased" approach if she hoped to pull it off outside the initial handshake.

Lauren continued her stroll down Main Street, looking at the window displays that alternated between mountain gear, mountain sportswear, and a surprising array of beautifully done art, sculpture, and hand-crafted jewelry, with the occasional bookshop and restaurant thrown in for good measure. Most of it immediately forgotten, as her thoughts continued to stray back to the impending dinner. She really wished she could get her mother alone, first to talk and, hopefully begin to smooth things over, before diving into the crux of why she'd come, much less meet the crux. But she didn't see that happening.

It was the beginnings of a tension headache that had Lauren impulsively pushing through the doors of a bike shop. The constant stress of her job had been taking its toll for some time, even longer if you counted in how long she'd stubbornly refused to accept the fact. Headaches had become the norm, not the exception, and, by the end of each day, her body had ached like someone twice her age. Her doctor—when she'd finally broken down and gone to see him—had given her solid suggestions on how to reduce stress. But his first suggestion had been to either manage her job better, or find another job. She remembered thinking he was over-exaggerating at the time, that if she simply followed a few of his other ideas, things would improve.

Well, one of the other things he'd recommended was walking, swimming, or biking. She walked—ran, really—all day, every day, it seemed, for her job. And while she wouldn't drown if she ever fell overboard, swimming for distance, or style for that matter, wasn't ever going to be part of her repertoire. Bike riding, on the other hand, had sounded like fun. Between riding on the Mall, around the Tidal Basin, or all the trails through Rock Creek Park, she had plenty to choose from. She'd decided that would be her gift to herself, her way of distressing. She'd even looked forward to doing it, imagined herself pedaling around town. She'd just . . . never gotten around to finding the time to actually get a bike. It had been on her to-do list. Along with making time to ride it.

She'd ceremoniously burned the list the day she quit her job. She didn't need reminders now. Her calendar was wide open.

"So," she said, "no time like the present, then." Because the present was definitely not the time to court a migraine-level headache. It could be the thin air, but more likely it was the only serious remaining source of stress in her life, which, when said and done, all boiled down to dinner. This evening. At seven.

Fifteen minutes later she was riding what they called the "townie" model, which essentially meant it had a bigger seat for her bigger caboose. One look at the narrow, rock-hard wedge that served as a mountain bike seat had her quickly swallowing any vanity she might have had on the subject, which had been ever-so-gently broached by the guy at the rental desk, and opting for the biggest, softest townie model in stock. It was pink. Very pink. She'd been trapped in navy blue and pinstripes for so long, she'd just instinctively pointed at it. The rental guy couldn't possibly know how un-pink her life had been. But he didn't laugh, or even look at her funny. He'd merely smiled as if it made perfect sense for her and handed her a matching helmet and water bottle. She decided the rental guy was her new best friend.

After a wobbling start in which she almost took out a sidewalk rack of fleece vests and an entire folding table lined with Crocs, she finally managed to find her pace, only to have to stop at the first corner as the one and only light in town turned green for cross-moving traffic. So, she took the opportunity to check out the map her new BFF had given her. He'd explained which trails were accessible to her on her "townie" and which were steep, mountain-bike-only trails. She didn't bother to even look at those. This was supposed to be fun and pleasurable, after all. And she'd already risked death today in the gum-wrapper-size plane she'd flown out here in. No need to taunt fate twice.

There were various points of interest on the map as well. The ski resort, of course, along with the Olympic training grounds, the Nicklaus-designed golf course, the rodeo and county fair-grounds—just west of town—and a wee bit farther up . . . hunh. "McKenna Flight School," she read out loud. "What do you know. He's a town landmark." Or his school was. She wondered again about what role he played, if any, in local pol-itics, or just as a local businessman. She'd had him pegged as the sort who kept his focus on his own work and out of others' business, but then, what did she really know about him? "Other than he didn't throw you under the bus when Arlen's secretary had come calling." And if that was all she had to go on—okay, that and the fact that he was lust on a stick—then she'd extend him the benefit of the doubt. For now.

She glanced back over her shoulder and realized she'd come farther down Main Street than she'd thought. Another glance at her watch showed she still had more than an hour before she was to report for dinner. Which felt more appointment than social engagement. She toyed again with the idea of trying to call her mother to break the ice a little, but she really wasn't ready for all the variables that action might lead to.

She purposely hadn't gone into any of the shops, either. Other than the rental guy, Melissa, and Debbie at the motel, she hadn't talked to any locals. "So much for your plan of playing super sleuth." She had a whole list of questions she'd planned on asking folks once she got into town, find out what kind of man Arlen Thompson really was, especially to the people who knew him best. Riding herd on the media during Todd's campaign had taught her a great deal about the dogged persistence of journalists and how they wheedled information out of even the most taciturn delegate. She'd always loathed their whatever-it-takes mentality, but now that she was on the fact-finding end of the stick, the education she'd inadvertently picked up was quite useful. Or would have been if she hadn't landed in Cedar Springs as some kind of pseudo–local celebrity.

She looked up as the walk light came on, and tucked the map back into her pocket before setting off again. The fact that she happened to be heading in the direction of the flight school was strictly coincidence. Jake had been kind enough to get her into town, then leave her be. She thought about their "date" and wondered if he'd even remember it come Sunday. That was days away from now. Or, perhaps after hearing the buzz of gossip spreading about the mayor's estranged stepdaughter being in town, he might decide she was too much trouble.

It should bother her, or at the very least be a red flag of some perspective-giving sort, that the idea he might back out on the date disappointed her the way it did. But, at the moment, he was the only person here she felt she could trust, ridiculous as that sounded. And now his school was on the map. She usually went with her gut, and she was rarely wrong. But maybe all the stress, combined with her rather abrupt, life-altering decision, had diluted her instincts. After all, she still had no idea what she was going to do with her life. Not exactly an instinctive move on her part.

Still, she continued pedaling without turning back.

Chapter 5

Jake hung up the phone and raked his hand through his hair. Again. It was amazing he hadn't pulled it all out. He'd spent the better part of what was left of his day after returning from Holden, talking to the guy he hoped was going to be his first corporate sponsor, then updating his crew, who were all chomping at the bit on whether or not to plan on being ready and available for the National Air Races next month. To which he, yet again, had to tell them, he didn't know.

The most recent debate was on how, exactly, the corporate sponsorship of the *Betty Sue* would be marketed. Jake was not going to slap their company name on *Betty Sue*'s perfectly restored and historically accurate skin. He'd agreed to a whole raft of corporate swag they wanted to hand out during the races, but he balked on plastering anything on the plane itself. *Betty Sue* had always been, and always would be, true to her original paint job. This was not NASCAR.

The corporate boys—bankers and stock traders mostly, all connected with the same investment firm, but more important, decade-long frat brothers—were still, at heart, a bunch of kids. Really rich kids, in this case, who were really excited about having a part in one of the fastest races on earth, and just happened to have a whole lot of spare change between them to make their latest dream come true. But they couldn't agree on anything to save their damn lives. Jake wouldn't put himself through it, and realized why his grandfather had balked at ever allowing someone's checkbook to dictate how he was going to take care of his baby, much less race her.

But Jake was more pragmatic about it, and more realistic. Patrick McKenna—Paddy to his friends and grandchildren alike—hadn't minded the side show aspect of the fair and air show circuit, and had made enough doing them to just barely maintain *Betty Sue* and, along with his old war buddies, get her race ready each year. Jake didn't really have a love for that part of the flying culture. He just wanted to fly. He loved the history of the planes, and the restoration work was very fulfilling for him. That it all culminated once a year in a week filled with heart-pounding racing . . . that was enough. And, for all that, he wanted to win, dammit. He knew she could do it. And now, he finally had a chance to put *Betty Sue* at the front of the pack. With a little—okay, a lot—of help from Roger and his investment banker–stockbroker frat buddies.

"I miss you, Paddy McKenna," he grumbled. "I hope I do you proud. But enough already with this crap." He understood now more than ever why his grandfather had balked at allowing others to dictate anything having to do with *Betty Sue*'s upkeep. Before he'd begun sticking with the show circuit as his only funding, Paddy had organized fund-raisers and even taken on one of the local banks as a partner for a short, ill-fated time way back when Jake was in grade school and the annual race had just been created in Reno. Paddy had naturally wanted to show off his baby, and Jake couldn't blame him. He'd bought the beat-up World War II fighter in 1955 and had spent almost every second of his spare time, along with all of his spare money, restoring it. Taking on his two grandchildren hadn't helped his hobby, but he made up for it by instilling the same love he had for flying, and old planes, in his grandson.

It had been his grandfather's dream to win the Gold Medallion race in Reno pretty much from the year they'd introduced the event, and given the dreams he'd made come true for Jake, it was the very least Jake could do to see it through. But after five long years spent just getting back in the race, and another five trying to do it Paddy's way, and failing, Jake had caved and finally looked to outside sponsorship as the only way to put *Betty Sue* in real contention. "And goddamn, Paddy, you're right. They're a major pain in my ass, but I'm trying." He shoved away from the small desk crammed into the makeshift office in the corner of the secondary McKenna Flight School hangar, the one Paddy had built to house only one plane, and walked back over to *Betty Sue*.

"You are a pretty, pretty lady," he said, still just as in awe of her now as he'd been at age six, when he'd gotten his first close-up look at her. "And every bit as high maintenance as one, too," he added as he bent over to start throwing tools back into his tool chest.

"Well, on principle alone, I should argue that, or the Secret Society of Women Who Can Take Care of Themselves might revoke my membership."

Jake was fighting a smile, even as he tossed the last wrench into the drawer and turned around. "If I said present company excepted, would that keep me from having to register for the Misogynists of America Club?"

She braced her hands on the handlebars of the pinkest bike he'd ever seen and tilted her head, as if giving serious assessment to the question. "I'd have to get to know you better before I can make a judgment like that."

"Well, at least only one of us is making sweeping generalizations."

She smiled, and suddenly the frustration over the phone call with Roger was forgotten. "True," she said. "Someone needs to keep things grounded in reality." She glanced at the plane as she slipped her helmet off. "Clearly, that wouldn't be you."

"Probably not."

"I'm sorry to barge in. Or roll in, as the case may be. I rented a bike."

"Yes. I can see that. Hope you got a really good deal on it."

"Now, why do you say that? And, be careful, your membership application might ride on your answer."

"It's just . . . not surprising that it was available."

"Nicely done," she said with a wry smile. "The people I work with would be impressed with your . . . mediation skills. Do you want a job? I hear one is available."

"I'll pass. Actively involving myself in politics of any kind gives me the hives. My apologies."

"Apology accepted. I understand the reaction."

"How did you get interested in politics?"

Her smile spread. "You mean, for a girl?"

"No. I actually adore women, by the way. Especially women who know their own minds. My curiosity was straightforward. I honestly don't know why anyone is drawn to it."

"For all the altruistic reasons that a person who really thinks they can make a difference is drawn to."

"And now?"

She lifted a shoulder. "I'd still like to make a difference, but I decided to focus my energies a bit differently."

"Such as?"

She paused, then said, "My policies and new strategies are still in the developmental stage."

"Ah," he said, the epitome of nonjudgmental. "Nicely done."

She did a little curtsy, which sent her straddled bike bobbling and its rider hopping on one foot as she tried to keep it, and herself, upright.

He moved swiftly forward, reflexively reaching for her, but she righted herself and the bike before he got to her.

"I'm really not a menace to society," she assured him. "But perhaps they should at least make you do a little course or something before letting a person loose on the streets with this thing."

He was standing much closer to her now and was disappointed to see her freckles had vanished once again beneath a thin veneer of makeup. In fact, he rather liked the bedraggled, foggy-framed, sodden version of Lauren Matthews to the freshly showered and expertly made-up version.

"What?" she asked, making him aware that he was staring. She patted her head. "Helmet hair, right? Come on, you've seen me worse."

Her hair was perfect. Too perfect, all sleeked back in a shiny ponytail. Yeah, messy and makeup free was definitely better. More . . . her. Which made no sense since, clearly, he was looking at the "real" Lauren Matthews. "No, not a hair out of place." More's the pity. "I wouldn't have picked you for a fan of girly colors, that's all."

"Why wouldn't you have thought me a girly-girl? Because of the lovely raccoon-mascara eyes and stringy wet hair I was sporting when we first met?"

"I really haven't the faintest clue why. Maybe it's knowing your Washington background and making subconscious assumptions. I'm not usually the type to jump to conclusions. But, it . . . surprised me, that's all."

"So . . . liking pink and being girly is a bad thing?"

"Not at all."

She laughed. "Liar."

"I'm not lying. A woman being feminine is great. Who doesn't enjoy a very feminine female?"

"You, I think. I'm guessing you prefer your women outdoorsy, natural, with a few tomboy tendencies thrown in for good measure." He paused just long enough for her to laugh again. "Nailed it in one," she said, sounding smug.

"We all have preferences. Doesn't mean I think the alternatives are a bad thing."

"Well, sorry to disappoint, but I'm not much of an athlete, and although I'd be willing, you really wouldn't want me anywhere near a power tool. Not if you value your extremities and keeping your arterial flow strictly internal. And, to be perfectly honest, working in a job traditionally held by a man, wearing overly conservative, asexually tailored business suits so I'll be taken remotely seriously, for the very fact that I'm built like a very feminine female, one who refuses to sleep her way to the top—"

"I thought there were laws regarding that kind of thing these days."

"Yes, there are. Laws regarding behavior that a smart woman finds other ways to deal with, because blowing the whistle on your male coworkers or superiors, which is the dominant gender percentage of your workforce, is not the best way to win friends and influence people. Namely the very people who would be in charge of promoting you."

"So, you're more Clark Kent than Lois Lane. Cloaking your super powers under a perfectly tailored suit."

She smiled. "Only if Clark likes to wear supremely feminine undergarments under those perfectly tailored suits."

He smiled at that, but his body was having an entirely more exaggerated reaction to the very sudden, very unexpected mental images that sprang to mind.

"My point was that, surrounded by a distinctly black suit and red power tie work world, of which I am also a part . . . I liked being able to look down at my sensibly manicured nails and know that inside my sensible pumps are pink polished toes, and that, possibly, under my straight-cut, unflattering skirt are stockings that aren't necessarily constricting me in places I don't need to be constricted, and be reminded at the end of another grueling, seventy-hour work week, where I have to prove my worth repeatedly to the Boys Club, that I am female and really—really—enjoy being one. So, I saw the pink bike, sitting there in a sea of blue and green and black ones, and thought, *mine*."

He didn't say anything for a long moment. He couldn't. Not without possibly growling, or worse. Which would be an entirely too Neanderthal response that would give her far too much leverage. All the leverage, really. Which, he was swiftly learning, she was likely to have anyway. But no point in revealing his weak spot any earlier than necessary. But sensible, sleek hair on the outside, and garters and pink toenail polish underneath? That . . . well, that was just playing dirty.

She finally laughed and said, "Hard to believe I ever conformed, I know."

"Actually, I was thinking that I can't imagine there is a tailor on earth who could make you look asexual."

Her eyebrows lifted in surprise, but it was the flush that rose to her cheeks that had him permanently changing his opinion on the color pink.

"Yes, well, it's been . . . something of a challenge."

"I've always thought most of the men in Washington haven't a clue what they're doing, and the fact they prefer you buttoned up and down just proves it."

"Your support is appreciated. You really should reconsider the job proposition. We could use more men like you on the Hill."

That earned a short laugh. "No, you couldn't. Trust me." He closed the remaining distance between them and rested his hand on one of the handlebars. "You want to park this thing for a bit?"

She lifted her face to his and he had to resist the sudden, very urgent need to rub at her nose with his thumb until he uncovered a freckle or two.

"I didn't mean to intrude on your work. I've already taken up far too much of your time today as it is. I just . . ."

He ducked his chin to catch her gaze when she looked away. It was so uncustomary for the woman he was coming to know, he found himself curious. "You just what?"

"Your flight school was on the map that the guy at the rental shop gave me, and I was heading through town, and . . . I guess I sort of ended up here. I was curious."

"About?"

"What a flight school looked like." She held his gaze then. "You."

He was already halfway hard from the previous mental image

parade, but that single word made him grow a step harder. He liked her better when she was direct . . . his body clearly did as well. But he also liked that, at times, she was flustered and talked really fast, and that, when he teased her, she either dished it right back, or got the sexiest blush, and that he never knew which thing was going to get which reaction. "I'm not all that fascinating."

"I feel like Dorothy, very far away from Kansas."

"We're in Colorado, not Oz."

"It might as well be, compared to home. You were right, about the mountains. Now that the rain has stopped, it's hard to really take them all in, the immensity of them. I love our mountains back home, but they aren't anything like this. I've been around them my whole life, but they don't prepare you for anything like this."

"You have ancient hills back east. Rolling and graceful. Ours are newer, more jagged and raw, not yet worn down by time, and a bit more challenging because of it. But I think yours are beautiful, too."

"You've been to the East Coast?"

"I've been to almost every part of our country."

"Oh," she said, but didn't say more, despite the questions he could see in her eyes.

"You want to know more. So ask me."

"I'm being nosy and rude and taking your time, when I really should be focusing on preparing myself for the inquisition later this evening."

He smiled, quite easily that time. It was funny how, when she was around, his problems seemed less pressing, the smiles came far more readily. "So, I'm a distraction, then."

"Maybe," she said, then smiled. "But a really good one."

"Well, then, you might as well take full advantage."

And there was that bloom of pink again. It made him wonder just where her mind had gone and how he could get it to go there more often. "Ask questions, satisfy your curiosity," he clarified. The color deepened.

"Oh."

His smile spread to a grin. "Oh, indeed."

"I really should be going."

He shifted a step closer and tightened his grip on the handle-bar, keeping the bike steady. "Should you, really?"

His body reacted further to the way her pupils expanded under his steady regard. He was dying to glance down, see how else his close proximity might be affecting her, but then she might glance down, too . . . and notice the same about him.

"I should. But only because I have to. And . . . thank you."

"For?" he asked, almost afraid to hear what it was she thought she should be thanking him for. "I already told you not to worry about pulling me away—"

"Not that, though I'm still grateful. I enjoyed the company on the ride in and . . . I'm glad I didn't make that trip alone."

He continued his steady regard of her face, her eyes, her mouth . . . and realized he felt very much the same. "I enjoy being in your company, too, Miss Matthews."

She opened her mouth to speak, but apparently was the victim of a suddenly dry throat.

He had to fight the urge to grin. But he was pleased to know he wasn't the only one feeling the effects. "So, is that what you wanted to thank me for? My brilliant conversational abilities?"

She did smile then. "You may not say much, but when you do, it matters."

He hadn't expected that, and now it was he who didn't have a ready response.

She filled the sudden silence. "I wanted to thank you for being discreet, about my whereabouts."

He frowned, too caught up in her eyes to comprehend what she was talking about.

"Arlen's—the mayor's—secretary came to see me. I was surprised to find her at my door, and she explained that she'd spoken with you—" She lifted a hand to stall his reply. "And that you needed a bit of coaxing to reveal any information regarding me. That was nice of you."

"Don't believe your day-to-day motions won't be discussed and talked about, but you'd mentioned there being a stressful situation with your mother and so I didn't so much mind if she had to work harder to track you down. I'm sorry I couldn't keep your whereabouts completely out of the loop, but I'm afraid that's an impossibility here in Mayberry."

She laughed at that. "Well, I appreciate the thought and that you were trying to be sensitive to my situation."

Now it was his turn to laugh. "Trust me, I never involve myself in other peoples' 'situations' so you can take it as a compliment, if you wish. But I'm also warning you that I'm no good at it, so don't go planning to hide behind me. This town, and everyone in it, is transparent to some degree. There is no place to hide."

"Good to know. And don't worry. I'm not much of a hider."

He smiled, liking her more by the second. Wishing he didn't, as it was going to complicate things, but he was afraid it was too late for that. "We still on for Sunday?"

"I hope so. I'll know better after this evening. I'll let you know tomorrow, if that's okay. Can I call you here?"

You can call me anywhere, anytime. "Sure. I'll be here. You might not be high maintenance, but Miss *Betty Sue* over there is very demanding. I'm beginning to think she'd never let me out of her sight if she had her way."

"Betty Sue?"

He nodded toward the Mustang.

"Oh," she said, looking immeasurably more excited now. "Is that what we're going to fly in?"

He laughed. "No, she's not in service at the moment. I'm getting her ready for the race next month."

"Right. That—she's—the Mustang." Her gaze stayed on the plane. "She's really something. I had no idea. World War Two you said."

"Yes," he said, feeling a ridiculous sense of pride, which was silly considering she had no real idea what she was looking at. But he didn't mind that she liked what she saw. Or that, when she turned her gaze back to his, the look in her eyes didn't change. "I can bore you with about a million details covering her entire life history whenever you have a few years. But, in deference to keeping you interested in me for more than five minutes, I'll spare you."

"Actually, I'd like to know more. You said you didn't fly in the exhibitions like your grandfather did. Does someone else fly her then? Or is she only flown for the race? She's really pretty stunning to look at. Hard to believe she was used as a fighter."

"No one has flown her since my grandfather did, except me—" He broke off, then shook his head. "—and he would shoot me if I scared off a beautiful woman talking about the only other woman in my life."

She laughed. "No need for the false flattery. Once a man has seen you with raccoon eyes, she's never going to believe any compliments—"

"You should. You have beautiful eyes."

She clearly wasn't buying. "I wear serious looking glasses, and—"

"And I can see right through them." He was beginning to see through a lot of things, in fact. He was beginning to wonder just how "sleekly pulled back, every hair in place and freckle covered" she'd be if left to her own desires. His smile grew when he realized he'd made her stutter to a stop. "Although if it makes me sound more sincere, I'll add that while I find the frames kind of sexy, in a 'I want to slide them off' kind of way, I do prefer the eyes behind them, without all the black streaks."

She both laughed and swallowed, hard, if the way her throat worked was any indication. And the tension between them both ebbed—of the awkward variety—and flowed . . . of the more intimate kind.

"I really would like to hear more," she said finally. "About the plane, I mean."

"Trust me, I'm doing you the favor. You really don't want to get me started."

He realized he was grinning. And she was smiling back. And

suddenly he was thinking maybe he owed his baby sister a big fat thank-you. Although only under penalty of death would he actually admit that.

"It seems a shame that no one else flies her. I mean, all that work, she should get a chance to strut her stuff more often."

Jake started to reply, then stopped. He hadn't really ever thought about it like that. He'd always just been happy to keep her flight-worthy and race-worthy. "Possibly. I'll just be happy if I can get her ready by race week." And for that, he needed Roger to commit, once and for all, and do it soon. And . . . he really didn't want to think about it, not at the moment, anyway. For the first time in a very long time, he had other things on his mind . . . far more pleasurable things, as it turned out.

"So, about the inquisition tonight," he said, changing the subject. "I take it you're meeting with your mother and the mayor later?" He lifted a hand. "Not my business, I know, so don't feel you have to—"

"No, no, it's okay." She cocked her head a little then, and a different look came into those eyes he was growing so quickly fond of looking into. Too quickly, most likely. But he didn't look away.

"You know, it's funny," she said, "and I don't know why, but—don't let this make you run screaming, okay?"

He frowned at that, confused. "Okay."

"Maybe, subconsciously, I came out here because I thought you—" She stopped, shook her head, laughed. "It sounds even more ridiculous when I put it into words. So, ignore that. Yes, I am meeting them tonight, and no, I'm not looking forward to it. It's a long story that might rival your ability to talk about *Betty Sue*, only for completely opposite reasons, so I'll spare you the gory details."

"I won't pry. But I'm sorry things aren't smooth."

"I appreciate that. I also appreciate you telling me that my mother was looking forward to my arrival. It was . . . good to know. I guess I owed you more thank-yous than I realized."

"For?"

"That, and not telling Melissa every last thing about me when she called you. For keeping my job status a secret."

"How do you know I—"

"You haven't said anything, have you?" she countered, seeming pretty sure of him.

He shook his head. "Nobody's business but yours."

"So . . . thank you. It's been a difficult enough thing, coming out here, needing to set things right with my mother. We've always been really close, but her quickie wedding—" She stopped and held up her hand. "Sorry. I'm very sure you don't want to hear about any of that and I don't want to put you any further in the middle of anything."

"What makes you think you have?"

"You belong here, you know these people, live with them, work with them. I don't want you in any position to be defending me or choosing sides, if, God forbid, it comes to that."

"What makes you think I'd have to do anything like that?"

"Let's just say that my arrival hasn't exactly been under the radar. I had no idea my presence here was going to be such a . . . a . . ."

"Newsworthy event?"

"Might be an overstatement, but that's what Melissa made it sound like. And Debbie at the motel. Even the bike rental guy knew who I was before I filled out the rental form."

"And your being that visible casts the family reunion in an even more stressful light, I take it."

"Exactly. Sorry."

"For?"

"Dumping."

"You're not dumping."

"I could. You make it . . . you're easy to talk to."

"Thank you. Trust me, it's not a trait generally associated with me. Except by my baby sister, but she believes it's the God given right of being family, and I try not to argue. It just prolongs the torture."

Lauren laughed. "You're trying to sound like the much put

upon older brother, but I find that hard to believe. I'm sure she feels very lucky to have you on her side."

"There are as many days when she's pressed just to admit we're related, so it all evens out."

"If you say so."

"I'm just being honest. Always am. Sometimes to a fault." He grinned. "Okay, most of the time."

"Well, it's been appreciated by me. Maybe it won't sound so crazy now, but I think that's why I came out here."

"What do you mean?"

"It's what I started to say earlier, but I didn't know how to phrase it without sounding over the top. I just . . . it's been a little overwhelming, not to mention disconcerting, being here, having people know who I am but not know me personally. And the only person who does know me is the one I am here to sort things out with. I have a lot to deal with, to think about, not only with my family situation, but with my job, with . . . a lot of things." She looked at him directly now. "And, with my seeing them again being imminent, I guess I rode out here kind of on instinct."

"I'm not sure I follow."

"Maybe I'm sounding crazy after all, but I think I needed to sort of touch base with the one person I knew here who would just say what he thinks, and not what he thinks I want to hear." She smiled, but her eyes were still a little troubled.

It bothered him that he was troubled by her being troubled. She was right in what she'd assumed about him, but that didn't mean he wanted to get in the middle of anything. She'd said herself she didn't want him there, either. So . . . what was she saying now?

"Don't worry, okay? I'm only saying it's nice to know you can count on at least one person to speak plainly."

"Given the world you just left, I can imagine that's a commodity in short supply."

"Very true." They held each other's gaze for a longer moment, then she finally broke the hold first and slipped her helmet back on, made a show of buckling the strap. "Well, I'm past the risk of overstaying my welcome, so thanks for letting me bend your ear."

"It was just a little tug." Jake couldn't help but think that if Ruby Jean were a fly on the wall in that moment, she'd own him for the rest of her natural life. The bigger kicker was, for all his concern about being, well, concerned, he actually didn't mind so much that she'd sought him out. Or that he'd helped her cope in some way.

She smiled. "I'll get out of your way now."

He let go of the bike, surprised at how reluctant he was to do so. For a few minutes, he'd gotten to step outside of the frustration that had shadowed most of his waking hours of late. He told himself that's all it was. Problem was, he was having a hard time believing it. "See you Sunday." He had no time to spend showing someone the sights. After succumbing to Ruby Jean's tearful plea, he had already figured out how to narrow the time down to the barest minimum and still fulfill his promise. Now . . . now he was mentally scrambling, trying to figure out how to juggle his time and his obligations so he could spend more time with her.

"I'll let you know tomorrow, for sure. What time, Sunday?"

Anytime. All the time. "We can figure that out when you call. Or, if you need to work off some steam, feel free to pedal on back out here. The exertion does wonders for pent-up frustration."

"Sounds like you have some personal experience with that."

He'd been thinking of a different type of exertion, due to an entirely different kind of frustration, but she didn't have to know that. "A little."

She adjusted her helmet strap and balanced her weight as she got ready to mount the bike. The vision she made, all pink-power girl, made him smile as she backed the bike up until she could turn it around, aiming toward the open end of the hangar.

His thoughts drifted, quite naturally, he thought, to other things he'd like to see her mount. The rear view, in particular, was extremely . . . inspiring.

"Well, we'll talk again, one way or the other."

He tugged the rag from the pocket of his jeans and wiped his hands, then shoved them both in his pockets when she glanced back at him, hoping she wasn't noticing just how much he'd been noticing her. Plus, with his hands in his pockets, he couldn't do something remarkably stupid. Like reach for her. He did something like that now, and he'd either be really sorry he'd pushed it . . . or she'd be really late for dinner. Neither possibility was a good outcome. So he kept his hands hidden . . . and other things hopefully camouflaged. "Sounds like a plan."

She nodded, then turned her attention back to the bike, which wobbled quite dangerously when she launched off. He almost trotted after her, but she steadied herself after a few rotations. So he made himself stay where he stood, all the while wondering what in the hell had gotten into him, as he watched her ride until she was out of sight. In fact, he had to force himself to turn back to *Betty Sue* instead of wandering closer to the end of the hangar, where he could watch her pedal herself almost all the way back down to town.

"Right, because you don't have about a hundred and ten things you need to be doing right now." Didn't stop him from thinking about her though. He slapped his thigh and called out for Hank. He heard a groan and a snuffling snort, then minutes later, his big old hound came shuffling over. "You missed her, you know. Not much of a watch dog."

Hank stared at him with soulful eyes.

"You'd like her. She's quite something to watch, too."

In response, Hank wandered over and sighed deeply as he collapsed in a boneless heap by an oil drum.

"She'd like you, too, I think." He smiled as Hank stretched out in a fading beam of sunlight. He turned and looked back through the open hangar door. And wished his life was simpler.

At that moment, an afternoon spent stretched out under the sun sounded almost as intoxicating as racing five hundred miles an hour, barely a breath off the ground. Of course, the former option he wouldn't have to perform solo.

"Yeah," he said, wandering back over to his tools. "You'd like her a lot, Hank. Problem is, I like her, too."

Chapter 6

Lauren smoothed her hair, then her shirt, then her hair again, for at least the hundredth time. She'd dressed casual-nice, despite the fact that, from what she could tell, the town at-large was almost universally casual-casual. Which normally would have suited her just fine. One of the things she'd immediately loved about quitting her job was not having to armor up every morning. But, when she was dressing for dinner, she decided she could use all the support she could get. She might not like the power suits and sensible pumps, but, in truth, she felt more in control while wearing them. Capitol Hill Lauren. Assistant to a powerful state senator, Lauren. Future-all-mapped-out Lauren.

Which was definitely better than newly jobless Lauren, no future plans Lauren, or wildly attracted to the local plane jockey Lauren.

No, what she needed to be was "ready to meet the man you can't believe your mother married Lauren." Yeah, that was going to take at least a few layers of well-tailored support.

Satisfied that she was as pulled together as humanly possible, she ignored the rampantly flapping butterflies in her stomach and pushed through the doors. She welcomed the cooler air of the restaurant and drew in a deep breath of it. But before she could even look for the table where her mother and Arlen were likely already seated, she was accosted by the hostess.

"Well, hello! Welcome to Ragland Gap. I'm Kim, your hostess."

Kim, another naturally caffeinated denizen of Cedar Springs. Lauren might have worried that she'd landed in Stepford-ville, except they were all so sincere in their friendliness, it was hard not to respond in kind. "Hi, Kim. I'm meeting a party of—"

"Oh, I know. You're Charlene Thompson's daughter."

It caught her badly off guard, hearing her mother called by her new married name. She'd never thought to wonder if her mother had changed her name. It just felt . . . odd. Okay, it felt downright wrong, but she was trying—really—to be the new and improved, less biased, more compassionate Lauren. Which was challenging enough without being known on sight to yet another complete stranger. "Lauren Matthews," she said, introducing herself.

"It's a pleasure to meet you. George—he's the owner—gave the mayor a private room so you all could reunite without any distractions."

"Oh," she said. *Great.* Everyone not only knew they were dining here, but it was also apparently common knowledge that it was also their first family meeting. Lovely. Well, she supposed she should be grateful, at least, for the private room. She had no idea how the next hour was going to go, but the less public the better. "Thank you."

"I'll show you the way. Follow me."

Lauren was probably imagining that everybody was staring at her as she passed through the crowded dining room. Surely they were all whispering about something else completely, and there really wasn't a hush as she approached followed by a sudden burst of conversation after she passed by. All in her head.

She tried not to make eye contact and just prepare herself for the imminent hellos, and felt entirely conspicuous as Kim nodded at any number of diners as they took what had to be the most convoluted path possible through the tables. She wondered if that had been on purpose, so everyone could get a good gander at the mayor's new stepdaughter. After all, the place seemed unusually packed for a Thursday night.

Then Kim ducked them through an archway and paused outside a curtained-off door. "Here you are, Miss Matthews."

"Lauren."

Kim beamed. "Lauren. It's a pleasure. Stephan will be here shortly to take your order. You have a great night."

"Thank you," she said, half wishing she could just stand out here and chat with Kim some more. Kim was an easy crowd to please. But the hostess bustled off—with a cheery wave of course—and Lauren turned toward the closed curtain. Another deep breath. After a six-month delay, it was suddenly showtime.

As soon as she ducked through the curtain, letting it fall shut again behind her, her mother immediately got up and came around the table, engulfing her daughter in a hug. "Lauren, I'm so glad you came, sweetheart. I've missed you so much."

Lauren's face was smooshed into her mother's soft silver hair, so she couldn't respond and couldn't get a look at Arlen, but it felt so good, after so much time, and so much emotion and heartache, to be hugged by her mom that she simply hugged her back.

It was long moments later before Charlene finally set her back, but such a load had already been lifted from her shoulders with that one, heartfelt hug that Lauren felt a rejuvenation of hope that maybe this could all turn out far, far better than she'd allowed herself to dream.

Lauren pushed her own hair from her face and blinked back the tears threatening to form. "I am, too," she said. *Could it really be this simple?* Guilt swamped her. She should have made the trip out sooner, carved the time into her schedule, her life, and not waited until it had become this cataclysmic. They'd just needed to see each other in order to regain perspective and get their priorities back in place. Their bond had always been so strong, it could weather anything. She should have never let it get this bad.

Then Arlen stepped into view behind her mother, and Lauren's stomach squeezed right back into a tight ball. She'd been so overwhelmed and happy to be reunited with her mother, she'd neglected to remember that the actual reason behind their estrangement had yet to be dealt with.

His face was a bit paunchier than the photos she'd found during her investigative forays, and his hair a bit thinner, but otherwise there was no mistaking that this was the mayor of Cedar Springs. There was also no mistaking that this was a man who oozed a particular brand of God-given charisma and natural charm. The kind that allowed him to work a room, shake hands, kiss babies, and shoot the bull with just about anyone, all without actually uttering a truly sincere word. Sort of like a really sharp used-car salesman. Or a snake-oil salesman.

And, for the life of her, she hadn't a clue what her mother saw in him.

The woman who'd raised her would never have fallen for that kind of skin-deep magnetism. She could spot a phony a mile away. Ten miles. In fact, it was partly her ability to read a person within five seconds of meeting them that had made her such a successful and popular hostess. No one could seat a room as well as Charlene Matthews. It was a special skill but was largely responsible for the success of whatever event she was helping to sponsor. And you couldn't do that if you didn't have a knack for instantly knowing who and what you were dealing with.

But, Lauren thought, struggling mightily—oh so mightily—to scrape together at least a modicum of objectivity, perhaps there were hidden charms to be found that his more obvious character flaws hid from plain sight. She'd do best to sit back and watch her mother interact with him and see if perhaps it all explained itself.

But to do that, she had to get the party started. To that end, she mustered up the fake sincere smile that her years on the political party circuit had honed to perfection and turned to face him. "Hello," she said, deciding to take the upper hand. It remained to be seen how long she held it. "I'm Lauren." She put her hand out to avoid any potential awkward attempt at hugging, as well as to establish that while she was going to be polite, she wasn't going to be insincere and say she was happy to meet him. Best to be as up front as possible with the man, no matter what her mother might be hoping for.

"Arlen," he said, thankfully dispensing with any formal or titular introductions.

Neither of which would have surprised her after reading a few of his speeches. In fact, when he stepped closer to take her offered hand, she duly noted the automatic "kissing babies stump speeching" smile she was certain came as easily to him as breathing, but was surprised to also notice that he appeared almost a little nervous. There was a thin sheen of perspiration on his forehead even though the temperature in the room was quite moderate. Could he really be so worried about whether or not his wife's new daughter gave them her blessing? From what she'd gleaned about the man, that wouldn't likely be the case. So . . . why the telltale flopsweat?

"It's a true pleasure to finally be making your acquaintance," he said, still sounding like he was stumping for votes. Some politicians were like that, she'd learned, adopting a fixed-smile social persona that they became so entrenched in, they found themselves unable to flip the switch to truly sincere when the moment—and the company—dictated it. Like, you know . . . with family.

Others, like Senator Fordham, were comfortable and easily and sincerely themselves in any circumstance, private and social. A shame Arlen didn't fall into her former boss's category. But then, if he had, she'd have understood more why her mother had fallen for the man and they wouldn't be having this awkward dinner meeting in the first place.

"Please, have a seat," he added, all fixed smile and perfect, dentist-enhanced teeth. And . . . nervous. Up close it was even more obvious. "I hope you don't mind the private room; I thought you and your mother would appreciate the privacy. I—"

"We do," she said, feeling oddly compelled to put him at ease. It threw her off a little, his slight lack of composure. She'd been certain he would ooze the same rather smarmy charm she'd noted in the few taped speeches she'd been able to scrounge up during her search. And the smarmy charm was definitely there on the surface; his plastered-on enthusiasm hadn't changed a flicker since she'd entered the room, but the underlying nerves didn't seem to match up right.

She wanted to believe it was just about a man wanting to please his new wife. But he hadn't so much as glanced at her since Lauren had entered the room, much less shown any kind of united front by standing next to her. Which left the other, less flattering, but far more plausible option, given what she knew. That his nerves stemmed from him wanting to make a good impression on her for personal reasons. In her case, she could only surmise that would be because of her connections to the power players in Washington. Though what good he thought that would do him as mayor of a small Colorado mountain town, she had no idea.

"Why don't we all have a seat." Her mother, ever the hostess, directed them to the table with a smile. "The wine steward should be here with our request momentarily. I hope you don't mind, Lauren, dear, but we ordered a lovely bottle of pinot noir, grown locally, in fact. We'll be more than happy to get something else—"

"That won't be necessary," Lauren said, allowing the mayor to pull her seat back for her before he rounded the table and did the same for his wife. She sat catty-corner to her mother and directly across from the mayor. She watched them, curious to see any byplay between them, anything to help her understand the magnetism that supposedly existed. But there were no little touches, no private glances, no silent communication. In fact, they seemed to just be going through the motions, not exactly strained, but each of them definitely seemed lost in their own thoughts. "I, uh, didn't know they grew grapes at this altitude."

"Well, it's not Napa Valley," Arlen responded jovially, "but we're pretty proud of what our great state produces."

"You're originally from California, right?"

"Yes," Arlen said, and seemed quite enthusiastic about being given the chance to endorse that little tidbit about himself. "San Francisco."

Lauren kept her own "circuit smile" on steady display. "Then I suppose you'd probably know a little something about those Napa wines, so I'm impressed you think so highly of the local wines here. I'm looking forward to trying it."

"I assure you, you won't be disappointed."

Small talk momentarily exhausted, when the silence went on for a beat too long, Lauren's mother reached for her menu, prompting them to do the same.

It was cowardly, she knew, to hide behind the oversized, faux-leather folder, but it gave her a much-needed moment to regroup and reorganize her thoughts without Arlen staring her down. Well, maybe stare was too excessive a description, but he'd kept his focus fairly intently on her since she'd entered the room. Even when he'd seated her mother, his attention had been on Lauren. It wasn't exactly creepy or anything, but it wasn't comfortable, either.

Lauren surreptitiously took peeks at both her mother and Arlen as they perused their menus. For all she knew, they ate here all the time and knew the course offerings by heart. But they both seemed pretty intent on examining every entrée. And not once, that she had noticed anyway, had they so much as glanced at one another.

Could it be, Lauren wondered, that perhaps her mother had already come to the same realization that her East Coast friends and Lauren had come to about five seconds after she'd announced her elopement? If so, Lauren would be profoundly relieved and grateful to have the mother she knew and loved back to her normal sane, rational self. But she also was well aware that Charlene was a proud woman who'd been raised to do well in anything she attempted—a goal she'd pretty much always succeeded in achieving—so would likely be embarrassed by this rather public and personal failing. Lauren vowed right then she would approach the subject delicately and with compassion.

She glanced at her mother, wishing again that she could have spent some time with her alone first, rather than this somewhat stilted, best-behavior, social call. The private room was nice, but only went so far. She couldn't ask her mother the things she was most dying to know, which was how in the worldwide hell, with all the distinguished and lovely gentlemen who had orbited her very active social circles since Lauren's father had passed away—and there had been no small number who would have given anything for even a personal smile from Charlene Matthews—had she ever, even in a weak moment, chosen this one?

Okay, maybe she needed to work on the delicate part of her approach. But even if her mother had realized her impulsive union was a mistake, Lauren was still curious why she'd been compelled to be so impulsive in the first place.

She thought perhaps she could catch the corner of her mother's eye and silently mouth something to her— about seeing her later, in private. But her mother had set her menu aside and was busy spreading her linen napkin neatly in her lap, her faultless southern Virginia manners as natural a part of her as her relentlessly graceful charm.

When the silence continued after they'd all set aside their menus, Lauren cleared her throat and said, "Cedar Springs is lovely."

Her mother's eyes sparkled at the comment. "Isn't it, though? Just like a page out of a magazine."

"Jewel of the Rockies," Arlen said, sounding less uncertain of himself now. Of course, that was because he sounded like a campaign poster. Which as mayor, was, generally speaking, his job.

Now that Lauren suspected he wasn't going to be in her or her mother's orbit much longer, it was easier to simply take him with a grain of salt and not be as tense or stressed over every single sentence.

"It's taken a good part of my time in office," he went on, "but we've managed to turn this town into a destination resort that rivals—and if you ask me, outdoes—its more glitzier counterparts to the south. Telluride might have its little film festival, and Aspen and Vail their constant stream of movie starlets, but Cedar Springs is a town that can embrace the worldwide adventure seeker, and still offer home and hearth to those residents who plan to live out their life in our little mountain paradise. It's becoming a generational town, where family names still mean something, and small town values remain high on our priority list, despite our reputation as a place that easily meets the needs of our most worldly and cosmopolitan travelers. From a five star resort, to award-winning restaurants, it really is—"

"The jewel of the Rockies," Lauren finished with him, wondering how often he'd given that exact speech. "I can see why." She turned her attention to him more personally, a pleasant smile on her face. In fact, she was feeling almost generous with the guy now. It was even a bit tempting to let him believe he'd won her over with his chamber of commerce, tourism board ad campaign, but given the amount of rhetoric she'd heard in her career, it would have taken a much better actress than her to pull that off. Besides, even her goodwill had its limits. Which was made, perhaps more clear than she intended, when, instead, she said, "I will admit though, I hadn't expected my arrival to be so . . . conspicuous."

"I'm sorry about that, sweetheart," her mother broke in to say. "It's just, with Arlen being the mayor, and my excitement over your visit, word spreads in a little town like this. Please don't feel pressured by it; everyone is excited to meet you, as well."

Lauren smiled at her mother and wished like hell the two of them were anywhere but here right now. This all felt so . . . staged. And she was pretty sure her mother was feeling the same way. But her manners would never allow her to tear away the veil of social propriety. And Lauren wouldn't put her in that kind of awkward position by doing it herself. At least, not blatantly anyway.

But at least she could look forward now to spending some time alone with her mother. The two of them could figure out how best to handle the next step so that her mother could extricate herself and return to her previous life with as little fallout as possible. Which . . . was going to call on every bit of campaign strategy Lauren had learned in her years in Washington, and then some.

She glanced back at Arlen to find him steadily regarding her. It caught her off guard, and he immediately glanced down and spread his linen napkin on his lap, but it was still a little unnerving. She told herself he was simply feeling the awkward tension in the room and had been trying to read her, figure out what would work. Politicians and businessmen did it all the time as they met with constituents, clients, and those who might be able to help them achieve their goals. She wondered if Arlen was good at reading people, or just thought he was good at it. She'd met both types. She hadn't learned enough about him to know, but his business successes would indicate he was pretty decently skilled. It was something to keep in mind. To not underestimate him. Especially if her mother was planning to ask for a divorce.

He had a whole town behind him. Her mother was an O'Grady and a Matthews, and back home both carried significant weight. But Lauren was well aware that her mother would want to preserve both her good name and her standing, at all costs. Pride and dignity being paramount in her world. So, if Arlen wanted to play dirty, he could easily have the upper hand.

Worth keeping in mind, in terms of staying on his good side. At least, for now.

Lauren picked up her menu again just as her mother said, "We're so sorry we couldn't meet you in Holden. Jake was very kind to do us the favor, but I understand the storm earlier kept him from flying you in."

"It did, but we made it in just fine." Lauren was careful to keep looking at her menu. Her mother had an almost supernatural ability to look at her daughter's face and know what she was thinking. Or, at least, who she was thinking about. There was more than enough tension swirling in the room already. And that was what they'd come here to figure out. Lauren didn't want to give her any excuse for a distraction, particularly when she wasn't sure how she felt about the distraction yet, herself. It was definitely way too early, on all fronts, to mention just how much she'd enjoyed Jake's company. Much less that she planned on enjoying it again. She assumed that word might get around after their little flight on Sunday, but certainly by then she and her mother would have a battle plan in place. And, considering Lauren wasn't all that certain she'd need to be here much longer than that, it wouldn't really matter at that point. "How do you all know Jake?" she asked casually. Better to know up front what the connection was. "Or is it that everyone knows everyone here?"

"Well, that much is certainly true," her mother said, "but, as it happens, Jake's sister, Ruby Jean, is Arlen's personal administrative assistant. Sort of like the job you have with Senator Fordham," she added with a proud smile. "Just on a somewhat smaller scale."

"Careful, dear," Arlen said with a chuckle. "You know we men don't like to have our egos—I mean, careers—sized."

He patted her mother's hand, which caused a totally inappropriate, almost visceral protective reaction in Lauren, which had her staring really hard at the menu rather than using it to swat his hands off her mother.

Who happens to be his wife, she reminded herself, which should have been totally unnecessary. Of course, she'd already come to the conclusion, given their behavior so far, that there wouldn't be any endearments or little touches, so it had just caught her off guard was all. Certainly, given they were trying to mend fences first, they'd want to keep up appearances in front of her. Although neither of them had been trying too awfully hard. She just needed to be better prepared to witness it, that was all. Once she'd had the chance to sit down with her mother and get this fiasco all out into the open, all the charade playing could finally come to an end. Which made her wonder . . . were both her mother and Arlen playing charades? Had Arlen also come to realize the depth of the mismatch?

That set Lauren off on an entirely new tangent of internal questioning. Lovely.

She'd just have to watch a bit more intently, then see if she could figure out the lay of the land. Her mother had smiled at his little joke, but then they both had gone back to their menus. Charlene had never once, to Lauren's knowledge, had any patience for men with practiced, well-rehearsed viewpoints. Pompous poseurs, she'd called them. Her mother responded to passionate defense of beliefs and a person knowing his or herself well enough to stand behind them and defend them well if called upon to do so.

Somehow, after listening to Arlen's chamber of commerce speech a few minutes ago, Lauren couldn't really fathom him giving an impassioned, original defense of . . . anything. He might be a practiced orator, but Lauren would bet money the words he delivered the best were generally written by somebody else.

Lauren glanced at her mother again and found her thoughts going back to how they'd ever become a match in the first place. Under what set of conditions would her mother have ever fallen for this guy? Lauren couldn't come up with any. Which led her to wonder again if, perhaps, there really was something wrong with her. She seemed perfectly fine, sharp, gracious, and on point as she'd always been, but perhaps there was something else going on beneath the surface. Not that Lauren wished her mother ill health over simple poor judgment, but there had to be something that would explain this . . . aberration. Something that Lauren was obviously missing.

She stared sightlessly at her menu and tried very hard to be objective. Daphne, one of her former coworkers, and the only one she considered a close friend, had said in response to Lauren's venting about all of it that perhaps her feelings about Arlen were just totally off base and skewed by her dissatisfaction with her own life. And that maybe she should trust her mother, who'd always shown good judgment, the same way Lauren expected that of her mother when Lauren had dated various men on the Hill.

Except Lauren hadn't eloped and moved across the country with any of them.

And she'd fixed her dissatisfaction with her life. Well, she'd taken the first step, anyway. And that hadn't changed her feelings about the elopement. She really didn't think that had anything to do with this.

The wine steward came in just then, followed by Stephan, their waiter, giving a much-needed break to the growing silence in the small room.

After Arlen pronounced the pinot noir palatable, everyone placed their orders, or should she say that she placed her order, and Arlen placed the order for both him and her mother. Even though Lauren hadn't seen him consult with her at all on any part of their order. Her mother was a connoisseur of good food and was known for her very discerning palate. Her menus were always discussed after any event and considered both classic and adventurous, mostly in terms of the combinations she would so cleverly decide upon. So . . . it was just odd to see her hand over the choice of what she was going to eat to someone else. But then, as Lauren had noted earlier, perhaps they came here all the time and their choices were already well established.

She looked to Stephan, the waiter, to see if there was any acknowledgment on his part of the First Couple being regulars of the establishment. But he didn't seem to treat them any differently than he treated her.

And Lauren knew her mother's expressions about as well as Charlene could read her daughter's, and Lauren didn't spy any dissatisfaction with the direction the evening was taking, overtly or subtly.

It was all so confusing, really. Possibly she was just over-thinking all of it, examining the details too closely, analyzing aspects that simply didn't require such close scrutiny. Okay, probably. But that still left her with more questions than answers.

They all handed their menus to Stephan, who slipped out as silently as he'd slipped in, taking her one remaining shield away with him.

Forced to make direct eye contact, Lauren chose her mother. "So, how did the charity luncheon go today?" Small talk. She hadn't seen her mother in six months, and she was making small talk. It was pathetic, and made her more than a little sad, but she felt really out to sea here, so, like her mother, she clung to societal convention like the life raft it was. At least until she felt she had a better handle on the real situation between her mother and Arlen.

"It went well, but ran quite long." Her mother smiled, clearly using the life raft, as well.

"What was the charity?" Lauren asked, fiddling with her napkin, smoothing the wrinkles flat.

And so the conversation went, stilted and staggered and so incredibly not how she thought it might go after that initial hug. She blamed it all on Arlen, or perhaps her mother's discomfort in knowing how to act around him. She still felt certain that she and her mother were on the right track, but she'd have paid large sums to have an emergency announced in the kitchen right around then that would force the restaurant to close early. A little dramatic, perhaps, but that's how she was feeling at the moment. Finally, Stephan—bless his heart—returned with their food. Which was probably delicious, but she couldn't remember a single bite of it. Mostly it had given her something to do. And do it, she did. She carefully cut and consumed that lasagna like it was her damn job. She listened as Arlen talked on about the town's accomplishments and future hopes, and her mother chimed in to talk about this person or that, trying to personalize Arlen's monologue, as if Lauren would be interested in minor details of the lives of complete strangers. But then, it struck her that the irony was, the people sitting across from her were complete strangers, so what difference did it make?

Dinner finally dwindled to an end, their meals finished, leaving Lauren to desperately wish she could claim some other engagement and take off. But she'd just arrived in town. Expressly to see her mother and meet Arlen. So, what else could she possibly have to do?

Jake's sexy, smiling face floated through her mind.

She floated it right back out again as Stephan returned to clear dishes and ask after coffee and dessert. Lauren had the strongest urge to wrap her arms around his waist and beg him to stay. Or take her with him. Thankfully, dessert was unanimously declined and coffee was ordered. How long could it take to sip a cup of coffee, then beg off with claims of an altitude headache or jet lag? Neither of which were true, but neither her mother nor Arlen, who were both searching for topics of discussion themselves, seemed all that intent on prolonging the agony, either.

The other irony was that there was so much she wanted to say, wanted to ask. But, instead they were stuck in some kind of horrific provincial play, acting out parts none of them felt comfortable playing, rather than just putting it all out there on the table. It was on the tip of her tongue to simply say it, dive in, but something held her back. Maybe it was the way she'd continued to catch Arlen kind of staring at her during dinner. Nothing overtly creepy or anything, just that . . . staring thing he did. He'd smile when she caught him, or look away and pretend he hadn't been staring at all. She supposed it wasn't weird, him wanting to get a look at the one person who possibly stood between him and a potentially happy marriage. Or! A satisfactory divorce. Ooh, maybe that was it! It made more sense than anything else. Her mother had probably let it slip that Lauren was also an attorney, though not a practicing one, but still . . .

perhaps it wasn't her political contacts he wanted, but her legal expertise that he was trying to avoid.

So many questions, but with that one thought, she knew there was no way she could force the conversation now. It would never be in her mother's best interests for them both to be blindsided with that kind of conversational gambit.

"Lauren, dear, are you okay?"

She realized she was balling up her napkin in her lap and carefully laid it on the table beside her water glass. "You know, with the flight and the storm and all, it's been a really long day. It might just be the altitude change, but I think the day is catching up with me."

Her mother looked sincerely concerned, and suddenly Lauren was fighting tears in her eyes because she was sincerely concerned, too, and she wanted nothing more than for them to move forward and get to the heart of things. She wasn't sure what moving down that path would entail, but they'd figure it out as they went along. She pushed her chair back and used the moment to will her tears to remain at bay. Her mother and Arlen both stood.

"I'm glad you came out to meet us," her mother said sincerely, but more cautiously now. As if she, too, was disappointed in how the evening had gone.

Lauren wondered what her mother's hopes had been for tonight. And what she was thinking and feeling now.

"I had a few things planned," she went on, "just casually, nothing written in stone, that I thought we could do together while you were here."

Lauren wanted to ask if "we" constituted only her and her mother, or all three of them, but it was beyond her at that point to figure out how to do so without seeming rude. "Okay. That sounds good. We'll talk tomorrow."

Her mom came around the corner of the table to hug her, and Lauren knew it would be her only chance to speak just to her mother. When she was enveloped in a tight hug, she whispered into her mother's ear. "I need to talk to you. Just you. Okay?"

Her mother paused in the way she was squeezing her daughter, but in no other way indicated that Lauren had said anything to her. She finally straightened and stepped back, but slid her hands down until she could join them with Lauren's. "We'll talk tomorrow after you've had a good night's rest." She was smiling brightly—too brightly?—but didn't say anything further.

"Sounds good." Lauren squeezed her mother's hands, then let them go and turned to Arlen. "Thank you for dinner. It was very good." She knew she should say it was a pleasure to meet him, but somehow the words just refused to come out.

Thankfully, mercifully, Stephan came once again to her rescue, arriving with the tray of coffee.

"I can find my way back," she said, stepping to the curtain as he set the tray beside the table. "Please, enjoy your coffee. I'll call you tomorrow, Mom. Or, better yet, call me when it's best for you." Which, she hoped her mother had figured out, would be whenever Arlen wasn't within hearing distance.

And, with that, while Stephan was dispensing mugs, creamer, and wielding the pot, Lauren fled.

"Well. That was fun," she muttered under her breath, after faking a smile at still-perky Kim and pushing through the doors into the chilly evening air. "Not."

"Not what?"

She stifled a squeal, but still pressed a hand to her suddenly thumping heart as she turned around to find Jake standing right behind her.

"Need a lift?"

"I—haven't you've rescued me enough for one day?" she said, mustering a half laugh from somewhere.

He stepped closer until she could see his face more clearly in the light of the streetlamp positioned in front of the restaurant doors. Apparently, that allowed him to see her face more clearly, too, because he said, "I'm guessing it's rare you ever really need rescuing, but you do seem a bit . . . flustered."

"What gave me away?"

"Nothing, really. You just pushed through the doors like the hounds of hell were after you." His lips curved. "Otherwise, I wouldn't have guessed a thing."

"What are you doing here?" She was smiling, but the words still came out a tad more edgy than intended, but she was kind of at the end of her emotional rope, and maybe there was some jet lag, and altitude lag, and just overall life lag, affecting her as well. She wanted to make a better impression on him, she really did, but it would help if he'd stop catching her at her worst. At least she didn't have helmet hair or raccoon eyes and post-traumatic flight shock, but still.

"I live here," he said mildly, still friendly, if not quite as amused as before.

"I mean, *here*, here."

"I . . . like to eat," he said with a shrug. "Sometimes more than once a day. I haven't had anything since we stopped for snacks earlier today in Kremmling."

She ducked her chin and blew out a breath. He didn't have to work hard to catch her at her worst, because, apparently, that's all she was offering today. "I'm sorry." She looked up, forced a smile. "You'd never guess, but I can be quite charming when I put my mind to it."

"I thought you were quite charming in all your pink cycling gear this afternoon."

Her smile relaxed a little as her cheeks warmed a bit. He had a habit of doing that to her, too. And she'd thought seven years of working on the Hill would have put her beyond blushing. Apparently not. But then, she'd never had such a sincere sounding compliment, delivered in such a deep voice, by a guy who made her pulse pound just thinking about him. "Thank you. Then, please," she bowed slightly, "remember me as I was."

He waited until she straightened, then looked her up and down, and suddenly her fatigue wasn't quite as bone-deadening as it had been a mere moment ago.

"You look pretty good in navy pinstripe, too, as it turns out." He leaned closer and dropped that deep, sexy voice to a rough whisper, which . . . wow. "Although, I should tell you, I think they outlawed pinstripes in Cedar Springs right after the town charter was signed. Probably no one told you because, being related to the mayor and all, they didn't want to hurt your feelings."

She couldn't help it; she laughed. Something she couldn't have imagined feeling like doing when she'd exited those doors. "Well, I appreciate your being bold and daring enough to brave the potential wrath of your town leader."

"It's not Arlen I'm afraid of."

"Oh?"

"It's your mother."

Surprised, she said, "My mother? Why?"

"I've learned, never come between a mama and her cub."

"I'm hardly a cub."

He smiled and reached out to catch a strand of hair that had caught across her face in the evening breeze. He untangled it and smoothed it away, but his hand lingered. "Where mothers are concerned, you're always the cub."

Her smile softened, as did a little spot inside her chest. "Yeah, I guess you're right." Tears threatened to spring forth again, and at the same time, she fought a sudden, ferocious need to yawn. Relaxing, even a little bit, had demolished whatever reserve of energy she'd had left. "Well, this cub apparently needs to head back to the den for some sleep."

"I'll be happy to drop you off. My truck is just down the street."

"It's not that far. I thought I'd walk." She wanted the time, the night air, the activity, before she ended up in bed, alone, with nothing more than her thoughts and several full-length, mental, frame-by-frame replays of tonight's dinner to occupy her. If she was lucky, walking the few blocks back to her motel would both give her a chance to do an initial postgame review and drain whatever was left in the tank at the same time, allowing her to drop right off as soon as her head hit the pillow.

"Care for some company, then?"

Then again, maybe a little distraction would be even better. She smiled. "Thank you. I'd like that."

He crooked an elbow, and she slid her arm through. She smiled, he smiled back, and the silence was easy and companionable, with just the hint of combustibility below the surface. It was . . . perfect. A little, but not too much. And exactly what she needed.

So much so, that she didn't even hear the restaurant door swing open behind her. Or feel Arlen Thompson staring at her back, frowning at the sight of the newest member of his family arm in arm with one of the older thorns in his side. He'd thought hiring his kid sister would make the guy a bit more amenable to throwing his family's name behind the plans he had for this town. He'd guessed wrong. When Charlene stepped out behind him, he turned, blocking the couple from view, and hustled her to the car parked a few feet away, thinking hard, thinking fast, about how he could make this latest ripple work to his advantage.

Maybe the night hadn't been a complete bust after all.

Chapter 7

They paused in front of the hotel. The glow of the vacancy sign illuminated her face. "So, I take it the dinner wasn't what you'd hoped," Jake said, finding it took surprisingly strong will not to touch her again. "Did you eat anything, or push your food around the plate?"

"I ate, thank you. And it went about like I expected. Well, maybe not exactly how I expected, but the end result is that things aren't fully resolved yet. But there were some hopeful parts."

"Wanna talk about it?"

She rolled her eyes. "Like I haven't disturbed you enough. Besides, you know the parties involved, and I don't feel right—"

"One of the parties is your mother, and I don't know her that well."

"You were right about her being happy to see me."

"Would that be one of the hopeful parts?"

"Most definitely. See, you know more about her than you think."

"And the other person—"

"Is the mayor. Who you have known your whole life. So I don't feel comfortable discussing my own personal opinions about the guy—"

"You discuss yours, I'll discuss mine." He grinned and she

smiled, then laughed. "Then at least we know where we stand, and who knows, maybe it will lend some perspective."

"As tempting an offer as that is—and you have no idea—I think I should probably figure this one out on my own."

"So noted." *Leave it alone, Jake. You don't need to make this your business. You never make things like this your business. Do not start now.* But no, he actually heard himself add, "I know you don't know me, but trust me when I say I'm about as far removed from the gossip mills here as you can get."

"But you live in a town where everyone knows everyone's business."

He chuckled. "True enough. I guess what I was trying to say was that, if you want to figure things out, and talking helps more than thinking, I'm a good sounding board. Anything said goes no further. I have no vested interest in spreading opinions about anyone, to anyone."

Her smile softened. "So noted," she said.

He shook his head and chuckled. "If you only knew how completely out of character it was for me to even offer—"

She placed a hand on his arm. "I think I have an idea. And please, thank your sister for haranguing you into playing airport taxi today."

"You met Ruby Jean?"

"No, but Arlen—the mayor—"

"I know who he is," he said with a smile.

"Sorry, I just—it's weird calling him anything at this point, and I didn't want to seem like I was name dropping."

"Cedar Springs is about as far removed from D.C. as it gets. You really can't name drop here. We all know too much about each other to pretend otherwise."

"I guess that would be true." She paused long enough that he thought she might be reconsidering, but went on to say, "Anyway, he told me your sister talked you into the favor today, so I wanted to extend my thanks to her as well. I'm . . . glad she did."

"Yes," he said after the moment spun out, and they were still standing there, smiling at one another. "I am, too. Although if you tell her I said that, I'll deny it."

She laughed. "Don't worry, I won't hold you to it."

Now his gaze turned considering. "You, I might not mind so much. When it comes to holding, I mean."

She smiled, and he thought he detected a hint of blush. He had that urge again, to smudge off her makeup, expose a freckle or two. Pull her hair out of the sleek bun it was all knotted up in, let it fall down and swing around her shoulders . . .

"I . . . should be getting in," she said, and he realized he'd been staring. "Long day. I'm sure you feel the same."

He had no idea what he was feeling, mostly because it was so foreign for him to be feeling anything. At least when the anything was what he was feeling right now. Sexual tension he was used to. But there were all these other layers here. Layers he really needed to remind himself he had no good reason to explore, or even peel back and take a peek under. She was in town temporarily, a brief walk-on role in his life at best. He had no business letting himself get any more intrigued by her than he already was. So, naturally, he said, "I'm not sure how I feel. Could be a long night. I'm very . . . distracted."

Her mouth quirked even more at one end, making her smile kind of crooked and totally endearing, and he had the sudden, most intense desire to kiss it. "Did you say you had plans already set for tomorrow?"

She held his gaze for the longest moment, then said, "No, I didn't." Then she grinned. "But if you'd like an itinerary so you know what places to avoid, so you don't have to play Good Samaritan again—and again—I'll be happy to let you know."

The urge didn't diminish in the least. He really should step back. Head back. Run back. Pay attention to all the warning signals flashing brightly inside his brain. Unfortunately they were drowned out by the thrumming of his pulse, and the rather loud, insistent hammering of a suddenly very demanding libido.

"I don't mind the occasional damsel rescue."

If his sister could read his thoughts at the moment, she'd have leverage for a lifetime. Which was good enough reason to break the moment. The moment that seemed to stretch out, where they both maintained steady eye contact, and smiled like six-year-olds who'd just been handed their first ice cream cones. To lick up all by themselves. Every last sticky, delicious drip.

Jake was already leaning a bit closer, but was saved at the last second by some shred of awareness that reminded him where they were standing, and that she might not need the added complication of anyone seeing her standing too close to him . . . much less kissing him. Clearly there were already some family issues going on. Just as clearly, he also couldn't help but note, she wasn't exactly leaping back out of his way.

He paused. "Lauren—"

"Thanks again," she said softly. "For everything."

He held her gaze a second longer, then dropped his chin. His smile was wider, and as sincere, when he looked at her again. "My pleasure."

A car drove by and the sound broke what little was left of the bubble they'd been existing inside of since he'd run into her outside the restaurant. Possibly since she'd run in from the rain at the airport.

"We're still on for Sunday?" she asked as she finally took that moment-finalizing step back.

"What happened to tomorrow?"

Her lips quirked up in that way they did, this time making the corners of her eyes crinkle. "I guess we'll find out tomorrow."

He could have pressed. Maybe it was the shock of how badly he wanted to that gave him the strength not to. "I can be spontaneous."

She nodded in appreciation. "Good. That's probably going to be the byword of my entire stay here."

"How long will that be?"

She lifted a shoulder, and a bit of that lost look she'd been wearing when she pushed through the doors came back. "It already feels too long." Then she smiled directly at him. "And not long enough." She took another step back, then turned and headed toward the stairs leading to the second floor of the motel.

"I guess time will tell," he said just loud enough for her to hear him.

He was still standing there when she glanced back and added, "It usually does."

He watched her all the way until she was inside her room, with a last little salute, before turning and beginning the trek back to his truck. A gentleman would have seen her to her door. Jake, on the other hand, would have seen her all the way inside to her bed.

He took in a deep breath of the crisp night air and smiled. Then he shook his head and laughed as he walked down the sidewalk, fighting the oddest urge to whistle. So . . . that's what it felt like, he found himself thinking. "And, of course it's going to be complicated. Why did I think, when it finally happened, it would be simple?"

He was reminded of Paddy's favorite admonishment when Jake complained about things being hard. "Something comes too easy," he'd grumble, "you don't appreciate what you got." Jake would always mouth the rest right along with him. Tonight he said it out loud as the words echoed inside his head, the memory, for once, making him smile. "Work harder, and the reward will be that much sweeter."

Lauren Matthews was pretty damn sweet. And Patrick McKenna was a pretty smart man.

Jake was whistling when he got to his truck.

"Sunday. You mean this coming Sunday?" Jake cradled his forehead in his palm as he continued listening on the phone. "But—"

"The guys want to see the plane before they commit, Jake. Come on. It's understandable, I think."

"Roger, I sent an entire portfolio, there's not really much more to—"

"You know, they want to see it firsthand, get as excited about the race as I am. I told them all about seeing it when I was up here last season, but they want to be more involved."

More involved. Oh . . . yippee. That's what he needed. A bunch of bankers and stockbrokers without a single pilot's license between them, telling him how to modify his plane. "Did you show them the race DVD?"

"Yeah, yeah, and they're on board with the whole thing, really they are, but if we could just get everyone out there, put on a little show—"

Jake straightened. "Show? Roger, maybe I didn't make myself clear. The reason I'm taking on any sponsor at all is because I need the influx of cash in order to make the kinds of upgrades needed to really compete this season. I've competed long enough now that I know exactly what I need to do, I just need a little faith and financial support. She's not in any condition to go up in the air at the moment, so—"

"I don't mean an air show, I meant a little show and tell, a little walk-about the hangar, show them what she's made of, talk her up a little, show them all those pictures you showed me of your grandfather racing her, the World War Two stuff, her history. You know, get them feeling like they're part of the whole thing."

Jake sighed. What Roger was asking wasn't unreasonable, or even particularly problematic, so long as the "guys" didn't try and tell him how to fly his plane. It was just . . . he had other plans for Sunday. "Okay, okay. What time were you planning on heading up?"

"Well, that's the thing. We're all in Vegas for the weekend, and I was hoping you could come get us. You know, really make a day of it."

Great. A whole day. And night of it, too. Roger had talked about his work buddies often enough that Jake knew exactly what was going to be expected of him. And a quick tour of the hangar wasn't going to cut it. "Let me see what I can do, and I'll get back with you."

"I'm heading out to the pool, then we've got a private game scheduled after lunch. Get back to me before then."

Roger was all jovial, all "good buddy" and excited little kid. But he was also ridiculously wealthy for a guy who'd just turned forty, and he'd earned it all on his own. As had his banker and broker buddies. They were understandably cocky with it and not a little self-important—and entitled. Irritating as their "you'll do it my way" attitude might be to Jake, he understood that this was what he had to deal with if he wanted them to throw any hard-earned play money in his direction.

"Will do," he said, then hung up and rubbed his hands over his face. "Will do, indeed," he muttered. He stared at the phone, knowing his next call should be to the motel, and Lauren. He wished he could move up their date to today, but with lessons scheduled all day tomorrow, today would be the only chance he had to get the place tour-ready and figure out exactly how he wanted to orchestrate the event for the guys.

As much as the whole thing left a sour taste in his mouth, he'd already come to terms with the fact that he wanted the win badly enough that he was willing to do what it took to get it. So there was no point in pissing and moaning now that it was within his grasp. And if he set up the day right, it was highly possible there would be a fat check in his hand when he dropped them off back in Vegas late Sunday night. Or Monday.

He sighed and picked up the phone again, started to dial information for the motel phone number, then put the phone down again. If he was going to lose any chance to see Lauren on Sunday, then the least he could do was apologize in person. And get a little face time as well.

He just hoped it wasn't the last face time he'd have. She'd been wishy-washy on the length of her stay, but given what he knew about her current employment situation, he understood there was no immediate need to fly back east. And since he was already rolling the dice with Roger and his crew, he figured what the hell. Might as well gamble on Lauren as well. If he could push her to extend her stay a little, then he wasn't above doing so. Not that he wished more family disharmony on her, but he wouldn't mind if it took a little longer than she expected.

He glanced at the large, framed black-and-white photo of a younger, beaming Patrick McKenna, and *Betty Sue,* taken the day he'd bought her. "You might not agree with my methods," he told his grandfather, "but I'll come home with a win."

He grabbed his keys and headed outside, not bothering to clarify to Paddy—or himself—whether he meant the race . . . or Lauren Matthews.

Chapter 8

Lauren was sitting on a small wooden chair at the tiny local library, head bent over a newspaper, when someone whispered in her ear.

"I hear they sell those for a quarter and you can read them anywhere you want."

Her heart stuttered. She smiled. And looked up at the man responsible for a good deal of lost sleep the night before. Which, considering the dinner she'd been at earlier in the evening, she was actually thankful for. "Not if you want to read papers from five years ago."

"True. We can be a little behind the times, but generally not that much." He pulled out the chair on the opposite side of the table and nodded to the stack of papers, some more yellowed than others, piled in front of her. "So, what's up with the reading material?"

She debated on what to say. As it was, she'd come in hoping to screen through microfiche at worst, or, at best, a digital database. But worst turned out to be digging through file folders of originals instead. No indexing, other than by date. And the only data search was the really old-fashioned way: reading the paper yourself. "Just doing a little research."

"On . . ." He craned his neck and lifted a few papers. ". . . Cedar Springs business, front page news. There's some exciting reading."

"It's actually been more interesting than I'd imagined." Which was true. She'd been born in Richmond, just south of metropolitan Washington, and a capital city itself, so she'd grown up with nationally known newspapers as her "local" paper. She'd found it illuminating to see what a tiny resort town tucked away literally in the middle of nowhere thought was the news its readers would most want to know about.

"Yes, well, the race for the local fire chief was looking like a slam dunk last year. And then Paul Mathison's book store burned down right in the middle of the chief's re-election rally."

"I'm guessing the incumbent didn't take it then."

"Nope. Sally Harper did."

"Sally. Wow, how progressive."

Jake smiled and lifted a shoulder. "In some ways, we are very forward thinking. She was the most qualified for the job, and her ideas on improving the safety measures in town were solid and well grounded. Of course, in other ways, we do get a bit stuck. Marsha Stinson tried to change the annual Christmas pageant to a more broad-scoped event that embraced multiple beliefs without focusing on any one in particular. Despite the fact that we have almost no cultural diversity here and pretty much everyone attends the same church."

"How'd that go over?"

"Better with the town council than her own family. She almost ended up in divorce court."

"Seriously? Why?"

Jake grinned. "Marsha's husband is our Santa Claus, has been for twenty-two years. His own beard and everything. He's also our minister."

"Ah."

"Small-town politics almost always get personal." He leaned back in his chair. "Interested in local politics? Thinking about relocating?"

It would have been easy enough to let him believe that. It would certainly be a reasonable explanation for why she was delving into the newsworthy past of the town. She'd decided last night while analyzing the evening that she needed to be prepared for any outcome when she sat down with her mother one-on-one, and though she was pretty sure where the conversation would take them, she needed to have some backup if she was off base. Meeting Arlen hadn't changed her opinion of him, and so it stood to reason that if she could back up her gut instinct on the guy with some kind of hard facts, it could only help her get her point across, or at least explain why she wasn't going to be his biggest fan.

And, to do that, she needed to keep digging. There was a lot more to access here . . . but everyone was watching. So she needed help from an insider . . . and Jake was the only person she'd trust. She just hated to pull him into this. He seemed like a decent guy. A decent guy who had enough going on without adopting the problems of a woman he just met.

"That's okay," he said when the silence extended past a reasonable limit. "It's none of my business."

"It's not that. Well, it is that, but only because I don't want to make it your business. You have enough, with the race and everything."

"Why don't you tell me what's on your mind, and I'll let you know when or if I don't feel comfortable knowing more or getting involved."

She smiled. "Bold offer for a guy who doesn't like to get involved even in his own town's business."

"Maybe that makes me the worst guy to confide in . . . or the best. I won't know until you tell me."

"My interest is in your local politics, but I'm not job hunting."

"Ah. So would this be about doing a little research on the new branch of the family tree?"

He made it so easy. And, for once, rather than being wary or guarded, as she'd always had to be when any helpful hand was extended in her previous job—helpful hands usually wanted return favors—she was simply grateful. "Yes."

"Anything specific you want to know?"

She laid the paper on the table and held his gaze. "Yes."

He was quick, Jake McKenna was. And for that, she was very grateful. His gaze sharpened immediately. "Okay. Shoot."

"How well do you know the mayor?" she asked, keeping her tone hushed in a library whisper.

He slid her papers into a stack. "Come on. Not here." He scooped up the papers and stood.

"I still want to look through those," she said.

"Not a problem."

"You can't check those out."

Jake just grinned. "Sure you can."

"But, the librarian told me—"

"You didn't give the librarian the first kiss she ever had."

Lauren arched an eyebrow, thinking of the young, attractive woman who'd been manning the front desk. "How long ago was that?"

"Oh, it's been a while."

"I bet," Lauren said dryly. "And you think it was so good that, all these years later, she still owes you?"

He smiled. "Well, in case time has dulled the thrill, there was that time I got her and her husband to a special care facility in Denver in the middle of a snowstorm when Daisy, their six-year-old, had an unexplained seizure in the middle of the night."

Lauren stopped and turned. "Are you a medical pilot as well?"

"I'm whatever kind of pilot this town needs. But I work with Doctors Without Borders, and our local hospital, which is really nothing more than a clinic. During ski season, which runs six to eight months of every year, there are always a string of emergencies where we need to get folks who have no business being on a mountain the size of ours and prove it by breaking something critical to their survival, to Denver so more practiced surgeons can hopefully keep their fool asses alive."

She smiled wryly. "Well, it must be reassuring for them to have such a compassionate pilot on hand."

He grinned. "I've never had one turn down a ride yet." Jake plopped the papers on the check-out desk. "Hi, Becky. Mind if Ms. Matthews here borrows these? She's been called away on some town business and would truly appreciate the chance to finish up with her reading before filing these back away."

Becky was a fresh-faced brunette who looked like she was in her twenties, but was obviously at least a decade older given Jake's revelation. Of course, everyone here was fresh-faced. Lauren had already decided she was going to start drinking whatever they were drinking. Heavily.

"Sure, Jake," Becky said. "Not a problem. Let me see if I've got a tote those can fit into."

"How's Daisy doing these days?" he asked, leaning on the counter as Becky hunted through some boxes.

"She just made the varsity ski team."

"God, I'm old."

Becky straightened and handed him a canvas tote with long shoulder straps. "Tell me about it," she said, still twinkling. "I watch her barrel down the side of that mountain with my heart in my throat and swear my hair will turn pure white before she sees graduation." She slid the stack of newspapers inside the bag. "Of course, Ray—that's my husband," she said to Lauren, "wishes he were still out there on the mountain racing right alongside her. He loves every second of it. I swear, one of them will be the death of me."

"They wouldn't last a day without you," Jake said, taking the tote before Lauren could reach for it. "Thanks for the favor." He slid the straps over his shoulder. "We'll get these back to you as quick as we can."

"No worries," she said, then smiled at Lauren. "How are you liking your stay? Has the mayor shown you around yet?" She glanced at Jake and her twinkle took on a teasing flair. "Or are you playing tour guide?"

Lauren started to jump in, wanting to save him from being any part of town gossip. It was one thing to fantasize about him and all the parts of her she'd very much like him to tour and guide himself into, but the town didn't have to be speculating that anything was going on.

However, he answered quite easily, and with no apparent concern for what it might make people think or speculate about. "I'm trying to talk her into a little air tour, but she hasn't decided if she can squeeze me into her very busy schedule." He lifted the tote. "So, I might have an ulterior motive for lightening her work load here a little."

Becky wiggled her eyebrows, then gave Lauren a conspiratorial wink. "Take the tour."

Lauren felt her cheeks flush a little and swore she'd never blushed so often in her entire adult life. But then, she'd never been so obviously affected by anyone, as she was by Jake. "I'm considering it," she said, not risking glancing at him.

"Smart woman." Becky leaned over the counter and whispered, "Not a bad kisser, either. Just sayin.'"

"I heard that. And we were eight-year-olds."

"Girls know these things," she said, then winked at Lauren again.

"Girls think they know lots of things when it comes to guys."

"I could give you confirmation from any number of local sources, if you—"

"Come on," Jake said, corralling Lauren toward the door. "Before she ruins any chance I have getting you up in that plane."

"The conversation was just getting interesting," Lauren protested, rather liking the suddenly self-conscious look on Jake's face.

"We can have our own interesting conversation."

Now she grinned at him. "Really? That sounds—" They stopped outside the door, just short of physically running into the woman about to enter. "Mom. What are you doing here?"

Charlene glanced between the two of them. "I stopped by your motel room, but you weren't in. Debbie was at the desk and said you'd walked into town. Then, when I was getting coffee at The Beanery, Maryann mentioned she'd seen you going into the library. So I took my chances you'd still be here. But if I'm interrupting something . . ."

"No, I was just leaving, but—"

"Lauren, thanks for your help with this," Jake said, patting the tote still slung over his shoulder. "I've got to get back, I have lessons off and on all day."

She caught his steady gaze and held it, reading between the lines, and very thankful he'd done the same. It seemed her trust hadn't been misplaced. "No problem. Glad to help."

He waved and was off, leaving Lauren with her mother . . . and thankfully not a tote bag full of newspapers she'd have to explain away. More tension and explanations they didn't need.

"If you've got some time, I thought maybe we could talk," her mother said. "You mentioned it when you were leaving, and I'd like that as well."

"Of course I have time," she said. "That's why I'm here." Conscious of Becky somewhere behind her and who knows who walking by out behind her mother, she quietly added, "Is there someplace we can go where the whole town won't be taking notes on our entire conversation?"

Her mother smiled. "I'm afraid that's asking a bit much around here, but if you don't mind walking, there's a really nice path through the park, which passes by the botanical gardens. That's about as private as it gets. Unless you'd rather go back to the motel, or out to our place."

"I like the walk in the park idea. It's a really pretty day." It put them on even footing, too, and gave them something to do besides stare at each other while trying to find the right words.

Her mother led the way, nodding hello to pretty much everyone they passed, stopping a few times to introduce Lauren and to engage in brief conversations. "Sorry," she said after they were stopped for what felt like the dozenth time, and they'd only gone two blocks. "Once we get off Main, it will quiet down. It's not normally this eventful."

"No problem, I understand. You forget, I used to shadow a senator."

"Oh, it's not political, sweetheart, it's just the way small towns are."

Lauren wanted to say that while she'd noted the friendly, outgoing nature of pretty much every man, woman, and dog in Cedar Springs, there weren't suddenly that many more people strolling Main Street by coincidence. "Give yourself a little credit. You're a draw. It's not surprising the street gets a little more crowded when you take a stroll."

"Well, to be honest, it's not me, it's you."

"Me?"

They turned into the park and crossed a short footbridge over the Panlo River that ran parallel to the town. "Trust me, while most everyone is happy enough with my arrival here, and in a rural mountain town such as this one, you don't even have to try to snoop to know everybody's business, it's not normally quite such a parade when I take a walk. I just didn't want you to feel self-conscious."

"Well, while I'm not used to the limelight being focused on me, I am used to being in the halo of the glow. It's a little odd thinking that everybody in town knows my whereabouts at any given moment." Making her doubly glad Jake took the newspaper-filled tote. Although she couldn't help but wonder if Librarian Becky was already on the phone spreading the word that she'd checked them out, with God knows what kind of speculation attached. Lauren would like to think she was being ridiculous, except, after the parade event she'd just contended with in a three-block stroll down Main Street, she was probably underestimating.

"They're interested because I've been here a while and you're just now visiting."

"People really care about the timing of my visit? Or do they know you and I have . . . that things have been a little strained since you moved here? Have you made some close friends? Would they, perhaps, be part of why people seem so caught up in my arrival?"

"I've made a throng of acquaintances, but no one close, yet, other than Arlen. Given my new role, I'm being careful and taking it slowly, getting to know everyone, feeling my way in, learning the backgrounds, the family histories, and all the politics, both professional and personal. But I like the town and most of the people in it, so I'm certain my circle will both grow and become more intimate as well as I learn who I can trust. Being the mayor's wife, even in a place this size, does come with a certain level of awareness and obligation, though it's nothing I mind."

Lauren's steps slowed. This did not sound like the talk of a woman who was planning a divorce. But perhaps Lauren had called it right the other way. That her mother was simply making peace with her choice and moving forward the best she could.

Charlene paused on the path, making Lauren stop completely. "You've met him now, but I can see from your expression that your opinion hasn't changed."

Lauren paused beside her, then noted a small bench located just off the path ahead. She motioned to it, and they both walked to it in silence. Once seated, Lauren tried to find the right words. "You were happy in Florida. The people there, both your friends who spend time there while away from Richmond, and the new friends you made . . . they all said the same thing, that you were happy, busy, fulfilled."

"I thought I was."

Lauren frowned, surprised by the comment. "What do you mean?"

Charlene turned her gaze away and stared across the path, to the fields beyond, the rolling hills, the mountains. Lauren had no idea what she was really seeing, much less what she was thinking. Finally, Charlene sat a little straighter and looked at Lauren with both deep affection and a bit of determination, as if what she was about to say was quite important and she didn't want to screw it up. Lauren could identify with that feeling.

"I loved playing hostess for your grandfather, growing up in Richmond," her mother said. "I loved being both hostess and partner to your father, for each and every wonderful year we had together. Raising you was a joy, as were all the other things I dedicated myself to over the years. I enjoyed being on various charitable committees, being involved, engaged, dedicated to something. It's been a very fulfilling, rewarding life and I'm proud of all the things I've done and the people I've helped."

"You did all those things in Richmond and in Florida, too. You seemed incredibly happy. You were happy."

"I was." She looked at Lauren. "I think it's one of those things where you don't even realize what you're missing, what might be truly fulfilling, to you, personally, as a woman, until it's standing in front of you. I didn't know . . . not until Arlen."

Lauren tried to take it in, tried to understand, but it failed her.

"I know you don't understand, but that's because your idea of me, your vision of who I am, is limited to who I have always been."

"Who you are and have always been is a pretty spectacular woman. Person. I could never hope to live up to your example, but it inspires me and has informed most of the decisions I've made in my life. You are this force to be reckoned with, all packaged up in the form of the most gracious, generous, kind, intelligent, and strong person I know."

Her mother's eyes grew a bit glassy. "That's really . . . something, to hear you say that."

"You know I've always admired you. I've told you time and again."

"And you have to know how proud I am of you, too. But . . . Lauren, I need you to look past this icon of a mother and woman you see me as being. Maybe I am the things that inspire you, and perhaps that's what I'm most proud of. But . . . I'm more than that woman, that icon. I'm . . . me."

Lauren shook her head. "I don't understand. You're . . . everything. What more could there be?"

"So much more, as it turns out."

Lauren fell silent, trying to take in what her mother was

telling her, or trying to. In all of her analysis, both before coming and after last night's dinner and meeting Arlen . . . she'd never once anticipated this. How could she? "I thought you were happy with your life."

"I was. I spent it in service to family, to community, and it was, by far, more fulfilling to me than it could have possibly been to anyone else. But it was fulfillment I drew from others. Not something I gave myself, for myself." She stopped, looked away. "I'm handling this badly."

"No," Lauren said, taking one of her mother's small hands between her own. "No, you're not. I may not understand this, and I might be surprised to hear you talk like this, but I want to know. I want to understand."

"I'm just beginning to understand myself. Maybe I can't completely put it into words as yet."

Lauren thought back through what her mother had revealed. "So . . . are you saying that Arlen, in some way, is the one who is showing you this new side of yourself? That he's the one who is making you see what you've been missing . . . or just hadn't gotten around to yet?"

"He was absolutely the catalyst, yes. I know you don't understand why that—"

"You're right, I don't," she said, trying not to sound defensive or lost even though she felt a little of both. The woman she knew, respected, loved, and idolized, above all others, and had her entire life, was suddenly transforming before her very eyes into a complete stranger she didn't know at all. And that was still too much to take in, so she focused on Arlen. That was the main thing, at the moment, the thing that started this . . . transformation. "It's not because he's from so far away, Mom. Or that he's a mayor of a small mountain town, when you've been wined and dined by statesmen, ambassadors, senators, you name it, over the years, and could have had your pick from men who were from similar backgrounds, who would understand who you are, what you've accomplished. It's not about what he does, or where he's from."

"But, darling, that's exactly what it's about."

"But, he's so . . . different. Not from them, but from you."

"Differences can be exciting."

"Agreed. But doesn't there have to be some common ground? I guess I don't understand where you are compatible. He doesn't seem your type in any way."

Charlene laughed lightly. "I wasn't aware I had a type."

"You know what I mean. Opposites attracting are one thing, but I watched you two last night, and I'm not sure I saw any obvious attraction. You've only known each other six months, are still newlyweds—"

"We're newly-everything, Lauren. We're still getting to know each other. Yes, what we did was incredibly impulsive, but—"

"But . . . he's a stranger. Or was, certainly, when you married him. Now that you've been with him, around him, getting to know him, living under the same roof, do you still feel the same?"

There was the slightest of hesitations, but she spoke before Lauren could call attention to it. "No, I don't. I feel . . . more."

Lauren took that in, but didn't know what to do with it. She studied her mother's face, her steady, tranquil, certain gaze, then tilted her head. "You don't love him," she said, more as a revelation than a question.

"Love takes time." She said that quite easily, as if she'd never have expected anything different.

"Agreed. So how could you marry someone you don't love? You'd have a fit if I did that."

"You're on the beginning part of your path, your journey. I've traveled a fair bit longer a distance down mine. I have the benefit of that experience, to allow me the latitude of risk taking at this point in my life, that I wouldn't have taken at any earlier stage in my life."

"So, is this some kind of midlife crisis then?"

She laughed again. "I'm a fair bit past midlife. And it was more a life reckoning than a crisis." She shifted in her seat and took Lauren's hands in her own. "I know you don't understand. Don't see what it is we see in each other, but we're quite content figuring things out together."

"Mom—"

"I was happy in Richmond, I love every street, tree, and shop as if it were family to me, because it is and always will be. But I was tired of being the social center, of the demand and the pressure . . . to be me."

"I didn't realize how personalized it had become to you, but I know you wanted to retire from the demands of the political and social scene there, which you'd certainly earned. I know, that's why you relocated to Florida, for the slower way of life, the more relaxed cycle of things."

"And, within months, I'd simply created a new social whirl-wind of activities."

"But you loved them. I never really thought you'd slow down, just that what you chose to do would perhaps not be as drain-ing and more fulfilling, because you could pick things you loved and not be forced into doing the things you did out of obliga-tion, to our family name, your family name, our collective history. But I never once saw you sitting still down there. You'd have withered without something—many somethings—to occupy your mind."

"You're correct. And I did choose things that gave me plea-sure. But the cycle was still more or less the same. I volun-teered; I agreed to organize, hostess, and manage this function or that because that's what I do; it's what I've always done; it's the only thing I know to do. Only . . ."

Lauren squeezed her mother's hand, truly stunned by all she was hearing. It made her feel, in some ways, horribly guilty, like the worst daughter ever, for not ever seeing any of this. "Only what, Mom?"

Her mother smiled briefly and cupped her daughter's cheek, as if to say there was nothing to feel badly about. "There's a difference in enjoying something because you're good at it, and knowing others will benefit from your dedication . . . and being personally fulfilled and happy. A part of me felt I'd done my share, fulfilled enough others' needs, been important to causes, worked tirelessly on things I believed in. It wasn't until I got to Florida, and essentially filled my life with similar things, that I realized I did it more because I didn't know any other way to live than because I really wanted to do that any longer. It's like I've been trained to be this one thing. And while I loved it once, I'm . . . I guess I'm tired of it. Tired of the demands of it."

"Then scale back; focus your attention on things that don't demand so much of your energy."

Charlene sighed. "It's not about physical energy, or even emotional energy. I could do most of the things I did in my sleep, I'd done them so often, and for so many years. They weren't stressful, especially once I relocated south. But neither were they really making me happy. The problem was, if I scaled back, as you call it, I had not the first clue where or what to turn my attentions to. I didn't have hobbies or interests that weren't directly related to my charitable work. I needed . . . something. Something that was just for me. That I did fully for my own personal joy and fulfillment and not a damn thing to do with anyone else. I just didn't know what. All I knew was that my new life was turning out to be just a retired version of my old life, and I wasn't happy with that. I wanted . . . I guess I wanted more. I felt ridiculous even thinking that and very ungrateful. I was—have always been—very blessed in my life. But—"

"Something was missing."

She looked at Lauren. "Yes."

She'd put more emotion, more passion, more . . . of herself, into that single word than Lauren had ever heard her invest in anything, which was truly saying something. Because her mother was nothing if not passionate about her causes. But . . . maybe she was right, and she'd done all that at the expense of never being passionate about herself. "And that something missing was a person to share your life with."

"As I said, he was the catalyst, so yes. No one will replace your father, and I don't know that the kind of relationship we had, which was at such a different stage in life, is something I'd even reach for now. Things are very different now. I'm very different. And what I want . . . and why, is also changing. I've been alone a very long time, and—"

"Please, you don't have to reconcile that part with me. I've been begging you to find someone to complement your life for years; you know it's not about that. I guess I just never thought— never saw you with someone like . . ." She trailed off, sincerely not wanting to hurt her mother. She'd had no idea how discontented she'd been. She felt petty now for depriving her mother of any part of the joy she was finding in her new life. "I didn't know," she finished quietly. "I'm so sorry. I had no idea." She looked at her mother, tears gathering in her eyes. "I should have known."

"There is no way you could have known, as I didn't know myself. We might be closer than most mothers and daughters, but I am and always will be your mother first, and because of that, your image of me will never be one hundred percent realistic. And that's as it should be. I am enormously proud that you think I'm worthy of looking up to, because that means, in the end, I did right by you, and that is one job I will never tire of or want to walk away from. I know you don't understand, nor do you see or understand what it is that Arlen brings to my world, and maybe, as my daughter, you simply won't ever be able to. All I can ask is that you trust that I know. And that I'm fully at peace with my choices."

Lauren nodded, because her mother was right. It was a lot to take in, but, in the end, her choice was still so out there. And while she knew with time to let it sink in, her reasons for choosing this new life would make sense, she wasn't entirely sure that her choice of Arlen ever would.

"I know he's not what you would expect." Her mother laughed then. "He certainly wasn't for me, either. He is so different, Lauren, yes, but we have a compatibility of a political life. Our backgrounds are both steeped in that world. I know how to be a good political wife, and he's originally from San

Francisco and appreciates that I do understand that role on perhaps a broader scale than one would presume to need here. It fulfills his needs, his personal wants, having me by his side."

"And that's not repeating things again? At least in part?"

"Yes and no, but not in the way you mean. Or I meant when I said I wanted out of that world. Cedar Springs is as far removed from the world I lived in, both in Richmond and Coral Gables, than anything I've ever known. I do get to continue, in some small form, in a role I'm very, very comfortable in. But the expectations, the day-to-day of it, are so entirely different, the people so genuine and nice, the circle of it all, so incredibly small and intimate, without any greater agenda . . . everything about it, Lauren, is just right. I suppose a little like Goldilocks finally finding the right bed." She laughed then.

"I love everything about being here. I feel like I fit in because of who I was, but it's these people, this town, this place, that is informing me about who I really am. It's completely reinvigorated me. And while Arlen and I might not seem the traditional newlyweds, even for a couple who ran off to elope, I assure you we fulfill things in each other that we both truly desire and cherish. The rest . . . that will come with time. Or it won't. I can't explain why that part, the part everyone looks to in order to define a couple, so completely doesn't matter to either of us. What I do have already is a priceless treasure. Whether or not you understand it, I hope you can at least appreciate what it's given me." She squeezed Lauren's hands. "And give me—us—your blessing."

Tears swam in Charlene's eyes, and in Lauren's as well. "I do, Mom. I do want you to be happy. I'm sorry I doubted you. It was all just so shocking, so . . . not you. Maybe because I didn't know you, this part of you, so I couldn't possibly make sense of it."

Charlene laughed even as she sniffled. She gently dabbed at the corners of her eyes so as not to disturb her always carefully applied makeup while whisking away the few tears that threatened to leak out. "I know. Which is precisely what makes it wonderful. It took this kind of shake-up, this monumental shift in my personal paradigm, to find what I was always missing. Or what I was missing now, anyway."

Lauren pulled her mother into a hug. "I'm sorry I rained on your lovely new parade."

"I'm just happy you're here and that we finally had a chance to truly talk this out. I know you were just worried about me, and I love you for it." She set her back. "I raised you right, Lauren Madigan Matthews. I knew you'd come around."

Lauren hoped that in her relief and happiness at their reunion her mother couldn't see the lingering threads of concern that Lauren simply couldn't shake. It was all wonderful on the surface, but still pretty out there. At least for the woman who had raised her, anyway. It was such a monumental shift. It would take time for her to truly come to terms with what she thought about all of it. But there was one thing she did know for certain. "I want you to be happy. It's all I've ever wanted."

"I know, honey." She let go of Lauren's hands, then patted her thighs before squaring her shoulders and standing up. She turned and pulled Lauren up with her. "Let's continue our walk. We've now exhausted the very dramatic Story of Me, and now I need to catch up on everything about you. We've—I've hated not being able to keep up with you, with what you've been doing. It's been a horrible gap in my days, in my life. My one and only true regret. It's only been months but it feels like lifetimes. I worry, too, you know."

"I know you do," Lauren said, feeling somewhat comforted by the familiarity of the routines and rhythms they were naturally returning to.

"I want you to catch me up on every last detail of the past six months. What's going on with Daphne and that Italian investment banker she was dating. Are they still together? Who are you seeing? Anyone? Have you talked to Todd about your schedule? I really think if you approach it as I mentioned, that—" She paused in the middle of the path and turned to look at Lauren. "Wait. Something just clicked inside my head. Back there . . . before we sat down . . . you said 'used to shadow.' What does that mean? Has something happened with Todd? Or, God forbid, his family? I have been completely out of the loop since coming here, which I confess has been mostly a relief. I've tried to keep up, somewhat, with Washington, just because we've been so disconnected, but it just made that more unbearable for me."

Lauren silently cursed herself for the inadvertent slip. They were just renewing their bonds. Now was definitely not the time to get into another potentially divisive conversation. But she also knew it was pointless to try to divert her mother from the subject. She was going to have to divulge the latest turn in her life at some point. She'd just hoped it would be after she'd had more time to reconcile the latest sharp turn in her mother's life. But maybe it was the very fact that her mother had made such a sharp turn that might give her the right insight to truly understand why her daughter had, more or less, done the same thing. "You know I've been unhappy. For some time now. So—"

"I know, sweetheart. But you're here now and I just know we're going to be fine now that we've patched things up. I hope you'll stay long enough to get to spend some time with Arlen and get to know him better. Or, at the very least, agree to schedule some time in for a real vacation out here with us. If you could do that, I know you'll feel even better about this change in my life. Arlen has just been beside himself with your impending visit. I know I've never seen him so nervous about anything. It was like you were a state dignitary or something. But I know it's just because he wants that part of my life settled and me reconciled with my only child."

"Does he have children? I didn't think—"

"No, life didn't favor him in that way. But he does understand my need to be connected to you, to keep our bond strong. That has to count for something, doesn't it?"

"Of course it does. Mom, I might not fully understand about the suddenness of it all, or how completely you changed your life in such a short time. But I am happy that you're happy."

Her mother pulled her into another tight embrace. "Oh, sweetie, this all means more to me than you can know."

Lauren could hear the thickness in her mother's voice again and felt her own throat tighten, but for different reasons. Lauren realized that her mother hadn't noticed she hadn't gotten an answer to her question. And, for now, though she didn't feel great about it, Lauren left it that way.

Charlene broke the hug and slipped her arm through Lauren's. "The botanical gardens are just around the next bend. Care for a stroll? Arlen was a major force in getting this park built ten years ago. He really feels strongly about preserving the beauty of our town, of our mountain way of life. Which, I tell you, is a challenge with the resort holding an iron fist on our town's revenue potential. It's such a fascinating blend here politically, with all the demands of a small, very close-knit town balanced against what amounts to the huge corporate presence of the resort and all that goes with it. It's an international draw, just as Aspen and Vail are, and it requires some pretty tricky maneuvering, let me tell you, to balance their needs with those of the year-round residents. Then there is the small college just outside of town, and the fact that part of the resort is used as an Olympic training ground; it's really an amazing mosaic."

"I never thought about it like that," Lauren admitted. But it explained, at least in part, why there was enough here to spark her mother's avid intellect and continued need to be dedicated to something. It was funny, but Lauren thought that it looked like Charlene had found a rather unique place to stretch her later-life wings, in a place where no one would have ever pictured her steel magnolia mother settling down.

However, the man her mother had chosen to settle down with, well, Lauren still didn't entirely comprehend that part. Her mother's love for Cedar Springs and her new way of life presented a strong possibility of what the draw might really have been, and yet she'd fallen for the man—married him in fact—before she'd even seen the town, so . . . go figure.

Lauren let herself be led through the iron gates into the park. It was quiet, with hardly anyone milling around the path that circled several small ponds. Various local varieties of plants and flowers were carefully tended along the trail, all clearly marked with signs detailing the information about the plant, as well as who was responsible for donating it. And almost every flower and twig had a sponsor. Not that it was unheard of for a county to expand its services on the foundation of private donations. Everyone benefited then.

But it did give her another place to continue her digging.

And she still had every intention of continuing with her private little investigation. Her heart was less heavy now that she'd talked to her mother, but . . . she couldn't help it, her gut was still insisting that something wasn't right. She might be able to better understand now why her mother had so abruptly changed her life to come to Cedar Springs with a man she hardly knew . . . but that didn't mean she understood why Arlen had made the same choice. Not that her mother wasn't the catch of the century for any man, but given the lack of any obvious passion between the two, and what she knew of the man thus far, it made her wonder what his motives might have been.

She made a mental note to tour the park again later, alone. With a camera and a notepad. Where she could start compiling a donor list. It wasn't much, but it was a start. And one that hopefully wouldn't so easily trigger the town radar where she was concerned. She'd known she'd have to be discreet in her digging, once in town, but she'd had no idea the level of scrutiny her every move would command. She didn't want to disturb or in any way threaten the peace her mother had apparently found here, but until she felt more certain that the man who was living under the same roof as her mother also had her best interests at heart . . . she'd continue to learn as much as she could about the man, professionally and personally.

"It's a lovely park," Lauren said as they made their way to

the front gate, which opened onto Main Street, on the east side of her motel.

"Do you have any plans for dinner?" her mother asked as they stepped back onto the sidewalk.

Lauren smiled. "What plans could I possibly have?"

"Well," her mother smiled now, too, and in that moment, it felt like old times. "You did seem rather . . . animated when I saw you talking with Jake earlier. I just didn't know if, perhaps, the two of you—"

"He's taking me for an aerial tour this weekend."

"That's wonderful! So you two are hitting it off."

"I think his sister asked him to do it. As a favor to the mayor." She didn't know that for certain, but she had a hunch the chauffer service and tour had been a package request. What remained to be seen was whether or not it still felt like a favor after they'd spent the afternoon together.

"I wouldn't doubt that's where the idea originated," Charlene said, the gleam still in her eye. "She's a wonder, Ruby Jean is. I don't know what Arlen would do without her. That was nice of her, to think of that. You'll be in awe, when you fly over. You'll see why I love it here so much."

There was no denying the grand majesty of the mountains, or how awe inspiring the scenery. Still . . . "Do you, Mom? Really love it here? I mean, not the political landscape or the small town embrace, but the mountains and . . . well, it's just so different from Virginia and Florida."

"The thinner air took some getting used to, and I definitely had to readjust my thoughts about snow," Charlene said more frankly than Lauren had expected. "We get a lot of it here. But it's just so stunning, this view. It gives a person a different perspective. I can't really explain it, but I feel like I better understand myself here."

"Jake said something similar . . . about looking at the mountains and understanding where you fit into the scheme of life."

"He's absolutely right. I didn't know this was where I belonged until I got here." She shifted her view from the mountains back to her daughter. "It's different, and I won't say it's come without compromises, but in a new relationship, there are countless give and takes."

"What is Arlen compromising?"

Her mother just gave her an admonishing look. "I've managed to come this far in my life without making any disastrous decisions. So you'll have to trust me, and, if I make foolish mistakes, now or in the future, you'll have to allow me to endure them, the old-fashioned way." She touched Lauren's hair and smiled. "Just like I do with you."

Lauren laughed. "I love you. And I worry because I do love you. But I do trust that you're here because you want to be. Seeing you, listening to you, there is no doubt about that." What Lauren didn't add was that while she'd heard the rhapsody and joy her mother professed to have in her life now when talking about the town, and the mountains that surrounded it, she hadn't heard that at all in her voice when she'd talked about her husband. In fact, other than to call him a catalyst, and reference his good deeds toward the community, she really hadn't talked about him much at all.

Lauren wondered if it was just as Charlene had said, that even though their impulsiveness about marrying suggested a grand passion, or at least highly engaged hormones, they'd connected on a more intellectual level and were content with growing their relationship slowly.

Charlene pulled her into another hug. "I've missed you so. I'm so glad you're back, that we're back." She slid her hands down Lauren's arms and squeezed her hands before letting her go. "I'm so thankful we had the chance to spend some time together. I really hate this, but I have a meeting with the women's council, and then—"

"It's okay, Mom."

"Arlen has asked if you'd come out to the house for dinner. Casual. We're cooking barbecue on the patio."

"What time?"

"Is seven okay?"

"Sounds good."

Charlene clasped her hands together, looking almost ridiculously pleased. "Good! Now, will you be okay on your own the rest of the day? Because I'm sure Ruby Jean—"

"Has done enough," Lauren said with a laugh. "I'm fine. I'm going to knock around a bit, maybe take my bike out again. The path we were just on looks like it might be good for a bike ride. In fact, if you're serious about it being casual, I'll bike over to your place this evening. That way you won't have to pick me up."

"Perfect! Debbie can give you directions. It's just outside of town, but not much of a climb. We'll see you at seven." She paused for a moment, then added, "Of course, if you'd like to ask someone along, we have more than enough."

Some things never changed. "I'm happy you're happy, Mom. And I'm perfectly happy flying solo."

"Okay. But the invitation stands if you change your mind at the last minute. I'm sure Arlen would love the additional company. We're used to entertaining. Wait until you taste the fruit salad I've put together. I even made a centerpiece."

"Sounds delicious." Lauren took a step back as two women approached, and paused, just outside their immediate circle, clearly waiting to speak to Charlene. "I'll let you go," Lauren said, nodding beyond her mother's shoulder.

Charlene glanced back, smiled at the two women. "Oh, hello, Lina, Beatta." She looked back at Lauren. "The offer stands. And . . . if you do bring a guest, you don't have to be quite as casual." She winked.

Lauren resisted the urge to roll her eyes. A part of her wondered if she'd actually missed this part of their relationship. "I'll be presentable."

"Fun, not frumpy," her mother said. "Those suits you wear—"

"Are not in my luggage."

She beamed. "That's my girl. See you soon." Then she turned around and was immediately ensconced in a conversation about some garden committee or other. It was clear the two older women were quite willing to pull Lauren into the conversation, so she politely said her good-byes and excused herself quickly, ducking around the trio and heading toward her motel. Never was she so thankful that she'd had the foresight to book her own room.

She even had a little time to do a bit more digging—for her own peace of mind, at this point, if nothing else—before dinner. And the best place to start was her tote bag full of newspapers. Which, she remembered now, were not in her immediate possession.

She smiled. Gosh. It looked like there was a trip to the flight school in her immediate future. Well, she *had* said she was going on a bike ride. . . .

She thought about her mother's obvious desire that Lauren would bring someone with her—a specific someone. It was a shame Lauren wasn't willing to fan the flames of her mother's matchmaking fixation, or subject Jake to what was sure to be another stilted evening, because she could dearly use the support, and the diversion.

But there were other flames that would be fanned then, too, and she wasn't sure that was a wise idea, either. Still, that didn't mean she couldn't stop by the school to see him.

After all, she did need those papers back. . . .

Chapter 9

She was waiting for him as he walked away from the Piper, back toward the main hangar. Jake's pulse kicked up a notch seeing her standing there. But first things first. "Good job, Ben," he said, patting his young student on the shoulder. "Best landing you've done to date."

"I really want my solo."

"You're getting there. Another couple of hours and it's all you." Jake could all but taste the impatience in the sixteen-year-old. He'd been much the same, and at a much younger age. "Next Tuesday?"

Ben looked wistfully at the plane. "Only because it can't be sooner."

Jake laughed and waved as Ben walked over to the bicycle he'd left leaning up against the fence. Then he turned his attention to the woman who was leaning herself against the side of the hangar, pink bike helmet under one arm, a contemplative smile on her face.

"Want a lesson?" he asked.

"I've never thought about it, but I admit, it does look like fun. Scary, and intimidating, but fun." She glanced at Ben who'd just taken off back toward town. "How old is he?"

"Just turned sixteen."

"How close is he to getting his license."

A GREAT KISSER 127

Jake grinned. "Not as close as he'd like to be, but he'll get there. He loves this more than anything."

Lauren smiled. "Even girls?"

"Well, just imagine how hot they'll be for him when they know he can drive at ten thousand feet."

She pushed away from the hangar and fell into step beside him. "Is that why you started flying?"

He shot her a sideways grin. "No, but when I was old enough to figure that part out, I can't say I was disappointed."

She laughed. "How young were you when you learned to fly?"

"I grew up in the cockpit of a plane. I was playing copilot to my dad, and my granddad, before I mastered a two-wheeler. They had to build a special booster seat so I could reach everything."

"Precocious."

"No, I imagine it would have been that way in any business if you're exposed to it young enough."

She gave him a considering look, then nodded. "I probably resemble that remark."

Jake laughed.

"Does your sister fly?"

"She'll tell you otherwise, but she missed her calling. And the military missed out on what might have been their best fighter pilot ever."

"She was in the service?"

"No. She just has the most uncanny ability to focus regardless of the chaos surrounding her of anyone I've seen. And she can handle a plane like it's an extension of her own body. A true natural. Remember I said my grandfather used to do air shows? Well, Ruby Jean was only twelve when she started actually performing with him."

"Twelve? Aren't there regulations?"

"There are. Just as there are ways of getting around them. At least in some of the more rural, remote places where they performed. Not everyone was such a stickler for those things. She looked a lot older. She got all her height and most of her curves pretty young. She'd also learned to fly even younger than I did and there was no disputing her abilities. Anyone who saw her fly never questioned it. Not that anybody would have guessed she was that young. Anyway, they only had a year together on the circuit before he passed away, but they were a big hit. Usually she flew, and he walked. But she was a good walker, too."

"Walker?"

"On the wings."

Lauren's eyes widened. "No way."

"Oh, yes, way."

"On the Mustang's wings?"

Jake laughed. "No, no, we had another plane back then that they used for that. Haven't had it now for quite a while. Paddy— my grandfather—left it to Ruby Jean. She sold it to pay, in part, for her college education. She earned the rest of her tuition from the air show circuit. She missed a few seasons after our grandfather died due to her age, but she got back to it, mostly flew in the aerobatics shows for other owners. She was pretty well known."

"What made her stop?"

"Her heart wasn't in it the same way, flying for other people."

"And you said that it wasn't your thing."

He shook his head. "No. I'd have done it for her, but she knew it wasn't where I wanted to be. I just like to fly. The annual race is icing on the cake for me, but the school is where my heart is. She stuck with it as a way to keep his memory alive, and later as a means to earn tuition money, but without him as a partner, she lost her desire for it and no one really stepped up to fill that role. Boys entered her world, and most of them weren't too impressed with the fact that she could out-fly, out-drive, and out-ski all of them." He looked out across the short runway toward the mountains. "She doesn't do any of it anymore. She turned her focus to school, then trying to figure out what she wants to do with her life. She's been with the mayor for almost two years now."

"Is she happier?"

"She likes it well enough. Ask me he's the one getting the better deal, but her options are limiting here. I'm not sure who or what she really wants to be, and I'm not too sure she's really come to terms with who she really is, or who she thinks she's supposed to be. But she's trying to figure it out." He looked back at Lauren. "That's all any of us can do."

"How'd she land the job with the mayor?"

Jake held the door for her and they stepped into the other side of the school hangar that was divided up into two small offices. He motioned her toward the first one. "Is that a making-conversation question, or a personal one?"

"Why would there be—" She broke off as she noticed the stack of newspapers, carefully sorted, on the surface of his desk. "Oh."

"I wasn't intending to snoop. None of my business. But I knocked the damn bag on the floor and the papers went sliding everywhere. When I was putting them back together . . . well, let's just say I noticed a trend in the specific issues you'd pulled."

"I told you I was here to get some questions answered. Here in Cedar Springs, I mean. I'm here, in your hangar, to pick up the papers, and to thank you, once again for being thoughtful and reading between the lines so I wouldn't have to answer any awkward questions with my mother. That was very appreciated. You don't know this, but I've already returned the favor by saving you, too."

He leaned against the back of his chair and folded his arms. "Well, I appreciate that, whatever you did, but I should confess that perhaps, in my case, I had an ulterior motive."

An immediate wariness entered her eyes, which made him wish he'd phrased that in a different way. Also made him wonder what in the hell she was really trying to find out. Something told him this was about more than merely fact-finding details on the latest branch on her family tree.

"Which would be . . . ?"

"Well, you did look awfully cute in your bike helmet."

She rolled her eyes, but he saw the tension leave her shoulders. "Be careful what you wish for."

Now he lifted one eyebrow. "Which wish would that be?"

"Getting my attention, with or without flattering my lovely helmet hair."

Her hair was pulled back in a sleek ponytail. It was all glossy and silky looking, and he wanted to pull the rubber band out of it and rake his hands all through it. "Your hair is beautiful."

"Remind me to come to you whenever I feel the need to fish for ego-boosting compliments. Which I wasn't, by the way."

"I know. Makes them all the more fun to give. And I'm being perfectly honest when I say that your hair was one of the first things I noticed about you."

She laughed. "That was because it was a dripping, stringy mess. Nightmares are hard to ignore."

"No, after you'd combed the stringy and dripping out of it. I thought then that you had pretty hair. And when it was drying, as we drove back, I thought it then, too. Want to know the second thing I noticed?"

Her smile turned dry. "My charming personality and sparkling wit?"

"Your freckles."

She immediately ducked her chin, more an instinctive move than a deliberate one. Which had him pushing away from his resting spot and standing directly in front of her. "Why do you hide them?"

She looked up at him. "Because I'm not twelve."

"You are charming, by the way, and they're adorable."

"Yes, just the trait you need when trying to be taken seriously on Capitol Hill."

He rubbed lightly at her cheek with his thumb. "You're not on Capitol Hill anymore."

"Force of habit. And maybe . . . maybe—"

"Maybe a little shield, even if it's illusory, goes a long way when you're in otherwise uncharted territory."

"You're a very intuitive man."

"You say that like you're surprised."

"It's not a trait I come across all that often."

"In men," he added.

"In anyone, really. Most people are too caught up in their own thoughts, their own business, their own orbit, to pay attention to details."

"But you do."

"Are you asking?"

"No. I'm saying. If it's something you're even aware of, it's presence or lack in others, then you aren't one of the oblivious ones."

"I can be."

"We all can be." He brought his other hand up to her face, pleased when she didn't pull away, or duck her chin from his touch. "Why are you here, Lauren Matthews?"

"Here, in your airplane hangar?"

"You're in my airplane hangar because I have something you want."

"Newspapers."

His lips curved. "That, too."

"I'm guessing you don't feel the need to fish for compliments too often."

"Are you telling me you're strictly here for that stack of newsprint?"

"I could have asked you to courier them, but I don't think that's a common service here in Cedar Springs."

"I suppose I could train Hank to wear dog-size saddlebags."

"Hank?"

Jake motioned to the inert pile of bones presently stretched out full length under the worktable visible through the door that opened back into the hangar. "Part hound, part floor cover."

"He does seem very . . . relaxed."

"Not exactly the watchdog I'd hoped for, but as a companion . . . well, he makes a great rug."

Lauren barely muffled a snort, but nudged at Jake's shoulder. "You'll hurt his feelings."

"He relies on me for food. And yet, he's still not exactly hell bent on changing my opinion. I don't think my insulting him is affecting him too greatly."

"How long have you two been a team?"

"Seven years."

"So, he's pretty secure he's not going anywhere."

Jake chuckled. "This is true."

"And, just a guess, but probably not exactly courier material."

"No, you're probably right about that. Which brings us to your only other option."

"Which is?"

"Admitting that you came in person because you wanted your newspapers, and you wanted to get another little buzz."

Her brow furrowed. "Buzz?"

"Of the natural variety." He shifted a bit closer. "What, am I the only one who feels it when we get within two feet of each other?"

He felt the light trembling beneath his fingertips.

"Possibly not," she said.

His smile spread. "Possibly?"

"In my former job, you learn to waffle, evade, and remain as vague as possible. But, given, as you mentioned, I'm not on Capitol Hill . . . maybe I could upgrade that to a probably."

"I never turn down a free upgrade."

Her cheeks warmed under his touch. "That's a good policy."

"You haven't answered my other question."

"I seem to have been sidetracked." Her eyes crinkled at the corners when she smiled. "What was the question?"

"I'm not sure I remember, either. I have a new one that seems to be taking up most of my allotted brain space at the moment."

"So . . . ask me."

"Lauren Matthews, recently of Capitol Hill, and lately a guest of Cedar Springs. A woman of mystery, purpose, and burgeoning mountain biking skills . . ."

"You do realize that using big words like illusory and burgeoning is totally turning me on."

"What, a plane jockey can't be well read?"

"He can be a lot of things, it seems. So . . . what was the question?"

"Can I find out if you taste as good as I think you do?"

She couldn't quite stifle the quick grin, or the light blush that sprang to her cheeks. "How can I turn down such a sincere request?"

"Oh, it's quite sincere."

She moved in closer and let her hands come to rest on his shoulders. His entire body went instantly rock hard.

"You had me at 'illusory.' "

"Well, damn. And here I've been wasting time talking when we could have been doing this . . ." He tipped her mouth up to his and slowly lowered his own, until their lips just barely rubbed against one another. If a body could sigh, his did. He kissed her softly, exploring a little, letting them both get used to the taste and feel of one another. It was both the most simple and most erotic thing he'd experienced in a long while.

Simple, because with Lauren, it was elemental. He wanted her, was attracted, stimulated in every sense, physical and intellectual. It was the easiest thing he'd ever done, wanting her. Erotic because she was unknown to him, as he was to her. So much to learn, so much to explore, the anticipation alone was almost enough to send him over the edge.

And the restraint needed to keep from pushing only enflamed him further. Kissing her so gently, respectfully, when what he wanted to do was back her against the wall and devour every last inch of her. Then take her right on top of his desk.

But this was where it started, that first taste, the first true hello between them. It only happened once, and he was damned if he'd rush through even a second of it.

And then she made this little noise in the back of her throat, and her fingertips bit into his shoulders. And any restraint he had, any sense of the bigger moment they might be engaged in, was lost.

He took the kiss deeper, his hunger for her creeping in, no longer willing to be tamped down to something civilized and gentlemanly. And she took that kiss, the way he opened her mouth, just as hungrily. He'd always suspected—known, somehow, some way—that when he found that person, that click, that fit, that it would be exactly like this, this perfect mating of want and need. The only surprise was that it was even better than he'd ever dreamed it could be.

He finally had to break it off before his head exploded. Both of them. He tugged her ponytail free and pressed his face into the tumbling wave of silk, ending the kiss, but unwilling to end the hello. "You taste incredibly good," he murmured. "And those little noises you make . . . make a man—this man—crazy."

"Good crazy?" she asked, her voice muffled from where her lips were now pressed to the side of his neck, doing completely insane things to his pulse.

"Oh, the best kind of crazy."

He felt her smile and his body twitched. Hard. "I'm about a second away from forgetting that I'm running a business here, and that I have another student showing up in about ten minutes, who, if she's early—"

"She?" Lauren lifted her head.

Jake grinned. "You know, it should worry me, that slight edge, but I kind of like it."

"What edge? I was just asking—"

He wound a silky tendril of hair around his finger. "You were just wondering. And I don't mind that you wonder. In fact, I want you to wonder, to ask. To know whatever you want to know. She's a classmate of Ben's."

"Do you have a lot of girls taking lessons?" She leaned back so she could look him in the eye, then had to take off her glasses to clear the fog.

He took them from her and slid them back on. "I like that I steam you up."

She pushed them up the bridge of her nose, and the most delightful blush deepened her already flushed cheeks. "I have contacts, but—"

"It's kind of like the freckles?"

She smiled that crooked, wry smile of hers that he was coming to like the most. "Kind of. And, to be honest, they're easier. I'm used to them. So I don't often—"

"I like them. They're sexy. And it looks like they make a fairly good meter of how I'm doing."

"Steamy glasses as a gauge of sexual attraction."

"Not the most technologically advanced method, perhaps." He leaned in and kissed her again, lingering longer than he meant to, but she just tasted so damn sweet. He lifted his head and smiled as he looked through the light haze on her lens. "But I'm kind of liking it."

She sighed, took them off and wiped them clean again, and slid them back on herself, but there was a quirk to the set of her mouth that told him she wasn't exactly immune, either. "So . . . about your lessons."

"Ah yes, back to me and other women."

"Believe it or not, I'm actually just curious. It's a traditional guy thing, so I think it's cool that girls are into it, too."

"Mostly guys, but there's a few." He watched and waited, but she didn't say anything more.

"What?" she finally asked, when his smile slowly spread to a grin.

"It's killing you, but I appreciate either the trust, or the respect."

"It's none of my business."

"See? You totally want to know."

"I'm human. But it really isn't my place to ask. We're attracted. We kissed. We didn't sign a contract."

"I could draw one up."

She laughed.

He slipped his hands to her shoulders, then up so his palms cupped her face. "I like that you wonder."

"Why? You like jealous, possessive types?"

"Are you one?"

"Not ever." Then her lips quirked into a wry grin. "Normally."

He wondered when he'd ever grinned this often. "I'm not a fan of jealousy, but I like it that you wonder, because that means it matters."

"It was a kiss, Jake."

"It was that." He sighed with contentment. "It was that, indeed."

"You know, you aren't like anyone I've ever met. Must be the mountain air."

"I don't know. I'm not like myself with you. Or maybe I'm just being completely myself with you. I haven't figured it out yet."

"How are you normally?"

"The sort who shies away from the slightest hint of being pressured into anything beyond the casual, no strings exploration of mutual interest. At least initially, anyway."

"I appreciate the bluntness. That's refreshing."

"I am always that. Blunt, I mean. And I'm happy to hear it's a refreshing quality to you." He grinned. "I hope you continue to view it in that light."

"I can't imagine I wouldn't. It's one of the things that I noticed first about you."

"One of the things?"

"Fishing, fishing . . ."

He attempted to look contrite. "We all have our fragile sides."

She spluttered a laugh.

"I think I'm wounded."

"I think you're full of it. But I like that about you, too."

"I think I've just been insulted."

"No, you're being yourself, and assuming other people will not be easily offended by every little thing you say, or every nuance and possible interpretation, and therefore watching your every word. You have no idea how totally refreshing that is, too."

"You say what you think, you don't dodge, and you don't pull punches. Yes, I know a little something about feeling refreshed."

She covered his hands with her own. "So . . . we're mutually revitalized."

He slipped his hands over hers and pulled them around his waist. It felt remarkably comforting and . . . right. She fit against him well, and there was no awkward adjustment; she just slipped right into the circle of his arms, the shelter of his body. "I think we might be mutually a lot of things," he murmured, pressing a kiss against her temple because it suddenly felt like ages since he'd tasted her.

"So," she said, closing her eyes and pushing a little against him, like a cat seeking continued stroking. "If, normally, you would run, and you aren't acting like you normally do, then does that mean this isn't a casual, no strings exploration of mutual interest?"

"Would it send you running if I told you I feel anything but casual at the moment?"

"It does a lot of things to me." She shifted, looked up into his eyes. "But making me want to run isn't one of them."

He was going to have to get used to grinning. A lot. "That's the best thing I've heard in a very long time."

"It's complicated. Or could be."

"Only if we let it." When she started to speak, he talked over her. "It's whatever we make it, Lauren. All that matters, right this moment, is that we are both buzzed. And we both want more. And there is not a single reason, for either of us, not to take more. Is there?"

"I'm an available, consenting adult, if that's what you mean."

"As am I. So we just figure out what comes next as it comes."

She smiled. "I can't decide if you'd make the worst politician ever, or the best."

"Good thing I never have any intention of finding out."

"Amen."

They both laughed and he was thinking that for him, what came next was hopefully a whole lot more of what they'd been doing a few moments ago, but a gentle clearing of the throat had him quickly reconsidering.

"Mr. McKenna? I'm here for my lesson."

Lauren started to pull away, but Jake merely straightened and turned, sliding his hand to the center of Lauren's back. He had nothing to be embarrassed or worried about and hoped Lauren felt the same. "Hey, Stephanie. Head on out, I'll be there in a second."

She smiled, revealing two rows of braces banded with purple wires. "I think today could be the day."

"It could be. It's been a pretty amazing one so far. I'll meet you out there. Go through your preflight check. Grab the log book."

She dumped her backpack inside his office door and all but raced back out the door.

"Looks like the other woman in your life needs you."

"That's me, always in demand."

Lauren smiled and eased out of his hold. "Why don't I find that hard to believe?"

"Because you're smart, beautiful, and amazingly intuitive."

"Such a silver tongue," she teased.

He snaked his arm back around her and tugged her close. "It does all kinds of tricks. Wanna see?"

She laughed when he leaned down and flicked the tip of it over the pulse on the side of her neck. He also felt the little shudder that went down her spine when he followed it up with a light nibble. He wanted to learn all the other things that made her tremble like that.

She ducked away before he could pursue that line of thought. "Me, getting my tote. You, teaching someone how to fly."

"Trust me, in a few years, Stephanie will be the teacher. She's a natural."

"What is she so hopeful that today's lesson will bring? She looks too young to be flying by herself."

"She is, but not by much. Age is just a number, and Stephanie defies a lot of statistics. But today she gets to be in charge of the takeoff."

"That's pretty exciting."

"Want to come out and watch?"

"Sure. I still have some time."

He stacked the piles of newspapers and slid them into the tote, then slipped the strap over her shoulder, tugging her in close for a hard, fast kiss. He was pretty sure his heart skipped at least a beat or two. It was both exhilarating and terrifying. Like racing a breath away from the ground. And, just like racing, he wanted more of her particular brand of adrenaline rush. A lot more. "Can you make some time for me later?"

Her voice was a bit huskier, too. "Remember when I said I saved you?"

"Sort of. Everything before the kiss is kind of a blur now. B.K. and A.K."

She laughed.

"You think I'm joking."

"I think you're always joking."

"I tease, but I never joke."

"Well, no joke, in return for your gallant save at the library, I saved you from suffering through dinner with my mom and the mayor."

"How is that?"

"You recall that my mother ran into us both leaving the library. Together. Meaning I was in the vicinity of an apparently healthy male who was not a coworker or a direct superior, and he didn't appear to be put out or off with me in any way."

"Okay."

"So, naturally, that makes you a target. Fresh meat, as it were."

"Ah."

"So."

"I was invited to dinner, was I?"

"You were."

"And you declined for me?"

"I thought it was the least I could do. You've been nothing but kind to me and it seemed rude to repay that kindness with such cruelty."

He smiled. "What are they cooking?"

"Barbecue."

"I like barbecue."

"Served by my matchmaking mother and . . . her husband?"

"You know, we're going to talk more about this thing with you and your new . . . whatever you want to refer to him as."

"Jake—"

"No, I'm serious. I know there's some stuff there that's not cool, and I'm thinking, given the research you were pulling, that it's not entirely just an attitude problem on your part."

"I'm not sure what it is yet. That's what I need to find out. For myself, and maybe for my mom, too."

"So, we'll talk. Or you can talk. I make a good listener. Well, Hank does, but I've learned a lot from him over the years. He can come, too."

"Jake, you don't have to do the barbecue. Things are better with me and my mom, but the rest . . . well, I don't know what that is yet. It could be awkward, probably will be in some ways, and who knows what else. Not exactly the meet-the-family moment I'd prefer. Not yet, anyway."

"I know. Just tell me one thing: would you deal with the evening better flying solo, or would you mind a little support?"

"You don't have any idea what you're really asking here."

"So, you'll tell me. Later. I have to go let Stephanie earn her wings." He kissed her again, then again, then stopped before it got completely out of control. He pressed his forehead to hers. "Seriously, I'm not running." And then he ducked out before she could come up with any more reasons why he shouldn't accompany her that evening.

More shocking, was that he was actually looking forward to it. Maybe not the barbecue part, but definitely the "spend more time with Lauren" part. And he was admittedly curious to know more about the dynamics of the situation. He'd talk to her about it, but being there, observing them, might give him some additional insight.

And why the hell he was wanting insight, he had no idea. For a guy who was perfectly happy keeping to his own business and focusing on his passion and leaving others to theirs, he was certainly sticking his nose in where it didn't belong all of a sudden, wasn't he? Way in, in fact.

But the truth was, he wanted to know more. And he wanted to spend time with Lauren. So, if it meant he nosed around, and asked a few questions . . . well, then, apparently that's what it meant.

Chapter 10

"Well, how do you like that, Hank?" Lauren said, surprised the lanky hound hadn't trailed after his master. Instead, he had plopped down right in front of her, giving her that saggy-faced, baleful look that had her searching the office for some kind of dog biscuit box. Something. "He wants to go to my mother's barbecue," she said, still searching. "Who does that? I mean, he seems like a very nice, stand-up, dependable guy, but that's just above and beyond. And he doesn't even really know me. Yet." She paused and looked back at Hank, who thumped his tail on the floor once, then sunk slowly down into a boneless heap, as if that single action had taken all of his remaining energy reserves.

"That's kind of how he makes me feel. Boneless. Just a look can do it, but wow, the touching part is pretty amazing, too," she said, knowing she should feel ridiculous talking to the dog. But it felt kind of good, putting the tumult of thoughts and emotions into words. She was a conflict of wants and needs at the moment, and wasn't sure if she could just adopt his "take it as it goes" demeanor. "I'm a planner, Hank. I don't do 'wing-it' very well. I need to know where I'm going." She glanced at the dog, who was already dozing, and gave up her dog biscuit search to lean her hip on the desk and sigh. "Of course, I did a pretty big wing-it when I quit before deciding what to do next with my life. So . . . there is that."

Hank lifted one droopy lid, waited for her to say more, or maybe cough up the biscuit, then slid back into doggy dreamland when neither was forthcoming, apparently content to let her resolve her own issues.

"Well, thanks for listening. Jake was right, you're pretty good at that." She bent down and gave him a scratch behind the ears, which elicited a little groan of appreciation and another single tail thump. His eyes remained closed, so that was apparently all he could muster. She hiked the tote handles farther up onto her shoulder and headed out, pausing once she was outside. She could hear a plane engine revving and whining as it geared up and walked around the side of the building to see Stephanie do her takeoff.

But she ended up standing there long past the moment the plane made its departure from the terra firma and marched majestically into the gorgeous, bright blue sky. She wondered what that would feel like, to possess the power and skill to lift away from earth like that, to have the freedom to soar through the sky. She felt a bump against her thigh and glanced down to see Hank had wandered out and was gracing her with his less than enthusiastic companionship. She scratched at his head, which, even sitting hit her about hip high. "Maybe I'll take lessons," she told him. "After all, if little Stephanie up there can do it, I could probably figure it out. I earned a law degree, after all." She glanced down to see Hank staring up at her, his enthusiasm limited to a few long-lashed blinks. She sighed. "Maybe I'll just get a dog instead. At least when I talk to myself, I won't sound quite as irrational."

Hank sighed and slid to the ground at her feet, resting his chin on his oversized paws.

"Your confidence in my abilities is truly heartening." She lifted her gaze back to the sky, but the plane was no longer in sight. She and Jake hadn't exactly firmed up their plans yet. He didn't even know what time the barbecue was slated to start. She had no idea how long his lessons ran. And she really wanted some time to dig through the newspapers before seeing the less-than-dynamic duo in action again.

Everything her mother had said was still swirling around and settling in Lauren's head. And in her heart. It was a significant thing, realizing that her mother was a different woman, or at least a woman with different needs, than Lauren would have ever attributed to her. Lauren was truly happy for her and felt a great deal more settled about the matter now that she had some sense, some reason, for why her mother had anchored so determinedly out here in the west. She'd witnessed, firsthand, the serenity and peace of mind it had brought to her, and she had no intention of doing anything to change that, nor would she if she could.

But there was still the issue of her mother's choice in husband. And while Lauren understood that where Arlen was concerned, if her mother was as settled with him as she was with her life here in Cedar Springs, then Lauren should accept that, too. Unfortunately, while she was at peace with her mother's happiness, she wasn't settled with Arlen. So, even if it was now only for her own illumination and enlightenment, she had every intention of seeing her investigation through to the end—discreetly—and find out whatever it was that she needed to know and understand in order to resolve it in her own heart once and for all.

If her mother planned on staying married to the man, which it certainly appeared she did, then that meant he was going to play a role in Lauren's life. And, because she loved her mother and planned to continue their close relationship, that meant she had to come to terms with her husband, too, and find a way to sincerely be okay with him on a personal level. To that end, she would spend time with him, like this evening, and get to know him better, continue to form her own opinions and let the ones already formed take better, more realistic shape with the additional information she'd gain from that personal interaction.

All while simultaneously investigating him to the very furthest of her abilities. Because that's what her gut was still telling her to do. And she was very much at peace with that.

She hiked the tote bag full of press articles about Arlen's

business dealings in Cedar Springs higher onto her shoulder and looked down at her newly acquired, four-legged sounding board. "So, I'm guessing if he doesn't come to his senses and decide to run, run fast, he'll come find me at some point. Right?" Hank didn't seem to be paying the least bit of attention. In fact, he appeared to be sleeping. Again. A slight snoring sound drifted upward, confirming her observation. She bent down and rubbed his neck and slowly extracted her foot from under his head. So much for her new best friend. "See you around, big guy."

Hank's response was a heaving sigh as he rolled over to his side.

"Right." She gave one last look skyward, then turned and headed to where she'd left her bike. "To think that senators and statesmen used to routinely hang on my every word. Now I'm reduced to begging attention from a narcoleptic dog." She scraped her hair back in some semblance of a ponytail and plopped her helmet back on her head, then slid the straps of the tote over her head so they crossed her body at an angle, keeping the tote tucked beneath her arm as she straddled the bike. She was halfway back to her motel before she realized she was grinning like a fool.

Compared to having conversations with flight school jockeys and disinterested hound dogs . . . talking to the country's most powerful movers and shakers was highly overrated. As it turned out.

"Who knew?" she murmured as she wheeled into the parking lot of her motel. Despite the fact that she could probably have left her bike in the middle of the parking lot and it would have been perfectly safe, she wheeled it into her motel room and propped it against the wall and felt better for it. You could take the girl out of Washington, and the girl might even like it, but there were some parts of the city that were just going to stick, no matter what.

She slid the stack of papers out onto the bed and grabbed a legal pad from her laptop case and a black pen, red pen, and yellow highlighter. It occurred to her that most people probably didn't carry legal pads, a variety of writing implements, and a handheld scanner in their computer bag when they were going on, what was for all intents and purposes, a vacation. Some people might not even carry their computer. "Yeah, well, some people don't have to dig up dirt on their stepfathers just to figure out what it is about them that gives them the creeps." Just thinking the word stepfather in conjunction to herself made her shudder a little. Her mother's husband. No, spouse. Yes, that's how she preferred to think of him. Her mother's ex-spouse would feel even better. "Except that's no longer on the table for discussion." Much as she might wish it were.

Which either made her a terrible, selfish daughter . . . or one who loved and cared about her mother so much that she was willing to do whatever it took to make sure she wasn't hurt.

Lauren pushed her glasses up her nose, which made her smile a little, then flipped the first paper around so the print was facing her the right way. She was skimming a story that had caught her eye on a business deal Arlen had brokered between the town council and the developers the resort owners had hired to expand the little nucleus of shops that were sprouting up right around the resort buildings, and was reaching for the phone to call the desk and ask where she could go to make copies, when she thought better of it. Normally she wouldn't think twice about asking a hotel desk about office services or any local services. But this wasn't any hotel. In any town. If she asked about making copies, somehow that would be news, and then her mother would be asking her what on earth she needed to make copies of and . . . well, some parts of city life were desirable. Anonymity, for one.

She tugged her handheld scanner out. It had been an invaluable tool when she'd been with the senator on long road trips, making speeches, talking to local businessmen, and the like. She would scour local papers, event magazines, cull local news interest stories from anywhere she could find them, brochures, talking to people, whatever it took, and put them together in a file for the senator to read over in between his meetings, to pick up talking points, find a way to connect directly to the people of whatever town he was in. She never went anywhere without her computer, the scanner, her PDA, wireless air card, and small printer. She'd brought all but the printer with her to Colorado, thinking, at the time, that she was actually downsizing fairly well.

She set everything up, but for whatever reason, though the first few articles scanned in fine, the one she wanted most was blurred and impossible to read. She even checked her glasses to see if they needed cleaning, then laughed at herself. The article read crystal clear; it just scanned poorly. She made some adjustments, but the end result was still far more frustrating to decipher than it was worth. Then she remembered, when she'd been looking for dog biscuits . . . Jake had a copier in his office. Duh.

He already knew she wasn't here strictly on a social, fence-mending call. And she had every intention of talking it over with him. She was more sure of him than she was of anyone else in town. And she needed the ear and perspective of someone who'd seen Arlen in action, especially over a period of time, in different circumstances. This was one case where the "everybody knows everybody's business" aspect of small town living should tilt in her favor. Jake had said he really wasn't partial to town gossip and tended to keep his nose out of it, but by simply living here he would know more than he might think.

She looked at her bike, then the clock, and then the papers spread on the bed. Maybe she should go through as many articles as she could, see what she found, if anything, then dress for the barbecue and bike back to the flight school. He'd probably be done with his lesson by then. And they could leave for the barbecue from the school. Besides, if he drove her to her mother's, then he'd have to take her back to the flight school—and presumably he lived somewhere in that vicinity, if not on the property itself—to get her bike back.

Not that she was planning anything. Really. But if they happened to be alone, and they happened to revisit the kind of "getting to know you" behavior they'd indulged in earlier . . . well, she was just thinking it might be better to be with him in the privacy of his space, then have him in her "less than private motel room right on Main Street" one.

Just in case. Anything might happen. It was good to have a plan. Planning was a good thing. Not that she had any specific plans to do anything . . . specific.

"Who am I kidding?" She forced her thoughts away from those few incredibly fantastic minutes she'd shared with Jake in his office today and back to the matter at hand. She had no time to waste. "He really is an amazing kisser, though. Just saying." She looked over, as if expecting to see Hank laying there, staring back at her, soundlessly judging her. "Right. Now I am talking to myself."

She slid her glasses up her nose and went back to reading the news story. Six papers later, she finally found something. She re-read the paragraph several times. Straightening up from the cross-legged slumped position she'd shifted into at some point, she slid the paper onto her lap, and read it a third time. "Well . . . that's interesting." It wasn't actual proof of any wrongdoing or any-thing, but it provided a bit more insight into the man her mother had married. Well, okay, the man Lauren wasn't taking a shine to was more accurate. Regardless, it was a good starting point for her talk with Jake.

"Because talking is what I want to be doing with Jake. Right." She glanced at the clock, and winced when she saw how late it was. "And I really need to either get a dog or stop talking to myself."

She slid the papers into the tote bag, with the article of inter-est on top, then jumped into the shower while planning what she would wear. Another plus to mountain town living. No panty-hose required. For that matter, no makeup required, either, from what she could tell. But she still had her workaholic Washing-ton pale skin. And even the freckles didn't give her that fresh-faced, mountain-air kind of look that everyone else in town had.

Besides, she couldn't really be expected to give up all her armor at once.

Twenty minutes later, her hair was combed back into a sleek ponytail, and she was wearing khakis, flats, and a sky blue camp shirt over a pale pink tank top. All freshly ironed, but still casual enough to survive the bike ride to the school, and all the way out to her mother's for that matter if Jake ended up backing out. Besides, she felt better if she at least started with freshly creased trousers and a nicely pressed blouse.

"So, in addition to a dog, and my own bike, I need a good dry-cleaner." She might be the only freshly pressed and creased person in Cedar Springs, but some things she simply wasn't going to compromise on, no matter what she decided to do with the rest of her life.

When she rolled onto the dirt walkway next to the little gravel lot, she could see Jake's plane—at least the one he'd been using earlier for lessons, parked in the distance beside the smaller hangar that she knew housed *Betty Sue*. So, unless he was up in a different plane, he should be in the front office, or maybe he was working on the Mustang. She'd check the office first, use the copier, then track him down if he wasn't there.

It was crazy to have the kind of butterflies she was having at the moment. They'd kissed. And boy, had they. But it wasn't like she hadn't done that before. And he seemed very straight-forward about his attraction to her. Also good to know. And much easier to handle than the typical mating dance guessing games that were the result of most initial attractions. He really was a refreshing change, and despite there being some complications—okay, possibly a lot of complications—maybe this could be the one thing she got to take pleasure in. A little oasis. A little balance. Something to simply enjoy. It could just be that.

She walked into the office front and saw him bent over the desk, his shaggy, sun-streaked hair curling against his neck. She noticed the way his old sweatshirt stretched across broad shoulders, the way his worn, grease-stained jeans showed off a decently muscled backside and thigh . . . and sighed. This was so going to be a whole lot more than simple.

"Hi."

He glanced up and smiled immediately. And the butterflies swarmed. In a good way. A really, really good way.

"I was just about to come find you," he said.

"I thought I'd save you the effort." She slipped the tote over her head. "And, maybe, beg the use of your copier."

"Sure. There's probably one in the motel office, too. Not that I mind if you use mine, but in case you needed one again later."

"Unfortunately the motel copier comes with motel employees watching. I'd rather not share all my business. As it is, there's probably speculation on why I checked out the stack of newspapers. Though why anyone would care is beyond me."

"Something to speculate on, because it's out of the norm. Most visitors come to town, do some shopping, see the local sights, take a tour, ski if there's snow, and eat some of the best cuisine this side of Denver. The library isn't usually on the list of Things To Do in Cedar Springs. And you're not just any visitor."

"Okay, so you make many good points. All underscoring the need to use a more discreetly located machine." She smiled and moved over to the copier. "Any special operational details I should know?"

"Face down, top left corner. Push the green button."

"Thanks."

She sat her tote on the floor next to the machine, which was catty-corner from his desk just behind him. She noticed he was watching her rather than returning to whatever he'd been doing before she'd come in. "I'm sorry if I'm interrupting. I can do this later."

"No, no problem. I was almost done anyway."

"So . . . don't let me keep you. I'm sure I can figure this out."

She looked over her shoulder to see he'd sat down and swiveled his chair fully around to face her. He'd crossed his leg over one knee and folded his arms. "I like watching you. Nicest view I've had all day."

"Considering I know you've been up in the sky, going over those mountains, that's really saying something."

"Yes," he said without hesitation. "It is."

Boy, he could say the damndest things. She hadn't blushed this much since, well, ever. "Jake—"

"Lauren." He reached out and snagged her wrist and tugged her closer until she more or less tumbled into his lap.

"Oh!"

"My." He settled her so she was half facing him. "Is it possible to miss someone you've just met?"

She shifted a little but didn't try and get up. His arms had settled around her and, well . . . she rather liked where she was at the moment. "I think it's possible."

"You want to tell me about those?" He nodded to the stack of papers she'd left on top of the copier.

"Actually, I do. I want to feel you out a little."

He wiggled his eyebrows. "Best offer I've had all day."

She pushed at his shoulder, but laughed. "I'm serious, though. You don't have to let me bend your ear, but I'd really appreciate your viewpoint."

"You know, normally I'd tolerate the ear bending, because it would serve the greater good. Which would be to eventually get you into bed."

The very idea made her shiver in anticipation, but her tone was dry. "At least you're honest."

"I'm a guy. It's what we do. But, I'll be honest with you, I've been curious about what's going on with you and your family and I'm generally not one to give a flipping damn about other people's business."

She smiled wryly. "You sound so perplexed."

"You have no idea."

"Well, since we're being frank here, I will tell you that even if you don't listen to my tales of woe, it's highly possible that with a little more behavior of the sort we practiced earlier in this very office that the bed scenario is probably not out of the question. And that's not normal behavior for me, either. So you're not the only one stepping out of the comfort zone."

"So why tell me?"

"Why did you tell me? I just thought maybe you'd like to save yourself the time and possible return of your Guy Club decoder ring when they find out you care about more than just getting laid."

"Oh, I care about that. I've thought about it. A lot. In fact, it's clouding my ability to get work done. You're proving to be a really big distraction."

"Am I?" It should have made her feel at least a tiny bit guilty, but . . . no, not so much. "Well, so are you."

He grinned. "Good to know I'm not alone."

"Nope. Definitely not alone."

He pulled her a little closer. "But I have the strangest feeling that I could take you to bed right this very second, and when it's all said and done, I'm still going to want to know what the deal is with you, and your mom, and Arlen."

"Hunh. Go figure."

"I know. What's up with that?"

They held each other's gaze with pretend stumped expressions for a beat too long. Jake cracked a smile first. Then she smiled. Then they both laughed.

"So . . . maybe you should tell me all about it first."

"And risk you changing your mind and running for the hills? Of which you have many. I'd never find you."

"Unless I wanted to be found. Would you search?"

"Depends on what part made you run. So, why risk it?"

"Because if we get all the talking out of the way first, it leaves us far less distracted to do other things. At length. Without concerns of conversations yet to happen." He started to toy with the collar of her shirt, then ran his fingertip along the vee neckline of her tank top, stopping where it dipped the farthest.

She sucked in a shuddery breath. "You continue to make some very good points."

He lifted her camp shirt away from her body and peeked inside. "So do you."

Her nipples tightened even further, and it took considerable will not to drag his hand to where it might actually do some good. And she'd bet he'd do a lot of good. Really, really good, in fact.

"We have a barbecue to attend," she said, hearing the slightly breathless quality in her own voice.

"Another excellent reason for you to tell me what's going on before our command performance, given it concerns them. The more I know, the better I'll be able to support you."

"Why? I mean, why do you want to support me? We only just met."

"I know. And I want to because I'm on your side."

"You don't even know the sides yet. Either of them."

"I know you're on one side, and your mom and Arlen are on the other. If, after you explain things, I think you're misguided or could use a little perspective, I'll tell you. Which still makes me on your side."

She smiled. "Because I'm the one you want to get into bed."

"Well, there is that. But you strike me as an intelligent, rational woman. So, in addition to wanting you, I want to help. I'm guessing you're not facing whatever it is you're facing without there being some merit to the problem."

"And being sympathetic will probably get me into bed."

He grinned. "Win win, really."

She laughed. "I appreciate the support, the willingness, whatever the motive, I do—"

"Kidding, and sex, aside, I'm here and I'm willing to listen. Just be prepared to hear whatever my reaction is. I won't pull punches."

"Good. Because I need your insight. Into the town and the people involved. Although, if there are any personal reasons why you might not be comfortable talking, then just tell me. I'll respect that." She grinned. "And possibly still go to bed with you. Just be honest. That's all I ask."

"That you can have. And so much more." He slid his hand down her side and slid it back up again, under her camp shirt, nudging up the hem of her tank top until he could brush his fingers against the bare skin just above the waistband of her khakis.

She was like this puddle of pheromone induced goo with him. Just his touch was driving her incredibly crazy. And he wasn't even touching anything important. Yet.

Maybe because she knew—could feel in fact—exactly how badly he wanted her. And because her own needs and desires easily matched his.

"There's not much time," she said. "We . . . really should go."

"We should," he said without the slightest bit of urgency in his tone. He slid his other hand up her back, then brought her head down closer to his, leaning the chair back until it hit the desk as he pulled her more fully against him. "In just a minute."

He tilted her head so he could take her mouth, pausing just before contact so that she opened her eyes. His were steady on hers. Then he grinned. It made his eyes twinkle. "I'm glad you're here." He said it with a little bit of wonder in his voice.

"I am, too," she said, wondering a little herself.

Then he kissed her. And it was a slow seduction, when no seducing was necessary. She could feel him grow even harder beneath her thighs, and they tightened against the sudden and very real ache between them. She'd expected something hard, fast, demanding. So this slow, languorous, "all the time in the world" kiss totally undid her before she had a chance to regroup. She was responding without thinking, because he made it so damn easy to do just that. Just . . . feel, taste, take, accept. Explore, want, desire . . . anything. As simple and natural and uncomplicated as she thought it would be, wanted it to be.

He was lifting his head just as she was about to sigh and really relax into it. "I want full, complete, uninterrupted time with you. No demands, nowhere to be. Days of it. Maybe weeks." His voice was a little rougher and, if possible, a bit deeper.

"Right at this moment, you have no idea how good that sounds."

"Oh, I think I do. I know we're on different paths, in different places, different demands, but I'm betting we would both love the escape."

"Is that what this is? What I am? An escape? I'm not blaming, mind you, because vacation flings can be just as good for the local as they can for the out-of-towner. Fulfill a few needs, no complications. Over at some point, the "going our separate ways" part already predetermined . . ."

"Except your way isn't determined at all, at the moment."

"No, but—"

He hushed her by brushing his lips across hers. "I have no idea what this is. Or what it can be. I do know I don't play local-and-tourist. Gets really old, really fast. This doesn't feel like that. At least to me. Maybe I'm just kidding myself."

"I don't play vacation fling, either, so I don't know what it feels like. But there are no premeditated parameters on my part."

"Good to know. Unfortunately, I also know that I have no time to truly escape, not at the moment. My schedule is insane for the next month or so, up to and including the race. I can't do anything about that. But you're here now, not a month from now. And I don't want to pass up the possibilities, even though I know I can't devote the time I want to figuring it out. You're important."

"How could I be important?"

"You matter."

"We haven't known each other forty-eight hours."

"A day, a week, a minute, a passing glance. That's not relevant. What's relevant is how being around you makes me feel. And I feel . . . different. Energized, happy, excited. And not just in the hormone-rush way it usually goes. Although, there is that." He shifted her on his lap and she laughed.

"Yes, there is definitely that."

"And . . . I don't know why it feels so different, but it doesn't change the fact that it does. Sometimes you just know. Have you ever just known?"

She didn't answer right away. Because maybe she knew exactly what he meant, but it was really too insane to even contemplate that it might be more than that rush of hormones she'd been trying to convince herself it was. Because, seriously, what else could it be? And she was nothing if not serious about things.

"I've never once met anyone so in tune with himself," she said.

"I'm just being honest. And maybe a bit more—okay, a hell of a lot more—vocal than I'd ever normally be. But I kind of feel pressured here."

"By me? I'm not—"

"By circumstance. You're here, but for how long? If I don't act, don't say what I'm thinking, how would you know? I don't have the luxury of taking my time."

"Are you always this impulsive?"

"Never," he said without hesitation.

She had no response to that.

"Don't mistake this for me pressuring you," he said. "I'm just putting it out there. You're free to do whatever you want with that. Of course, the fact that you're in my lap and not struggling to get out, even with me acting like a completely deranged fool, is definitely encouraging."

"I'm—I have no idea what I'm feeling. I'm not as organized about it as you are, not just yet. I guess I'm basically sort of winging it."

He chuckled. "You don't strike me as the winging it type."

"I'm so not. Never used to be, anyway. Until recently. I'd say I'm pretty much winging everything right now."

"Understandable."

"Not really. I'm a planner. I love to plan. It makes life so much more pleasant when things are structured. So much of life you can't structure, so managing and organizing what you can, builds at least a foundation to work from."

"Until now." She nodded. "So . . . how is the whole winging it thing going so far?"

She smiled at him, still settled in his lap. "At the moment, I really can't complain."

He grinned. "Have you ever been married? Ever been close?"

The question was just so unexpected, even in the context of the very unexpected conversation they were having, that she just gaped at him.

"Don't worry, I haven't gone completely insane. I'm just going back to a previous point. Have you ever just known? That a particular person is the one?"

"I—I've been close. Yes."

"What happened?"

His frank openness was so new and different, she really didn't know how to handle it, other than to be as frank and open in return. "I—I guess I thought I knew, but then I realized it wasn't right. For any number of reasons. But knowing . . . works both ways, I guess. I blame me. Nothing was wrong. It was just . . ."

"Not right."

"Exactly."

"Did it take a long time to figure out? The knowing, then the knowing it wasn't right?"

"No. I just knew. And probably did all along. You can talk yourself into believing a lot of things when you want what you want. But eventually, I had to admit that just because I wanted it—him—didn't make it right. It would never have worked, and I always knew that, but chose to ignore it. Until I couldn't. So, you're right. You do just know. I guess I've never known the other way. When it really is right. Have you?"

"Up until now, no. I've been more like you. Liked it, thought I wanted it, but knew somewhere deep down that it really wasn't it. That it couldn't be. That the real thing would be different, would be . . . more."

She was too afraid to ask him why he thought this time could be different. She wasn't sure she wanted to think about it herself yet. This was supposed to be simple fun. It was definitely fun . . . but nothing about Jake McKenna was turning out to be simple. "Maybe this isn't it, either," she said, putting it into words, thoughts, she could handle.

"Maybe. But it is . . . more. And that's a damn good place to start."

She thought about that, thought about the hormone rush she'd gotten in the past when meeting someone who attracted her. And not always simply physically. She'd had all her senses engaged before, thought there was a pretty strong chance it might be "it." But she'd definitely never met anyone who so fully engaged her, who was so open about the process while it was happening. She'd never met anyone so unafraid of challenging her, of being so completely himself, and so completely open about whatever was going through his mind. He said he was never impulsive, and neither was she. So . . . it only stood to reason that if she could act so completely out of character, so could he. And . . . if they were both compelled to do so with each other, then maybe it did demand a little bit of thought. Maybe a little bit of hope.

"Wheels are grinding," he said with a chuckle, and tapped a gentle finger on her temple. "I can hear them."

"I'm used to analyzing data, extrapolating patterns, searching for clues to help hedge current and future potential against previously calculated and collected material."

"How is that working out for you in this case?"

She smiled. "The applications really don't seem to apply in this instance. It's all very frustrating, actually."

"Not everything can be calculated against past data to insure future success."

"I think it's the lack of current data that's making it hard to assess what actions are best taken."

"That's where gut instinct comes into play. Or winging it, as it were. Don't you ever—in your job, or in your life—have to just go with your gut? Even if it forces you to base your decisions on something completely new and untested?

"Yes. I don't generally like to, but yes, sometimes you aren't given the luxury of prolonged study."

"Exactly."

"Don't you think, though, that gathering more information before making a judgment call one way or the other, helps to prevent—"

"Sudden losses? Failure? Otherwise known as getting hurt?" She nodded, then pointed to herself. "Remember, planner."

He smiled. "It might, but sometimes it just is what it is. Time doesn't always play a role with instinct. Or impact at what point you know what you want. And once you do, can you really slow it down? The instinct to go after something you want? Be it a relationship, a job, whatever. You might pretend to pace yourself, or make yourself not take the leap, because you want to be more certain, or even for appearances' sake, but that doesn't stop the urge to leap in the first place. It's just . . . there. Whatever arbitrary rules you put on it, isn't really stopping it from being there."

"No, I guess not. But, by nature, I keep a lot of that part of the process to myself until I know more."

"I do, too. Makes sense. Self-protection is smart. I can pretty much say I've always operated under that code. Probably too much. I might have missed out a few times because I was being too cautious, despite what I was feeling, what I was wanting. No one wants to be wrong, or rejected, or hurt."

"Exactly."

"But you can't win if you don't play."

"And life offers no guarantees," she added. "I know."

He cupped her face with his hand. "So . . . I'm playing. And I'm letting you know, I'm in. If that makes you want to pull the shields up and batten the hatches, do whatever you have to do. And if you want to leap, do that, too. I'll hold your hand and leap with you."

"Doesn't that unnerve you? Just a little? Don't you think it's probably just initial attraction and chemistry? When you get to know me, there are a thousand reasons why you might wish you'd never leaped."

"And I won't get to learn a single one if I don't take the chance and jump in." He tugged her closer. "And yes, it's the most unnerving thing in the world. It's also damned exciting. It's . . . well, it's a lot like taking off for the first time, and wanting to stay up there as long as you can to enjoy every last bit of the rush. You don't think about the landing, not the first one, because you don't want to ruin the high of it. You'll come down eventually. You have to. And it will either be devastating, and horrible. Or it will be a soft touchdown and all you'll be thinking about is getting back up there again. And the more often you touch down smoothly, the more confident you are about getting back up. It's addictive and it never gets old." He rubbed his thumb over the corner of her mouth. "Some things, the best things, never do. That I do know, and that I believe. I've just never found it in a person before."

"What are the chances you will now?"

"Haven't a clue." His eyes twinkled as the skin crinkled at the corners. "But . . . this is more," he said simply. "So, I sure as hell am going to do what I can to find out."

Lauren felt like she was grabbing onto the tail of a comet. Like she was about to take the ride of her life. He was right, it was both a terrifying and exhilarating rush. "I've never met anyone like you."

"Good. Let's hope it only takes knowing one." His grin widened further. "Me."

Chapter 11

He had completely and totally lost his mind. It was the only explanation, really. He'd only just met her and there he was, spouting ridiculous amounts of bullshit, which, if he could honestly say it was for the greater good of getting laid, he wouldn't be that upset with himself for having spouted. But no . . . he'd actually meant every single goddamn word. And he hadn't planned on saying any of them. Because . . . who would plan on saying all of that? Out loud? He'd gone totally around the bend. Altitude sickness. Something. So what if he'd lived his whole life at eight thousand feet? Maybe the thin air was just now catching up to him.

He glanced over at the woman sitting next to him and wondered what she'd think if she could peek inside his head at the moment. Relief, probably, that he really wasn't as loco as he'd sounded now that he had come to his senses. It was to her credit that she hadn't fallen in some kind of swoon, listening to him spout off, but what did it say about her that she hadn't flown out the door, either, finding anywhere else to be but with the touchy-feely nutjob who'd just gone all Dr. Phil on her?

Maybe it says that she's cautious, but willing to take you at your word . . . and think about it. A rational, sane woman, giving you the benefit of the doubt that you really, truly believed what you were saying.

Crap.

If she'd taken off, then he could kick himself for being an idiot and not taking her to bed first. And then he'd have gotten over it, as he did with all life's disappointments, and gone back to the business of, well, doing business. But no. She'd stuck it out. Neither swooning or running screaming. Being, in fact, exactly the type of woman he thought she was, which was the exact kind of woman who'd inspired his little "I like you I really really like you" speech in the first place.

So . . . what in the hell was he supposed to do now?

She caught him glancing and smiled. And his heart did that thing it did when she looked at him like that. His heart had never behaved like that. Not even when he thought undressing Jenny Kistlinger, twenty-one-year-old college senior, was the best thing an eighteen-year-old high school senior could ever hope to do in his whole entire life, had he felt this particular brand of butterflies. And he was older now, far more experienced—thank God—and knew better than to feel any such sort of fluttery little feelings. Horny feelings, yes. Twinges of affection, even deep affection, certainly. He'd even fancied himself in love a time or two. But not . . . whatever the hell this was. And not five seconds after meeting.

He glanced back at the road. "So, you want to talk about the articles?" Real life, that was what he needed. To get his head out of the clouds and back on real-life issues. Like talking about why she was in Cedar Springs, reading everything she could get her hands on about any business dealings concerning her new stepfather. Not the myriad of political moves and public announcements, interviews as mayor, and things like that. What she'd pulled had to do with the handful of times Arlen's personal business had made it into the news. And, given some of his connections, it was only surprising he didn't land there more often.

"Well, the bare bones basics are that I hadn't quite given my blessing to my mom and Arlen—not that they need it—but I was worried. About my mom, about why she made the choices she did, how it all came about. How it came to be Arlen."

"You said your talk today helped?"

"It did. A lot. There were things about her . . . about what she wanted in her life, what she didn't want any longer, that I didn't know. I do now, and a lot of things make more sense."

"Except?"

"Except her choice in husband." Lauren lifted her hand. "I'm not trying to insult your mayor, although I know I am, but . . ."

"It's okay. It might ease your mind to know he's not my favorite person. Or maybe it will make you more worried. Nothing horrible, I should say up front. We just don't see eye-to-eye on a few things." Lots of things, actually, but he didn't elaborate. Yet.

"That's a little part of it, or was initially. From what I've learned about him, just politically, I'm surprised my mother doesn't feel the same."

"Do you all usually share the same opinion? About politics, men?"

"Hardly, but this isn't about her agreeing with my point of view. This is about me knowing her point of view—on both men and politics—and wondering how it meshes with someone like the man she chose to very suddenly marry and change her entire life for."

"In that context, I'd be concerned, too. What do you want to know? I'll try to be impartial, and I'll let you know when I can't be."

"Which is more than fair. Thank you."

"Go ahead."

"Okay." She shifted in her seat so she was facing him. "I did a lot of digging into his political career when I heard about their elopement, but other than being surprised by the fact that they're not exactly on the same party page, there wasn't anything else there that caught my eye."

"Have you thought . . . and no insult intended, but your reservations came before you'd even met him."

"Yes, they did, but they weren't automatic, if that's what you mean, because he married my mother. I'm not the overprotective, spoiled only child here, although I definitely don't want to see my mom get hurt."

"Is she prone to making rash, potentially harmful decisions?"

"Never."

"Well, then . . ."

"As I said, given that, it was shocking when I got the call. But, even then, it was just shock, not a condemnation. But then she started to describe this man she'd run off and married, after being a single widow for a very long time—and trust me when I say she's had many opportunities to change that status, and I encouraged her to get out and find someone."

"So, what triggered the protective daughter part to come out?" He glanced at her. "I didn't say overprotective; there is a difference. A good one, in your case."

"Thank you. Well, of course I was curious, to say the least. Then I listened to her talk about him and there wasn't really this gush of lust or a rational explanation, it just . . . I don't know. It was kind of odd. So I started doing a little research. Given we were both in politics, I had some access that others might not have and I pulled some strings and favors."

"And?"

"Well, I found the opposite politics aspect kind of confusing, and I can't say that I liked the man based on either his politics or what I got to read and see of him in action as the mayor. Mostly, it all just really stumped me. And I'm not paranoid or suspicious by nature, but my job has certainly put me in the position, constantly, of having to vet every new situation and extrapolate what the dangers might be. So I know I'm predisposed to seeing things that way. I really tried to be objective, but—"

"You just didn't like the guy your mom abruptly married and you wanted to figure out why."

"Exactly. So I went to my mom and talked to her about it. We've always been really, really close, so—"

"Did it hurt that she got married and told you after the fact?"

"I—well, it was surprising, of course, shocking really, but no, if she was deliriously happy and the man she married was in any way to her like my father was—"

"They had a good marriage?"

"A great one. One for the ages. It was, in large part, why she never remarried."

"But you wanted her to."

"Of course I did. I mean, I wanted her to be happy, and if that was something that would, then yes, I absolutely pushed for that. I loved my father and we were very close. I went into law because of him, and my grandfather. But he was gone, and I'm not the sort who believes you should wallow. So I nudged, I pushed, I even set her up a few times."

"So, it's really just about Arlen, then."

"Well . . . yeah. I want to like him. I do. I want to be on board with this relationship. I am on board with the fact that it clearly makes my mother happy, but to be honest with you, in person I haven't seen even the tiniest inkling of what they see in each other. It's not even obvious they're in love with each other, much less newlyweds. And . . . meeting Arlen in person didn't . . . well, it didn't really change my opinion of the guy. Something about all of this just doesn't seem right and I don't know why."

"Does your mom know you still feel this way?"

"She knows I'm happy for her, and we've mended most of the fences that got torn down, heck, destroyed, over the past six months over conversations we had about the marriage and my concern for her."

"I'm glad you've patched that part up, and if your gut isn't good with Arlen personally, or them together, then maybe you're doing the right thing in trying to figure it out for yourself."

"They're going to be together, so yes, I need to come to terms with him. I don't want to make things difficult for my mom, and I don't want to have to pretend not to feel odd whenever I'm in the room with him."

"Odd how?"

"I don't know. He just . . . he looks at me. Not in a perverted sense, just . . . like I'm being studied. It's unnerving. And well, he's kind of a blowhard, in that used-car-salesman kind of way that doesn't endear me."

"And, I suppose, makes you wonder why in the hell it would endear your mother."

"That, but even more odd, to me, is that she doesn't seem particularly endeared to him, either. It's just . . ."

"Odd," Jake asked with a smile, earning one from her in return.

She nodded. "So . . . I just feel I need to keep trying to figure it all out. It's . . . off. For me. He's off."

"And if you figure it out, do you plan to share it with your mom?"

"I don't know; I guess it depends on what conclusions I finally come to. It might just be that I don't like the guy and can't figure the two of them out, and if that's what it is, I'll have to deal with that on my own."

"But you think there's more."

"I—I guess, yes, I do. There just has to be. At least that's what my gut tells me. I need to know, need to figure it out. What 'it' is, I'm not sure. And maybe I'll never feel right with it all. But I'm going to at least dig until there isn't anything left to find."

"So . . . what do you want to know from me?"

"First, I want to thank you," she said.

"For?"

"For listening, hearing me, not judging me."

"I understand why you're doing what you're doing. You're confused by something that makes no sense to you. You don't want to hurt your mom, but you don't want her to get hurt, either. Why wouldn't I understand that?"

She smiled. "Because I'm still trying to figure it out, but just putting it all into words has helped a lot."

"Good," he said, and found that he meant it. He wanted her to figure things out. In fact, he was kind of curious now, too. "So, what can I tell you that might shed some light?"

"I know almost all of his political background, but what do

you know about Arlen's personal business? His personal life? I know some of the general parts—"

"You know about his family connections?"

"I know he was married to a local heiress and, from what I read in the papers I got from the library, I know her family played a large role, or seemed to, in his rise up the ladder here."

"That is definitely true."

"Since she passed away, which was almost twenty years ago, from what I read, he and his former in-laws have remained cordial, and the Covingtons have had some business dealings with Arlen, but—"

"They are careful to keep business business, and in that family, it's all business."

"What do you mean?"

"The Covingtons run the largest ranch in central Colorado, which, if you saw any of the spreads as you flew out here, you know is saying something. The resort owners here have a pretty good stranglehold on commerce in Cedar Springs, and if the resort isn't successful in bringing in the vacationers year-round, skiing in winter, golf and fishing in summer, then a large part of the town's commerce would shrivel up. Used to be that mining, ranching, and logging made up most of the commerce out here, but in Cedar Springs, it's ultimately the resort now that keeps the town afloat. So while the Covingtons have enormous pull, both politically and financially, they are careful in how they leave their footprint."

"Do they also rely on the resort being a success?"

"Not really, but neither do they want to do any harm to Cedar Springs."

"So, what does that have to do with their dealings with Arlen?"

"Well, Arlen was the one who reunited them with their lovely only daughter, who, story has it, ran off to the West Coast to pursue her dreams, much to the disapproval of her family."

"I read that she and Arlen met when she worked on his campaign in San Francisco, for councilman I think."

"Yes. He's from a suburb of San Francisco originally and still has a few business interests there I think. He had run for town council, that sort of thing, but he wasn't moving up the ladder maybe as fast as he wanted to. Then he meets Cynthia Covington, oldest daughter of a very old, very wealthy cattle and mining family. He was an okay businessman, but it's a big city and he didn't have the family name or backing. Blue-collar background with both his parents, which he plays up big during election time, especially in these parts, but wasn't helping him with the blue bloods and the like in California."

"So, his aspirations were bigger and he thought she might help him achieve his goals."

"That's the generally accepted view."

Lauren glanced at him. "Meaning? Was it her, personally, or just her bankbook, that was the lure?"

"Oh, she was beautiful enough to turn any man's head, but I think the bank balance certainly didn't hurt." Jake glanced over at her. "Not to stick my nose in, but are you concerned that Arlen might be after your mother's money?" He hadn't thought about that, as Arlen was one of the town's wealthier citizens, but then he remembered what Ruby Jean had inadvertently let slip, about Arlen still apparently having bigger political aspirations than remaining mayor for life of Cedar Springs. Which put another new wrinkle on things. He'd wondered if Arlen was interested in Lauren's connections . . . but maybe her mother had connections of her own. The kind that came with lots of zeroes attached.

"It's . . . crossed my mind."

"Well, if it eases your mind at all, Arlen isn't exactly hurting."

Which was true as far as it went. But it took a lot more than a fat personal account to mount a campaign.

"In a few of the more recent articles, it seemed to me that, perhaps, there has been a bit of a cooling off between him and his former in-laws. Will that affect his personal bottom line? I guess what I'm asking is, how much does he rely on the Covingtons in his personal business dealings?"

"I'm not sure what might be going on between him and the Covingtons," he said, which was absolutely true as he really didn't make it his business to keep up with any of that. That was Ruby Jean's territory. And anything she'd said to him would have gone in one ear and out the other, which was a long-ingrained habit whenever she started in on what she'd heard. "But I don't think it would really make that big a difference. If they'd had any real falling out, the whole town would have heard about it." He wouldn't have been able to avoid it.

Lauren seemed to ponder that bit of information, then said, "Do you think they—the Covingtons—like him personally, or—"

"I think, from what I know, that they will always hold him in special regard, because it was due to his connecting with their daughter, and eventually marrying her, that she came back to Cedar Springs for good, which is where they'd wanted her all along."

"Tight-knit family?"

"Most are out here. But they are particularly so. It's a very patriarchal family, with very old-fashioned views. The elder Covingtons are in their eighties, and their only remaining child, Charles, Cynthia's younger brother, pretty much oversees all their interests now."

"And how does he get along with Arlen?"

"Fine, as far as I know."

Lauren fell silent again. "Did his first wife resent having to come back home?"

"I was too young, really, to remember all of that when it was happening, but the story goes that she wasn't totally thrilled. When Arlen came back to meet her folks, they got to talking about his political aspirations, and I think they saw an opportunity there."

"Provide him with backing to run for mayor, and thereby keep him, and their daughter, in Cedar Springs," Lauren said.

"Pretty much."

"And she came around to that idea?"

"I don't really know. Like I said, I was barely a teenager at the time and we were dealing with a lot in our own family."

"I'm sorry."

"Nothing to be sorry about, just a fact of life. It's not town lore, if that's what you mean. I'm sure most of the older residents probably have some take on their relationship, as they'd have socialized with them, but my parents didn't, to my knowledge, and I know my grandfather didn't."

"Something specific, or just that their paths wouldn't have crossed?"

"Oh, everyone's paths cross out here, but it was more than that. Patrick, my grandfather, wasn't particularly fond of the way that the Covingtons lorded it over the area. He was excited when the resort developers came to town, thinking that would balance the political scales a little because the Covingtons had pretty much ruled the area's interests for a long time. Patrick saw it as a way to help keep the town from dying out, which was something even the Covingtons couldn't control, as more and more of the younger generations were leaving to find careers elsewhere."

"Did it?"

"Definitely, but you have to remember, those developers bought the initial property for the resort—"

"From the Covingtons."

"Exactly. So, at least at first, nothing really changed much. I only know this from listening to my grandfather gripe about it all the time."

"How long has the resort been here?"

"Almost as long as I've been alive. About thirty years."

"So it was up and running before Arlen came to town."

"Yes, why?"

"No reason, just trying to add in all the details I can. Does Arlen have any direct business dealings with the resort owners?"

"He's mostly into cattle ranching, here at least, which relates directly to his relationship with the Covingtons, and it's something he's maintained and grown even though they are no longer directly related. If he has any personal dealings with the resort, I don't know about it. As mayor, he's been very much a part of keeping the peace between the ranching community and the resort community. But that's all I know."

"Did the resort help your grandfather's business in the long run?"

"Oh, absolutely. He was very much for it, which didn't make him a favorite of the Covingtons or the other ranchers, but he thought it was what saved Cedar Springs and I'm sure he was right about that. It wasn't only the newer generations leaving and not staying to maintain their family holdings. Ranching, mining, all of it, isn't what it used to be in terms of its continued viability. Tourism, on the other hand, is something that is always viable if you have the right product to sell. It kept Cedar Springs from going the way of a lot of the other small mining and ranching towns you saw that we drove through on the way in from Holden."

"Yes, I remember. What else can you tell me about Arlen? I know he married again, about five years after his first wife died. He would have been, what, in his mid to late forties then, right? He married Cynthia Covington in his midthirties and she died a few years later."

"They were married about seven or eight years. Car accident. It was a real tragedy here. Her family was just beside themselves. And as the mayor's wife, it was . . . it was a tough time for everyone."

"Was she well liked?"

"Well respected was more like it. She was every bit the local heiress, our own Jackie O of sorts."

"Did you know her?"

"I remember her, but no, not really. I mean, we all knew each other to a certain degree, but I was definitely not from a family with that kind of pedigree. Even in a small town, there are social strata. We didn't run in the same circles, even as small as those circles might have been."

"But people looked up to her."

"Envied her, certainly. I don't really know much beyond that. I'm a guy, we don't pay attention."

She smiled. "And you were a young teenaged boy, so I'm sure you had a few other things on your mind."

"Exactly."

"They never had any children. Was that any kind of a 'thing' or was it just the way it was."

"As I recall, there was some talk of whether or not they'd start a family—everyone wants newlyweds to have babies, after all."

Lauren gave an exaggerated shudder. "Not every newly-wed."

Jake laughed. "Sorry, I wasn't thinking."

She laughed with him. "Go on."

"Anyway, I just remember there being talk, mostly, I think because of the money, her family, having an heir and all."

"Did her brother ever have kids?"

"No. Never married."

"Gay?"

Jake slanted her a dry look. "Not in that generation."

Lauren shot one right back at him. "But is he?"

He smiled. "I don't honestly know."

"So there is no direct heir, then, after him?"

"I guess there isn't. I don't know about Lars Covington's re-lations—he's the senior Covington—so there might be someone on the family tree somewhere."

"But not directly in the picture?"

"No, I don't think so."

"Would Arlen be in line for any of it?"

"I don't know the details of Lars's will, or what he'd be likely to do. Not a big one for talking—never was. But, I guess it's not outside the realm of possibility. It's not talked about, though, so if he is, it's not common knowledge I don't think."

"When Arlen remarried, did it anger the Covingtons?"

"Not that I know of. I don't think they're the type who'd expect him to mourn for the rest of this life. It was several years later that he began seeing Paula Slattery, and they were married a few years after that, so there was no scandal that I can recall."

"I dug up a story about their divorce that said their marriage was strained due to their inability to have children."

"She was a lot younger than he was, wanted kids. I don't know that Arlen did or didn't, but it was talked about in town circles. Gossip mostly. I didn't really pay attention, but it wasn't exactly a secret that the mayor's wife's clock was ticking."

"Did their inability to conceive bother Arlen?"

"Well, I can't imagine he was happy about it, at least in the sense that he's a man's man kind of guy, and in the west, well—"

"I get it. It's not macho to be infertile, even if it's the wife's problem."

"More or less," Jake said wryly.

"So, their marriage lasted about as long as his first one, until he was in his early fifties; she was almost forty. Was it just about not having a family?"

"So the gossip goes, yes. And before you say anything, there is no escaping some gossip here. But beyond that, they kept their personal life very personal. Paula was not like Cindy Covington, not remotely. She didn't really involve herself in town functions or organizations and pretty much stayed out on their ranch most of the time."

"Polar opposite from a Jackie O type."

"Very much so."

"How did the town react when they divorced?"

"No scandal. I don't think anyone was surprised. Arlen is definitely the sort to want something bright and shiny on his arm—" He glanced at Lauren. "Sorry, I didn't mean that the way it came out. I don't mean he escorted sweet young things, but he is a social creature and everyone thought he'd marry someone who was far more like Cindy."

"Was Paula connected?"

"Do you mean was she loaded?"

Lauren's smile was dry. "I meant did she have political or family connections that might have benefited Arlen? And yes, that would extend to whether or not she had personal wealth. I ask, because if she wasn't the social butterfly Arlen would have typically gone after, then I was just thinking maybe there was another reason."

"Maybe he just loved her."

"Is that what you think? You know him."

"Not well enough to know that kind of thing, but I think we're all prone to falling. Even—"

"—someone like the mayor? Meaning that you'd be more inclined to think he'd marry for . . . other things?"

"Again, this is where personal disposition comes into play, and I'll be up front and tell you my answer would be colored by my personal feelings of the man."

"So noted. And?"

"He might have been in love, but I don't know that he'd have married her if he didn't think there was something else in it for him. Sorry."

"Nothing to be sorry for. Do you think the same about his marrying my mother? And you can be frank; it's okay."

"He's gone it alone for a much longer time this go around, so I really don't know. And I'm being honest. A man gets to be in his senior years, and it's hard to say what might motivate him to pair up again."

"But putting that aside, it would be keeping with character for him to choose a mate for things other than his heart being in play?"

"I feel like I'm not really in a position to know that. But I know what you're getting at, and my gut answer would be yes." He looked over at her. "Again, I'm sorry. And, also again, I don't know at all that my opinion there means squat when it comes to your mother. I really don't."

"Well, to put your mind at ease, he may love her for love's sake—after all, they did run off and elope—but my mother is definitely connected, both politically and financially. So she wouldn't be outside the norm for him, in terms of choosing a mate. Other than the fact that she's more East Coast blue blood than western royalty. I imagine the two cultures are vastly different."

"I'd agree. Although the bottom line might be the same. I'll be honest with you and say I see more of what he'd see in her, given his attraction to Cindy, who might have come from ranching royalty but went to college on the West Coast and definitely had big city polish—"

"But do you see the reverse attraction?"

"I don't know your mother. Other than socially, and even there, it's not much more than a nodding acquaintance and that mostly because of Ruby Jean working for her husband."

"Well, I do . . . and there isn't anything in her history that would make falling for someone like Arlen—not insulting, just saying—seem reasonable. Given her past and her choices. I'm still stumped."

"Still think he has ulterior motives?"

"I'll just say I'm not convinced he doesn't."

"I hope I haven't colored your thinking too much—"

"I wanted your honest opinion and I thank you very much for giving it to me. You seem a pretty good judge of character and not someone who shies away from honesty or the truth. Beyond that, I can come to my own conclusions, and yours is just one opinion." She smiled. "It just happens to coincide with mine, so I find it particularly insightful."

"As long as you're keeping perspective."

"Right." She laughed, then she sighed. "I wish this weren't so complicated. And I wish my gut wasn't so intent on telling me something isn't right. My mother seems happy. Very happy, actually. But the bond between them is . . . well, not awkward exactly, but not how you'd think a newly married couple would be. Especially a 'we had to elope' couple."

"Maybe they were just going out of their way to be respectful of your discomfort with their marriage."

"Maybe. But it did come up today, and . . . I don't know. Maybe tonight will help a little with giving me better perspective with that."

"I hope so. One way or the other."

They pulled off the main road and started down the long gravel one that led to Arlen's ranch, which spread out across the flat acreage to the west of the drive. All along the right the ground surged up abruptly into sharp, jagged peaks. They climbed a little before dipping back down to circle around the side of the sprawling ranch house. The elevated part of the drive revealed acreage that extended down a high valley, almost as far as you could see. Not nearly in the realm of what the Covingtons' holdings were, or even several other large ranches in the nearby area. But it was substantial enough. And impressive enough.

Jake wondered if her impressions were changing at all, now that she was seeing what Arlen had backing him up. Jake would have said that he didn't see Arlen marrying for wealth or connections at this later stage of his life, but given what Ruby Jean had let slip, it all was questionable now. He didn't know what Arlen had in his sights and debated on mentioning that to Lauren, but opted to discuss it with his sister first. After all of this, he wasn't going to be the one spreading unfounded gossip.

"Thank you, again," Lauren said as they pulled in behind Arlen's pickup truck, which was one of several vehicles of varying sizes and uses parked in the larger paved lot. "For being willing to be honest with me."

He shut off the engine. "My pleasure." And despite all the turmoil roiling around, both inside her head . . . and very likely inside that ranch house, he realized that he absolutely meant it. Which was kind of shocking when he thought about it like that. But at the moment, he was far more concerned with being there for her in whatever capacity she might need him this evening, than whatever his personal discomfort might have been with the proceedings. "Come on. Might as well jump in."

"Might as well," she said, sounding very unenthusiastic.

He came around and opened her door and helped her hop down. He kept his hands on her waist. "Should we have a signal?"

"You mean a 'get me out of Dodge' kind of thing?"

He smiled. "Something like that."

"I'll let you know if I need rescuing."

"Somehow I can't see you ever *needing* rescuing—"

She laughed. "Says the man who's done more of it with me than anyone in recent memory."

"Well, you might not need it, but if for any reason you want it—"

"Just . . . be there for me. Steer me if I inadvertently go off in a direction that's not going to help my cause."

"Help you read the room? The once-executive assistant to a state senator needs my help with reading a room?"

She smiled back at him but he could see the uncertainty in her eyes. "It's a pretty intimate room. And I'm obviously a little too close to what's going on to perhaps see things as clearly as I should. So, it'll be nice to know I have an outside observer keeping my back."

"I don't know how outside I am . . ." He leaned in and brushed his lips over hers. "But I'll do my best to get us both out of there in one piece."

"Ulterior motives again?"

He slid his hand into hers. "Maybe."

She held on, then squeezed. "Probably."

They headed around to the gate that led to the back of the property, where the rich scent of smoke barbecue filled the evening air. "Is that going to be a problem?"

"No." She looked up at him as he held the gate and smiled. "It's probably going to be my salvation."

He stepped in behind her, and felt her tense as her mother

and Arlen approached. "I'm good with that," he murmured in her ear.

"Good," she whispered. "Here we go."

Yes, he thought, feeling his heart flutter again, as he watched her step forward to greet the pair. *Here I go, indeed.*

Chapter 12

"Lauren, sweetheart, I'm so glad you made it." Lauren's mother enveloped her in a quick, tight hug. "And I see you brought Jake with you; that's wonderful." She smoothly turned Lauren with her and extended her hand to Jake. "I'm so glad you could join us."

"The pleasure is mine," he said, taking her slender hand and briefly covering it with his own instead of shaking it.

Her mother beamed at Lauren. "And such nice manners, too."

Lauren couldn't help but smile. Her mother was as short as her daughter, but where Lauren had inherited her looks from her father's side of the family, where the women had dark hair and lush figures, her mother was diminutive in every way. And though there wasn't a fragile bone in her body, nor in any essence of the way she carried herself, men generally fell all over themselves in a rush to see to her every need. Her mother took that with good grace as well. Despite the fact that she needed rescuing even less often than her daughter did.

Arlen stepped up then. "Glad you both could make it out this way. Barbecue is coming along nicely. Know anything about using cured wood to smoke meat?" he asked, directing the question to Jake.

"A little."

Arlen chuckled. "More than I know, then. Come on over

here and look at this new smoker. I think I've got it going along okay, but it never hurts to get a second opinion."

Jake glanced at Lauren, who gave him a quick, almost imperceptible nod, then he smiled at the mayor. "I'm not sure what my opinion is worth, but I'm happy to oblige."

The two men turned toward the back of the house. "Well, gives me someone else to share the blame if we burn anything. Come on back."

Lauren watched them depart, thinking the easy conviviality would have gone a lot further toward soothing her concerns if Arlen's pasted politician smile and canned laugh hadn't been in full force. But he was making an effort, Lauren told herself, and she could, too. So she turned back to her mother with a sincere smile. "Thanks for inviting us both."

Her mother was studying her, but her smile was soft. "I'm glad you brought him." She tilted her head slightly. "Is he just a very nice-looking barrier, or of any real interest?"

"I just met him, Mom."

"Well, now, I know a little bit about short courtships." Her mother's smile deepened slightly, but Lauren noticed it didn't entirely make it up to her eyes. So there was still some concern on her mother's side, too.

She'd always been able to read her daughter, so Lauren shouldn't have been surprised, but she hoped that this evening could just be about relaxing and enjoying each other's company.

"Don't get any ideas," Lauren cautioned, keeping it light. They were finding their way back to how it used to be, and she wanted that trend to continue. Although, looking around at her mother's new life, the one she shared with Arlen, she wondered if things would ever really be the same.

"Would you like the tour of the place?"

"I'd love one." She followed her mother toward the side door, through a small, lovingly attended garden. "This is beautiful. Truly."

"Thank you." Her mother beamed. "The beginnings were

already here. Arlen had a professional design the basics that surround the house when he had it built several years ago, but I sort of claimed this little spot as my own. Gets a little of the morning sun and the evening sunset. I like it out here."

"It's lovely. Peaceful." She paused, then said, "I didn't know you—"

"Gardened?" her mother finished with a laugh. "I didn't. Never had the time. Despite being on the boards of two garden clubs in two different states back when I was married to your father. We all had gardeners then and some of us might have puttered in a little greenhouse or potting shed, but it was all rather silly, really, when you think of it. I didn't even have a hand in the cut flower arrangements in the house."

"So, what made you take it up, now?"

Charlene opened the door to the side entrance. "I might not have made the time before, but I did always have the interest. And now . . . I can finally indulge myself. There are a lot of things I'd have liked to indulge in, but always thought I never had the time for. I think back, now, about the choices I made and how I invested my time—"

"Do you have regrets? I always thought you thrived on the organizations and activities you devoted yourself to."

"I did, I did. And I had myself convinced that that was all the fulfillment I needed. When your father and I were married, that was probably more true than it was after he passed away. He always kept me afloat, I think."

Lauren laughed a little. "I think he'd swear it was the other way around if you asked him."

Her mother's smile was warm and filled with good memories. "We propped each other up. We also pushed and supported each other. It was the best kind of teamwork, I suppose. I did thrive. And . . . when he was gone, I suppose I just kept on doing what I knew how to do. It might not have been as fulfilling as it once was, but there was solace and comfort in the familiar." She shrugged. "And I guess I enjoyed being needed."

"I always needed you," Lauren said, squeezing her mother

around the shoulders. "But I know what you meant. I'm sorry I wasn't more aware of how lonely you must have been. You always seemed so busy, so . . . well, if not happy, at least not at first, at least at peace. You seemed . . . better when you were involved."

"Oh, I made sure I was always that." She squeezed Lauren's shoulder back and showed her the rest of the garden. "I guess it wasn't until I moved to Florida that I had to ask myself what I really wanted, what would really make me happy."

Lauren debated biting her tongue, she really didn't want to bring it up, but the opening was there, and given her mother was clearly aware of her continued misgivings, maybe it was best if she simply asked the questions that were nagging her. "I meant what I said, earlier today. I do love that you found happiness here, Mom," she said. "And I know it's still early for you and Arlen, but . . . does he make you feel like Dad did?" She raised a hand before her mother could respond. "I don't mean that the way it sounded. I know Dad was Dad and you're not looking for a replacement. What I meant was, you talked about teamwork, and feeling supported, and knowing you were the one he'd come to for that same support. Do you have that with Arlen? Or do you think you ever will?"

Her mother didn't answer right away, and Lauren noticed she'd turned her attention—and her eyes—away from her daughter, staring instead at the array of brightly colored flowers blooming by the garden swing. "I don't know that I need that same kind of teamwork," she said. "My life is different now; the demands are different." She turned to her daughter. "I'm focusing more on myself. I think I've earned that."

"You have. We should all take care of ourselves like that—"

Her mother raised an eyebrow. "Says the pot."

Lauren smiled, but her gut tightened. Now was not the time to talk to her mom about her recent job shift. Okay, job end. She hadn't exactly done the shifting part yet. "I've been doing a lot more thinking about that lately than ever before. Actually, it was your move to Florida that made me start to question what

I wanted for my big picture." Lauren moved toward the side door and her mother's innate hospitality had her moving to intercept and open the door to usher her daughter inside.

She stepped inside and was immediately enveloped in a very warm, homey kitchen room that was decorated in a country prairie style that was about as far away from her mother's elegant southern roots as Lauren could have imagined. But it was beautifully done and she felt immediately at ease, surrounded by the gleam of walnut, offset with the red, yellow, black, and white accents in the window treatments and tiling. "Wow, this is really eye catching." She caught her mother beaming. "You did this?"

"Don't sound so surprised," she said, taking Lauren's hand. "I have many hidden talents."

Lauren squeezed her mother's hand, then let go so she could stroll around the room, looking at the antique kitchen implements that decorated the opposing wall, interspersed with black and white photos of Cedar Springs, all taken back in the fifties or earlier. "This is really wonderful. Hard to believe you've only been here six months."

"Well, when I got here, Arlen had more or less had the place decorated in early hunting lodge."

Lauren laughed then tried to cover it with a polite cough. "That's . . . so not you."

Her mother smiled, and it was great to see that mischievous, assertive light come back into her eyes. "You're right about that. I've made a lot of adjustments to the more rugged, rural life out here in the mountains, but I drew the line at looking at eyes that could look back at me while I was eating. Other than Arlen's, of course."

Lauren kept her smile on her face, but turned her attention back to the décor. "Of course."

"Sweetheart—"

"Why don't you show me the rest of the place? How many rooms did you make over?"

"Just a couple of them," her mother said, leading Lauren

into the large dining room. "So far," she said, a twinkling smile on her face as she looked over her shoulder.

Where the kitchen had been all warm and homey, the dining room was far more formal, with a glossy maple table and high back chairs to seat ten, and a full china service displayed in a matching glass case on the far wall. "Now, this looks more like you," she said.

"It's all like me. Now, anyway. To be honest, this turned out to be my least favorite room. I thought it would be comforting, a reminder of—"

"This isn't our old—"

"No, dear, all that is still in storage from my move to Florida."

"What did you do with your place down there? I never asked."

"I still have it. In my own name." She smiled, but there was a bit of smug in it. "I'm not quite the foolish old woman you think I've become."

"Mom, I never said—"

"You didn't have to."

Lauren sighed a little. "I'm sorry. I wasn't trying to insult you. I was worried."

"You still are. Despite seeing how happy I am."

"Actually, I am surprised at how well you've made a home for yourself out here. I'd . . . well, I'd have honestly never placed you in this kind of setting, but you're—you're glowing."

Her mother beamed, and this time the smile easily reached her twinkling eyes. "You have a bit of that glow about you, too. Fortunately, we can blame it on the gorgeous mountain air."

Lauren couldn't duck fast enough to keep her mother from seeing the roses that bloomed lightly in her cheeks. "Yes, well . . . the mountain air is certainly . . . stimulating." She glanced over at her mother in time to see her do the ducking and turning. Hmm. She turned to face her mother. "I do know you're happy here—"

"I am, Lauren. I think . . . I don't know. I feel more truly re-

tired now. Life is a pleasure. I do what I want, explore new av-
enues about myself that, frankly, I never would have in
Florida."

"You seemed happy there, too—"

"Not like here."

"No," Lauren said, admitting what was easily observed.
"Not like this."

"I think I still didn't know how else to live, to organize my
time, my days, other than how I'd always done it. Florida was
different, a slightly slower pace, warmer, certainly, and a lot
less stressful than the life I led, both with your grandfather and
your father and beyond. I was doing what I wanted, but it was
more or less the things I'd always done, just in a different climate, with different motivations." She turned and looked out
the big picture window that filled most of the back wall of the
room. "Here . . . here nothing is the same. The old rules, my
old life, none of it applies. I had to find out who I really was."
She turned to Lauren. "What I really wanted. And what I want
is to be here."

Lauren nodded. She was absolutely certain her mother meant
every word. What bothered her was that she'd noted once
again that, at no time when discussing what made her happy,
had her mother included her husband. She talked in glowing
terms about the town, the mountains, her home, her new hobbies, interests. Other than in passing, she rarely seemed to mention Arlen at all.

And Lauren didn't think it was because her mother was trying to spare her admittedly touchy sensibilities by avoiding him
as a topic. It went beyond that. A person who was newly married, newly in love, newly . . . anything with someone couldn't
avoid talking about him if they tried. She'd certainly witnessed
it time and time again with her friends . . . and was experienc-
ing a bit of tongue-biting herself at the moment, thinking about
Jake out there with Arlen and not being able to pour out the
myriad confusing and conflicting feelings she was having over
him to the one person she'd always been able to talk to.

Which made her wonder if her mother was also biting her tongue about her own possible conflicted emotions. She'd enjoyed a closer than usual relationship with her mother, both before and, especially, after her father died. Growing up, her mother had been parent first, friend second. But, as adults, they'd become a pretty good team, too, continuing the open dialogue her parents had always encouraged, and deepening it into something mature and special. They'd been able to talk about anything, despite not always seeing eye-to-eye.

Which made what was happening now an even more fragile time. She needed her mother now more than ever, to talk about the major change she'd made in her life, the man who'd recently entered it . . . so many things. And wondered if her mother was feeling the same thing about her major changes . . . and the man she'd brought into her own life. She wondered if by being so openly stunned and disconcerted by her mother's abrupt life change, if she'd made her mother feel now, as time had moved on, as if she could hardly bring up any discontent she might be feeling, if only to avoid the "I told you so" conversation that would likely follow.

Lauren liked to think she was more sensitive than that, but here they'd found themselves, anyway, her hiding things from her mother, and her mother possibly doing the same.

Well, they both clearly didn't want it to be that way, and that was a start. But one of them had to start the conversational ball rolling, so, taking a steadying breath, she turned around with the intention of doing that very thing. And she'd start by revealing her own secrets. Then perhaps her mother would feel comfortable enough to reveal her own. "Mom—I need to tell—"

"Supper is about ready," Arlen called out, choosing that exact moment to stick his head in the kitchen door.

"We'll be right out," her mother called from where they still stood in the dining room. "I'm sorry. What were you about to say?" she asked, turning back to Lauren.

"I—nothing." Now was definitely not the time to embark

down that path anyway. She should have known better. "We should get outside. It smells delicious."

Thankfully, her mother didn't press and they both went back through the garden, around to the rear patio that was as sprawling as the ranch home itself. "You have a beautiful place here," she told Arlen, speaking honestly. She'd had the right mind-set at the start. Keep it relaxing and enjoyable. There'd be time to get answers later.

At the moment, there was delicious smelling barbecue to eat, a sexy flight school owner smiling at her . . . and the perfect opportunity to observe her mother with her new husband, and perhaps draw some additional conclusions on her own.

"Thank you," Arlen said in response to her compliment. "I had it designed by a fellow I know in Denver. He's a real whiz at building green, if you know what I mean."

"Yes, going green is a huge topic back at home, as well. I think that's great," she said, and meant it. Thankful she could be sincere.

"Well, he's an innovator, Dave is—Dave Brumfield's his name—knows all kinds of ways to keep from impacting the environment without making your house look like something from a science fiction movie." He chuckled, clearly expecting them all to laugh along, which they dutifully if not heartily did.

"You'll have to show me some of the innovations," Lauren said, thinking he had a way of making any conversation sound like a sales pitch, no matter if he was sincere or not. "When did you rebuild?" At his questioning look, she added, "I mean, when did you 'go green'?"

"Arlen's previous home burned down quite some time back," Charlene said, pausing in the middle of arranging the place settings on the large, rectangular glass table that dominated most of the lower part of the patio. "So, he took the opportunity—well, you tell them," she said.

"No, no, that's okay." He looked at Lauren and Jake and finished the story anyway. "It was a difficult time," he said, "but something good came out of it." He gestured to the home behind them.

Lauren glanced between the two, but there was no overt tension. Her mother was smiling as she went smoothly back to her role as hostess, leaving her husband to make the small talk. Lauren couldn't help but wonder if it wasn't a strategic retreat to something that came as second nature to her. She still hadn't seen any clear sign of "newly wedded bliss." Or even simple affection. It would almost be more believable that they'd been married for decades and had settled into their own routines, each comfortable in an orbit that didn't necessarily include the other.

"What happened?" Lauren asked, more as a means of continuing the conversation than anything, then realized how that might sound. "Sorry, that's none of my business. I just—it must have been horrible, losing your home." She risked a glance at Jake, but he was tending the ribs on the open grill, while Arlen was still stationed by the smoker.

"It was. A real tough time. Summertime, real dry, lightning strike. Spread all the way to my back acreage. Took out four of my best bulls along with a good quarter of my land, and my house."

"That's terrible," Lauren said, and meant it. She couldn't imagine losing everything like that. "Was anyone hurt?"

"Mercifully, no. And it was contained before it spread any farther through the valley." He turned and started moving the meat to the platters on the sideboard. "Took a while to go through all the legal processes, insurance and such, so I had time to think about what I wanted. I considered moving into town, but I've grown attached to living out here, seeing all this every day." He waved his long handled fork toward the mountains, but didn't really look at them. "So, I did some research on architects and Dave happened to be in town on vacation, and the rest just sort of sprang from that." He did look up then, looked at his house. "I'm real proud of what we accomplished here." He glanced at Lauren. "We talk about the environmental issues, but it's time more of us put ourselves into the picture intimately, if you know what I mean. It's been something of a personal movement of mine ever since."

Lauren smiled and nodded, even though now he sounded like he was stumping his cause on the campaign trail. Maybe he simply couldn't help it. Maybe he'd been mayor for so long, politico-speak was his normal conversational style. But she also couldn't help but think if he was so environmentally conscious, that his 'personal movement' would have been more readily reflected in the press she'd been poring over, both back in D.C., and, more intimately, the past day or two.

She glanced at her mother, to see if she could gauge her expression while listening to her husband pontificate, but she was still busily arranging everything just so. "It's a beautiful table, Mom," she said, awed, as usual by how her mother made it all look so effortless. "You really always amaze me with how you put things together." She laughed a little and looked at Jake. "I take after my father. We couldn't arrange plastic silverware on a picnic table if our lives depended on it."

"Oh, it's just force of habit," Charlene said. "You do anything long enough it becomes second nature." She primped the last napkin, then, looking satisfied and pleased despite brushing off the compliment, she spread her arms to them. "Fill your plates and come have a seat. I'll get the lemonade and the tea."

"Would anyone care for wine?" Arlen asked. "Beer, Jake?"

"I'm fine with lemonade," Jake said. "Haven't had any in a long time and it sounds good."

"Me, too," Lauren said.

"I can bring out a bottle of cabernet, if you—"

"Don't bother with it," Arlen told Charlene. "If you can't beat 'em, join 'em. I'll have some lemonade, too."

Conversation ceased as they all went about filling plates from the sideboards, giving Lauren more time to think. Other than Charlene's aborted attempt to talk about the house, neither of them included the other in their conversational efforts, nor did they comment on what the other was saying. When she'd commented on the lovely table, she'd half expected Arlen to give her props as well, saying something about her mother's wonderful hostessing capabilities, but he'd said nothing. Maybe he wasn't paying attention, or the sort who passed out compliments. Hard to say. The air between them wasn't strained. But it was hardly convivial or teamlike. Much less affectionate. She just didn't get it.

Fortunately, this time she had Jake with her, as a second set of eyes and ears. Maybe she really would just not ever get it and had to simply get past it. Or maybe Jake would confirm what every second spent around the two of them continued to reinforce inside her: which was that these two people may be happy in their life here, but they weren't exactly happy with each other. Much less in love.

"Hey," Jake said as he moved in next to her while she used the tongs to grab a roasted ear of corn.

"Hey, yourself," she said, feeling ridiculously breathless just by his very nearness. She bobbled the corn and Jake quickly moved to cover her hand with his own.

"Careful there."

"Got it," she said, delivering corn husk to plate. "Thanks."

"Anytime."

She glanced at him. He was still leaning in closely, so she could talk without being overheard. "I mean for all of it. You really didn't have to come here tonight. I can't imagine this is great fun for you."

"So far it's just been handling the rituals surrounding the manly art of barbecue." He leaned in front of her to snag his own ear of corn and used the motion to catch her gaze with his own. "How are you holding up? How was the tour?"

"Good."

He quirked a brow, but led her on toward the smoker as Arlen and Charlene made their way to the grill.

"That sounds . . . less than enthusiastic."

"No, not at all. We're good, or getting there. I'm way more encouraged than I was. She's truly happy here and it shows in what she's done with the house. I'm finding out all kinds of things about her I didn't know. I guess she didn't really, either."

"But?"

She glanced at him. "You're way too good at reading me, for knowing me such a short time."

"Maybe we're just in tune."

Maybe they were. She heard his words from earlier in the day echo through her mind. *Sometimes you just know.*

"We'll talk later," she said, feeling her mother and Arlen drawing closer. "Just . . . watch them together."

"What do you—"

"Are you all getting enough to eat?" her mother asked as she stepped in behind them. "Please, there's enough here for a week of leftovers. Jake, I hope you'll consider taking some home with you."

"Thank you, Mrs.—"

"Charlene," she said. "Please."

"Certainly. I appreciate your generosity in inviting me this evening, but please don't feel—"

"Please, otherwise I'll be having barbecue for a week. You'd be doing me a favor. Since Arlen got this smoker—"

"I thought you were enjoying it," he asked as he joined them.

"I am," she said, carefully shifting between Lauren and Jake so she could serve her plate.

"Here, let me," Jake said, quick to take up the tongs. "What can I get you?"

"I'd love some ribs," she said. "And I do like the smoker," she said to Arlen, "but you have to admit we've had just about everything you can smoke on it over the past few weeks." She smiled to smooth over any possible ruffled feathers, ever the perfect hostess.

Arlen chuckled, but looked a bit ruddier about the cheeks. Could have been the heat from the barbecue and smoker. "What can I say, when you do something, you should keep doing it until you get it right."

"Here you are," Jake said, taking care of serving Charlene.

"I think we've perfected it with this batch." He wiggled his eyebrows a little. "And, you know, winter will be here sooner rather than later, so you can always get retaliation with a Crock-pot."

Lauren and her mother both started laughing, leaving Arlen and Jake looking perplexed. "Long story," Lauren said, "but suffice it to say that Matthews women and electrical cookware . . . not a good match."

Jake gently nudged Lauren. "Good to know."

"The secret is out," she said, still smiling.

Arlen finished filling his plate at the smoker. "You already know what a great hostess Charlene is," he said, "but we do try and leave the cooking to others."

"Now, Arlen, you know I make a perfectly respectable dry martini."

Everyone chuckled and Charlene led them and their loaded plates to the table. Lauren relaxed a little. Finally, a little banter. It was about time. She tried to catch any further byplay—shared glances, anything—between the two, but Jake stepped in front of her to help pull her chair out, and they were both seated across from them by the time she'd unloaded her plate and taken her seat. "Thank you," she said, glancing up with a smile as Jake helped push her chair in.

"My pleasure." He took the seat next to her, so they both faced their hosts. "You do set a beautiful table, Mrs.— Charlene," he said, quickly correcting himself. "Are those flowers from your garden?"

"In fact, they are. As you probably know, Arlen was very involved in getting the botanical gardens started in Cedar Springs some years ago. So I had the very fortunate privilege of working with the head gardener there to get some clippings and some advice."

"A very nice perk," Lauren said.

"You know something about that, I suppose," Arlen said. His tone was entirely conversational as he started digging into the ribs on his plate. "Perks, I mean. Working for Senator Fordham must come with a few. He's pretty highly placed."

Lauren felt rather than saw Jake come to attention at the comment, which she found equally interesting. She'd have to ask him his thoughts on that, too, later. But while she'd have much preferred to eat her dinner and let her mind wander to the possible directions her evening might take once they departed the ranch house, she couldn't afford to let Arlen's conversational gambit go to waste.

"I would say the sacrifices are greater than the perks, but some of them aren't all that bad." She smiled. "Still the stuff you put up with makes it a little easier to take advantage of the perks you do receive without feeling too guilty about it. They're usually well earned. You probably feel the same, having been mayor for so many years."

"I do my best not to take advantage, but in a small town, we all rub each other's back, as it were." He settled into his meal but lifted his gaze to meet Lauren's. "How long have you been in D.C.? Your mother tells me you rose pretty quickly in the ranks. Impressive."

Lauren risked a glance at her mother, but she was busy skewering her corn cob with little red-and-black-checked glass chickens. She realized they matched the kitchen décor, and wondered again at the change in her mother. She'd never thought of her as particularly whimsical. At all, actually. Pragmatic, steady, determined, gracious, with an amazing eye for detail, her style had always been understated southern elegance. In a million years she'd have never expected ceramic chickens and antique baking implements used as room décor, no matter the room.

But Lauren loved her mother's new kitchen, loved the warmth, the ambience. And while her mother had always been nothing less than a warm and welcoming hostess, and made certain her home reflected those same sensibilities, that warmth had generally been established by the polish in the fine oak and heritage furnishings, the perfectly constructed and color-coordinated window treatments, all contrasted with the bright colors of the fresh flower arrangements that always filled their home. Whimsical, her childhood home was not.

And yet, her mother's exquisite eye hadn't failed her in her most recent stint as home designer. So the whimsy was all hers. And Lauren found she really wanted to get to know the woman who had chosen a checkerboard backsplash and ceramic chicken and rooster salt and pepper shakers. She thought she knew her mother better than anyone. But now she wondered if her own life upheaval had skewed her perceptions of . . . well, everything in her life.

"Lauren?"

She jerked her gaze away from the little cob skewers she'd been fiddling with. "I'm sorry, I lost track there for a moment."

"Arlen was just commenting on your impressive rise through the ranks back home," Jake said, resting his palm on her knee beneath the table and giving her a reassuring squeeze.

Lauren fully trusted he wouldn't say anything about her recent exodus from the ranks, and was struck again by how well they'd connected in such a short time. Reassuring, indeed. "Well, I don't know how impressive it is," she said. "It's just nice to be rewarded for hard work. And the work is a lot easier when you believe in what you're doing."

"Todd is very lucky to have someone like you at his side," her mother said, "and it's good to see he knows it."

"How was it you came to work for him?" Arlen asked.

"I had just taken my bar exam and, growing up as I did, have always been interested in both the law and politics. Todd was running for county commissioner then, and I was on a committee offering him some volunteer legal advice on a few items of local interest that he might want to address in his campaign." She lifted a shoulder in a half shrug. "Things just moved forward from there." She took a bite of her ribs, really wanting to change the subject to . . . anything else. "This is really delicious."

"It really is," Jake said, picking up her cue. "Now I'm going to have to think about getting a smoker. My grill is about worn out."

"Don't you have a catalog from the company?" her mother asked Arlen.

Arlen responded that he did, and the conversation moved mercifully off in the direction of men and their toys. Jake and Arlen were in a discussion of gas versus charcoal grills, when Lauren shifted her chair back. Jake started to do the same, but she put her hand on his shoulder and squeezed. "No need," she said. "I just need to find the powder room."

He covered her hand with his own, then laughed when he got barbecue sauce on her fingers. "Sorry, let me—"

"I'll take care of that, too," she said, hoping he was getting what she wanted from him, which was to keep her mother and Arlen occupied for a few minutes. Or longer. "I won't be long."

He glanced up at her and she met his gaze for a moment, then smiled at their hosts and excused herself.

"It's just down the hall, dear, to the left." Her mother started to move her chair back, but Lauren stopped her.

"I'll find it. Please, enjoy your food. Besides, they may need a referee," she added with a laugh. As if they were all just one big happy, jovial family. Which, despite every effort being made here, they were not.

Lauren let herself into the house and quickly rinsed her fingers off in the kitchen sink before heading down the hall. Only she wasn't looking for the bathroom, she was looking for . . . "Bingo," she breathed, as she cracked a door open and saw a number of antlered heads lining the walls. She glanced over her shoulder, but could still see everyone gathered on the patio through the big bay window in the breakfast nook.

She pushed the door open just enough to slip into Arlen's office. And immediately found herself agreeing with her mother. All those hollow stares were more than a bit unnerving. She couldn't even name the species of half the things lining the walls of his very heavily masculine study. With a little shudder, she tried to avoid a direct look into the eyes of any of them and did a slow circumference of the room. It was a fairly decent-size home office, with three of the walls lined with floor-to-ceiling bookcases, all filled with both books, and interspersed with framed photos, the occasional award, and a few small pieces of art. The fourth wall was dominated by a large fireplace and a very, very large moose head mounted over it. "Sorry, Bullwinkle," she said as she side-stepped around the extensive antlers, despite their being well over her head. She hadn't thought, from the outside, that the ranch style home would have supported cathedral ceilings, but it was a must in a room like this, housing the type of things it did.

She stepped over to the first bookcase, interested to see what kind of books he collected, and was drawn instead to a few of the framed photos tucked here and there on each shelf. More of them dotted the wall by the mantle and the door. She didn't recognize the people in the photos, but enough of them were known to her to realize that they were all either political figures or well-positioned businessmen. Which, she knew, were often the big pockets needed to build a successful campaign war chest. She couldn't say for sure, but given the subtle and not-so-subtle changes in Arlen's general appearance and the suits he wore, it appeared the time frame of these photos spread over several decades, at least.

She glanced at the door again, then moved behind his desk. She had no business, none whatsoever, even thinking about snooping through his personal things. But . . . something just wasn't right. Her mother and Arlen's continued outward appearance of being more associates than spouses being just one of the more overt signals. But despite the smiles and surface ease, there was an unmistakable undercurrent here that Lauren knew had to be attributed to more than her sudden arrival in their lives. She just needed . . . something, some concrete little something that she could put her finger on. It didn't necessarily even have to be anything nefarious or even bad, just . . . something. Something that would explain why every time she looked at Arlen Thompson, she felt her stomach knot.

Squashing any guilt she might have had by telling herself she was doing this to protect her mother, she tugged gently at first one desk drawer, then another. Locked. All of them. Which . . . wasn't that kind of odd in the very rural home office of a small town mayor? What did he have to lock up? Wasn't the only other person here her mother? Maybe they had cleaning staff, she told herself, trying to play devil's advocate, striving to really be open minded. Maybe he was just a private person.

She tugged at the long center drawer and was surprised when it slid open. But there was nothing in there but the typical office detritus of pens, pencils, paper clips, and the like. The top of his desk was completely clean of all items save the leather blotter in the center. Not so much as a Rolodex or daytimer, or even an old-fashioned blotter. She slid the drawer shut and turned around to look at the shelves behind her. More framed photos of Arlen and the parade of politicos. She tilted her head to read some of the titles of the leather-bound and hard-cover books.

"You have an interest in political history?"

Lauren started badly, instinctively pressing her hand to her suddenly thumping heart. But she quickly regrouped and was smiling when she turned to face Arlen, who was standing in the open doorway.

"Sorry, you startled me. And I didn't mean to intrude. I just . . . I saw the shelves through the open door and I was curious. So many books. Quite a collection."

"Yes, it's both my vocation and my hobby." He stepped into the room and it took considerably more will than it should have for Lauren to remain standing where she was. She attributed it to her own guilty conscience more than any overtly threatening feel on his part, but the end result was the same. She wanted to throw up.

She forced a smile. "An impressive collection of photos as well. Seems like you're the one with the connections here."

"I've made my share over the years." He walked toward the desk, but stopped short of coming around to join her on the other side. For which she was eternally grateful. It was silly to still feel so . . . spooked, for the lack of a better word. She hadn't broken into anything or seen anything she shouldn't have, so despite being here uninvited, she really wasn't doing anything wrong. Besides, it was her mother's house, too.

She wished any of those rationalizations would help to slow her still thrumming heartbeat, but they didn't.

"Did you ever have the desire to run for office?"

"No," she said, taking the opportunity to return her gaze to the books and photos . . . and slowly ease herself along the wall of shelves and farther away from him. And his desk. "I like being behind the scenes, helping to put things in motion. Being in front never really called to me."

"A shame."

"Why do you say that?"

"Well, it's not like in my generation, when women were expected to be standing behind the man, in the supporting role. These days you all step right to the front. You're smart, educated, assertive . . . just seems like your party would love to have someone like you running on their ticket."

Lauren had no idea where he was going with this, or what might be prompting it. She turned to face him. "It takes a lot of those same people to help run the offices of our elected officials. I'm more suited to that challenge."

Arlen lifted a shoulder as if to say he didn't really understand how anyone could not want the limelight role, but said nothing more.

"You seem to be pretty involved in politics beyond the local scope here," she said, pointing to even more photos, these obviously more recent, hanging on the wall next to the fireplace. "Did you ever have aspirations beyond mayor of Cedar Springs?" She lifted a hand. "I meant no offense, just—"

"No, no, I understood the question. I hope you didn't think I was insulting your chosen profession, either. I just wondered why you didn't reach further, is all. What with all your family connections, you really have the path there for you."

"Maybe, but just because the path is there, doesn't mean you have to take it." She looked back at the photos. "Do you wish you had? Taken a different path?"

"This town might not be the place I was born, but in every other way it's my town. I take great pride in it."

Lauren turned, still smiling. "As well you should. It's a great little town. But did you ever think about stepping beyond the smaller, more intimate stage here, to a larger arena, where you could take your enthusiasm and direct it toward broader goals?"

"Life has a way of making its own plans while you are naïvely, perhaps, making your own."

Again, she noted the dodge, but it prompted about a dozen other questions. And she wanted to ask him about her mother and why he'd been attracted to her. With all the talk of political aspirations and goals, maybe she'd get a better peek at what had instigated their initial attraction to one another.

But just then Jake stuck his head in the door. "Charlene is getting ready to serve something very chocolate that looks pretty damn amazing. I thought you might like to join us while there's still a chance of there being anything left."

Lauren smiled at him and caught his gaze when she moved between him and Arlen, when only she could see his face. He mouthed the words, "Sorry," then stepped back so they could exit the room.

"No need," she whispered as she moved past him. She wasn't sure if he was apologizing for the intrusion or taking so long to come to her rescue. She was warmed by either thought. And exhausted by all the mental gymnastics she'd been vaulting around all afternoon and evening. What she really wanted was to have a few bites of very decadent dessert . . . then make up any excuse she could come up with so she and Jake could leave. And have, perhaps, a few delectable moments themselves.

Arlen paused before exiting the room, doing a quick visual cataloging of the room. His gaze snagged on the almost closed top drawer of his desk. He stepped out and closed the door. The door that was always closed, whether he was in the room or out. Which would have made it pretty damn hard for Lauren to see the shelves of books she claimed enticed her into his personal space.

He walked down the short hall, and back toward the patio,

watching through the bay window as Charlene laughed at something Jake said.

Lauren moved beside her and the two served dessert with the deftness of longtime partners. They were close, those two, with the kind of bond he might not fully understand personally, but could certainly recognize. And that was despite the estrangement.

He'd have to do something about that. And, well . . . he'd given Lauren every opportunity to tell him, and her mother, that she was no longer working for the senator from Virginia.

What to do . . . what to do . . . And, most importantly, how to do it.

Chapter 13

Jake closed the door after climbing into his side of the Jeep.
"Everything seemed to go pretty well, you think?"

Lauren settled into her side of the front seat and reached for
her seat belt. "Yes, I think we all behaved like adults and played
well together."

"But?"

She flashed him a quick smile, which he returned as he backed
out of his parking space. They both waved to Charlene and
Arlen, who were standing beneath the extended awning off the
side of the garage. Side by side, and yet, not overtly together.
He hadn't seen Arlen so much as accidentally brush against his
wife all evening.

"But, I'm still not getting the greatest vibes from Arlen," she
said, still smiling as they waved. "Or my mother and Arlen, together."

They finally turned the Jeep around and headed out to the
main road back into town.

"What was your perception?" Lauren asked. "And be honest. I'm fully aware this unease I feel could just be a selfish reaction to losing my mom at the same time I've decided to leap
from pan to fire in my professional life."

"You haven't lost your mom. Anyone with eyes in their head
can see how close the two of you are. She might be geographi-

cally farther away from you, and you might have good reason to be concerned, but your bond is clearly there and very strong."

He caught Lauren blinking a few times, quickly, as she looked out the side window.

"Lauren, I didn't mean to—"

"No, no, don't apologize. You have no idea how reassuring it is to hear that from someone with no agenda in the matter." She looked at him then, eyes a little glassy, but chin set. "Both about our obvious closeness, and what you said about having reason to be concerned. Did they not seem very . . . newly wedded to you? I mean, yes, they might have been 'sparing' me, but there's only so much a couple that's supposedly in love with one another can hide or stifle."

"Maybe it's a generational thing," Jake offered. He had definitely noticed the lack of both physical and spoken affection in the partnership between the mayor and his new wife. But there was also no doubt in his mind that Charlene was quite happy and content in her life there. And Arlen . . . well, he was just the same as he'd ever been, but he certainly hadn't seemed unhappy or distressed. Jake had caught him watching Lauren pretty closely a few times, however. "Maybe they're just not big into outward displays of affection."

"My mom wasn't like that with my dad. Or even her own father. She's southern, she's . . . naturally affectionate and generous."

"She seemed pretty happy, though," Jake offered. "I don't think that was a put on, she really did seem—"

"Content," Lauren finished. "I know, and she is. It's so funny, but for as close as we are, and as much as I feel I know my own mother, she really surprised me today."

"In what way?"

"Her garden, the way she decorated the interior of the house. It was—she was—different from the woman who raised me, who I thought I knew." She looked at Jake. "But you're very right, she's definitely content. She's found this whole new self, this side of her she'd never really let herself get to know. And I honestly think she's reveling in it and the continued discovery process."

"Then maybe whatever the deal is between her and Arlen is worth the price of getting everything else she wants in life."

"That's just it, she doesn't need Arlen to have those things."

"Except it was through marrying him that she discovered them in the first place. Would you consider her to be traditional and old-fashioned enough to honor the marriage, regardless of what she's discovering in her new partnership after the fact? It's not so hard to believe that she's chosen to look at the bright side, even if she's regretting some part of the impulsiveness now. Or perhaps her need for companionship, or the type of companionship, is different now, at this point in her life."

Lauren didn't respond right away, but seemed to be thinking over his comments.

"For what it's worth, I do think there's a lack of . . . connection, or something with them. They seem very at ease around each other, and in some ways, like an older married couple who have just settled into their respective routines and no longer bother to key into one another."

"I thought the exact same thing. Except they've only been together for six months."

"I know. Which is why it was noticeable. But, perhaps, they've both come to realize that even if their rush to the altar might have been a little hasty, that there is value in the companionship and have settled for that. Neither of them seemed tense, or stressed, they were both quite relaxed. Even if not appearing particularly couple-like."

"I know," Lauren sighed. "And you're exactly right. I thought much the same thing."

"And yet, it's just not feeling right to you." He said it as more statement than fact.

"No, it's not. Something about Arlen . . ." She let the sentence drift, but Jake noticed the way she rubbed at her arms. "I guess I'm just going to have to get over it. I haven't found a single thing to prove there is any real reason my mom shouldn't stay with him. She's a grown woman, and as we've said, clearly happy with the predominant part of her life. And, apparently, okay with her partner. I wondered if maybe she was feeling she had to stay with him because of all the fuss over her elopement."

"Would she do that? Just to save face?"

"See, that's just it, no, the woman I know wouldn't. So, I guess I spent the evening trying to figure out why she is sticking. Your explanation is as good a guess as any. But I don't see any honest affection or love there."

"You could talk to your mom about it, just to clear the air, make sure she's really happy and okay with her current circumstances. Make sure she understands that her happiness is all you care about. It is a small town, and perhaps she's sensitive to that, too."

"Meaning the gossip that would ensue if she were to want a divorce so suddenly after marrying him."

"Especially if she'd want to stay on in Cedar Springs afterward."

Lauren nodded. "Meaning it might be the easier path to just go with the flow and keep things as they are. Especially if Arlen is open to the same arrangement, which from everything I could tell, seems plausible."

"You should talk it over with your mom," Jake said, reaching over to put his hand over hers. "Your heart is in the right place with this, Lauren. I'm sure she knows that. And . . ."

She looked over at him. "And?"

"Well, you are going to tell her about the change in your employment status at some point, right?"

Lauren sighed. "Definitely. I just haven't figured out when. Or how. All this has turned out to be complicated, which—my fault, I know. But that doesn't make it any easier to untangle."

"I just think it would be better coming from you than her finding out another way. We may be a small town stuck out in the middle of nowhere, but Denver is just a few hours east and we do get national news here."

"I'm sure my leaving the senator's staff isn't going to be national news. If there'd been some kind of scandal, maybe, but that wasn't the case. I'd be surprised if it gets any mention at all beyond local comment." She lifted her hand to stem his response. "But I do want her to know about it from me, so your point is well taken. We talked about getting together for a late lunch tomorrow, so I suppose that will be my chance."

Jake squeezed her hand, then turned it over so he could lace his fingers between them. "So I guess any chance I had at talking you into a quick trip to Vegas—" Her look of alarm was so unexpected, he frowned, then realized what she'd assumed. He laughed. "No, no, I wasn't going to encourage you to follow in your mother's footsteps." He chuckled, even as she continued to stare at him. "I'm sorry, I am. I wasn't even thinking about that." He held on to her hand when she went to tug it free.

"So . . . Vegas?" she asked, still clearly confused. And wary.

His laughter faded. "You're really still worried, aren't you?"

"No. Yes. I don't know. Maybe it's just I've been carrying around the concerns for so long it will take a while to shake them. Especially given I didn't come here to discover them all happy and cozy in their little love nest." He felt a little shudder go through her.

"A blessing in disguise, perhaps," he said, dryly.

She nodded, then forced a smile of her own. "I should start counting those." She looked at him. "So, what's this about Vegas?"

Now it was his turn to sigh. "With everything going on, and maybe being a tad bit distracted by you, I forgot to tell you my schedule has changed for the next few days." He took heart in the fact that she looked instantly disappointed. "I have to fly to Vegas tomorrow and bring back the group of guys who are going to invest in *Betty Sue* so I can get her race ready for next month." He smiled and winked. "I thought maybe I could get you out of Dodge for the day and convince you to go with me."

She smiled then. "You have no idea how tempting an offer that is. Seriously, tempting. In fact, I'm probably an idiot for not taking the out." She turned his hand over and covered it with her other hand. "But I think I should stay here, work things through with my mom." She glanced from their joined hands, to him. "But I'd have otherwise loved to spend the time with you, getting the chance to fly with you."

"Speaking of which, because of having the guys in town, I won't be able to keep our date for Sunday, but if you're not in a big rush to leave Cedar Springs, then I'm hoping I can convince you to stick around so I can keep that date next week sometime."

Her grin was quick. It made her eyes light up. He caught himself thinking that he could easily see going to great lengths to make that happen as often as possible.

"I think I could be persuaded to stick around for that," she said.

"Good." He tugged her hand closer and kissed the back of it, before sliding his hand free so he could steer them up the winding lane toward the flight school. The dark shadows of the hangars were illuminated against the night sky by the moon making its ascent overhead.

He pulled around toward the gravel lot, but slowed to a rolling stop before actually parking the Jeep. He shifted his weight and turned more toward her. "It's getting pretty late. Why don't we grab your bike and let me take you back down into town?"

"We could do that. I can't say I'm all that excited about a night bike ride down a still unfamiliar path."

He reached over and pushed back a few silky strands of hair that had escaped her ponytail in the evening breeze. Then found his fingertips unwilling to leave the soft, smooth feel of her cheek. He drew them down along her jawline and felt her tremble. "What would excite you?"

She trembled again as he continued his exploration and traced his fingers over her lips, down to her chin, then back up to her bottom lip, which he pressed down on, slightly, until they parted. "I—" She didn't finish, but instead let out a little gasp as he cupped her cheek and slid his thumb a little farther into her mouth.

She bit down gently on it before pulling it in deeper.

Now it was his turn to tremble a little.

"Lauren," he said, surprised at how gruff and raspy his voice was.

"Jake," she said, holding his gaze so directly with her own it was impossible not to see the need there, the want.

"Stay." It was all he could manage with his heart in his throat, and the rest of his body on fire. "Please."

She bit down gently on the pad of his thumb, then covered his hand with her own, withdrawing his thumb, but keeping his palm against her cheek. "I told you I wasn't leaving, at least until—"

He searched her eyes intently, and went for broke. "Tonight." He didn't know how much time they had, but he sure as hell was going to grab every second of it he could and hold on tight. And damn if he'd apologize for it.

Her eyes flared, and her fingers tightened reflexively against the back of his hand. "Here?"

He nodded. "I want what I want, Lauren. And I think I've made it clear what I want is you. If it's a no tonight, I'll wait until it's a yes, but you should know, I'm going to push. You've got some big life decisions to make . . . and I'm going to do what I can to make sure I'm part of them."

Her eyes were dark and the intensity between them was palpable. So it only served to jack him up even higher when she smiled, brightly, boldly, in the midst of all the uncertainty swirling between them.

"Pushing is good." She leaned forward, pulling him toward her. "Makes it easier for me to say yes."

His body leaped at her response . . . and so did his heart. It was the damndest thing. "Are you saying yes?"

She nodded. "To tonight."

He threw the truck into park and an instant later was pulling her across the seat, into a half sprawl across his lap. He cupped her face with both palms and took her mouth like a dying man might take his last sip of water. To his immediate and utter gratification, she kissed him back like she was starving, too.

Things quickly spiraled. The windows fogged over as their breaths grew shorter, more labored. He was tugging at the buttons on her camp shirt that she'd done up as the night had turned cool and she was pushing his shirt open, when some shred of rationality wound its way into their heated frenzy. "My place is . . . top of the hill."

She was exploring the side of his neck with her tongue . . . and her teeth, and he thought she might well have the rest of her life to get tired of that little combination.

"Top of hill sounds better than front of Jeep."

He laughed, and his body surged even more achingly tightly against the fly of his jeans. "Top of hill it is."

She sighed wistfully and started to slide back out of his lap, but he clamped one arm around her and used the other to shift the truck into drive. "I could do this blindfolded," he said. "Stay with me."

She kissed the skin exposed at the vee opening of the front of his button-up shirt. Just the feel of her warm lips made him grow hard to the point of pain. A condition he was quickly realizing was going to be a continual issue every time he was around her. He was willing to deal with it. "It drove me crazy, trying to keep my hands off of you today," he said.

"Why did you?"

"I thought it might be nice to make a good first impression with your mom."

She laughed against his throat. "True. Although I think she wouldn't put up much of a fuss if we were together."

"No?"

Lauren smiled and kissed his chin, following it with a little nip on his jaw. "No."

Jake swerved around the last curve and swung into the driveway. "Good to know," he said, leaning down to kiss her again. "Very good."

"Your house?" she asked, a bit breathless as he continued kissing her. She slid her glasses off and dumped them blindly on the dashboard.

"Mine. Looks down on the school and whole valley below."

"Can't wait to see it in the daylight. Did you grow up here?"

"No, we lived on the other side of town, closer to where your mom and Arlen live. And my grandfather lived just off Main, right in the center of town. I inherited his place—Ruby Jean and I did—but I stayed out here more often than not. So I finally built this. It was completed about three years ago. The land is part of school property."

"*You* built?"

"Mmm hmm," he said, kissing her temple, then her forehead, working his way down to the tip of her nose. "Took four years and a lot of blood, sweat, and swearing. And a little bit of help. Maybe more than a little in some cases." He smiled against her mouth. "Would you like to see it up close and personal?"

She smiled back. "I thought you'd never ask."

He popped open his door, and rather than let her wiggle back off his lap, simply pulled her out with him and swung her up into his arms.

"Jake!"

"What?"

"I'm—you don't have to carry me."

He grinned down at her. "I know, that's what makes it fun."

He climbed the steps up to the deck that wrapped around three quarters of the house, all of which hung off the side of the mountain.

"What I can see of it, in the moonlight, looks gorgeous," she said. "I love the log cabin look, but wow, that front window, it soars up at least—"

"Two and a half stories. Come on." He turned so he could unlock and open the front door, still carrying her.

She craned to look down. "Where is Hank?"

"Oh, he likes it down at the school. The hangar is home to him. He can wander up here whenever he wants, there's a back trail that is a shortcut up the hill, but mostly he likes sprawling out down there."

He let her legs slowly slide out of his arms, until she was

standing hip to hip, inside the circle of his arms. "I know I'm pushing you—this—a little, but—"

"I don't get pushed anywhere I don't want to go."

He smiled and grabbed another quick kiss. Her quick smile, her confidence, her vulnerability . . . it didn't just grab at him, it clutched him. Hard. Why wasn't he running, looking for an out, or at least a safety net? Instead he was scrambling to find a way to get her to leap with him. "I could give you the tour now, or—"

"In the morning," she finished for him, pulling him into a deeper kiss. "When do you have to fly out?"

"Fly out?" he said, his head spinning as she took control of the kiss, capturing first his mouth, then his tongue, all the while working her fingers up the back of his neck and into his hair. She had the rest of her life to cut that out, too.

"Vegas?"

"Right," he mumbled against her lips. "Vegas . . ." He back-walked her to the nearest wall and pinned her against it. He loved the feel of her lush, tight curves pressing into his body. Made him crazy. The feel of her, the scent of her. "In the morning." He took her mouth again. And again. He hiked her up, wrapping her thighs around his waist, then slid the band from her ponytail and finally, mercifully did something he'd itched to do all night, and drove his fingers into her hair. "We have hours."

"Hours," she gasped as he moved his mouth along the side of her neck. Her nails were digging into his shoulders. The little sounds she made drove him wild. She moved against him when he bit her chin.

"All night." He groaned and pushed his hips into hers, making her gasp and buck up against him. All he wanted to do was strip them both naked, or as naked they needed to be so he could drive every aching inch of him into every welcoming inch of her. "Lauren—"

"Jake," she said, her voice raspy, husky as she broke their kiss and began kissing the side of his neck, raking her fingers up the back of his neck and into his hair as she arched her back away from the wall.

He kept her shoulders pinned with his weight but slid his hands down to palm her hips, pulling her up and onto him, so he could move against her, thrusting, pushing. She was groaning now, grinding right back on him. And those guttural, grunting noises accompanying her little moans were his. "You—I want . . ." he started, but couldn't finish because she was robbing him of his breath and every last scrap of control. Not that he minded in the least.

"Take me to bed, Jake," she managed. "Or right here. But, for the love of God—"

He pushed her shirt and tank top up and she slid her arms up over her head, helping him get them both off of her. He kept her arms pinned above her head, pushing her spine back up against wall again as he slid his hands down her arms. He shoved her up higher as his fingers slid down her spine, making fast work of the hooks there, his mouth already on the front of the pale pink silk and the hard bud of her nipples.

Her breathing was coming in pants . . . and so were his. Her fingers were in his hair again, nails raking his scalp, her thighs wrapped around his ribs as he slid the straps and helped himself to the warm, scented skin of her breasts. Full, ripe, they filled his palms and his mouth.

She was writhing in earnest now, wild as he teased one nipple with his fingertip while tasting the other with his tongue.

"This—you—" All she could manage was a hoarse whisper.

"Yes," he said, his heart pounding. "This—us."

He swung her away from the wall, catching her to him when she gasped in surprise at the sudden move. His face was buried in her breasts, and he let her slowly slide down until she settled around his hips . . . and his mouth could once again find hers. "Us."

"Yes," she panted. "Yes." Then took his mouth, took him into her mouth, joining them in the only way they could truly mate.

Something he intended to correct. Immediately.

"Hold on to me," he said, wrapping her more tightly as he stumbled them both down the hall toward the master suite that was, essentially, the entire back half of the house. Built, literally, halfway into the side of the mountain, the only source of exterior light were a series of reinforced sky lights that formed almost all of the ceiling. It was a bitch keeping the snow from piling too deep on them in the winter . . . but the payoff was sleeping under the most brilliant carpet of stars in the universe.

Somehow, tonight, he didn't think he'd be seeing anything but the equally brilliant glitter of desire in Lauren's eyes. And he was perfectly content with that.

He lowered them both to the bed, pushing her back until he could pin the full length of his body over hers. Her legs still wrapped around his waist, and he lifted her hips up as he pushed hard between them.

"Too many clothes," she managed.

"Way," he grunted.

She unbuttoned the rest of his shirt; he unzipped her pants. He slid down her body, pushing her farther onto the wide sea of his bed so he could feast once again on the lush fullness of her breasts. Her hips moved sharply beneath him as he suckled her nipples, teasing the turgid tips with his tongue.

"Jake, please . . ."

"Please, what?" he asked. He reluctantly left her nipples, damp and tight, and oh so incredibly perfect . . . and began a slow, winding trail of kisses down to her navel.

"Just . . . please," she said, a thread of humor in her breathless voice. "Me," she added, a definite smile in her tone now, her hips moving restlessly now as he teased his tongue along the open zipper of her pants.

"Your wish," he said, then slid her pants down her hips with his hands . . . and her panties down with his teeth. "My command."

"If I'd only known it was so simple . . . oh!"

He slipped his tongue over her, knowing from her heady scent she was ready for him. Which was going to come in really handy since he wasn't sure how long he was going to be able to sustain the playing part. Any other time, he'd want to prolong this moment, these small intimacies, for as long as he could, learning her body, imprinting her scent and taste onto his very psyche, until he'd know her blindfolded in a crowd of thousands. But this time was different. His body was like a coiled spring, even pressing against the mattress was shooting him to the edge. Certainly sliding his tongue into her was going to—

"Oh! Jake..." That last word had come out on a low growl; primal, it vibrated against something so deep inside him he hadn't known it existed.

She began to move against his mouth and he couldn't keep from pumping his hips into the bed, the need to take her, claim her, to join himself with her in the most basic way a man could with a woman—his woman...he couldn't begin to describe the power of it. He'd never felt the need to possess...or the feeling of being possessed. It should have terrified him, and maybe the magnitude of the emotions rocking through him, so foreign, so fresh, did, just a little. But the anticipation of finding out what happened next, and where giving in to the needs and wants that were now driving him would take him—take them—was far more intoxicating.

She started to tremble, and her moan took on a deep, almost keening sound. Her fingers were wrapped in his hair, her hips twisting as he took her, literally, screaming, over the edge.

And that was where his control ended. He should probably temper the ferocity of it all, but when she reached for him, pulling him up and over and into her body, any rational thought fled. Replaced by the pure, primal need to mate.

"Lauren—we need to—"

She took his face, so close to hers now, with her palms, so their gazes met, and locked. "It's okay. I'm—we're okay."

He trusted her. He'd have never done that before, no matter

what his partner said—not the first time, anyway. He was a cautious man. But he was there, and she was everything. Holding him so tightly, so perfectly . . . so naturally.

"We're more than okay," he said, then, keeping her gaze, he started to move inside of her.

There was nothing in the heavens or on earth that could match the wondrous sparkle of desire, want, and need that lit her eyes. She never left him, not her body, not her hands, not her gaze. She was completely, beautifully and fully open to him.

He could only hope she saw the same thing in his eyes.

"It's crazy," he said as she pressed her knees into his hips, crossed her ankles over the lower part of his back, and lifted up so he could push even more deeply into her. He'd have sworn he'd have taken her wildly, but the rhythm they established right from the start was steady, and deep, and made all the more powerful for the way it allowed them both to feel every push, every slide, every pulse, and quickening.

"What's crazy?" she murmured, lifting her head up to take his mouth, her eyes drifting shut as she claimed him with a kiss that was every bit as deep and profound. They were so fully joined.

He closed his eyes, too, and was stunned further by the emotions that rocked him as he felt himself gather, felt her body tighten instinctively as she felt him climbing higher, faster.

He was thrusting now, deeper, harder, and there was this rushing sensation that overtook him, all of him, heart, mind, body, soul, as his climax thundered toward release. She was with him every inch, every pulse, whimpering, moaning—or maybe that was him—he honestly couldn't tell where he ended and she began.

And when he came, it was almost with a violence that left little stars twinkling in the periphery of his vision. Or would have if he could open his eyes. He tried not to collapse on top of her, but she wouldn't allow him to shift his weight, pulling all of him down on all of her.

"Stay," she murmured, keeping him wrapped up in her body.

He gave in without a fight, as it was exactly where he wanted to be, in this moment, and for as many other moments in his life he might be lucky enough to have. He buried his face in her neck, striving to regain his breathing, feeling the racing of her heart match his, the pulse in her neck rippling against his cheek as they both tried to find their next breath.

Their breathing slowed, though their skin was still warm and slick from all the exertion. She played with his hair, trailed her fingernails on the back of his neck. He hummed his approval and rolled to his side, taking her with him despite her protesting his leaving her. He groped over his head for a pillow and dragged one under his cheek, even as he curled her into his body, pulling her leg over his, her cheek pressed against his chest. Against his heart. Which was in a wild freefall that he knew it wasn't going to recover from anytime soon.

"What's crazy?" she asked again, slipping her arm around his waist, nestling in closer, making herself at home in the protective circle of his body. He wanted nothing more in that moment than to keep her right there, just like that, forever.

He kissed the top of her head and debated saying the words that were circling around and through his mind. And his heart. It *was* crazy. And speaking them out loud, saying them to her, especially in such an emotionally charged moment, would be both crazy and foolish.

She shifted her head back and tilted her chin up so their eyes met. She searched his for a long moment as he fought speaking his mind, saying the words that were bursting forth, clinging to the tip of his tongue.

Then she said, her voice soft, and still deep and a bit raspy from their lovemaking. "Is it crazy that I already feel things for you that I've never felt for anyone in my life?"

And that was it. Done deal. His heart was totally and completely hers. "I thought it was . . . but I've changed my mind."

Her lips curved just the tiniest bit as she searched his face, looking for whatever signs she needed. And he prayed she found whatever it was she was looking for, because he was pretty damn sure she was feeling the same thing he was. What in the hell were the chances of that happening? And how on earth had he gotten so lucky to have it happen to him?

He wanted to take her all over again. He wanted to jump on his bed and sing the hallelujah chorus. So this is what they wrote poetry about, why music was made, and stories written. He got it now. He so got it. And thanked God he hadn't missed out on it.

"Good," she said at length, reaching up to push his hair off his forehead, then trace the contours of his face with her fingers. "Because otherwise I'd be so seriously crazy right now that I might need to be committed."

Jake laughed then, and she giggled, and they laughed together. And it felt equally as good as the shattering climax he'd just had. "There's only one place I want you committed to. But don't worry. Because I plan to join you there."

Chapter 14

Lauren stretched as she slowly came awake, a smile still curved on her face. She was pretty sure that had become a permanent expression at some point during the night. And she was perfectly okay with that. Her yawn turned into a short squeal when a heavy male arm snaked around her waist and tugged her back against a very warm, very broad chest. And a very ready body.

Her body instinctively moved back onto his, but she couldn't help the little inhalation of breath as he pressed against what was now some fairly tender flesh. "I could die a very happy woman right this very second, but honesty compels me to admit that I'm also a slightly sore deliriously happy woman."

"No worries," he said against her neck, shifting her body so he wasn't pushing against her softest skin. "I was about to suggest a nice, long, restorative shower."

She smiled and pulled his arm more tightly around her. "If you were thinking of joining me, I'm not sure any amount of tenderness could keep me from trying to have my way with you."

"Then I'll just have to have enough willpower for both of us."

She snickered at that.

He nipped at the side of her neck, then laughed, too. "Okay, so I have no defense there."

"No, you don't. You're like the bionic man or something. You'll have to give me time to get used to you."

"Us," he gently corrected. Then he chuckled and rolled her to her back, tucking her to his side, pinning her with the weight of his leg. "And as far as I'm concerned, you have the rest of your life to get used to us."

Her heart flipped over, possibly skipped a beat or two somewhere in there as well. There was absolutely no hesitation in his voice, and his gaze was squarely on hers. Last night, after the first time they'd made love, he'd said some things and so had she. Intimate things that linked them together in ways other than the physical. The other times they'd come together during the night had been more a slow, languid, joining of bodies and souls, with the only communication that of touch and taste.

Now it was the light of day. And if they'd been crazy to half admit what they'd half admitted in the immediate aftermath of a very intense passionate first coupling, that was almost understandable. It had felt rather life altering in that moment. And what had followed through the night merely an underscore of that intensity.

But what did it say now, that fully clear of mind, and of heart, staring into eyes she knew she could look into for a very, very long time . . . that she still felt exactly the same way. "Better be careful what you offer," she said softly. "You might get exactly what you wish for."

His smile was blinding and sexy, his eyes so full of life and . . . other things she badly wanted to believe in . . . it made her want to leap fully and completely off the cliff and into whatever danger may lay ahead.

If she were honest with herself, it was possible she'd already done so . . . she simply had to accept it. And decide what she was going to do about it.

"Poor me," he said, tracing his fingers along her cheek. "I'll risk it."

He was really irresistible. She was reaching for him despite her body's tender spots, when another thought popped into her head. "Your flight," she said, suddenly remembering that his very immediate future involved leaving for Vegas.

"I know." He made a face. "I don't wanna."

She laughed. "That's a pretty good pout."

"Is it going to get me anywhere?"

"I don't know. Will it work on the guys who want to throw money at your plane?"

He frowned. "Party pooper."

She laughed. "One of us has to be the pragmatic one."

"Funny thing is I'd have always sworn that'd be my job."

"We can take turns. I'm sure there will be times when I'll employ the pout and whine, too."

His devilish grin flashed again. "Yeah, but I'll warn you, it's probably always going to work on me."

"Good to know." She caught him off guard, rolling him to his back, then scrambling across him and off the bed.

"Hey! Wait a minute!"

"Last one in the shower has to wash the other's back first."

"That's not exactly going to motivate me to move any faster," he said, climbing out of bed after her.

But, for a big guy he moved deceptively fast, catching her up against him just as she reached in and turned on the hot spray. "Can I decide which side of you I get to soap up first?" he murmured against her ear, then dropped several resistance dissolving kisses along the side of her neck and shoulder.

"I'm thinking you can probably do anything you want right at the moment," she said, sighing and leaning back into him. "But then, I can almost guarantee you you're going to be late."

"You know, I don't have to race planes," he said, then made her squeal when he scooped her up and walked them both into the oversized walk-in shower. Steam billowed around them, enveloping them quickly.

"Right. That's what I want to be, the woman who made you give up your passion."

He moved them under the drenching spray and pulled her tightly into his arms. "A man can have many passions. I seem to be all caught up in one right now."

"Imagine that," she said against his lips. "So am I." Then she gave in and let him have her. She wanted him to have her all the time. Every second was all his for the taking, that's how she felt. Unapologetically so.

But he kept his word and took wonderfully careful, gentle care with her, making her ache in ways that had nothing to do with being tender from all night lovemaking.

They were drying each other off and she was thinking she still needed to search for her clothes, when he said, "Do you want a quick breakfast?"

"That's okay. I can ride my bike back down if you need to get going."

He tugged the knot in the front of the towel she'd tied around herself and pulled her up against him, then slid his hands around to cup her backside through the soft terrycloth. "I'm not thinking you're going to want a bicycle seat pressing against these."

She winced at the thought before she could stifle the reaction. "You're probably right. I could always call my mom—"

"I'll take you back to your motel."

"But—"

He kissed the tip of her nose. "It's fine. Truly. They're in Vegas. I'm sure a few minutes one way or the other isn't going to ruin their day."

"Okay, okay." She giggled when he gently squeezed her backside and kissed her nose again. She'd become a giggler. And she was unapologetic about that, too, as it turned out.

"I'd work harder at talking you into going with me, but I know how important it is for you to get some time with your mom."

Her heart did that fluttery, beat-skipping thing again, and this time she kissed him on the tip of his nose, though she had to wobble on tippy toes to do it.

He laughed and wiggled his nose. "What was that for?"

"You. Being all good guy and understanding and saying the exact right thing. Where have they been keeping you?"

"First off, please remember this moment, and allow me to use it as evidence for when I say the wrong thing at the wrong time, which could happen at any moment. And, secondly . . ." He lifted her up against him and backed them up against the wall next to the towel rack. "They haven't been keeping me anywhere. I've been right here all along. Just waiting for you to find me."

She sighed. Her heart sighed. And she gave herself into the kiss and let the tenderness and intensity of her response hopefully speak all the words she hadn't exactly figured out yet.

They somehow managed to dress and get all the way to his Jeep and down to the flight school without ending up back in bed. Or on the floor. Or up against the nearest wall. Although there were a few close calls.

It was crazy. How happy she was. How much she completely didn't care that this was the most impulsive thing she'd ever done. That she didn't even really know Jake McKenna, but that she was already half head over heels for him. She glanced at him. Maybe more than half. She wanted to hug herself and dance a little jig, that's how stupid happy she was. It wasn't lost on her, the irony that it was her mother's own, similar impulsive act that had brought Lauren to Colorado in the first place.

She wondered what her mother was going to say when she told her. And Lauren had already decided that today she was going to tell her mother everything. About her job, about her continued concerns where Arlen was concerned . . . and about Jake. She wasn't exactly sure how she intended to explain any of it, the least being that last part, but if they were going to find their way back to the relationship they used to have, then they both had to be completely open and put everything out there.

She only hoped her mother felt the same way. Because now that she was here, and the wall of miscommunication and hurt feelings had finally been dismantled . . . she wanted to ask her mother some direct questions, as well. And hoped she'd answer them honestly.

"Didn't you leave your bike next to the front office?"

"What?" She'd been so lost in her thoughts she hadn't been paying attention. "My bike? Yes, I just leaned it up against the hangar when I came in looking for you. Why?" She looked at the hangar and door to the front office. "Where's my bike?"

"Exactly what I was wondering."

"Would someone have taken it? Or borrowed it, maybe? One of your younger students?"

Jake lifted a shoulder, but a frown still creased his forehead. "I don't know. I wouldn't think so. Not without leaving a note. And it's not like Cedar Springs is rife with crime. But I guess there's a first time for everything."

"Maybe you should go in, look around, make sure nothing else was taken." She looked back toward the other hangar. "What about Hank?"

"Oh, I'm sure he's fine, probably slept through the whole thing. Not much of a watch dog and anyone whose been up here would know that." He popped his door open. "But I should take a look around. I don't remember if I locked up before we took off last night or not."

"Is that pretty much the norm? Not locking up?"

"I keep the hangars locked, but there's not much in the front office worth taking. Sometimes I do, most times I forget. Like I said, Cedar Springs isn't exactly a hot bed of crime. In fact, Gerald—that'd be the police chief—spends most of his time over at the firehouse, mooning around after Sally. She stays a lot busier than he does. Mostly he deals with the occasional altercation out at the resort. Drunk and disorderly, cars banging bumpers when the roads get bad, that sort of thing. Can't recall him ever having to deal with a break-in, or worse. There's been a few cases of shoplifting, but that's about as exciting as it gets."

"Which . . . sounds about exactly how I'd imagine the town to be like. All of which doesn't explain—"

"Where your bike is," he finished. "I know. But, as I said, always a first time for everything. Let me go in and do a quick check, then I'll get you back to town."

"Should I call the police chief?"

"I'll drop you off at the rental shop so you can let them know what happened. Who knows, maybe someone found it and turned it in."

"How would they know—"

"Big sticker on the side of the bike. Plus . . . hot pink isn't a regular color you'd find at the mountain bike shop."

She flashed a smile. "You making disparaging remarks about my bike, mister? Because I'm kinda liking the whole biking around town thing. I might just look into getting a fancier mountain bike of my very own. And when I do?"

He chuckled. "Uh oh. I've created a monster."

"A hot pink one. With accessories," she called out of the Jeep window as he stepped into the front office.

He was still smiling when he came back out, lifting his shoulders to indicate that everything seemed normal. "Who knows," he said as he climbed back in. "Let's get back into town. Maybe it's turned up."

"You know," she said, thinking as they wound their way back to town, "my bike did tend to stick out a little. At least I haven't seen another one that color since I've been here. And, come to think of it, I stick out, too. And I've ridden it all over the place, so it stands to reason people would associate the bike with me."

"What are you saying?"

"Just that whoever took the bike might have wanted a less conspicuous ride if they were hoping to get away with the crime."

He chuckled. "You watch too many cop shows."

"No. I live in D.C. It's its very own cop show. Daily. Hourly, in fact. Live, and in person."

"Probably truer than I'd like to believe, so that's fair. But, around here . . . I don't know. I'm figuring there's a good reason."

He pulled over in front of the bike rental shop. "You want me to go in with you?"

"No, I'm a big girl." She laughed. "I think I can handle the Big Bike Scandal of Cedar Springs all by myself."

"Call me and let me know if you find out anything."

"Won't you be in the sky heading south?"

He grinned and took her hand, tugging her a little closer. "I have to land sometime, and finding a message from you would be a nice thing to look forward to."

She dipped her chin and shook her head. "Seriously," she said, "they don't make guys like you back at home."

He tipped up her chin. "For which I'm eternally grateful." He searched her eyes. "I'm dying to kiss you."

"Well, we don't need the head of McKenna Flight School expiring right here in the middle of town."

"No, we really don't. But we are right here in the middle of town."

She smiled, understanding. "We had dinner at the mayor's home. How long do you think it took for that to spread like wildfire?"

"Faster than an actual wildfire, which is saying something. But that doesn't mean we have to fan the—"

She shut him up with a kiss. Then laughed at the somewhat stunned and happy look on his face when she lifted her mouth from his.

"They don't make them like you, either, Lauren Matthews." He shook his head as he shifted back into his seat. "No, indeed, they don't."

She slid out of the Jeep and waved at him, enjoying that she could rock him the same way he so effortlessly rocked her.

He gave her a short salute, then pulled a u-turn right in the middle of Main Street and headed back toward the flight school. There might have been a slight squealing of wheels. And she could have sworn she heard a holler. Or two.

Grinning in a way that couldn't be erased by a simple bike theft, she went to push through the doors but they were locked. She backed up, looked at her watch, and laughed while shaking her head again. They'd been so wrapped up in each other they'd forgotten it was barely eight in the morning. "Ha," she said, then continued laughing as she walked back to her motel. At least they were both acting equally sappy-mushy-googly-eyed. "Because that makes it ever so much more dignified."

She figured it was just as well. She'd have a chance to change into something other than what she wore to the barbecue the night before. Not that her apparel was under speculation. At least she didn't think the townspeople's fascination with her extended to that degree. Which was a good thing, she decided, looking down at the hopelessly crumpled camp shirt and multiple creases in her khakis. "A fashion plate I am most definitely not."

She skirted the front office and whoever was behind the desk—just in case—and headed up the steps to her room. She was already reliving several of the more spectacular moments of the night before as she unlocked her door. So she was caught totally off guard by the discovery of her bike, leaning against the wall inside her room, right where she normally left it. Only, she hadn't left it there. She'd left it at Jake's.

And it hadn't been mangled. The way it was now.

"What the—" She dropped her purse on the bed and leaned the bike away from the wall. It looked like it had been run over. Several times. The wheels were completely torqued and bent beyond repair. The frame was crumpled and—she leaned closer—yep, those looked a lot like tread marks on the paint. Her nice, hot pink paint.

She leaned it back against the wall and straightened, still staring at it. "Well, at least they knew where to bring the dead body." Apparently she hadn't been far off in her assumption that everyone in town had seen her on that bike. She had no idea what had transpired between the time it was stolen from Jake's school and left here, but clearly, "I had a much, much better night than you did."

She sighed, pouted a little—her pretty pink bike was toast—then silently thanked the gods that she'd been smart enough to get rental insurance. She decided she needed a shower before figuring out what her next step should be and started stripping as she headed in that direction. She'd showered at Jake's less than an hour ago, but, whether it was staring at the mangled bike or having had to put on yesterday's outfit again this morning, she needed more than a fresh set of clothes.

Jake. He'd asked her to call when she found anything out. He was probably still prepping his plane, or had just taken off by now, she couldn't be sure. She didn't know how long that kind of thing took, but he'd been up pretty quickly the other day with his student. She opted to put off calling him until she'd at least gone to the bike shop or found out anything about what had happened.

Almost a full hour and a very restorative shower later, she was freshly dressed, hair pulled back, and the most minimal amount of makeup she'd applied in the past nine years. Colorado was starting to wear off on her a little.

She debated on trying to get the bike to the bike shop, but unless she was going to carry it on her back, there was really no way to get it there. Which begged the question: who had dragged it up to the second story of the motel and left it in her room?

She detoured away from Main Street and went into the tiny front office of the motel instead. Mabry was on duty that morning and was looking as disgustingly chipper and happy as Lauren herself had felt . . . until about an hour ago.

"Hello, Miss Matthews—"

"Lauren, please."

"Lauren," she said, nodding. "What can I do for you?"

Obviously, Mabry knew nothing about the bike. "I was away last night and when I got to my room this morning, my rental bike was there, all mangled and bent up. Do you know anything about that? I had left it up at McKenna's Flight School yesterday, but we discovered it was gone from there this morning."

The older woman frowned. "And where did you say you found it?"

"It was in my room. Do you know who put it there?"

Her eyes widened a bit at that piece of news, so it didn't look promising that she was going to be much help. "*In* your room? And you hadn't loaned it to anyone? The bike, I mean?"

"No. I didn't loan out my room key, either. So I was just curious if someone here found it and realized it was mine."

"I'll have to ask. I just came on at seven."

"Who was on the shift before you?"

"Debbie. I'm sure she knows something about it, but just forgot to tell me. We had a lot of late-night check-in's for the weekend, so it was crazy busy last night into the early hours."

Lauren nodded, thinking. "When does she come on again?"

"Oh, she's off this weekend, going out of town with her husband—that's my son, Danny—to a rodeo in Wyoming. My grandson competes," she added proudly.

Lauren smiled. "That's great. Do you think you'd have a chance to speak with her before she goes? Or I could contact her if—"

"Oh, I'll definitely do my best to get in touch. Once she's over the pass to the north, though, we won't be in touch till she gets back. No cell service up that way."

Lauren's smile was a bit more forced, but she nodded. Figured. "I really appreciate anything you can do. I'm going to have to find some way to get it back over to the rental shop—"

"Can't Jake take it over for you?" As soon as the question was out, her cheeks flushed a little. "Small town," she said by way of explanation.

"No, that's fine, but he won't be available—"

"Trouble?" she asked, frowning, then smiled, her faded blue eyes twinkling unapologetically despite the next words out of her mouth. "Sorry. Truly. None of my business. You'll have to forgive me. I'm really not the town gossip. Well, we all are, to be truthful, but what else have we got to do, right?" She laughed and shrugged. "Trust me, everyone's happy to see Jake smiling and happy."

Lauren remembered what Jake had said about Mabry being a character, but really good people. She found herself agreeing with that summation. And it was nice to hear that people in town cared about Jake. "Has he been particularly unhappy lately?" The question was out before she could think better of it. But now that it was, what the hell? Besides, she wanted to know.

"No, not in any troubling sort of way. It's just, he works real hard, takes care of his school, and his sister, Ruby Jean—have you met?"

Lauren shook her head. "Not yet, no."

"Well, she's just the sweetest person you'd ever want to meet. Sharp as a tack, too. Anyway, they both work real hard and are good people."

"He says the same about you."

She swore the older woman blushed. Apparently Jake had that effect on women even when he wasn't present.

"Well, Jake, you know he's like the town's eligible bachelor, so—"

"So, you all aren't upset that he's spending time with an outsider?"

Mabry laughed like she'd said something particularly foolish. "You're not an outsider, honey. You're the mayor's daughter. Stepdaughter," she added cautiously, apparently seeing something in Lauren's expression she hadn't been quick enough to mask.

"It means a lot to me that you all have embraced my mom the way you all have. I've truly never seen her happier. So, for that, I'm forever indebted."

"Well," Mabry said, eyes twinkling, "then we'll be grateful if you can prove us all wrong."

"Wrong? About what? About the mayor? Oh, you mean Jake?"

"There have been bets for years on when he'll settle down. Most of us have changed our bets several times as the dates pass us all by. Some of us have changed them to never." She winked at Lauren. "But now that I have insider information, I might be swinging my vote the other way. Could rack me up some spending money."

Lauren wanted to believe Mabry was just kidding about there being an actual pool going, except she was pretty sure she wasn't. "I'll let you know how things are going."

The older woman laid her hand on Lauren's arm and squeezed. "And I'll see if I can't track my daughter-in-law down for you."

"Thank you," Lauren said, smiling sincerely now. Mabry might be a little bit much, but Lauren found it almost impossible to resist her relentlessly sunny nature. Since sunny was like the town default disposition, she might as well get on board with it, and Mabry seemed as good a place as any to start. "I really appreciate any help you can give me."

"If you call Steve or Randy over at the rental shop, they'll help you get the bike back over there." She gave Lauren a pained look. "Please tell me you took out insurance."

"I did."

She blew out a breath. "Well, at least there's that bit of good news. I can't possibly begin to imagine what happened to your bike, and I'm real sorry for the scare it must have given you, finding it in your room like that. I'm sure someone was just trying to help. One thing about this being a small town, it'll all come to light at some point. But in the meantime, Steve can hook you up with a new ride."

"I was thinking about maybe going ahead and buying a bike. Any good deals in town?"

If possible, Mabry's smile widened. "Does that mean you're going to be staying?"

"I'm not sure, but I can always stash the bike out at my mom's place for when I visit."

"Try Alpine Racing in town. Ask for Barnabas. He's an old coot, but a fair one." Her cheeks grew a little pink again. "Tell him Mabry sent you."

"Okay, I will." And, without thinking, she leaned closer and lowered her voice slightly, although there was no one else in the little registration area but them. "Something I should know about Barnabas?"

Mabry's flush deepened and her laugh was suspiciously giggle-like. Normally that would have made Lauren want to roll her eyes. Except she'd sounded suspiciously similar earlier this morning. In fact, she was feeling downright bonded with Mabry in that moment.

"He can be an ornery son of a gun," Mabry said, "but he's my ornery son of a gun. Or would be if he'd just open his fool eyes to what was right in front of him."

"So why don't you tell him?"

Mabry chuckled. "I know you're from the East Coast, but out here? We're still pretty old-fashioned. At least in some ways."

"Well, I think you should just march in there and tell him what's best for him and the heck with the rules. How long have you known each other? Is he new in town?"

That set Mabry to laughing all over again. "Oh no, honey, we've known each other almost our whole lives. Married other people, divorced other people, married again, me widowed, him divorced. Never was our time, I suppose."

"So why are you wasting precious time now?" One thing that watching her mother blossom at this later point in her life had already taught Lauren was to not waste time. Maybe meeting Jake had a little something to do with that mind-set, as well.

"I'll keep it in mind." She laughed again. "I can just see his face if I went marching in there." She was laughing too hard to go on, tears gathering in the corner of her eyes. "Might almost be worth it."

Lauren smiled and shrugged. "It just might be."

She left the motel office in a much better mood than she'd been in when she'd entered. Yes, her bike appeared to have been stolen and involved in a very unfortunate accident, but in the big scheme of things, it was likely not something to get all that worked up over. She'd get a new bike, a brand-new one, maybe. And, Mabry was right, it was a small town; sooner or later they'd piece together what had happened. At the moment, she was excited about her possible new purchase, and even about the prospect of finally having a long sit-down with her mother.

Things were looking pretty good in her world. She took out her phone and left a quick voice message for Jake. Just hearing his recorded message made her feel all goofy-mushy-tingly. She was definitely getting her own bike. Hot pink. If she had to order it and have it shipped.

"Look out, Cedar Springs," she said under her breath. "Lauren Mathews has come to town."

Chapter 15

"There she is, gentlemen." Jake led Roger and the others into the hangar that housed *Betty Sue*.

This was a moment he'd been working toward almost since the day Paddy had passed. Securing their help meant he had a shot. To many it would seem a frivolous pursuit, putting so much energy and time into one race. But it had meant everything to his grandfather. Jake had no idea what the future held, but he wanted it to include that big, shiny trophy and a framed victory photograph to put on the flight school wall, a fitting bookend to the long line of *Betty Sue* photographs, chronicling her long, storied career from fighter jet to race champion. Paddy would have gotten such a charge out of seeing her story play out as he'd always intended.

Jake hadn't really thought much past winning that race, where racing or *Betty Sue* was concerned. It had all just been working up to this moment. Now there was Lauren. Who had nothing to do with the impending race, or any future races . . . except that he was distinctly distracted at a time when he couldn't afford to be.

Even now, as the guys ooh'd and ahh'd and made the predictable testosterone-fueled comments regarding the P-51 Mustang—and there was plenty to ooh and ahh over if you asked him—his thoughts continually strayed elsewhere. Namely, to a certain curvy little brunette who dominated his thoughts to the point of—

"Earth to Jake." Ben, one of the stockbrokers, waved his hand in front of Jake's face. "Adam just asked you if you have any photos of the plane back during the war. Do you know any stories about it?" He turned and looked back up at all the gleaming silver, and Jake had to smile.

It never got old. He very likely had that same look on his face the first time he saw Miss *Betty Sue*. He'd been barely old enough to ride a bike, but that hadn't stopped him from imagining himself as a World War II fighter pilot, strapped in and ready to take on the bad guys! He'd stopped envisioning the war part pretty early on . . . but strapping himself in still held enormous appeal. He only wished he got to fly her more often.

"I do, in fact. Come over this way." He led them over to the Wall of Glory, as Paddy had often called it. Rows of photos, dating back over seven decades, lined almost an entire section of the hangar wall. There were framed news stories from the time of the war; only two were about *Betty Sue*, the rest referred to the P-51's contribution to the war, and, much later to the world of air racing. Then there were photos with various town officials standing in front of her through the years, here in Cedar Springs, back when Paddy had done stunt flying as well as the aerial shows. There were pictures of him and Ruby Jean, too. Jake smiled as he looked at the ones of RJ in her flight suit, barely twelve years old, but beaming with such confidence as she'd taken her first official photo as *Betty Sue*'s aerial show pilot.

She'd led quite the storied life, his Mustang had. And Jake was determined to get her that championship race title. Her, and Paddy. And Ruby Jean, too. They'd all earned it. He'd earn it.

He walked the wall with the guys, explaining the photos, who was in them, regaling them with the same stories, told in almost the same exact words as he'd heard his grandfather do countless times over the years. As they completed their tour, he could look at their rapt expressions and know that if he somehow blew this, he'd only have himself to blame.

"Can she still fly more than one person?" Ben wanted to know.

"Any chance we can—or some of us can—get up in the air?" Roger came around from the nose. "She's really something."

"She is, indeed. Flying her is a privilege." Jake grinned. "And an absolute rush. After the race, I'll make sure you all get some air time."

The men all grinned; there was back slapping and fist pumping.

Adam pointed to the pilot name stenciled on the side below the pilot seat. "Your grandfather?"

Jake shook his head. "No, that's the name of the original pilot who flew her. Those insignias underneath are her stats from the war."

Adam moved closer to the wing. "You keep them painted on?"

"She's kept just as she was flown. The colors, the stripes, the name. That's why I had to nix the corporate mention. No sponsors on the plane. We keep her accurately represented." He smiled. "It's not NASCAR."

The men chuckled and Roger stepped forward. "Now that I see her, and all of her history over there on the wall, I understand and appreciate your position a lot better." He threw an arm around Jake's shoulders. "But I do want to talk coffee mugs, pens, T-shirts. Of course *Betty Sue* here will be the prominent feature, but we'll get a little logo on there, something not too ostentatious."

"I've got no problem with that," Jake said.

Roger grinned, glanced over at his buddies, who all nodded, then back at Jake. "Then I think you have yourself a corporate sponsor."

Jake shook his hand and endured more back claps and bro hugs from the rest of them. They were all grown men making middle six figures, but something like this reduced them to the frat brothers they originally were. He didn't mind; he loved their enthusiasm. It was exactly what he needed to get his head back on the race, balancing keeping the school going and getting *Betty Sue* prepped to take her first trophy.

Roger walked over to the nearest flat surface and pulled out his checkbook. A moment later he was tearing it off and handing it to Jake. "Enough zeroes there for you?"

Jake looked down and had to do his damndest not to goggle. He'd never once been in the position to write a check for an amount so high, much less to tear one off and hand it away on what was, for all intents, a whim. "You can get a whole lot of coffee mugs and T-shirts for this," he said, trying to be nonchalant about tucking the check in his back pocket.

Adam waved. "We'll take care of that. Write off." He nodded at the check. "That's just to get *Betty Sue* up in the air. Pay for whoever you need to come in and help you out. You mentioned you had a crew—"

Jake nodded. "I do. Mostly friends of my grandfather's, all retired. They're just waiting on the word and they'll be here." He patted his back pocket. "This will cover any additional expenses." And then some, he wanted to add. "I'll keep a tally of—"

Roger waved him off this time. "Just win that race. Give us all our five seconds of borrowed glory."

"And a ride in that rocket," Adam added with a grin.

"I think this calls for a celebration."

Another round of high fives and Jake was herding them over to the other hangar to show them around the school. "Just let me make a call, get us some transportation."

They all went wandering into another hangar and it was on the tip of his tongue to caution them against touching anything. Then he thought about the size of the check in his pocket and resisted the urge. Damn, but it must be nice to have that kind of play money.

Grinning like a Cheshire cat and not caring who knew it, he

slipped his cell phone out and went to hit the speed dial for Ruby Jean when he saw the text from Lauren.

He'd just spent an entire fifteen to twenty minutes not thinking about her. Almost a whole half hour being the old Jake. The old Jake who was unattached with no one to consider but himself. Other than his sister, but he didn't answer to her. He'd always been Mr. Pick Up and Go. Jump in a plane, head out. Moment's notice, that was all he needed.

Now . . . now it was different. He was different. Everything was different. He looked at *Betty Sue* and back to his phone. Things were changing, and changing fast. And he had to think about what that meant. What he wanted. And what he was going to do about it.

He clicked open the message: *Found the bike. Bought a new one. Yes, of course, it's pink. Tell you about it later. Call when you can. Oh, and stay away from the roulette tables. . . . I'll tell you about that later, too.*

He smiled and read the note again. Yep. Heart still doing that fluttery thing. Only it was worse now. Because now he knew what she tasted like. How she sounded when she climaxed. How good it had felt to wake up next to her. And how much he wanted to repeat that entire chain of events many times over.

He glanced across the tarmac, watching as the guys strolled through the bigger, open hangar. And wondered how he was going to juggle everything he needed to juggle. Because he wasn't going to pass up the chance he'd waited his whole life for.

Either one of them.

His phone buzzed in his hand, startling him. Smiling, he put it up to his ear. "I was just about to call you."

"Well, it's about damn time," his sister retorted. "I have to hear from Mabry about you and Lauren playing footsie? And later, at lunch at Wynn's about you out at the mayor's last night. What, you can't tell your sister these things so I don't look like a loser?"

Jake grinned. "I love you, too. In fact, I love you a whole lot right at the moment, so stop sniping at me."

Her voice immediately softened. "Why, what did I do?"

"You had faith in me, RJ. You supported me going after a sponsorship. And right this very second, I have a big fat check in my back pocket to show for it."

He heard her gasp. "They're in? They signed on?"

"They did."

She hooted so loudly he had to hold the phone away from his ear. "Tell me everything!"

"Well, if you don't mind coming up and helping me shuttle the guys down to Ragland's for dinner, I'll bore you with every detail. That is, if you can peel yourself away."

"Peel myself away from what?"

"The men you'll be chauffeuring."

"What about them?"

Jake told her the amount of check they'd just written him. "Play money. And all but one is single, as far as I know."

"I'm still processing that number you just told me. Wow."

"That pretty much sums it up, yes."

"But even for that much money, I'm not dating an old guy."

"They're in their thirties. Right around my age."

"Like I said."

Jake snorted. "The oldest one isn't ten years older than you, the youngest not more than five."

"I can't believe you're recommending I date someone a decade older than me."

"Tell me you've met a single man your age who you haven't run circles around? Maybe you need to focus on someone who is more your speed. It would take someone at least five to ten years older to catch up."

Ruby Jean laughed even as she pretended to be miffed. "I'll come help out, but that's all I'm doing."

"Oh no, you're celebrating, too." Then he paused and felt his heart squeeze inside his chest. He wanted to remember this moment, this feeling. And he was glad he was sharing with the only other person who'd been there through it all. "We're going to take the trophy home this year, RJ. We're going to finally do it."

She laughed. "You know we are. I'll be up there in about fifteen minutes. I want to know how it all happened. Every. Last. Detail," she warned, then hung up.

He clicked off the phone and looked over at *Betty Sue* and grinned. "This year it's all yours, baby." Then he clicked his phone on again to re-read Lauren's message and invite her to join them at Ragland's. He wanted her to meet Ruby Jean . . . and he might as well get through all the gloating his sister was going to do early on. But there was another text waiting for him, saying her lunch with her mom had been moved to dinner. He was surprised at how disappointed he was. He wanted to have everyone with him who mattered on one of the most important nights of his life. And she mattered.

He smiled, then, thinking they'd just have to have a more private celebration later. He sent a text message back. *Have a good time with your mom. And I want to hear all of your stories. Especially the bedtime ones. I'll be there by midnight. Keep my side warm for me.*

Chapter 16

L auren checked her hair again, then rolled her eyes and made herself walk out of the bathroom. She paced her motel room instead. It was ridiculous to be nervous about meeting her own mother.

Of course, Lauren knew why she was nervous and it had nothing to do with having limp hair issues at eight thousand feet. There was a lot to talk about. And then lunch had been postponed to dinner. And since Jake was still tied up with the guys from Vegas, it hadn't mattered to her. Except it had given her way too much time to think. About everything.

She thought about the message Jake had sent earlier, which prompted as big a smile now as it had when he'd sent it earlier. She could have been put off by his presumptuousness. That just because they'd spent one night together, that he assumed he'd be spending tonight as well. Except she could hardly be insulted by the assumption when she'd been hoping for the very same thing. They'd just begun. And she wanted more. A whole lot more. And not just Jake in bed. She wanted as much time with him as she could get. Doing anything and everything they could do together. A lot of anything and everything.

It was such an entirely different kind of relationship than any she'd ever had. Partly because of where she was, both literally and figuratively, in her life. She'd have never met anyone like Jake in her day-to-day life back in Washington. And partly because the intensity and immediacy of their attraction and bond was such that . . . well, it simply didn't compare to anything she'd ever felt. Maybe that was tied up with where she was, too, here in Colorado, and in her professional career. Maybe it was just the thin air and the fact that she was wildly attracted to him.

Mostly she was just happy that, for whatever combination of reasons, he seemed to feel the same way. If anything, he seemed more sure of it, of them, than she was. Which . . . "Insane," she whispered. "Truly. We're both nuts." Thank God.

Which was the only conclusion she'd come to after spending far too many hours alone with her own thoughts. Well, maybe not entirely alone. There had been the phone call from Daphne. Lauren still wasn't entirely sure what that had been all about. Someone had called her former co-worker and best friend saying they needed to ask a few questions as part of the hiring process. So Daphne had called to let Lauren know she'd vouched for her friend, and to excitedly ask what job, exactly, Lauren was going for, since she hadn't caught the full name of the company from the person making the call.

Lauren had no clue where any of that had come from, unless Todd had put her name forward to a friend or contact, thinking he was doing her a favor. Which wasn't outside the realm of possibility, as he'd offered it more than once when they'd talked about her leaving his team. She'd have to contact him on Monday and see what was up.

In the meantime, no matter what had prompted the call, it had been wonderful to talk to someone who was outside of her personal emotional whirlwind, even for a few minutes. Daphne had been cut off by work demands, but had promised to call her back later so they could gab at length, for which Lauren was eternally grateful. An objective opinion right now would be very welcome. On any number of topics. She'd all but begged Daphne to keep that promise, and given she was never the one with private life stuff to talk about, she was pretty sure her friend would follow through. Besides, she also wanted to hear how things were going with Natalie, her successor, and things in general since her departure.

A quiet knock on the door mercifully interrupted her thoughts. "Yay." She went to the door, peeked out—habit—and smiled as her mother smiled back. She opened the door and did the most natural thing in the world, which was to hug her mother as if this were their first meeting after a long separation. And in some ways, despite the fences already mended, it felt that way. Maybe because she was going to get the chance to tell her everything and finally be completely herself again.

Her mother hugged her back just as tightly. "It feels really good to be able to do this. Having you here makes me realize how much more I missed you than I even realized." She stepped back, still holding on to Lauren's arms. "And I missed you a lot."

Lauren felt the quick sting of tears and blinked them away as they continued to beam at each other. "I know. I did, too." She ushered her mother into the room, but Charlene stalled out in the hall.

"I was thinking, it's a gorgeous afternoon, well, early evening, anyway. Maybe we can go for a drive out in the mountains, see the sunset. Just the two of us. We'll have the same privacy, and you'll get to see a bit more of my new home."

"Let me grab my purse." Hours spent cooped up in her room made her mother's offer sound like round-trip tickets to an island getaway.

"Yours?" Lauren asked in surprise as her mother opened the driver's side door to a small SUV.

"A concession to mountain living. I still have my car, but we might travel roads that aren't paved to perfection, so opted for this instead for today." They both climbed in. "I'm glad you thought it was a good idea."

"Great idea. Jake was going to take me up in the plane today, but—"

"Investors, in from Vegas," Charlene finished. "I heard from Ruby Jean," she said by way of explanation. "She was heading out as I was leaving, going to help Jake ferry them into town for dinner. I'm guessing that's good news if they're staying for dinner? Something to celebrate?"

Jake hadn't said one way or the other in his text, but she assumed she'd hear it all later. She hesitated to tell her mother that she'd be seeing Jake tonight, then reminded herself that today was all about putting everything on the table. "I hope so. I'm sure he'll fill me in tonight."

Her mother cast her a quick glance, her expression carefully pleasant. "So . . . it's going well with him, then? I enjoyed his company at the barbecue. I'm glad you brought him along."

"I am, too. And, yes . . . it's going well. The fact that there's anything to go anywhere is something I'm still getting used to," she said with half a laugh. "I certainly wasn't looking to start anything with anyone when I came out here, but . . ." She wasn't really sure what to say. It was one thing for her and Jake to make all sorts of wild revelations to one another. Another thing entirely to try and explain that to her mother, about a man she'd known for such a short time.

"I wasn't planning on running halfway across the country and eloping either, but . . . these things happen," Charlene said.

"I guess they do," Lauren said, thinking it was very different what was happening between her and Jake, and whatever it was that had happened between her mother and Arlen. And it wasn't about age, or the ick factor of thinking about your own mother in a heated, passionate relationship . . . just that she hadn't witnessed anything between them to make her feel that was possibly the case.

"You two didn't seem like a newly dating couple," her mother went on to say. "It was almost as if the two of you had been a pair for some time. Which is funny, because I don't know that I'd have picked someone like Jake—much as I like and admire him—for you, but I suppose that's because I wouldn't have thought of it, in the context of your life."

"I guess we both have men in our lives we wouldn't have pictured ourselves or each other with." When her mother didn't directly comment on that, Lauren bravely pushed on. She wasn't going to back down this time. There were no interfering townsfolk or barbecue meals to be consumed. It was just the two of them, no interruptions. So it was now or never. "I was thinking about that, today. He and I have each commented on how swiftly we've . . . connected." Lauren debated how to phrase the question that was on the tip of her tongue. It was one thing to want to clear the air and another thing to actually blurt out what was most on her mind. "If I can be candid . . ."

Her mother laughed. "Why stop now?"

Lauren flushed, but smiled, too. "I know, but some things . . ."

Her mother's smile faded. "What is it, sweetheart?"

"I think you sort of hit it on the head, about me and Jake. It's crazy how quickly and, well, intensely we've hit it off. With you and Arlen . . . on the surface, it would seem that it's the same kind of thing, given the sudden elopement. But . . . now that I've spent time with you both, and in your own home, your own surroundings . . . well, I don't mean any disrespect, and I'm not questioning your contentment, I see that part loud and clear, but that connection is mostly with Cedar Springs. I don't see that same kind of obvious connection with Arlen. In fact, it's harder for me to believe now that I've met him that he swept you off your feet."

"I just said the same about Jake. He's not exactly your type, or the type you've always dated."

"I don't mean just that. I'm . . . well, I guess I'm just not seeing you two, you know, as a couple. You don't act very couple-like. In some ways, you act as if you've been married for years."

"Well, then—"

"So many years that you've grown comfortable in your separateness. That's not how newlyweds act. I don't see you being affectionate with one another, or making eye contact, or finishing each others' sentences, or even really including each other in the conversation. I could assume it's just generational. Jake says maybe it's out of deference to my stated discomfort with the union from the start."

"You've discussed my marriage with Jake?"

"I'm here for the sole purpose of meeting Arlen, and figuring things out between us, so it stands to reason that we've talked about that, yes. I don't mean to make it sound intrusive, or like any kind of betrayal of privacy on my part, but he's actually been very helpful in being objective eyes and ears for me, and the voice of experience in knowing Arlen."

Her mother's smile was brief, but it didn't reach her eyes. "Well, I appreciate that much, anyway."

"I'm not trying to be critical, really, I'm not. You're obviously happy with your partnership. I'm just trying to explain why it's still hard for me to wrap my head around it, that's all. I guess I thought—hoped—that spending time with you two, there would be this undeniable . . . I don't know, vibe or something. I'd witness this powerful connection you must have had with my own eyes, and feel better about all of it."

"Powerful connection. You mean like you and Jake have?"

"Well . . . yes. Like Jake and I have."

"So . . . it's serious then. Or could be."

"Yes," she said, seeing no reason to beat around the bush with it given the direction of their conversation. "I can't explain how or why it's happening, but it definitely is. It's just the beginning, and I don't know where it will lead, but I guess I want to find out."

"Could it lead to you relocating here?"

"I haven't thought that far ahead."

"Would he leave Colorado for you?"

"I don't think so, but I wouldn't ask—"

"Arlen wouldn't move to Florida, either. But then, I was retired and he's mayor here. His roots are here. And I was rather . . . rootless."

Lauren reached over and covered her mother's hand. "I know. I mean, I didn't know, had no idea really, how you felt about your life. But I do now. And regardless of what I say about you two as a couple, I have absolutely no doubt in my mind that you're happy here. And for that alone, I'm happy for you. But you don't have to stay with Arlen for appearances, or to guarantee your place here. People like you, I see that when they talk to you. I don't think it's because you're the mayor's wife."

"My, my, you already have me divorced and moving on with my life."

"Mom, can you look me in the eye and tell me you love him? That you're happily, blissfully in love and thrilled to be married? It's only been six months. And after waiting so many years to finally fall in love again . . . I think you'd be positively giddy with it. I guess that was part of why it all just struck me as so . . ." She lifted her shoulders and let them fall, suddenly tired of talking about it. Maybe she should just let the whole thing drop. It really wasn't her business. Did it really matter what she thought? Her mother was, as she'd stated, a grown woman with her own mind. So what if the new love of her mother's life didn't fit Lauren's preconceived notions about how those things should be? So far she hadn't turned up anything between the two that would suggest her mother had gotten in over her head, or wanted out. Or that Arlen was overtly bad for her in any appreciable way. She should just drop it. Once and for all.

Her mother glanced over briefly, then kept her eyes glued to the road, both hands on the steering wheel now, her grip tight, if the strain across the back of her hands was any indication. "Not all matches are about wild and uncontrollable lust," she said at length.

Lauren choked on a surprised half laugh. Hadn't she just, more or less, been thinking that very thing? But hearing her mother put it like that, well . . . "Is that how you see me and Jake? We hardly touched each other in front of—" She broke off, but her mother sent her a knowing look anyway. Now it was Lauren's turn to look out the window.

"I'm simply stating that, especially at my age, it can be as much about companionship as—"

"Pardon me, but bullshit." Lauren sighed and realized she wasn't quite ready to let it go after all. She shifted in her seat so she faced her mother a bit more directly. "You're the most passionate, affectionate, life-living person I know. I cannot imagine you settling for something as—as sterile as what you're describing."

"I never said it was sterile, merely that it might not be as, well, physically tempestuous—"

"You would thrive with a tempestuous partner, Mom. Dad certainly was, your own father was larger than life. You've been surrounded your whole life by—"

"And maybe that's precisely why calm and more reserved is suiting me more these days."

Lauren didn't immediately refute that, in fact she sat back and thought about it for a few minutes. "Okay."

"Okay?"

"Okay, what you say might make sense."

"For someone else, you mean," she added with a tired laugh.

"I said okay."

Her mother merely slanted her a dubious look, then went back to looking at the road ahead.

"So, tell me how quiet and reserved equals running off to Vegas? How does one lead to the other? What's not tempestuous about eloping? I just can't see the two of you doing it, that's all."

"Well, we most certainly did. We met, we got along, extremely well, and he—he's different. From any man I've ever known. He's smart, city born and raised, shares my passion for politics even if we don't always share the same views . . . actually, we share very few of them."

"So, why do you—"

"It was rather nice talking, debating—rather spiritedly debating, actually—the various topics of the moment with someone who wasn't trying to win me over by agreeing to every little thing I said. Someone who wasn't being patronizing, even if unintentionally. You have no idea how refreshing that was." She sighed. "I can't remember a time when I've enjoyed arguing so much." She laughed a little. "No one ever let me argue a point of view on policy. They either agreed with me or patted my hand as if I couldn't possibly really know anything about it. I got used to it and started keeping my opinions to myself. In fact, I wasn't aware just how many I had, until Arlen and I started talking—debating really—at the luncheon. It was very intriguing to me."

"I'd never really thought about it like that. Opposites attracting, I guess, is what you're saying."

"In some ways, perhaps, yes. I might not have gotten swept up in him, Lauren, in the way you're describing, but I was very swept up in the idea of him, of what he represented to me, what being with him could mean for me. He offers me a life free from worry and from the one I've always known. In that way, it was a rather tempestuous thing, running off, changing my life so suddenly and so dramatically. It was damned exciting, actually. More exciting than I can recall being in some time. That feeling alone told me I was doing the right thing."

Lauren listened, truly listened. "And now that you're here, living under the same roof as a committed couple . . . has it continued to be what you wanted? Is it fulfilling enough?"

"We might not match your vision of a newly wedded couple, but we are most decidedly that. And we're happy."

"Are you? Truly?"

Her mother looked over at her. "I can look you in the eye and tell you I've never been happier, and I'm living a life I never thought I would. For all of that, it's been the best six months of my life, and I can't wait to find out what the next six months has in store." She slowed and reached over for her daughter's hand. "I know you might not understand my connection with Arlen, and it might not be the relationship you'd have wanted for me, but hopefully it will be enough for you that I'm blissfully happy here. And that I have absolutely no regrets."

She squeezed her daughter's hand, and Lauren squeezed back. "I'm sorry I'm dampening what should be—is—such a happy time, I'm just—"

"Looking out for your aging mother, I know. And I love you for it, dear. But you're here now, and you've met Arlen, and you've seen how happy I am. Of course I hope that, over time, you and Arlen can develop some kind of relationship with one another. But, ultimately, I hope you'll give me your blessing and let go of your reservations and simply be happy that I'm happy."

"I am. Truly. And I know you are. I'm sorry that I'm not as infatuated with your husband as I am with your new life here. For that part, I am supremely grateful. And while I'll be perfectly honest and say I can't see Arlen and I ever being chummy . . ." She thought about the way he'd been watching her, the way he was looking at her when he'd caught her, so to speak, in his library. "I'll do my best to keep my feelings where he is concerned to myself. I'm a big girl, and though it still doesn't completely make sense to me, to what I know about you, or thought as I did, it is—he is—what you want. And that's what matters most. That I can wholeheartedly accept. I thought our tastes were more closely aligned, but then you're making a lot of changes I wouldn't have prescribed to you, and they're obviously good ones. So I'll hold my tongue."

Charlene sighed. "I hate it that you feel you have to, but I guess once it's all been said—"

"It's all been said," Lauren agreed. "I won't bug you about it any more, promise."

Her mother slid a sideways glance her way, her smile knowing. "Okay."

Lauren laughed. "Really, I'll do my best."

They drove on in silence for a few minutes, then Charlene said, "So, do you think your suffering Arlen in silence is something you're going to have to do more often?"

"Are we back to my possibly moving here?"

Her mother smiled now. "Your turn to be grilled."

Lauren smiled, too. "I thought it was feeling a bit warm.

And the answer is, I don't know. But there is something else I have to tell you."

"Okay." Charlene looked over at her. "Sounds ominous and from the look on your face—"

"I quit my job." There, she'd said it. Finally. It didn't feel as good as she'd hoped. Her mother didn't say anything right away, but when Lauren dared look over at her, she couldn't say she looked exactly . . . surprised, either. "I expected shock. You don't seem all that surprised." Then her shoulders fell. She'd waited too long. "Did you already know? I'm so sorry you had to hear it elsewhere."

When her mother did look at her, it wasn't with the disappointment or concern Lauren had feared. It was with hurt. "Why didn't you tell me?"

"So, you did know. I'm so sorry. I was trying to find the right time. How did you find out?"

Charlene sighed. "Well, this isn't likely to win Arlen any points—"

"*He* told you? How on earth did he know? I thought maybe you'd heard from one of your old Washington connections. I was hoping, being out here, you wouldn't be in as direct contact . . . but it never occurred to me you'd hear it from someone here, especially not . . ." She let the thought trail off as she worked through it mentally. Lauren knew that the only person she'd told was Jake, and he wouldn't have mentioned it to her. And Lauren sincerely doubted he'd shared the news with Arlen over the smoker at the barbecue last night.

"I don't exactly know, dear, but he keeps up with national news. In fact, he follows the politics in Washington very closely. I can only assume it was mentioned in a local article back home."

"How long have you known?"

"He told me this morning. Said he thought you'd tell me yourself last night, but when you didn't mention it, he told me over breakfast."

Lauren replayed the dinner conversation and the short talk

they'd had in Arlen's den. "So that was why he was asking all those questions about my working with the senator. He knew all along."

"Maybe he was just trying to give you the opportunity to talk about it. I guess he knew we were meeting today and thought if you didn't tell me today, either, I should tell you I already knew to ease whatever anxiety you might be having. I'm sure he was only thinking to help. He knows how tense things have been—were—between us."

"I'm sure," Lauren said, working hard to keep her tone neutral, because, at the moment, she felt anything but. All those questions about her running for office herself and being a credit to her party. They'd been alone then, which her mother likely didn't even know about. Arlen had every opportunity to tell her he knew, to tell her he wanted to help, if that was in fact his goal. She couldn't shake the way he'd watched her, talked to her, perpetuated what he knew was a lie. Or at least not a whole truth. It just churned things up all over again.

Which was another reason to keep her mouth shut, at least until she'd had time to think it through. It felt like a betrayal, or worse, like he was purposely trying to do quite the opposite of her mother's supposition and shove the wedge even deeper between them. She knew that was purely an emotional response to a man she didn't like, and it was very likely just as her mother had said. But her gut told her otherwise.

Of course, her gut had told her otherwise about their marriage being a happy one. So what did she know?

What she knew was that the more she learned about Arlen, the less she liked him. *Helping, my ass.* She was unable to shake the reaction. She'd talk it over with Jake later. He was the voice of reason where she was not, and had the added advantage of town perspective. She found herself wanting to smile a little. How was it in such a short time, it was already as natural as breathing to think of him as someone to turn to. Her backup, so to speak. Her . . . partner. She'd never had that before. Not in this more intimate way. It felt pretty damn good.

"What I don't know is why you quit," her mother said.

Lauren wrapped her arms around her middle as if trying to lock in the warmth that she always felt when thinking about Jake. She'd need all the warmth she could get from the looks of things.

"I . . . I wasn't happy. I guess that's the bottom line."

"You mean working for Senator Fordham? I thought you really admired and respected him."

"I do respect him and if I was going to keep on in my career . . . I'd most definitely want to be on his team while doing it. But that life wasn't satisfying to me. I was becoming more jaded by it, more cynical about it, and no matter how hard I try to cling to my ideals, I don't like the person I'm becoming." She lifted a hand. "I know it could be argued that to do otherwise is to be hiding my head in the sand, avoiding reality, but there is a difference between knowing and having a deeper appreciation for the world we live in, including the not-so-lovely parts, except I was feeling like I was part of the not-so-lovely sector, and I guess I'm no longer starry eyed enough to believe I can make a difference. At least not the kind of one I'd have to make to keep my soul intact while doing it."

Her mother didn't respond right away, but one of the things Lauren had always loved and appreciated about her was that, unlike her daughter, she thought through things before speaking, at least when confronted with something new and outside her comfort zone.

When she did finally speak, she said, "I had no idea you were so unhappy. I thought you thrived on that life, much like your father. I always thought—knew—I'd have never survived it. Feeling much the same as you apparently feel now." She eased off the gas and reached across the seats to squeeze Lauren's knee. "Maybe you have more of me in you than you thought." She laughed shortly. "Sorry about that."

Lauren quickly covered her mother's hand before she could pull it away. "Don't say that. I'm grateful to be able to feel anything. And that is largely thanks to you. I did thrive on it, once.

But I'm not like Dad. Or Granddad, as it turns out. I don't have the stomach for it. But I didn't know what else to do. That is what I do. That is who I am, or what I am."

"So what made you finally take steps to change your life?"

"I know this is going to sound funny, or ironic, or both, considering how against it I've been . . ." She looked over at her mother. "But it was you. You suddenly just picking up and changing your whole life. Even if I didn't understand it, I saw you reaching for what you wanted, or at least thought you wanted—initial perspective, not the current one—and it really made me take a look at myself. Especially given how unhappy I was with you running off like that. It made me question all kinds of things, about you, about us, and a lot about me." She laughed a little, but there wasn't much humor in it. "You know, there was a part of me that was just so insanely jealous when I found out. And not because you'd found love, or a partner, but because you escaped. Because you just went and did it. And I didn't think I could do that. Had no real clue that that was even a real possibility." She smiled then, and it was sincere and heartfelt. "But look at you. I thought moving to Florida was a huge change for you, a step into the life of a content retiree, and wondered how you'd manage the transition given how busy you'd always kept yourself. But I'd never in my wildest dreams imagined you'd reach for, or want, this life."

"I wouldn't have, either," Charlene said. "If anyone in my acquaintance had told me a year ago I'd be living in the mountains, driving an SUV, and wearing Birkenstocks, I'd have asked if them if they needed their medication adjusted." She laughed. "But, as we learned with losing your father so suddenly . . . the world moves in ways unrevealed to us until it's time for us to know it. It's what we do with it when it is revealed that matters." She looked over at Lauren. "I chose to grab hold."

"And I chose to let go."

They both laughed and Charlene drove on in silence for a

bit, and they both watched the sun setting in spectacular fashion over the western ridge as they drove toward it.

"Have you any plans on what you want to do? Were you
thinking about getting back into law? Do you have something
already lined up?"

"No."

Her mother did send her a surprised look then, and she
laughed again. "My, we are a pair, aren't we?"

Lauren shook her head and smiled ruefully. "A pair of what
I don't know, but at least we're a happier pair."

"Are you?" her mother said when their laughter drifted to
silence. "Happier?"

"Yes, most decidedly. I have no regrets about leaving. It was
abrupt to everyone else when I gave notice, and I talked at
length with Todd first, so he wasn't blindsided. But I'd been
thinking about it for some time by then, and I knew if I didn't
just sever the tie, I'd never leave. Because I had no idea what to
do next, but I couldn't even think, couldn't organize my thoughts,
my life, because it was dedicated twenty-four-seven to the work
I was already doing." She took a restorative breath, and realized the knot had eased in her gut. "So I talked it over with the
senator, and he couldn't sway me to stay, which just confirmed
my convictions, and he handled it as well and respectfully as
could be expected. He's offered to help me find something I
love—I think he's even put my name out there; Daphne called
me today to say someone called her as a reference—"

"Is it something you want?"

"I don't even know what it was all about. I'll contact Todd
on Monday. I need to check in with him anyway, and it's a
good excuse to do so without seeming like I'm missing my old
job. I am curious how it's going and plan to talk to Daphne
again later, but it's more a natural curiosity, not a homesick
feeling."

"And so, now what?"

"I don't know. I decided to come out here, see you, to fix

what most needed fixing first, then maybe I could think more clearly on the rest."

"And . . . ?"

She laughed. "And I am just figuring out the fixing us part."

"And now there's Jake."

Lauren sighed, but she was smiling as she did. "Now there's Jake."

"How long were you planning to stay out here?"

"As long as we needed; I really had no timeline set up. One thing about being a workaholic for the past ten years is that I am in the comfortable position of not having to rush into anything right away." She looked at her mother. "I have time to figure things out. I want to enjoy some time with you. I've really missed you, missed us. And, now . . ."

Her mother's smile was knowing bordering on wicked. "There's Jake." She even wiggled her eyebrows.

Lauren swatted in the general direction of her mother, but also spoke before thinking. "See, that's the passionate, tempestuous woman I know. I can't believe you're stifling that part of yourself in any way."

Her mother's expression immediately shuttered a bit and Lauren wanted to kick herself in the ass. Or tape her mouth shut. "I'm sorry, truly. I was just—"

"No, it's fine." She looked at her daughter, all sober, serene, and looking wise beyond her years. Or maybe wise because of her years. But Lauren also noted, for the very first time, the weariness there. Or maybe it was resignation.

And she started to worry all over again. Dammit.

"Let's look at the sunset and just appreciate that we're here. Together. And we're good," her mother said. She pulled the truck over at the crest of the next ridge, and the valley spreading below them was breathtaking, aglow with the colors of the setting sun behind the rigid and jagged peaks rising above it on the other side. "We are good, aren't we?" she asked quietly, a few moments later.

Lauren hated with a passion the renewed niggling in her gut. "We're the best," she whispered. "The very best."

Maybe just as parents worried about their kids no matter their age, kids worried about their parents, too. It was natural, normal even. A sign of a loving partnership. At least that's what she told herself as they finally turned around and headed back toward home.

Home. As the light faded, and they drove on in what she desperately wished was companionable silence . . . she found herself wondering how that word applied to her life now. And realized she had absolutely no clue.

Chapter 17

R uby Jean threw her arms around Jake's neck and held on
tight, kicking up her heels and making him grunt as he
grabbed hold of her to keep from tumbling them both to the
ground. "Paddy would be so insanely proud of you right now."
The widest smile split her pretty face.

"You think so? I'm not so sure. But it was my only choice."

"He just hated the commercialization that came with investors. You kept control of how the *Betty Sue* would be maintained and marketed. Besides . . ." She bussed him noisily on
the cheek as he set her on her feet again. "You bring that trophy home and put it on the wall, next to his picture, and he'll
be smilin' in heaven for all eternity."

Jake laughed, feeling too good to argue the point. "I wonder
if you can claim bragging rights in the afterlife?"

"Oh, I'm certain if there's a way, he'll be the one findin' it,"
she said, affecting the brogue that always grew far more pronounced whenever their grandfather was exercised over something—which was almost always—and despite the fact that
Patrick McKenna had spent all but ten of his seventy-five years
on American soil.

"I'm sure you're right." Jake glanced over his shoulder at
Roger and the group, who were presently arranging rooms at
the resort registration desk. They had consumed, perhaps, a wee
bit too much celebratory champagne, and while Jake was per-

fectly sober and could have flown them back to Vegas, they'd opted to return in the morning. Jake had had to scramble to re-arrange two of his lessons, but a bit of inconvenience was more than worth it, considering what they were doing for him. And for *Betty Sue*. "Sorry, about earlier. I know they got a bit out of hand."

Along with the celebratory champagne, a few of the guys had been more than a little obvious about wanting to do some celebrating of a more personal nature with his sister. And while he'd teased her about their availability, in no way did he expect her to put up with that nonsense.

"If I'd had any idea they were going to behave like that, I'd have—"

Ruby Jean put her hand up. "I can handle myself, big brother. They were just excited about the prospect of seeing big jets fly at ridiculously fast speeds. It's a testosterone rush and I was an available outlet to cut it loose on. But, trust me on this, no one manhandles Ruby Jean McKenna." She flashed her dimples in a sweetheart of a smile. "At least not without her explicit permission."

Jake groaned and clapped his hands to his ears. "I do not need to hear about this, much less think about it." But his sis-ter had been telling the truth about being able to handle herself. She'd handled their drunken advances with an easy demeanor and quick wit that kept things friendly, but made it perfectly clear she wasn't going to play.

It was funny, though in some ways Jake had always been a little in awe of his baby sister, from how young and how quickly she'd taken to flying, to her daredevil nature, but in most other ways, she was, in fact, his baby sister and always would be. So, it always kind of set him back a step when she showed just how mature and responsible for herself she really was. She might come crying to him about, well, almost everything, or so it seemed, but when it came down to it, she was a smart, resourceful, highly ca-pable, independent young woman.

She frowned. "Why are you looking at me like that?"

"Like what?"

"Like a proud principal or something. What'd I do now?"

He hugged her. "I know I hassle you, and that's largely because you drive me crazy on a regular basis, but if I haven't told you this lately, I really am proud of you, Ruby Jean McKenna. You've grown up good."

She eyed him warily. "I'd have sworn I didn't see you drink more than a half glass of champagne."

"I didn't."

"So . . . where is this flattery leading?"

He managed to look affronted. "It's sincere flattery. Can't I tell my sister I'm proud of her?"

"Sure. Right after you tell me you've decided to go back to the state fair air show circuit with *Betty Sue*. Because there's about as much chance of that as—"

Now he frowned. "I'm not that bad, am I?"

"You didn't used to be," she said, then nudged him in the ribs.

"Ow," he said, rubbing the spot. "You have the pointiest elbows."

"It's a girl weapon. Shh, don't tell."

The guys called out that they were heading up, and Jake and Ruby Jean both turned and waved to them. Then RJ slipped her arm through Jake's and turned them both in the direction of the doors. "But now you'll understand why I've been so set on finding you somebody. You were getting downright cranky."

"I wasn't cranky. It just takes a lot to keep the school going and trying to figure out how I was going to get *Betty Sue* race ready and—"

"And you needed to get laid. Regularly. And by someone who knows how to do it."

"Seriously, stop before I need therapy."

She stopped them both short, just as they stepped out of the wide glass doors and into a clear, star-studded night. "So, *that's* why you're being all nice to me!"

"I'm always nice to you," he said, truly affronted now.

"You . . . and Lauren Matthews. You're not just getting laid regularly, you're—oh, my God." She didn't wait for him to say anything, not that he knew what he'd have said, but threw her arms around his neck and hugged the breath right out of him. "Oh, I'm so happy." She leaned back and looked at his face. "It's so obvious, I can't believe I missed it. Of course, I don't think I've ever known exactly how you were going to look when you finally got hit with the arrow, but wow." She punched him on the arm. "It looks good on you. You're actually glowing."

He rubbed at the spot on his arm. Ruby Jean was no featherweight when it came to punching. "You missed your calling. Professional wrestling could make a fortune with you. And I don't glow."

She was too busy smiling and buffing her nails on her shirt. "And I take all the credit for being the one to hook you two up."

Jake groaned, even though he knew this moment had been an inevitability. "You already knew I was seeing her. You told me so earlier."

"Yes, but I thought . . . well, I thought you were just, you know . . . being how you usually are with women."

"Meaning?"

"Meaning you enjoy their company, but you always pick women who have no chance of turning into anything permanent." Her expression suddenly fell. "Wait, you . . . what are you going to do about her being from Washington? I mean, you wouldn't follow her back, would you?"

"First of all, you know me better than that. And it's not that she's not worth changing my whole life for, but she wouldn't expect me to and I don't know that it's going to be an issue."

"Why? Isn't the senator she works for like in line for the presidency at some point?"

Jake knew that Lauren hadn't told her mother yet, but that she'd planned to tonight. Still, he couldn't be the one to share her secret, not even with Ruby Jean. "We just started seeing each other. Trust me, okay?"

"Why, so you can let her walk away? Jake, I swear—"

"You don't have to. And I have no intentions, at least at this point, of letting her walk away from me. I don't know what or where or how, but we're both interested in figuring that out. And that's the best I can offer you. That, and that I've never been this sure of anything in my entire life."

She goggled, then beamed. "Wow, now look whose gone and grown up." She hugged him again. "I'm so proud of you."

He laughed and hugged her back. "Thanks."

She linked her arm through his again as they walked over to where they'd parked their cars. "If there is anything I can do, anything—"

"I appreciate the offer, but I think we can handle it."

Ruby Jean snorted.

"You just said how proud you were, remember?"

"Yes, but your track record, frankly, sucks. Remember?"

"I never wanted any of them to stick around. This is completely different. And I'm usually pretty good about getting what I want."

Ruby Jean laughed. "That much is true. Well, the offer stands. I'm more than happy to provide a united front and do what I can to help win her over."

Jake grinned. "Oh ye of little faith."

"Oh, I know you know how to hook them, why do you think I asked you to escort her in the first place? But keeping them on the line? Novice."

"Says the woman who hasn't dated anyone for more than a month in the past four years."

She merely lifted a shoulder. "Haven't found anyone I want to stick around longer than that. But I always had hope that I would. I don't think that you ever hoped for that; in fact, I was beginning to think you preferred to keep your single status in check."

"I don't know that I thought about it one way or the other. I had other things on my mind, and it wasn't a particular goal, but it wasn't something that ended up just happening, either."

He stepped closer. "I do want you to be happy and . . . you know, you're bright, smart, sharp as a whip, and well, RJ, you're too good for Cedar Springs. Arlen doesn't know the goldmine he has in you. I really think you should consider maybe heading out to a more populated place like Denver, or beyond. Lauren might even be able to help you with that. I know she probably has some great contacts and I'd have to ask, but I can't imagine she wouldn't be willing—"

Ruby Jean put her hand on his arm. "I don't want to leave Cedar Springs—well, you. I don't want to leave you. You're all I've got, Jake."

"You've got the whole world, Ruby Jean. And I'm not going anywhere; I'll always be right here. So spread your wings a little. Think about flying a little farther from the nest." He shook his head when she started to speak. "Just think about it. Okay?"

She looked into his eyes for a long moment, then took a breath and said, "Remember the other day, when I was asking—begging—you to go pick up Lauren?"

He smiled. "It's now a day I'll never forget."

The sweetest smile flashed across her face. "I like you like this."

"I like me like this, too. So, go on . . ."

"Okay, so remember when I told you that I had aspirations with Arlen, that I see a ladder to climb there?"

"Yes, you did say something about Arlen wanting to campaign for some other office, but didn't mention which one. Why, what does he want to run for?"

"You can't say anything." Then a stricken look crossed her face. "Wait . . . you're seeing Arlen's stepdaughter. I wasn't thinking about that."

"Just tell me, RJ. I'm always first with you and you with me. I'll deal with the juggling."

"Okay. And I'm sorry in advance, but . . ."

"Just tell me."

"He's gearing up to make a run for governor."

"Governor? Of Colorado? Does he have the right connections for that? I mean, I know he's got a history in California, but that was a very long time ago."

"I think his time as the Covingtons' son-in-law sort of got him noticed and he's been working toward this for a long time, more than anyone knows. Certainly more than I did. I figured he was considering retirement, not . . . well, not this."

"How could the whole town not know about it?"

"I'm not kidding when I say he's been super hush hush about this. No one on his staff here knows. I didn't either, until it kind of slipped when he was asking me about Lauren. I guess because we're such a small town, he doesn't want to make it known until he actually declares."

Which was understandable, but still . . . "Governor. I didn't think he still had any aspiration for higher office. I'd have thought, especially now with being married that he'd be eyeing the other direction. Retirement."

"Me, too. I think everyone is thinking that. And I think he's letting them think about his replacement, only he doesn't plan on riding off into the sunset; he plans on hitching his ride to a whole new star."

"Does Charlene know?"

"I have no idea. But when he was talking to me about Lauren, about being worried about her estrangement from her mother, and let it slip that he couldn't afford to not have family harmony if his plans for . . . and then he broke off. I waited for him to elaborate, but he didn't. So I asked him, plans for what. I told him that, as his executive assistant, I was on his side, in his corner, and would do what I could to advance his cause. So, he told me in strictest confidence that he was being considered by his party as a possible contender for a bigger role in Colorado politics, but that it had to remain under wraps for now. I can't think of any other role he's ever wanted but that one. Ever since being part of the Covington family and their talk of helping him get the nod."

"Does he still have their support?"

"I'm not really sure what he has. He didn't tell me anything else. I'm frankly surprised he trusted me with as much as he did."

"You're his senior assistant."

"I know, but . . . I don't think he's working with anyone here on it."

"Meaning he has someone somewhere else helping him?"

"I don't know. Maybe it is just Lars and Chuck Covington helping him lay the groundwork. All I know is that if he declares, then I want to be in the best possible position to be on the team that runs his campaign. And then, who knows?"

Jake shook his head. It was a lot to take in. On many levels. "Is this what you really want to do? Do you really support him as a man, or is this just your ticket out?" He lifted a hand. "I'm asking sincerely."

"I'm not offended, Jake, because I don't really know. I didn't picture this for me, either, but there aren't exactly any other pictures falling into place, and so this seems like the best, I don't know, launch trajectory, for lack of a better description. I don't necessarily want to leave here and I definitely don't want to leave you, but maybe I just need to put myself in a place where more options are available, where I can see and learn about new things." She smiled. "Find my picture."

"I think that's a great plan." He was happy to hear she wasn't planning to hitch all her dreams on Arlen's star, because he was the type to use people up and spit them out when they no longer served their purpose . . . and that was just here, in small town Cedar Springs. If he had more power, greater leverage, who knows what he'd become. "And no clue on whether Charlene knows about this?"

"No, but I'd have to assume she would; she's his wife."

"Right." And that just launched him on a whole other path of questions. Well, he would have a lot more to talk about with Lauren tonight than he thought. "Do you know, at all, what his immediate plans are? When he plans to throw his hat in the ring?"

"I don't know. I really don't. I think he was really nervous about Lauren coming, about getting that settled, first. But it has to be soon if he's going to have any chance at next year's election."

Jake had stronger feelings now about why Arlen was so concerned about his new family's reunion, and most of them weren't charitable. "Would you do me a huge favor, and when you know, let me know?"

"Of course." She frowned. "Is there something else going on?"

"You know things are a little rocky with them, and they're working on it, but . . . well, this just adds to it."

"Jake, you can't say anything. You can't. If anything is said, like in the heat of the moment, he'll know it originally came from me. My career would be immediately over. It would jeopardize everything for me."

"I know. I understand. I won't do anything to compromise you." Which was a promise he had every intention of keeping, although possibly not the way Ruby Jean assumed he would. There were all kinds of thoughts and questions swirling around in his mind now. And they not only possibly affected Lauren, but her mother, and now his sister. No way was he just going to sit back and see how things worked themselves out. He just didn't know the exact path he was going to take just yet.

"Jake," Ruby Jean said, a note of warning clear in the single word.

He kissed his sister on the cheek. "I've never let you down, have I?"

"I shouldn't have told you."

"Yes, you should. In fact, it might have been the smartest thing you've ever done. And given how smart you are, that's saying something."

She sighed. "You are a really bad suck-up, you know that?"

"Yes, but you're my only sister, so you have to love me anyway."

"I do." She hugged him again. "I really do." She looked up at him. "So much going on. With both of us. It's scary and exciting all at the same time."

He grinned. "Just focus on the exciting part. Okay?"

"I'll try."

"Thanks for tonight, for helping out, for . . . everything."

"Anytime. Let me know when to come back and help you ferry these guys back to the school."

"The hotel will shuttle them up, no worries."

"Good. Okay." She opened the door of her SUV and slid in, then shot him a knowing smile. "Have a good time with Lauren tonight."

"You're my sister. To you, I'm a monk."

"Right. You're so lame. Go have fun."

"I will. And don't ever expect me to say the same thing to you when you have a guy waiting."

She rolled her eyes. "I won't. But I love you for watching over me, even if you make me crazy." She closed the door and lowered her window. "And who's to say I don't have some guy waiting for me tonight? Maybe two guys!" He could hear her laughing as she zipped the window up and pulled out of her space.

"Not funny!" Jake called after her.

But she was gone with only the echo of her laughter in the night air.

He shook his head, but he was smiling. Things never changed, and everything was changing, all at the same time. What a day. What a night. And he still had to talk to Lauren. He'd been excited, all but climbing out of his skin, all day, wanting to get back to her. Which, given how amazing a day he'd had, was really saying something. But the whole time all he could think was how much better it would have been if he'd been sharing the whole exciting day with her. That was such a first for him.

He climbed in his Jeep and gunned the engine. He couldn't wait to get to her. He wished they didn't have so much to talk about. He wanted to scoop her up, tell her about the deal, his plans for *Betty Sue*, then take her to bed and make love to her until they were blind with exhaustion.

But now there was the possible campaign. He needed to

know what she'd told Charlene today. And if Charlene had revealed anything about her spouse and any possible plans for
their future. Maybe that explained Arlen's allure. First Lady of
Colorado had a pretty nice ring to it. Not that he saw Charlene
as a gold digger, whatever the gold, but he didn't really know
her. Even Lauren said she was learning all kinds of new things
about her, and she was her daughter. The Matthews background was pretty heavy on political achievements, so it wouldn't
be out of the realm of supposition anyway.

One thing he did know was that family could make you think
about things differently . . . and he wondered what Lauren was
thinking now, about her future, maybe even about him.

He had to figure out how to make sure she had the knowledge she needed to make things right with her family . . . and
also protect his sister. He knew he could trust Lauren to keep
his sister's best interests at heart. But if she was put into the position of having to decide between her family and his . . . well,
that was also a first for him. He'd never had someone who
meant as much to him as his family, so he'd never been put in
that position. But he was there now, he realized. And it was
hard. Not to mention a little scary. He wasn't sure what Lauren
would do, because he wasn't sure what he'd do. Dammit. He
hated complications.

He pulled out of the resort lot and headed into town and
Lauren's motel. Unfortunately, he didn't have any better answers when he got there. Maybe they'd just have to figure it out
together.

The idea that he had someone to help him figure things out
was another in a series of the day's little revelations. It was a little disconcerting . . . but it was a whole lot more comforting.

As long as he didn't screw it up.

Chapter 18

Lauren tossed her purse on the bed and pulled open the nightstand drawer, then frowned. "I could have sworn . . ." She turned around and scanned the room, then crossed over to the desk. No laptop bag, which wasn't surprising because she was positive she'd put it in the nightstand. She crossed back over, pulled the drawer out again—like it was magically going to reappear, which of course it didn't—then started to close it when she caught sight of the black zippered bag tucked between the nightstand and the bed. She slid the drawer shut and pulled the bag out, frowning, as she laid it on the bed and sat on the edge of the mattress.

Had she put it there? She always tucked it out of sight when she left her room; it was an old habit from spending a lot of time in hotel rooms while on the campaign trail. Her room had been cleaned while she was out, so it could have been moved, but why would the maid take her computer bag out of the drawer and put it by the bed?

Lauren was unzipping the bag with the intent of sliding the computer out to turn it on to make sure nothing else odd was going on, but paused when there was a knock on the door.

Her face split into a wide grin and her heart skipped a few beats. She immediately decided the computer mystery could wait until tomorrow and slid the computer, bag and all, back into the nightstand drawer where it belonged, and all but bounced off the bed. She didn't even pause at the bathroom mirror. It was ridiculous how much she'd missed him today, probably foolish, but that didn't keep her from racing to the door. She peeked out of the peephole, and her pulse jumped another notch as she slid the chain and opened the door. "Hi," she said, knowing she must look like a giddy schoolgirl, all but bouncing on the soles of her shoes.

"Hi," he said, a slow grin spreading across his face. Then he did the perfect thing. He slid both palms onto her cheeks and leaned in for a kiss, backing her into the room as he did and kicking the door shut behind him. "I missed you."

Her heart, already in a free-fall after last night, picked up speed. "I missed you, too." God, she sounded like a giddy schoolgirl, too.

Damn, it felt good.

"So?" she asked a bit breathlessly as he backed her up against the mirrored closet door, peppering her mouth, her chin, her temple, the side of her neck, with kisses. She could hardly think. "It went well?"

"Best." He stole another fast, hard kiss. "Ever." He lifted his head, his eyes were all twinkly and sparkly and she didn't think she'd ever been so attracted to anyone in her whole life. "The meeting was good, too."

She spluttered a laugh, then grabbed the collar of his shirt and yanked him back for another kiss.

"Wow," he said against her lips. "Remind me to compliment you more often."

He pushed his hands into her hair, sliding her ponytail free, and cradled her face again as he angled her mouth so they could take the kiss even deeper. Finally he lifted his head so they could catch their breath. He was studying her eyes and she was lost in his.

"What?" she finally said when he continued to just look at her.

"It went well?" he asked in return.

She smiled, feeling a tug on her heart. She'd been thinking

about him all day, about how the meeting was going, if it was going his way and how exciting it all must be, and so it felt beyond good to know that even with all that going on, he'd been wondering how her day went as well. Funny, it wasn't such a big thing, really, and yet it felt wonderfully huge to her. When had someone other than a coworker cared about her day? "Yes. Yes, it was really, really good."

He stroked her cheeks with his thumbs. It did things to her insides, the way he touched her so naturally, but so . . . intently. So perfectly. "I can't seem to keep my hands off of you."

She covered his hands with her own. "I like it when you touch me. I like it a lot."

His smile spread. "Good. Because it's a condition I don't see recovering from for a very long time."

She moved her hands to his shoulders and slid them around his neck so she could toy with where his hair brushed the nape of his neck.

"You have hours to cut that out," he said, groaning a little. "Possibly days."

She grinned. "Hmm, learning your hot spots might be fun. I'll start keeping notes."

He made her squeal in surprise by spinning her suddenly around and carrying them both back onto the bed. He braced himself on his forearms as he hit the mattress so his weight wouldn't crush her . . . but covered her just exactly right.

"So . . . about your hot spots," he murmured, nuzzling her neck. "I'd like to start mapping some myself. In fact . . ." He nipped along her jaw, making her squirm in the best of ways. "I think I've already determined a few of the coordinates."

"Oh," she said, her breathing already a bit ragged, grew even more so. "I—I think you're doing a really fine job already."

He chuckled, and just that reverberation against the tender skin of her neck made her skin tingle. Made lots of things tingle.

"So," he said, shifting to drop kisses along the curve of her shoulder, which continued to do wonderful things to those tingly spots. "Did you get the chance to tell your mom everything you wanted to?"

She framed his face until he looked at her. "Yes, but first . . . did you get enough financing to get *Betty Sue* race-ready in time?"

He grinned. "I did."

"And did you get the concessions you wanted, about their marketing ideas?" They'd talked about his meeting with the Vegas guys on their way down into town that morning. She really wanted to hear more about it, about the plane, what would happen next, the race. All of it fascinated her. Jake McKenna fascinated her. Period.

"I did, but you don't want to hear all the de—"

"Actually," she said, pulling him in for a hard, fast, kiss. "I really do. I think it's exciting. And you've worked hard for this. I'm excited, too."

"Okay," he said, chuckling. "I'm kinda liking it when you get a little demanding."

She just wiggled her eyebrows. "I'm serious, though. It's interesting to me. When, exactly, is the big race? I know it's next month, but when?"

"We've got six and a half weeks. It's going to be killer crunch time trying to get her ready to roll."

"And is your help going to be able to come? Your grandfather's buddies?"

He nodded. "They'll help me get her ready to race, then I have a team of guys that will also be there to crew for me during the race itself."

"They must all be so excited."

"I haven't called them all yet." He blew out a short breath. "I guess I'll be doing that tomorrow in between lessons and a run back to Vegas."

She smiled. "Is that offer still open?"

The twinkle deepened as his eyes grew darker. "Which offer is that?"

"To be your totally inadequate, completely useless copilot."

"Ah, that offer." He rolled to his back and took her with him, sprawling her across his body. His hands slid down her back and cupped her more closely to him. "I wouldn't call you inadequate or useless."

"I meant in an airplane cockpit."

He squeezed her cheeks. "There, either."

She laughed. "One-track mind."

"Guilty as charged. Since the moment I left you this morning." He dipped his head down and kissed her. "Are you saying you haven't?"

"Who me?" She batted her eyelashes and laughed with him.

He sunk his fingers into her hair again, and watched it slip through his fingers. "Is it just me or is this incredibly fantastic?"

She bumped her hips a little. "This?"

"No," he said, pulling her mouth her down to his for a long, slow, devastatingly tender kiss. "This."

"Oh," she said, her voice little more than a rasp. "That."

"Yeah," he said, that slow, devastating smile curving his mouth again. "What about that?"

"It's . . . yeah, incredibly fantastic is a pretty good description."

"That's what I was thinking. And I'd love it if you would come to Vegas with me."

"What time?"

"First thing in the morning."

"Okay."

He smiled. "Okay."

She should have felt more . . . shy, or something, or at least awkward or uncertain. But it was already like the most natural thing in the world. Falling for Jake was so easy, too easy. She should be worried about that other shoe, the one that had to be dropping at some point. Things just didn't go this smoothly. It should be complicated. Or more complicated than it was. And, so far, it was amazingly and almost completely uncomplicated.

He tapped her temples. "What's going on in there?"

"Shouldn't this be more complicated?"

He barked a laugh. "You're looking for problems?"

She smirked at his laughing face. "I'm wary of the fact that there don't seem to be any."

A look . . . something, flashed across his face, so swiftly if she hadn't been looking at him so intently, she'd have missed it. "What?"

"No, it's . . ." But he didn't finish.

"Nothing? I don't think so."

He wavered, but only for a split second, then he sighed. "Yeah . . . maybe not."

Her heart stuttered, literally, inside her chest. "Go ahead."

"It's nothing that matters right this second, okay? Besides, I was kind of liking where we just were."

"Yes," she responded, working really, really hard not to let the vise that was presently squeezing her heart reflect in her expression. "Fantasy land. Who wouldn't like it? So . . . spring the real-life part on me."

"Wow, you sound so abruptly fatalistic."

"I work in Washington, D.C. It goes with the territory."

"*Worked* in D.C."

"It hasn't rubbed off yet."

"Or Colorado hasn't had enough chance to rub on."

She just held his gaze until he finally dipped his chin and sighed a little again. Not the best sign. He was supposed to be reassuring her that whatever it was he was struggling with or stumbling over wasn't really a big deal. Not that it was just something they could put off till later. "Putting things off till later is rarely the better plan, Jake. Just tell me."

She struggled mightily to build some really fast walls and barricades around her heart, but quickly realized it was already far too late for that. Stupid, stupid her.

When he lifted his gaze to hers again, his looked far more somber than she'd ever seen. And any sliver of hope she'd been clinging to slipped slowly from her grasp. "Jake."

"That's just it. I can't."

She immediately slid off of him, the movement so abrupt he

didn't have time to grab hold of her. She rolled over and sprang off the bed. Pacing was good, better, anyway. Movement, anything, something to help her steady her swirling thoughts. She turned around at the far end of the room, arms folded. "Why? I mean, seriously, Jake, you can't just say there's some problem, some complication, then not tell me what it is. I doubt waiting until some later time is really going to make it better."

He was already sitting on the side of the bed. "Come here, sit down." He looked at her. "Please."

"You're supposed to be telling me it's no big deal and I'm overreacting. Reassure me that I'm blowing this out of proportion."

He stared her for several seconds, then simply said, "Would you just come over here and sit down for a moment?"

"Just tell me, are you dying? Is it something horribly tragic?"

He looked momentarily surprised, then laughed. "We're all dying."

"Not funny."

"No, I can see that. No, I'm in no immediate danger."

"So, what is it then . . . married, engaged, otherwise involved?"

His eyes popped wide. "What? No, of course not. Why in the hell would you think that?" He shook his head a little as if trying to make sense of her. "I mean, I know this is fast but I sure as hell thought you had a better opinion of me than that."

"I did. Do. I don't know. Yes, the man I was falling for wouldn't—didn't—seem like that kind of guy."

"Because he's not," Jake said, and she could hear the edge of temper, or maybe it was hurt, in his tone. "We even talked about that, about how we feel about relationships. I'd never . . ." He trailed off, shook his head, more wearily this time.

She was torn, between feeling really badly for insulting him, for jumping to such a suspicious, insecure conclusion, for not giving him the benefit of the doubt, whatever it was. "I'm sorry."

He looked at her. "Thank you."

"And I mean it. I'm not usually that cynical. Truly. But when you said what you said . . . it's just . . . I didn't—couldn't think—

what else would be a complication to our relationship moving forward other than you dying or being already otherwise involved."

"Family," he said.

She frowned, thrown by that. "Family? Whose? Yours or mine?"

"Both."

Now she crossed the room and sank down on the bed opposite his, so their knees almost brushed. "Why can't you just tell me?"

"Because I promised." He eyed her. "And I'm the kind of guy who keeps his word."

"Jake, really, I don't know what else to say. It was a knee-jerk reaction." She couldn't manage a smile, but her tone was at least rueful when she added, "Emphasis on the *jerk* part. But this all came out of nowhere. And if it has anything to do with my family, then don't I deserve—need—to know what it is?"

"That would be the complicated part."

"Okay. But if we're going to move forward with each other, then I'd like for us to do it together, face things together, because that's what we'll need to do. I mean, trust me, I'm no more used to having to confide in or consult with anyone when it comes to making decisions on how I want to handle things, but with you . . . I'm actually enjoying that. I even look forward to it. I already find myself thinking, well, what would Jake say about that? or I'll have to ask him about this. I wanted to tell you about today, share it with you, get your feedback. That's all very new to me, but it feels really good. It's like . . . I don't know, knowing someone has my back, now. At least that's what I want us to have.

"But if we're not telling each other stuff, or being selective in what we share, then that foundation will always be shaky. Not to mention the fact that you said it was my family, too. How can you promise someone else that you won't tell me something that involves me so directly?"

"Because it was my sister."

"Oh," she said, her shoulders slumping a little.

"Exactly. I really . . . I hear everything you're saying and I couldn't be more in sync with your vision on how things should be, trust me. This is just as new for me, and I am feeling all those same things. It's just, I've never been in this position before and I want—need—to do the right thing, by both you and Ruby Jean. I couldn't lie and say oh yeah, everything is perfect, no clouds. But . . . it's—"

"Complicated," she finished for him, nodding in understanding. She might not know the details, but she did comprehend his problem. It's not a place she'd want to be stuck, either. And the fact that it was clearly bothering him, enough for them to even be having this conversation, meant she mattered to him. On par with the only other person he was truly connected to—his own sibling.

He raked his hands through his hair, swore under his breath. "This is so not how I pictured this evening going."

"Me, either," she said on a sigh. She still felt bad, but now that her heart had stopped cartwheeling, she was beginning to recoup a little. "But, while I do appreciate the spot you're in, you can't bring something like this up, then get all mysterious and close-mouthed about it, and not expect me to want answers. Yes, I overreacted initially, and I have to think about that, about why I was so convinced this couldn't work that I jumped so hard on the first little sign that there might be a problem with Paradise—that's on me. But you're also part of why we're sitting here like this right now and not tearing each other's clothes off, and that, I'm afraid, is on you." She rested her forearms on her thighs and reached her hands across the small gap between her knees.

He took her hands immediately in his, and it might be the most foolish thing she'd ever allowed herself to feel, but having the warmth and strength of his hand in hers made her believe that, no matter what it was, it would all be okay. As long as they tackled it together.

A ghost of a smile crossed his handsome face. "You wanna just forget it came up and get back to the ripping clothes part?"

He was too damn charming by half. She should be mad, or at least miffed. But she felt her lips twitching. "I haven't crossed it completely off the list."

His smile was there, but there was true regret in his eyes.

"I guess . . . can you tell me why you can talk to Ruby Jean about whatever this is, but not me? Is there a reason she's concerned?"

"She doesn't know you, and while she's wild about the idea of us being together—do not doubt that for a second—this is important enough to her, to her future, that she doesn't want to risk screwing it up by bringing someone else in—also with a vested agenda in the situation—and trusting them not to inadvertently ruin things for her if put between a rock and a hard place."

"Wow."

"Don't take it personally, Lauren. And know that I stood up for you in this. She might not know she can depend on you, but I do."

She tilted her head to the side a little, because he'd ducked his gaze right there at the end. "Do you? Really?"

He squeezed her hands, lifted his gaze to hers. "As real as I can know it to be, yes. And don't take that as a slight, but you have an agenda in this, too, stakes in the outcome. And I . . ."

"You're stuck in the middle. Right where I know you'd rather not be."

"Pretty much anywhere else, yes."

"But you trust me. To handle Ruby Jean's . . . situation? Whatever you want to call it . . . you know I wouldn't do anything to jeopardize you in any way, and, by extension, I wouldn't to your family, either."

"Yes . . ."

"But—"

"I just need to think on it some, figure out the right way to do what's best for . . . well, everyone."

"Is there anything I can do to make that easier?"

"Actually . . ." He pulled their joined hands up and kissed

the backs of her knuckles, then tugged a little and she fell across the gap between them, and he used her forward momentum to pull her all the way on top of him as he fell back on the bed.

"Jake, this is a great solution to a lot of things but—"

"Shh," he said, leaning up to kiss her lightly. "I just like us better when as much of your body is touching as much of my body as possible."

"Think more clearly that way, do you?" she asked, the wry note back in her voice. Not that she was struggling. Because, truth be told, whatever it was he had to figure out, this was where she'd most like to be while he did it.

"No, but it's a lot more fun this way." He scooted farther back on the bed and shifted her so she was curled up against his side. He reached up and dragged a pillow under his head, then snuggled her closer.

She liked the steady beat of his heart beneath her cheek. She slid her arm across his waist, and at his urging, tucked one leg between his.

"Better?"

"Much. Is this a good thinking-it-through position for you?"

"Best one to date. Though I'm open to improvements." He toyed with the ends of her hair and lightly stroked her back.

She smiled against his chest. "Okay, so we're laying here, thinking caps on . . . what part can you tell me? I'm assuming, if it has to do with both our families, the common thread is Arlen." She tipped up her chin. "One blink for yes, two for no. Then you won't have technically tattled."

He chuckled and wrapped her closer to him. "I know this seems really unfair and frustrating to you, and it is, but it's not a place I've ever been before. I wouldn't let anything bad happen. To you or Ruby Jean. So don't think, if push came to shove—"

"That you'd put your only sister above the woman you've only known for less than a week, or that I would put you before, I'm guessing, my mother in this case, as she's the only real family I have." She lifted her head slightly. "Or did you mean Arlen when you said both of our families, because, seriously, if you think you need to protect him because of our relationship, please don't go to any great—"

"Arlen is in the middle of this, and no, he's the last one I'm worried about and I know you share that sentiment."

"Okay. Good." She settled her head back on his chest, and he resumed playing with the ends of her hair, which felt ridiculously good, while they both thought things through in silence for a few minutes.

He spoke first. "Can you tell me what you and your mom talked about today? I mean, specifically? Did you tell her about your job?"

"Yes, but she already knew."

"She did? How? News from someone back home?"

"No, news from her new husband."

Jake lifted his head and looked down at her. "Arlen told her? How did he know?"

She lifted a shoulder in a half shrug. "I have no idea. And don't worry, I know you didn't tell him."

"No, I didn't, but I appreciate the trust." He kissed her hair. "Truly."

"I knew you wouldn't do that. Charlene says he keeps up with news in Washington, apparently somewhat avidly, so she assumed he heard about it that way."

"How long has he known? For that matter, how long has she known? When we were there for the barbecue, I can't believe she could have known something like that and let him go on about your working for Fordham like he did, and not ment—"

"She didn't know then. When I didn't say anything to her about it that night, and Arlen heard we were getting together today for some private mother-daughter time, he made the decision to tell her. This morning. At breakfast."

"Why?"

"My mom, of course, thinks he was telling her so she'd be able to talk to me about it if I didn't bring it up. According to

her, Arlen said he was telling her to help with our reconcilia-
tion, in case I was afraid to tell her. He was helping us."

"And, from the slight edge I hear there, I'm assuming you
don't assign the same benevolent attributes to his revelation."

"I'm fully aware I'm still heavily biased against him, despite
having a really good, very frank talk about their relationship—
or lack of obvious one—with my mother today. So I get that
my perspective is warped, but, well, no, I guess I don't. That's
just not the vibe I get from him. When we were at the house,
Arlen and I had a little . . . conversation."

"You mean right before I came to get you for dessert?"

"Yep."

"We didn't get the chance to talk about that, but I'm assuming that whatever was said didn't alter your opinion of him
any."

"Hardly."

"Can I ask why?"

She sighed. "Yes, and I wish I could give you a more specific
answer than I just didn't like the way he was looking at me."

Jake leaned back a little and tilted her head back so he could
see her face. "And how was that?"

"Don't worry, it wasn't anything creepy or lascivious, if
that's what you're thinking."

"No, I didn't get that particular vibe from him. At all. But, I
noticed him watching you at various points in the evening, too."

"Did you? I did, too. When we were alone in his office, I didn't
feel threatened in any way, but it was still . . . I don't know.
Creepy, just in a different way. Cold, I guess. Calculating. I caught
him a few other times, too, after that, watching me. That's the
best way I can describe it, too. Not looking at me, but watching
me. It feels different."

"Like he was, I don't know, studying you or something, trying to figure you out."

"Exactly. You pegged it. Did it seem like he was a bit too . . .
intense about it? Not bad, not good . . . just really focused?"

"That's as good a way of describing it as I can think of."

"So, I think it was that, and the fact that I don't see him and my mother acting very . . . well, newlyweddish, that is keeping me from changing my initial instincts about him."

"You talked to your mom about that part?"

"At length, yes."

"And?"

Lauren reviewed the high points of the conversation she'd had with her mom as Jake listened, explaining about Arlen treating her differently than other men, challenging her opinions, being open to debating them with her, no kid gloves. "I had no idea she felt so sheltered or taken care of, although I know that's exactly how men do behave around her. I always thought it was sweet, but from her perspective, I can see how patronizing it must have felt, to be so respected for what she did so well, but never assumed that there was an avid brain behind the beauty and elegance. So I guess I can see the attraction, purely from that standpoint, but . . . I just don't like the guy. I can't help it. Actually, the whole topic came up because she was talking about us."

"What did she have to say about us?"

"All good, trust me. She likes you a great deal and is happy to see me happy. So I said that it was the very thing she was seeing between us that I wasn't seeing between her and Arlen."

"But she said she was content."

"Well, she didn't use that word, no, but that's when she told me what it was about him that had initially attracted her. I did talk to her about the passionate and tempestuous parts that I didn't see them having, and she more or less said she was okay with the status quo, then tried to sell me on what you'd been saying might be the case, which is that she didn't need the passion and excitement at her age."

"Well . . . ?"

"I called her on it, because, Jake, I know my mother, and I don't care if she's in her nineties instead of her sixties, she's not someone to settle. For anything. She's just . . . not."

Jake pulled her closer and rubbed a comforting hand up and down her arm. "Maybe she's not settling."

Lauren looked up at him. "What do you mean?"

"I mean that maybe the fulfillment is coming from those other things. She might not be having it all, in the broadest sense, but maybe she's not settling as much as you think. She does seem very happy."

Lauren sighed. "I know. I guess it's just I know her pretty well, and this doesn't seem to fit with the woman I know."

"You're learning there's a whole lot more to her, too," he said gently.

"I am. I know. And I feel horrible that I never saw that part of her in there, dying to get out."

"How could you when she apparently didn't, either?"

Lauren paused, then smiled and looked up at him. "You know, you really are good at the 'saying the right thing' stuff."

"Just keep track; I'm sure I'll screw up."

She hugged him again. "I already did tonight and I'm still sorry."

He rubbed his hand over her arm. "It's water under the bridge now. So, how did you leave things with your mom?"

"That I'd stop badgering about it, and do my best to be supportive, and assured her I was completely supportive of her happiness."

"And Arlen, how did you leave that topic?"

"Well, I didn't sugarcoat it, she knows how I feel, and that while I support her, and her new life in general, that he's not someone I feel entirely comfortable with."

"Entirely?"

"Okay, not even marginally. But she knows my feelings about it haven't changed, just that I'm trying to maintain a new perspective on the matter that will help me see things her way a bit more. I think we both felt like we'd made as much progress as we could with just talking about it and that the rest will simply have to come over time. I told her I'd do my best to look for positives . . . and she accepted that I'd try."

He hugged Lauren closer and she wrapped her arm more tightly around him, amazed at how much better a sounding board he made than thinking things through in her own head. The snuggling while talking definitely earned two thumbs up from her, too. Which reminded her. "Oh, and I didn't get to tell you about the oddest thing that happened today. Well, maybe not the oddest, but it was kind of strange."

"Was it about Arlen?"

"No, it was about the bike. And tonight, there was something else."

"Hold that thought, for just a second, okay? There was another thread of what we were talking about that I wanted to follow up on before we change topics."

"Okay."

"You said you told your mom about quitting your job?"

"Yes, and that she already knew about it."

"Right. Arlen told her. She felt he'd told her to help the two of you mend fences, but you didn't think that was his motive."

"I didn't tell her that part. I kept that to myself."

"She didn't say how he found out?"

"No, she didn't, but she wasn't at all surprised. Like I said, he apparently follows Washington news very closely. He's a resort town mayor, but he still has his San Francisco big-city roots, I guess. She didn't think it was out of the ordinary." Lauren lifted her head so she could see Jake's face. "Why?"

"So, he wasn't mad that you hadn't told her?"

"I'm guessing, from what she said, that he was more disappointed, because he felt that meant I wasn't completely on board with them as a couple, that we hadn't fully made up. He knew how close we were and that in other circumstances I'd have told her the minute I'd made the decision."

"Charlene said all that?"

"Not in so many words, but that's my take on her thoughts about it." She lifted up more and braced herself on his chest so she could hold his gaze more directly. "Why are you so interested in this part of our conversation? Does it have to do with what you can't tell me?" She smiled, wanting to keep things okay between them this go around. "I'm a lawyer, remember; you can't distract me with miscellaneous details."

He smiled back, but there was still a renewed tension between them, which she already hated but didn't know how to resolve. She vowed not to jump to conclusions this time.

"They're not miscellaneous details; it's your life, and your relationship with your mother, that I am interested in."

Her smile grew. "You sound almost surprised by that."

"Trust me, I am. Like I told you in one of our earlier conversations, I never ingratiated myself into anyone else's personal business unless absolutely necessary. But I care about you, so I want you to be happy, and that means mending fences with your mom. And figuring out where you stand with Arlen, or her marriage to him."

"Or both."

"Or both, yes. And so I was just curious if that whole revelation changed the tone between you and your mom. Both that you didn't tell her, and that you quit your job."

Lauren laughed, which clearly surprised him. "Actually, she was more interested in whether or not me quitting my job might mean I'll pursue my burgeoning relationship with you, and if my not having any immediate plans for my future, if things progress with us—"

"That she'll have her daughter living in the same town."

"She was certainly invested in the potential, yes."

Jake smiled. "Which I'm taking as a good sign."

Lauren gave him a wary look. "I haven't made up my mind about anything. Yet. And don't get hurt or wounded, I'm just saying that—"

"I'm not asking. Yet," he said, still smiling, but there was a definite added gleam in his eye on that last word. "I'm just happy that things are heading in the direction they are. There, is that nonthreatening enough?"

Now she laughed, albeit a bit ruefully. "If you team up with my mother, I don't stand a chance."

His grin was downright devilish. "Good to know."

"I walked into that one."

"You did." Jake rolled her to her back. "Now, how can I walk you out of your clothes and under the covers of this bed?"

"You can tell me why you were mostly interested in the discussion with my mother as it pertained to Arlen."

"You already supposed he was the common thread."

"And that tells me exactly nothing."

"Okay, let me ask you one last thing."

"Promise?"

"No," he said, "but yes, for the moment, anyway. Then I plan on focusing all of my mad interrogation skills on getting you naked."

"Oh sure, keep secrets and don't tell me what's going on, but still expect me to go to bed with you? Good luck with that." Her retort would have carried a lot more weight if she wasn't grinning while issuing it.

"I'm feeling pretty lucky today."

She pushed at him, and he slid his hands into her hair, bracing his elbows on the bed as he leaned down and kissed her. But rather than a heated, claiming, "make her mind go numb" kiss, it was tender, and slow, and . . . almost poignantly sweet. When he finally lifted his head and stared intently into her eyes, all signs of that mischievous smile gone . . . she really didn't know how to feel or what to say. Just when she thought she had him pegged, he'd always go and do something like that. It had been like that since she'd pegged him as some kind of plane jockey and he started talking about the power of the mountains and his place in the universe.

She really had to stop pigeon-holing him . . . and perhaps, in doing so, underestimating him.

"What?" she finally asked, as he continued looking into her eyes as if he could keep doing so for hours. She couldn't help wonder what it was he was finding there.

"It's not because I don't want to," he said, and she didn't have to ask what he was referring to. "And the moment I have this all sorted out, and I will, you'll be the first person I talk to. I'm going to ask that you trust me, and trust that I have your best interests in my heart at all times. Just as I have Ruby Jean's."

"I do," she said, and realized she meant it. "But if there's a conflict of interest—"

"Then all bets are off. Meaning if I can't take care of both of you my own way, then I bring both of you into the loop and we try and figure it out together."

"I guess what I don't understand is why we aren't doing that now?"

"It's—"

"Complicated. Rrrrr," she fake-growled.

"I know." He stroked the hair from her forehead, then toyed with the ends, sending the most delicious shiver up her spine. "But this way I can keep from putting either one of you in situations that you'd be a lot more at peace with not being in. I know that doesn't make any sense—"

"Actually, it does. So . . . you're protecting me, then?"

"Trying to."

"From myself? Because that's a little patronizing, don't you th—"

"You're not used to anyone stepping in to do that, I get that. But I'm stepping. And you're going to have to adjust a little, because while you are someone I look at as an equal partner, I'm also going to want to take care of you. Sometimes, you're just going to have to let me, in my own clumsy male way, do that. Trust me, it will never be because I don't think you can handle it. But because you simply don't need to. You have enough . . . I'll deal with this."

She held his gaze for the longest time, and saw—knew—there was no condescension in his attitude. Still, it wasn't easy to capitulate. It wasn't something she'd ever willingly done, because getting ahead in her career precluded that, on every level, every step of the way. "It's not easy, what you're asking. You need to know that about me. I might always push, and fight you on things like this."

He smiled, and it was such an easy smile and so full of honest affection, any possible grudge she could hope to nurse against him was simply impossible to sustain.

"And you need to know that I'm going to push anyway, and stomp around on your heretofore list of things that you would never let someone else help you with."

"You're not helping; you're superseding my help and circumventing me being a part of any of this. I don't even know what it is you're helping me avoid having to deal with."

He kissed her nose. "Exactly."

"I should be so frustrated with you right now."

"And you're not?"

She tugged him down and kissed him hard and fast, and then more slowly, and deeply, until they were both breathless again. "No," she said roughly, when she finally pushed him back slightly.

"Could have fooled me."

"I trust that you won't let anything bad happen to me without telling me . . . so I guess I can afford to sit back and see how this goes. Then, next time you pull this kind of thing, I'll know better just how frustrated I should be." Now she smiled. "And how, exactly, I'll fight you on it."

He grinned right back. "At least you're already conceding there will be a next time . . . and that you'll still be around to handle it."

"We'll see."

Even that pseudo-warning didn't seem to phase him.

"Yes . . . we will." He slid his weight more fully on top of her. "Now, what do you say we get ready for bed. We have an early flight in the morning and I have to get my pilot's beauty sleep."

She feigned an innocent look. "You were thinking we'd go right to sleep, did you?"

"Well, not until you tell me a bedtime story." He started to unbutton her blouse.

"Bedtime story . . . what about?"

"That's for you to decide, but I really like the one about the damsel in distress."

"I might have a hard time with that one."

He slid his hand inside her blouse and rubbed his finger over her quickly hardening nipple, making her gasp and reflexively pump her hips.

"There's all kinds of distress . . ."

She closed her eyes and arched into his hand more fully. "Why yes . . . you might be right about that."

He continued undressing her. "Once upon a time," he urged.

"There was a headstrong prince who thought he knew every damn thing . . ."

"Oh, I'm liking this one already." He slid her shirt open and replaced his finger with his mouth, suckling her through the silk cup of her bra.

Lauren gasped again, and her hips continued to twitch.

"Knew every damn thing," he prompted as he started to slide down her torso, undressing her as he went.

Her thighs were literally quivering as he tugged the edge of her panties down . . . with his teeth. And the ache that had sprung to life between them was sweet torture. "Yes. Right," she managed.

He moved his fingers . . . and his tongue, right to where she wanted them both. "And?"

Her hips were bucking now and he pinned her to the bed, while he continued his torturous assault on her most sensitive skin.

"And . . . maybe he knows a few damn things. Oh, my Go—"

Jake was chuckling as he drove her up and over the edge, so effortlessly she should have felt cheated, except while every nerve ending in her body felt like it was still quivering in plea-sured response, he was shoving off his clothes and sliding up her body . . . and pushing deep and hard and fast into hers, his stroke so sure and steady, she climaxed instantly, all over again, and he kept her there, humming, as he moved inside her like he'd been built exclusively for that purpose.

By the time he had continued, pushing deeper, faster, and moving her higher . . . and higher still . . . she swore she was seeing stars when her final climax drove him over the edge at the same time.

He collapsed, his skin slick, on top of her, and she reveled in the heaviness of his weight on top of her, inside of her. "A few damn things indeed," she choked out, her throat dry from moaning—okay there might have been more than moaning—and her heart was still pounding.

He half chuckled, half rasped, "And don't you forget it."

From somewhere, she found the strength to roll him to his back, making him half laugh, half gasp in surprise. "And don't you forget that it takes two to achieve what we just did."

He smiled, shook his head, but defeat was clear on his face as he pulled her close and kissed her. "Right you are." He kissed her again. "Two is always better than one."

"Glad you know that damn thing, too."

He traced her mouth. "We'll figure this out, I promise."

"I'll hold you to that."

He pulled her close. "You'd better."

Chapter 19

It wasn't until they were at the hangar the following morning and he was prepping the plane for takeoff that he realized he'd never remembered to ask Lauren about the odd thing she'd started to tell him about the night before. About finding the bike.

He glanced over to where she stood, just inside the open hangar door by his office drinking coffee and making small talk with the guys, who were all quite a bit more somber—hungover was more like it—this morning. He smiled and went back to his checklist as he moved to the other side of the plane. It was still amazing to him, pretty much all the time, how easily she'd slipped into his life and filled in all the cracks. He hadn't even known he'd had cracks that needed filling. He'd always thought a long-term, committed relationship was more work than payoff, or at least not potentially worth the trouble over the long haul.

But last night, dealing with the sudden rise in tension between them, and disagreeing on how to handle resolving it, showed him they could be on opposite sides of an issue . . . and still be okay.

When he woke up beside her this morning, for the second morning in a row, things were so crystal clear to him, he wondered how he'd ever been so blind. Well, he knew why. He'd never met Lauren Matthews before. When it was right . . . it was ridiculously easy. Even when it was hard. Without question, he'd go through a hell of a lot more than a little tension and the continued complications of Arlen, his sister, and whatever else life threw his way, if it meant waking up to her every morning.

And it had been a pretty damn fine morning.

He made a mental note to ask her later, after they'd dropped the guys off, what it was she'd wanted to tell him. And to also tell her how much he appreciated that she'd stepped back and respected that he needed to handle things his own way, despite clearly not being all that crazy about that option. "Just don't screw this up, McKenna," he muttered under his breath.

Checklist complete, he walked back inside the hangar. "Ready to board, gentlemen?"

"You know," Adam said, following Jake out to the white and blue Cessna, "if I'd known the women got prettier and more interesting the farther west into the Rockies I went, I might have reconsidered making Denver our base of operations."

Jake smiled easily, but admittedly liked it—a lot—when Lauren slipped her arm through his and laughed just as easily. "And if you all ever want to take your smooth-talking ways to Washington, I know some people who could really benefit from your skills."

All the guys laughed good-naturedly, and in no time at all, they were all inside, strapped in, and ready for takeoff. Jake looked over at Lauren, who was next to him and clearly nervous.

"Just don't touch anything and we'll be fine."

"Oh, have no fear. Just don't go having some kind of malfunction where I have to take over, like every airplane suspense movie ever. Because then we're all doomed to die. I'm just saying."

He laughed as he ran through his cockpit preflight checks. "You might surprise yourself. In fact, I think you'd love to fly."

"With lots of instruction and lots of practice, maybe. Even probably. But today, it's all you."

"You know, about that instruction part . . . I do know somebody who might be able to help you with that. And he loves practicing. In fact, he's a firm believer that practice makes perfect. Or at least perfect practice."

Lauren smiled and settled in as Jake started things up, then radioed in his flight plans and listened to the return report. He shifted to look over his shoulder. "And we're off," he told them. "Sunny skies all the way to Vegas. We'll be there before your coffee has had a chance to work its magic."

"Did you get any? Coffee, I mean?" she was quick to add, raising her voice to be heard over the increasing whine of the engines.

He reached over and briefly wove his fingers through hers. "I got all the magic I need right here."

She rolled her eyes, but his grin grew wider as he spotted the bit of pink blooming in her cheeks. Lauren might have been a Washington power player, immune to most bullshit . . . so he kind of liked it when he slipped past her defenses. He liked it a lot.

They slipped on headphones that allowed him to hear her as he taxied out to the runway, then started down the narrow strip of pavement.

"Oh, wow," she breathed as she watched them head directly for the ridge in the distance.

"My sentiments exactly," he murmured. "Every time." He loved how the flight school had been constructed across the long, flat top of a ridge that was just above town, but central enough between the two larger ranges, to allow relatively easy takeoffs and landings. It could get windy in certain conditions, like a dustbowl, but was generally also protected well from the worst of the air conditions that plagued any pilot when dealing with flying in and around mountains. On takeoff, it did look as if he was launching himself like a slingshot, right at the highest visible range, just to the north of the town. Landing was equally stunning, as you could see all of Cedar Springs, sprawled out below.

"I'm sorry we couldn't get up for a solo tour, but—"

"It's okay," she said, her voice still hushed in awe. "This is like the most amazing ride in the best amusement park ever. I can see how a person gets hooked on it. It's a totally different experience, sitting up here. Look at the mountains!"

Jake grinned and continued doing his job as he listened to her running commentary. His love for flying, and his mountains, had never dimmed, but it still excited him to hear someone else's initial reaction.

All too soon they were landing in Vegas.

"It's so . . . brown," she said, trying for enthusiasm and failing by a mile.

He slid his headphones off and smiled. "Maybe Colorado is rubbing off on you after all."

She shot him a grin. "Something is rubbing off on me."

"Good to know. I like things rubbing where you're involved."

She was laughing as they debarked and went through the motions of saying good-bye to the guys. There was back slapping and last minute reviews of earlier discussions, as well as a reiteration of his promise to get them some airtime in *Betty Sue*.

"We'll make it happen," he assured them, and then they were waving their final good-byes as they climbed into their waiting limo and slowly drove off. Jake turned back to the plane. "I have to go inside, have a quick conversation, then refuel and we'll be back up in the air. I'm sorry we can't take advantage of being in Sin City, but—"

Lauren laughed and held up her hand. "I got any urge to gamble out of my system after working on the senator's first two re-election campaigns. He wins, I keep my job, he loses, I have no career. I prefer my entertainment not to have such monumental consequences."

Jake moved in closer and put his hands on her hips, tugging her to him. "So, I suppose I should be flattered that you're willing to risk something so precious with me."

She put her hands on his shoulders, toyed with the hair on

the nape of his neck, a habit of hers he was quickly becoming addicted to. "And what precious item might that be?"

He lifted a hand and drew a little heart on her shirt, directly over her heart. Her entire demeanor changed, he was discovering, when he said or did things like that. Not that he planned them, but he liked that her confident, take charge, independent self always seemed just a little bit undone by the way he slipped past her carefully built guard. Her eyes went a little dreamy, her shoulders curved more softly, and her lips parted the tiniest bit as she exhaled softly in wonder while trying to regroup.

"If it makes it any less terrifying," he said, tugging her closer still, until their hips bumped. "You're not the only one gambling."

Her mouth curved then, and back was the confident smile, the witty, easy bantering gleam in her eyes. But there was a lingering softness, too, an honest affection, that meant more to him than all the heated looks and pent up desire she had to offer.

"Not remotely less terrifying," she said as she leaned in for a kiss. "But I'm glad I'm not the only one shooting craps with her heart."

Jake laughed and when she lifted her head, he pulled her back for another kiss, a little bit longer this time, slower. "I have to confess," he said as he finally lifted his mouth from hers, "I'm getting used to this."

"It's not exactly a hardship," she agreed, her pupils wide with desire, her lips a bit softer, fuller looking, from his kisses.

"In some ways, it blows my mind pretty much every waking minute, how quickly and vastly my life has changed."

"For me, too . . . which is saying something given how drastically it had already changed just before I met you."

"Do you ever think, or wonder, if it's because you're in such a state of flux, and emotionally maybe a bit more taxed due to your issues with your mom, that—"

She pressed a finger to his mouth, gently, teasing him as she rolled her eyes. "I don't think you caught me at a weak moment, if that's what you're angling at. But I do think that if my life hadn't been in such a transitional state, I'd have never allowed myself to look at you, much less get involved."

"So, if you'd come out here as the senator's still very much employed assistant, same reasoning, to talk to your mom, mend fences, same storm, same hired chauffeur . . . that there would be no chance we'd still be standing here right now?"

She tilted her head a little, taking his question seriously. "I'm—I don't know. My first impulse would be to say no, we wouldn't be. Because if I was still working for Fordham, I'd be umbilically attached to him twenty-four/seven by some technological device."

"Even if you're here on personal time?"

She laughed. "Personal time. You're so cute."

Now he laughed. "So you'd have been too busy, too worried, too stressed out to give me the time of day."

"I'd have said so, yes."

"Do I hear a but?"

"Are you so hard up for compliments that you have to go fishing?"

"I'm just curious."

"But, now that I know you . . . I don't know. I can't say definitively that you wouldn't have found a way to slide behind all my carefully constructed defenses."

It was so close, almost verbatim, to what he'd been thinking earlier, he couldn't help but grin. "I'm stealthy like that."

"Yes," she said, tipping up on her toes to kiss him again, then taking a step back. "You most definitely are. So, to answer your original question, no, you're not tricking me into anything, and—"

"Hey, that's not—"

"And I'm not going to wake up tomorrow, or probably any other day that we're together, and suddenly freak out and run back to my life in Washington." She grinned. "At least not without telling you first."

He groaned. "You're killing me."

"I'm here. And you're here. We're spending every waking minute we can together and I'm really, really good with that."

"Me, too."

"Okay, then."

"Okay, then."

"Figured out yet what you're going to do about this big Top Secret problem you have?"

"Can't we go back to talking about how much you want to be in my personal space, with my hands all over you, all the time?"

"Is that what I was saying?"

He spanned her waist with his hands and lifted her up against him, then wrapped her tight and close, keeping her feet off the ground. "That's what I was hearing? Was I wrong about any of that?"

She giggled. He loved it when she did that. "Um . . . no. No you weren't."

"Right again, then. Just, you know, for the record."

"Yes, Mr. McKenna. Right, again. My faith and trust in you, once again, growing by leaps and bounds."

"Hold on," he said, and nudged her legs around him as he carried her around the plane and up the steps. "Duck your head." He tucked them both inside, then set her gently into one of the passenger seats.

"Jake—"

"Just relax and let me take care of a few things."

"I thought maybe you were bringing me in here to show me your . . . owner's manual. Or something." She tried batting her lashes, but it made them both laugh.

"No, I brought you in here so I didn't pull you down to the tarmac and ravish you like I was wanting to."

"Pity."

"I was thinking the faster I got you home, the faster we could be somewhere far more private and far more comfortable."

"In addition to being right—again—you're also pretty smart and forward thinking. I like that about you."

"Good to know." He started to back out of the plane because it would be all too ridiculously easy to stand here for the better part of the day and just banter back and forth with her. He ducked out, then swung around again to face her. "The other thing I was going to say, back there, when I was talking about this being amazing."

"Yes?"

"Was that it also feels like the most natural thing in the world. Crazy, huh?"

"Crazy, indeed."

He paused, then said, "You, too, then?"

She nodded, that sweet affectionate look stealing into her eyes again, only this time he wasn't even sure what he'd said to earn it. "Yes, me, too. You know, you're also very cute when you're vulnerable."

"Hmm, the soft underbelly was showing, was it?"

"A little. I kind of like it. Matches mine."

"Good to know."

He was whistling as he jumped off the stairs and headed toward the hangar offices.

They were halfway back to Cedar Springs, smooth flight, when he remembered to ask her about her story from the night before. They'd been flying in companionable silence for a while, so he reached over to touch her knee so he wouldn't startle her. "Last night—"

She smiled immediately. "Mmm, last night. Yes?"

He laughed. "That, too. But you had started to tell me something, before we got . . . sidetracked. About the bike? You said you found it, in the text you sent me, but that it was odd."

"Oh, right! I can't believe I forgot to tell you. It was in my room when I got back, but—"

"*In* your room?"

"I know, right? But that's not the odd part, or the only odd part. I figured someone found it, turned it in to the motel staff, knowing it was mine—"

"You'd think they'd turn it into the rental shop, but—so, did Mabry or one of her staff put it in your room?"

"That's just it, we don't know. And there's more. It was totally busted and mangled, like it had been run over. Several times."

Jake's eyes widened. "Have you talked to Mabry, or—"

"I did—you're right, she is a character—but it was her daughter-in-law who was on duty that night, and she's out of town, out of contact for the weekend with her husband and son, so we haven't been able to verify how the bike got into my room."

"Where is it?"

"The guys from the rental shop came and got it. I had insurance, so that wasn't a big problem, but they were just as stunned as I was."

"Did you call the chief?"

"The police chief? No, I figured the bike was back and it'll be covered. Wasn't sure really what else there was to do about it."

"So that's why you bought a bike."

"Well, that and I was thinking about getting one of my own anyway. I ordered it from Barnabas over at Alpine Bike and Ski." She grinned. "Did you know Mabry was sweet on him?"

"Sweet on Barnabas? Are you kidding?"

"Not kidding. She told me."

Jake shook his head. "I guess I really have managed to bury myself away from gossip. How'd I miss that?"

"Well, apparently Barnabas is playing hard to get."

Jake laughed at that.

"I told her she should just go in there and tell him."

"You told Mabry to—" He shook his head in disbelief. "Okay, you're definitely, officially part of the town now."

At that, Lauren grinned a bit smugly. "I think I already was. They like that we're together."

"Do they?" he said, not knowing if he really wanted to think about the town discussing his love life, even though he knew it was inevitable. Didn't mean he had to ponder what was being said. "Well, that's good to know."

Her smug smile didn't abate.

Jake glanced over at her again. "What?"

"There's a pool."

"A what?"

"A pool. On when you'll get taken off the market. Apparently the kitty has gotten pretty steep."

Jake opened his mouth, then had no idea how to respond to that, so he wisely closed it again.

"I think Mabry is my new best friend because she now has insider information."

"What kind of information?"

"She told me where to go buy a bike. And she put two and two together and figured that if I was buying transportation, maybe I intended to stick around a while."

"That's insider information I'd like to know, too."

"I told her that I could always store it out at my mom's to use whenever I visit."

"Hmm." He kept his gaze forward. "And what did Mabry have to say about that?"

"I think I got a knowing smile."

Jake slid her one of his own. "Hmm."

"Yeah. Hmm," Lauren repeated, smiling that crooked smile of hers. "Oh!" she added. "I almost forgot the other odd thing. I never checked it out, either."

"What other odd thing?"

"Well, two more, I guess."

Now Jake frowned. The bike was weird enough. "What two more?"

"When I got back to my room, after going out driving with my mom, my computer bag was between the bed and the nightstand."

He glanced at her. "What's odd about that?"

"Nothing, except I left it in the nightstand drawer. I always do. I was going to check my laptop, but then you got there, and . . ." Her lips curved. "Seems it's slipped my mind since."

He smiled briefly, but something about this was niggling at him. And not in a good way. "And the other thing?"

"Oh, right. My friend, Daphne—a former coworker and closest friend I have back in D.C.—she called me yesterday."

"Everything okay back on the home front?"

"Yes, as far as I know—you know, she was supposed to call me back last night. I guess she got hung up."

"Or we just missed the call."

Lauren smiled. "I've looked at my phone today and there were no missed calls. I'll have to call her when I get back. But the odd thing was that, the reason she called was to tell me she gave me a good reference."

"For what?"

"A new job. Problem is, I haven't applied for any."

"Did she say who it was with?"

"She didn't catch it at the beginning of the call, then it ended before she could ask again. We're both thinking that maybe the senator was trying to help and put my name out there, but Daph said it sounded like they'd interviewed me. At least, that's the vibe she'd gotten from the headhunter who called her."

"Did she keep any notes, get a number?"

Lauren shook her head. "She didn't think to, at the time, which is understandable. She thought she was just giving me a good reference."

"Did they ask any unusual questions?"

Now Lauren frowned. "You know, I didn't think to ask her that. I'd chalked it up to it being Todd trying to help me out. It's definitely something he would do. I know he was really concerned that I was flying free with no safety net in place."

"You're going to contact him tomorrow?"

"I was planning on it. I'll get in touch with Daphne, too. What is your take on it? You seem pretty concerned."

"I don't know. It just seems like an unusual sequence of events, that's all. Could just be coincidental. The bike could have been borrowed by someone who'd intended to bring it back, then maybe it got banged up so they just left it at the motel to avoid getting in trouble. Maid could have moved your computer, and your former employer could have set up the headhunter. All plausible."

"Except?"

"Nothing, I guess. It is all easily explained."

"But you think it's something else." She didn't make it a question.

He didn't correct her. The more they talked it out, the less his reasoning felt right. But that's all it was, a gut feeling. "What's your take?"

"I hadn't really thought of them in conjunction with one another like that, so I don't. I guess . . . the bike part definitely freaked me out a little, not knowing how it ended up in my room. But, like Mabry said, it's a small town; the story would come out eventually, whatever it was. So I sort of tucked it away until we could talk to Debbie. The other things didn't really connect—"

"You were the one to mention that a few odd things had happened, so it didn't feel right to you, either."

"They were odd, but I don't know that I assigned anything more to it than that."

"Okay."

She looked at him. "Okay, what?"

"Nothing. If you're not feeling weird about it, then . . . okay."

"What do you think I should do?"

"I guess exactly what you're already doing. Contact Debbie when she gets back, check out your laptop when you get back tonight, and call the senator and your friend this week and find out what they know."

"Okay."

Now he shot her a look, but she immediately shook her head. "No, I actually mean that sincerely. I think it is the best approach. But, I won't lie, your reaction is freaking me out a little and making me a bit more concerned about the whole thing."

He covered her hand with his free one. "I'm sorry, I didn't mean to."

"But you do think I should look into it."

"You were already, right?"

"Right." But she was still looking pretty wary.

"Until we follow up, let's not get ahead of ourselves, okay? I just thought it was odd, too. I didn't mean to worry you."

She laced her fingers through his and squeezed. "Okay."

Jake held her gaze a moment longer, then chuckled. He already knew her well enough to know that she'd be on this the moment the wheels hit the ground. But much as he didn't want to worry her, he'd feel better the sooner they got some answers.

The whole business with Arlen's possible run for governor cast everything having to do with Lauren and her weird vibes about the man into a different light. If it wasn't for the fact that his sister worked for the guy and was hitching her star, at least for the immediate future, to his, Jake would be a lot more direct in how he handled it. But the last thing he needed was to jeopardize Ruby Jean's plans . . . or for that matter, strain the relationship between Lauren and her family more than it already was, all because he had an odd, unsubstantiated feeling.

Still . . . perhaps it wouldn't hurt to do a little digging on his own. Roger was invested in local politics in Denver, and Adam, if he recalled, did his master's at Stanford, with possible connections there as well. Those guys could care less about the small town goings on of Cedar Springs, so a few discreet questions shouldn't affect anything on the home front and might give him some insight into just how seriously Arlen was really pursuing his dream.

Jake found it really hard to believe that no one knew anything about his aspirations here in town. Just as he found it hard to believe that Arlen had ever let anything slip accidentally. Especially to Ruby Jean. Not that she couldn't be trusted. No one was more loyal. But Arlen had never struck him as the kind of man who made accidental slips. He'd informed Ruby

Jean for a reason. And Jake had a feeling that reason was sitting in the cockpit beside him.

All he had to do was figure out how it was all connected and what Arlen hoped to get out of the deal.

As soon as the wheels touched down, he'd be making a few calls of his own.

Chapter 20

Lauren had loved flying with Jake, both because she enjoyed any time spent with her copilot and because it had been such a rush sitting in the cockpit like that, with an eagle's eye view of the world. She left the airstrip seriously considering talking to him about lessons. Unfortunately, it was precisely because he had lessons, the ones he'd rearranged for the Vegas trip, that they didn't get the chance to spend any additional time together once they'd arrived back on the terra firma.

Which was probably just as well. Okay, not really. She wanted all of him she could get. But she did want to follow up on the things they'd discussed on the flight back, and while she didn't want to call Todd on a Sunday, she had no such qualms about getting in touch with Daphne.

She pulled Jake's Jeep into the motel parking lot, thinking it felt odd to drive again after steering only a bike for most of the past week. Jake had offered it to her because he'd had students pulling in even as they'd walked back to the front offices. Which had also kept their good-byes brief and a lot more chaste than she'd wanted. Darnit.

She smiled as she walked toward the registration office. They'd make up for it tonight. Jake had already invited her to stay with him for the night. In his magnificent home. With the even more magnificent bedroom. And, at the moment, other than the call to Todd and follow-up on the bike, she didn't have anywhere she had to be tomorrow. She did plan on continuing her look into Arlen's business, but otherwise, the day was her own. Maybe she'd see if she could drag Jake away for an hour, but between classes and *Betty Sue*, she highly doubted it.

So . . . maybe he'd let her take the Jeep for a solo ride out into the mountains. She hadn't really had the chance to properly enjoy them on the ride in during the storm, and had been mostly preoccupied talking with her mom during their road trip, so she was anxious to head out and see things for herself without distractions. Well, Jake would always be a distraction, even when he wasn't around. Maybe the drive would give her a chance to step out of the pheromone fog and think through things with a clear head. Both the Jake thing and the Arlen thing.

The little bell jingled as she stepped into the front office. No sign of Debbie or Mabry. "Hi," she said, introducing herself to the short brunette.

Of course, the woman grinned widely and spoke in a perky Minnie Mouse voice. "Hi, Miss Matthews, I'm Jennifer, Mabry's daughter. What can I do for you?"

"Lauren, please. And I was wondering if Debbie had checked in, or if you knew when she would be back."

"Oh, right! Mom told me about that. So odd! And I talked to Debbie right when she got off shift and was heading out and she didn't say a word. I know she was excited about the weekend, but I can't help but think she'd have mentioned it. A real shame about your bike. Did you have insurance on it?"

Lauren nodded. "I actually ordered a new one, so that part all worked out okay. But I was—am—curious about how it got back into my room. Especially if Debbie doesn't know. Does someone other than the three of you have access?"

"Well, the maids do, of course, and the service technicians, but I can't see Marci or Georgeann either one hauling that bike up those stairs."

"Could they have gotten one of the service guys to help?"

"Probably, sure. But I can't see them doing something like that, even thinking they were helping you out, and not mentioning it to us. That would be really out of character for either one of them. And Andy, one of the service guys, has been covering almost all the shifts since Joe's been in and out of the hospital with his wife." She smiled and waved away Lauren's concerned look. "She's due with their first, and let's just say they're a wee bit over-anxious. Anyway, Andy'll talk your ear blue if you let him, so he'd have mentioned that bike."

"So . . . what's your best guess on how it got put in my room? I'm not upset or anything, but curious for obvious reasons."

Jennifer reached across the desk and touched Lauren's arm. "No, no, of course. You've every right to be upset. We take security here seriously, even though, to be honest, we have basically no crime. I can't believe the whole story hasn't already come to light, but I'm sure it will. Nothing stays a secret in this town for long."

Lauren would tend to agree, but clearly somebody knew something they weren't sharing. "I guess we'll wait to ask Debbie tomorrow. When will she be on?"

"Not until the afternoon. And you're right, it's possible in her excitement to get out of town, she just plain forgot. If you'd like, we can call Gerald—that's the chief of police—and get him involved on it. I'll be happy to make the call."

Lauren shook her head but was glad to hear they were, at least, treating this with sincere concern. "I don't think that's really necessary. We got the bike back and it was covered, so . . . I'm not really sure what I'd have him do. Hopefully Debbie will solve the room mystery and whoever stole the bike is probably feeling a bit sorry considering they have to be sporting a few bruises or something given the state of the bike."

Jennifer was nodding. "All true. But if we can't solve the mystery to your satisfaction, you just say the word and I'll be on the horn to Gerald."

"Thanks for your help." Lauren left and went up to her room, only remembering about the computer mystery when she got inside. It was where she'd left it this time, so that was a bonus. She had it on the bed, screen up, when her phone rang. She checked her phone, smiling, thinking it might be Jake. It wasn't, but she was still smiling when she answered. "Daphne, you were next on my call list."

"Sorry I didn't get back to you yesterday—"

"No worries, it turned out to be kind of a crazy evening."

There was a pause, then Daphne lowered her voice a little and said, "Really? How crazy is crazy? Do tell."

"Normally I'd say you know me too well to even go in that direction, but in this case . . ."

Daphne gave a little hoot. "I knew it!"

"You knew nothing of the sort."

"You said you needed to talk and I knew it wasn't about your mom."

"Well, I need to talk about that, too."

"But?"

Lauren knew she was grinning like an idiot. "But, there might be more to discuss."

"A-ha!"

She laughed. "I'm here for my mom, and I'm still confused about a few things, not so much from my mother's viewpoint, but there's just something about Arlen—"

"Hey, don't let me forget, I wanted to mention something about that, too, it's why I called, actually, but first . . . spill everything! You met someone, didn't you?"

Lauren frowned, wanting to pursue that line of conversation, but she knew she'd get nowhere until she told Daphne about Jake. "I did."

"And?"

"And he's completely not like anyone I'd have ever met in D.C."

"Thank God."

Lauren laughed. "Come on, they're not all that bad."

"Sure they are. The investment banker I was seeing, Steven? Yeah, he decided it was too difficult to date during such a fluctuating time in the economic marketplace. He's having too much work anxiety to be emotionally available."

"Do you think it was just a line? Is he seeing someone else?"

"No, I actually think he means it."

"Seriously?"

"Could I make this stuff up?"

"Right. I'm sorry."

"No, that's okay. Steven is sorry. I'm simply available. Again. So . . . let me live vicariously through you."

"For once!"

Daphne laughed. "It was bound to happen, right? So, details, details. You sound giddy. You are so not a giddy person. I want to know everything."

Lauren filled her in on her less-than-lovely entry into their first meeting, her amazement at how swiftly things were moving, and how simple it all seemed, even counting the little glitch from the night before.

"Sometimes," Daphne said, "when it's right, it is that simple. Why needlessly complicate things because they're going along too well? Just thank your lucky stars that two compatible, right souls have actually crossed paths. That alone is a rare occurrence. So enjoy it for the beauty and uniqueness of what it is and stop looking for trouble."

"I'm not looking for trouble. It's already here, anyway."

"It just sounds to me like he's trying to work something out for his sister that he can't really confide in you about because it has to do with her job, and her boss is—"

"Don't say it."

Daphne sighed. "Still that bad?"

She filled her in on the barbecue, her talks with her mother, and her still iffy feelings on the subject of Arlen.

"Well, now that you mention it, I might be able to shed some light on that, or possibly just add to the creepy factor."

Lauren clutched her phone a bit more tightly. "How do you mean?"

"Nothing awful, don't panic or anything, but you're telling me you're getting off vibes about this guy and I'm just saying that maybe your gut isn't so far off."

"Why, what do you know?"

"Well, after we talked and I realized you knew nothing about the headhunter who called me, I happened to have a meeting with Todd and I was able to bring it up—"

"What did you say?"

"Nothing, other than to ask if he'd put any feelers out on you, job-wise. He was happy to know we'd talked; I told him you were doing well and that you'd talk to him next week, and he said he was looking forward to it. He also said he was absolutely still willing to help you with the job search, but out of respect for your wishes he hasn't stepped in."

Lauren's shoulders rounded a little. "Hunh. I really figured it had to be him. Who else would—"

"Well, I thought so, too, so I did a little digging. I went back to the call logs for that day. With all the new security measures, they keep track of all incoming and outgoing calls, including all numbers dialing in. So, out of curiosity, and because I was so swamped when the call came in that I didn't take any notes like I usually do, I checked the logs for that headhunter call."

"And?"

"And the area code is Colorado. Cedar Springs, to be exact."

Lauren's eyebrows lifted. "Really? Did you call it? Whose is it?"

"I didn't call the number because I wasn't sure what to say and I wasn't sure what all was going on in your world there, so I figured I'd just call you and let you know about it; go from there."

"Do you have the number?"

"Do you have a pen?"

Lauren simply tapped open a notepad document on her computer screen. "Shoot."

Daphne recited the number. "So, what are you going to do with it?"

"Not sure yet. Do a little digging here. What I wonder is

how anyone here had our direct office line? I haven't given it to anyone. Well, my mom has it, of course, but she wouldn't—"

The pause lengthened, then Daphne said, "I'm pretty sure we're thinking the same thing here."

"But what purpose would he have in calling and pretending to be a headhunter? What kinds of questions did you get asked?"

"Well, firstly, you should know, the caller was a woman."

Lauren got up and paced. "A woman." And she hated where her thoughts went from there. Was this the little problem that Jake was having? Had Arlen, for whatever reason, put his personal executive assistant—Jake's sister—up to calling her private office line disguised as a recruiter? And either Jake had gotten wind of it, or Ruby Jean had told him about it, but either way, it put Jake squarely in the middle. It explained a lot. Too much, really, for it to be anything else. "So . . . do you think it was Arlen putting Ruby Jean up to the call?" she asked Daphne after explaining her thoughts. "But, if so . . . why? What would he hope to gain out of it that he couldn't get just by asking me directly? What kinds of questions did she ask?"

"I've been wracking my brain, trying to remember exactly, but it was standard stuff. Job performance, compatibility with coworkers, confirming you'd voluntarily left and hadn't been fired, that sort of thing."

"They knew that you weren't my superior, right? Did they ask to speak to Todd?"

"I'm not sure about the first part, but on the latter, no, but I thought that was because he was the one who recommended you for the job, and I was a reference you gave them."

"Did they ask you personal questions? I mean, as if you were a personal rather than business reference?"

"Other than the trustworthy, dependable, loyal type stuff, no. She did ask if you were fielding other offers, which is a bit unethical, but not entirely out of line if she's being aggressive. I told her I didn't know."

Lauren fell silent, trying to find a linear path through the course of events that made sense. "You know, Arlen told my mom about me quitting my job before I did."

"Seriously? How did he know?"

"My mother says he follows political news and the Hill quite closely."

"Okay, but your leaving Todd's team wasn't exactly big news on the media circuit, so how would he know that?"

"I know, I thought about that, too. I'm not really sure, unless, after marrying my mother he was keeping specific tabs on me."

There was a pause, then Daphne said, "Well, that could either be really sweet and conscientious . . . or kind of creepy."

"I've met him, and I'm voting on the latter. Maybe creepy is too strong. He's not horrible or anything, but there's just—"

"Something about him. That's gut instinct talking; don't ignore it."

"I'm not. I'm just not sure what, if anything, there really is to do about it. I've looked into his political leanings, his business dealings. I've just begun on the latter, really, but nothing is leaping out at me. It might just be that I don't like the guy and my mom does—end of story."

"So, she's crazy about this guy? I guess she must be given the elopement, but if you're this naturally averse to him, what do you think she sees in him? No offense, just—"

"None taken, truly. I've been wondering the same thing."

"Have you been able to discuss it with her? I know you two have really had it rough this past six months, but I was hoping with you being there face-to-face . . ."

"We've definitely patched things up. And she's done her best to explain Arlen's appeal to her. It's certainly not the love match of the century, and she says she's okay with that. There are certain things she gets from him, or from being married to him, that have enhanced her life." Lauren went on to recap the highlights of her conversations with her mother, prompting a few surprised comments from Daphne who had met Charlene on numerous occasions during the time they'd worked together.

"Wow, I never really figured her for wanting an escape hatch. I thought she reveled in her life, her world. I was always a bit envious of how certain she was about her . . . point, I guess, for lack of a better word."

"I know, right? But I tell you, Daphne, she's happier than I've ever seen her, almost gloriously so. So, it makes it hard to fault her judgment on marrying Arlen when it's brought her joy and contentment."

"So . . . what are you going to do?"

"About my mother? Nothing. She's happy and I'm happy for her. We've mended fences, and I've more or less told her that I'll come to terms with my own feelings about Arlen and deal with that on my own."

"And she's okay with that? She's not pushing you to have a chummier relationship with him?"

"No. She's—we're—just respecting each other's decisions and feelings."

"All good. Except he still gives you the heebies."

"Exactly. So I figured I'd just keep digging until I at least figured out where those feelings are coming from. For myself, at least. If I can put my finger on something, then maybe it will lead to a better understanding."

"Or not."

Lauren sighed. "I know. You're right. But should I just pretend all is hunky-dory and not try and figure it out for myself?"

"No, no. I'm all for figuring things out. So, are you going to investigate this latest wrinkle?"

"Yes, of course. If someone is making phone calls, asking questions about me, I want to know who it is and why they're doing it. I'm just not exactly sure how to proceed."

"I think you should talk to Jake. Sounds like he's rational and pragmatic. And maybe this will resolve the other issue at the same time. If you let him know that you know about Ruby

Jean's dilemma, then perhaps it can all be put on the table and dealt with, once and for all."

"That might not be a bad idea. I didn't want to chance making it worse, but it might be the best way to just get it all out there."

"When do you see him again?"

"We just got back from Vegas—"

"Excuse me? Now *you're* running off to Vegas? Do not tell me—"

"No, no," Lauren said, laughing. "Nothing like that." She explained about the race and the investors.

"So, where was I during this lovely plane ride filled with rich, single men?"

"I know, what's up with that?"

"Maybe I need to book a few vacation days myself."

"I wouldn't turn down the company, or having another voice of reason. You could even bunk with me."

Now it was Daphne's turn to laugh. "Right. I'll just pretend I don't notice you and Jake in the other bed."

Lauren actually felt her cheeks heat up. She really had to learn to control that, but with Jake, she seemed destined to become a blusher.

"I'd say you already have enough bunkmates."

"You might be right about that." Lauren was grinning again. It was hard not to when she thought about a certain pilot who would be sleeping beside her that night.

"I'm glad I'm right about that, by the way. Besides, I can't book any time off right now. My best friend went and ditched her job, so I'm stuck trying to train her replacement."

"Very funny. Natalie is like the bionic woman. I'm sure she'll be better in my job than I was."

"She certainly has the right barracuda tendencies for the job."

Lauren laughed. "See? I knew there was something lacking in my approach."

"Mine, too, if that's what they're looking for."

"How is the dynamic with her and Todd? I thought she'd be good for him. I don't think I realized how badly I've been burning out until I worked with her briefly, prepping her, before I left. She's—"

"Bionic. You're right. And yes, she's working with him fine."

"You don't sound overly enthused."

"Oh, I'm fine. She's good, great even. But we won't be best buds. Hard to make friends with a machine. I just miss you and I'm whining a little. I'll get over it. When are you coming back?"

Lauren paused. And then the silence lengthened.

"Seriously?" was all Daphne said.

"I don't know," was all Lauren could say.

"Well, and I mean this, despite the fact that I already know there's a pint of Ben and Jerry's in my immediate future at the prospect of losing you forever, I'm happy for you. And I hope things work out, whatever that means. Your mom is out there now, and your man is there, too. No reason on earth why you shouldn't join them, if it's what you want."

"It's not that simple. I have to figure out who and what I want to be when I grow up. Again." She laughed. "But, in the meantime, while I'm working that part out, no, it's not a bad place to be at all."

"If there's anything I can do to help with the other little detail, please let me know. I don't mind doing some digging of my own, if you need me to. Or making calls to Cedar Springs for you, so you don't have to be obvious about tracking down whoever is making calls about you. Just give me the word."

"Thanks, Daphne," she said, never more sincere. "And, for the record, I don't miss my job, but I miss you terribly. And I do wish you were here."

"Ditto. Hey, I have to run. Let me know how it all shakes out."

"I will." They hung up and Lauren stared at the computer screen and the phone number she'd typed in. She slid in her air card and went online to the reverse directory, but the number came up as unlisted or unknown. "Of course, it couldn't be that simple." She was tempted to just use her motel room phone and call the number—see who answered. But she wasn't sure the direct approach, in this case, was the wisest. Someone was making calls about her and she'd rather not tip them off that she knew about it until she knew a little something about them.

She started to close her computer, then remembered why she'd gotten it out in the first place. She clicked to her desktop, but her neat little rows of shortcut icons were all still lined up, right where she'd left them. She wasn't sure what she was looking for, really. Other than the file she'd scanned some of the articles into, she wasn't actively working on anything, and her e-mail account was security coded. She clicked on that, typed in her password, but nothing new popped up. She went ahead and opened the scanned files one at a time. All of them were there, just like she left them. She sighed. "This is silly." She was playing like she was some kind of super sleuth. "And acting like there's something to be sleuthing." So the maid moved her computer, so what. Stranger things had happened.

Her hand paused on the lid before clicking the screen shut. Stranger things . . . like her bike being stolen, mangled, then returned anonymously to her hotel room. Like someone from Cedar Springs calling her former coworker and asking a bunch of questions about her. Strange things, indeed. She propped the screen back and right-clicked on one of the scanned files, then clicked on Properties. Her fingertips stilled on the mouse buttons. There was the date when the file was last saved. And it was after she'd left her motel room yesterday with her mother . . . but before she'd returned last night.

She curled her fingers inward and moved her hand away from the keyboard, as if it might suddenly bite or something. Her heart rate picked up some speed, but she tried to ignore that and think rationally, calmly. There was an explanation. A simple one. She was sure.

She turned her gaze toward the door to her room. "Yeah," she murmured, "and the easy explanation is that someone has been in my room. More than once." First the bike, now this.

Her first instinct wasn't to call Daphne back, or even her mother, the two go-to people in her world. No, her first instinct was to call Jake. Or better yet, go see him. Only this time it wasn't a flimsy excuse to be in his personal space, nor was it to talk to him about the fact that his sister might be the entire shortlist of who Lauren suspected was behind the disturbing goings-on, or at least strongly involved. Although both of those things were definitely in play. No, her instinct to turn to him was precisely that. She was confused and had some questions, and regardless of what they were about, he was the one she wanted to talk to about them.

"So . . . how about that." She did close the computer then and stood up, needing to move, to think, to not do something foolish because she was thinking with her heart instead of her head.

Should she try to discover the owner of the phone number first? Go to Jake only when she had something concrete to tell him or show him? Would he tell her the truth if confronted without any actual proof?

Wearing a track in the carpet, pacing, wasn't doing anything to solve her dilemma. Jake was trying to protect his sister from something. And he'd also said he was trying to protect her. If she went around digging and inadvertently caused more trouble, for any of the three of them . . . "I need to talk to Jake." One way or the other, that was where whatever happened next had to begin. She crossed to the bed, slid her computer back in the bag, and hefted the shoulder strap over her shoulder. The phone number was there, as were the accumulated articles she'd scanned and the ones she'd copied. It wasn't much, but it was all she had.

She wasn't sure if he was up in the air with a lesson or working on the ground at the moment, but that was okay, she'd wait.

Just as she was heading to the door, someone knocked on it. She froze, then shook her head at herself. "You've got yourself spooked now." She went to the door and peeked through the hole. This time when she went still, it was with reason. She recognized the blond woman on the other side of the door, but only because she'd seen pictures of her when she was much younger. Standing with her grandfather, next to the planes they'd flown in air shows when she was twelve.

She wasn't twelve anymore.

Lauren took a calming breath, squared her shoulders, undid the lock, and opened the door. "Hello, Ruby Jean."

Chapter 21

Jake sat in the front office, looking through the stack of news-papers Lauren had checked out of the library, waiting for Roger to come back on the other end of the phone. She'd meant to return the papers on her way back to town, but had forgotten them with the flight to Vegas.

He flipped through several of them. Most were recent, the past few years, but some were dated some time ago. He'd looked through them once before, when he'd first taken them from her when her mother had unexpectedly shown up. He hadn't done much more than realize that the stories were about various business dealings Arlen had been involved in locally, as well as a few things he'd accomplished as the mayor.

"Hey, Jake, sorry to keep you on hold."

"No problem," Jake said, frowning as he thumbed through one of the older issues Lauren had checked out to read the rest of a smaller front page article. "I hate to bug you with something like this, but I thought you or one of the guys might know something about it."

"Nothing immediate is coming back, but I'm waiting to hear from a few others who might be more connected to what his party is doing in Denver—what their plans are for the upcoming election."

"I really appreciate you looking into it."

"Hey, listen, no problem. Happy to help. So, you looking to back the old man? Because if you think he's a good candidate—"

"It's not that. He's recently married to Lauren's mother. I'm just doing a little background check, is all."

"Ah, I see."

Jake knew that Roger didn't really see that much, and he wanted to keep it that way. "Just trying to figure out the lay of the land, that's all. Lauren's mother is pretty well connected herself . . ."

"Right," Roger said, picking up on his drift. "You just want to make sure the new stepfather isn't taking advantage of the new wife."

"Something like that, yes. And I appreciate you keeping the source of the questions quiet. I don't need to cause any family discord, just—"

"Protecting your own. I completely understand, I'd do the same. You're a stand-up guy." He chuckled. "And your taste in women is certainly not in question, either. Both your sister and your significant other. What do you all drink out there in the hills anyway?"

"It's the clean air. Listen, if I can ever return the favor—"

Roger laughed. "Just win that race and get us up in that clean air in that sweet ride of yours, and I'll be a perfectly happy man."

Jake grinned. "I'll do my best."

"I know you will. That's why we're a team. I'll be in touch."

Jake hung up the phone and checked the clock. He had one last lesson that afternoon, but that wasn't for another hour. He started to gather the stack of papers, then remembered that last little story. It was about the fire out at Arlen's place, the one that had burned his house down. Jake was pretty sure Lauren had snagged the issue because of the big article on the business page about Arlen trying to push through zoning that would enable the resort to extend its commercial properties, which it in fact had, and the town had gone on to benefit pretty handsomely.

Nothing really earth shattering, but part of the pattern that the articles continued to prove over the years.

He flipped the paper in half and read the small blurb in the local news column about the house burning down. It had apparently happened several weeks before this issue had come out and was mostly just a follow up to what had probably been a much bigger story in a previous issue. This was just a tiny side note saying that the fire marshal hadn't been able to determine conclusively what had started the fire.

Jake leaned back in his chair. He was certain Arlen had said it was started by a lightning strike. Jake didn't know a lot about fire investigations, but he didn't think that one would be all that hard to prove, but maybe he was wrong. Arlen seemed certain enough of it. He read through the short column again, but there wasn't even a mention of lightning even being suspected.

Jake started to flip the paper shut, then stood and made a copy of the article for Lauren first before gathering all the papers into a stack. A quick check of the clock showed he had plenty of time to get the papers back to the library before his next lesson. Time enough to look back a few issues and see what had been said when the fire had actually occurred. Not that it mattered, really, but . . . all the same, he was curious now.

He ducked into the library, relieved in this case to see that Becky wasn't on duty. He could avoid making small talk and explaining why he needed to sift through more back issues. It was old Mrs. Peabody instead. She was somewhere between eighty and a hundred, had been head librarian in Cedar Springs as long as Jake had been alive, but now just worked weekends. She'd always favored Jake and Ruby Jean since their parents had died. "Blessed orphans" she'd always called them. Disconcerting when he'd been a child, but oddly comforting since he'd grown up. As he'd explained to Ruby Jean at the time, more people looking out for them was never a bad thing.

"Hello, Mrs. Peabody," he said, raising his voice above the strict library whisper because she was hard of hearing. "You're looking very nice today. New hairstyle? I'm just returning some papers I borrowed from the back room. I'll put them back for you, not to worry." He kept on moving, smiling as he passed by the front desk.

"Why, it's Jake McKenna," she said in her warbling voice, patting her hair and smiling faintly as he went by. "I thought perhaps you no longer took time to read. I haven't seen you in here in ages. Your sister, now, she comes by all the time. Blessed angel, that girl."

"Yes, she is definitely that." He kept on moving. "I won't take long."

"Keep things orderly, young man," she directed to his back, still sporting quite the commanding edge to her wavery tone.

"Yes, ma'am," he said, smiling to himself, comforted by the routine of it all. It was nice that some things never changed.

He already had the stack Lauren checked out in chronological order, so he worked from newest to oldest, sliding the issues back where they'd come from. When he got to the final one, he pulled out the entire hanging folder and starting thumbing through them, assuming a fire taking out the mayor's home would make the front page. "Bingo," he murmured, sliding an issue dated two weeks prior to the one Lauren had checked out. He skimmed the article, looking for any mention of an electrical storm or lightning, but it was something else entirely that caught his attention.

He frowned. "That's . . . interesting." He wasn't sure it was anything more than that, but it got his attention. It was just a few lines in the story. A mention that the fire was an unfortunate tragedy coming at a difficult time for the mayor, who had just recently finalized a divorce with his second wife. Jake hadn't remembered that, but then he'd been too young at the time for those kinds of things to matter. It went on to mention that Paula Thompson had resided in the home after their separation, but had recently relocated out of state. No details had been released regarding where she'd moved, other than a repeat of her formal statement asking that her privacy be respected.

Jake skimmed through the article again, but there was nothing else of interest other than the standard line that the source of the fire was unknown and a quote from the fire marshal assuring that he would be looking into it. Jake wondered what kind of insurance Arlen had had on the house and assumed it was the fire marshal's inability to determine an exact cause that led to the insurance payout, which, in turn, had financed the rebuild. He pulled out the other paper again, but there was no mention of where the mayor was temporarily residing, any insurance issues, or whether he planned to rebuild.

Jake sifted through the papers published for the seven days following the fire, but, other than a comment Arlen made thanking the citizens of Cedar Springs for their support during a speech given at an awards banquet for the local high school sports teams, he couldn't find anything. He checked his watch, swore under his breath, then did a quick search back through another month of articles, not having much time to do more than skim the front pages. He found two articles regarding the mayor's divorce. Without questioning the instinct, he slipped those issues, along with the one containing the story on the fire, into the tote.

He wanted to show them to Lauren, but first he wanted to run the subject by his sister. She'd been far too young to really remember anything about the fire or divorce back when it had happened, but Ruby Jean had an interest in town lore and a knack for recalling an almost disturbing quantity of details on even the most arcane of town topics. Couldn't hurt to pick her brain over anything she might have gleaned about the town's view on both events in the mayor's life.

He glanced at his watch and quickly slid everything back where it belonged. He debated on explaining to Mrs. Peabody that he was borrowing a few additional back issues of the local paper and risk being late for his next lesson, but when he emerged from the back, he found her in conversation with Arlen's secretary, Melissa, who was heaving a stuffed tote bag onto the return counter.

He gave them both a smile and a nod. "Thank you, Mrs. Peabody."

"Surprised to see you here. I thought Ruby Jean was the big reader in the family," Melissa said, turning so he had no choice but to slow down.

"I was just saying the very same thing," Mrs. Peabody offered.

Jake forced a smile. Melissa had moved to Cedar Springs several years before. She was around RJ's age, but that hadn't stopped his sister from trying to fix them up. After all, Melissa was single with a pulse. She seemed like a perfectly nice woman, was attractive enough, and had made it clear on more than one occasion that his interest would likely be returned, but he'd never pursued it. He'd told himself it was because she worked with his sister, but the truth was, she simply wasn't his type. Which he couldn't have described . . . until recently.

"Well, I'd read more, but between the two of you, it appears there isn't much selection left." He nodded toward the bulging bag.

Melissa laughed. "Oh, those are donations. The mayor donates back issues of his magazines and has urged the local businesses to do the same. Just doing my bimonthly collection run." Her smile brightened. "I don't suppose you could be talked out of copies of *Aviation Monthly*?"

"Those are sacred, I'm afraid. Sorry to run off, but I have a lesson waiting. A pleasure seeing you again, Mrs. Peabody. Keep doing that thing with the hair. Very flattering."

Mrs. Peabody's papery smooth cheeks flushed and Melissa laughed. "Now I understand why I could never turn your head. You prefer a more mature woman."

Jake kept smiling and heading out the door, but almost stumbled over his own feet when he heard Mrs. Peabody reply, "Oh, his head has been turned all right, but not by my thin blue hair."

Jake opted not to listen in on where that particular conversation was headed. He had no problem with Mrs. Peabody spreading the word that he was otherwise involved, especially to Melissa. It just felt somehow . . . naughty that the octogenarian he'd known since prepuberty had any knowledge of his very adult social life. "Bad images," he muttered with a little shudder, and immediately turned his mind to other things.

Like getting through this next lesson so he could see Lauren.

"Definitely better images." He slid his phone out as he climbed into Xavier's borrowed truck and punched the number for his sister. He wanted to get her take on things before talking to Lauren. Plus he wanted to persuade her that bringing Lauren in wouldn't jeopardize anything.

Ruby Jean didn't answer, so he left a quick message, then got a beep telling him there was a message waiting. It turned out to be a voice mail from Roger. Who, as it turned out, had some interesting information of his own. He clicked off after listening and tried Ruby Jean again. They definitely needed to talk. The sooner the better. It went straight to her voice mail. "Call me, RJ," he said, "we need to talk. It's four now. I'll be teaching for the next hour. Better yet, be waiting for me when I touch down. It's about . . . the matter we discussed the other day."

He clicked off, tossed his phone on the passenger seat, and slid on his sunglasses. All traces of good humor gone.

Chapter 22

"I hope you don't mind my barging over like this without calling first, but—I've been dying to meet you!"

Ruby Jean was a bundle of beautiful blond ringlets bouncing around a face that belonged on a forties' pinup calendar, complete with rose bud lips and sparkling blue eyes. Her smile was bright, her laugh infectious, and she was basically impossible not to like on sight. Which made the whole phone call thing a bit more challenging to confront.

"No, no, not at all," Lauren said, scrambling to figure out just how she wanted this surprise meeting to go. What to say, what to reveal. Maybe it was best to focus on meeting her as Jake's sister, first, then see how things progressed from there. "Come on in."

"Oh," Ruby Jean said, noting the computer bag on her shoulder. "You were just heading out, weren't you?"

"I—" Lauren looked at her bag and slid it from her shoulder. "Nothing pressing, really." She propped the bag next to the sliding closet door. "I wish I had something to offer you, but—"

"No, not necessary." She laughed. "I'd ask you out to have a drink and a bite, but then we'd be on the six o'clock news."

"You have a local news station?"

Ruby Jean laid her hand on Lauren's arms and squeezed as she laughed again. "No, no, I was just kidding. But, wow, you should have seen your face just now. Have we truly been that awful?"

It was really, really hard not to like her. In fact, had they met under any other circumstances, despite the obvious difference in their ages, Lauren would have bonded with her instantly. "Well . . ." She let the word trail off, but smiled herself—it was impossible not to—and shrugged.

"I'm really sorry. I officially apologize for every man, woman, and dog in Cedar Springs. Twice for the women, because they're the ones probably talking the most. We're really not that bad." She sighed. "Okay, we're totally that bad. Worse, probably. But to know us is to love us . . . warts, gossip mongering, and all. We're not close minded, and if it makes you feel any better, everything I've heard about you has been positive. Well, except perhaps for a few of the singles who were holding out hope that Jake might still look in their direction."

"Ruby Jean, I—"

"Don't you even think about apologizing for snatching my brother from the jaws of bachelorhood. If they could have pulled that off, they'd have done it by now."

Lauren smiled. "I'm glad you feel that way, because I wasn't going to say I'm sorry. He's about the best thing that's ever happened to me. I was going to say I hope you can get used to him dating an outsider, since I'm pretty sure neither one of us is interested in stopping." Her smile grew to a grin. "And I'd hate to come between a guy and his sister."

Ruby Jean took a step back and sized her up and down. "Damn, but I like you. Thank God my blind brother finally opened his eyes. I guess now that I've met you I can see why he's waited all this time."

Lauren breathed a sigh of relief. "And I'm really glad you're okay with it, because he loves you more than anything and I'm pretty sure nothing is ever going to come between that bond. Nor should it."

"I wouldn't be so sure about that," she said, a considering

note still in her tone but approval still on her face. "Hopefully we won't ever have to find out."

"Hopefully not, no."

Now that the pleasantries were out of the way, Lauren wasn't really sure where to lead the conversation. She'd just gained favor with the person most important to Jake and so it seemed foolish to jeopardize that, but . . . she had to know eventually, so might as well ask now. "Can I ask you something? And I hope you take it in the spirit it's intended, which is just pure curiosity."

Ruby Jean looked intrigued. "Sure, anything."

"If you love your brother even half as much as he loves you, and I can see the bond is tight both ways, then it makes sense that you'd want to make sure anyone he's seeing is on the up and up . . ."

Ruby Jean's smile faded, but her expression was simply one of open curiosity. "Go on."

"So . . . by any chance, have you been doing any, well . . . background checks on me? Or, you know, just fact-finding kind of stuff?"

Now she frowned. "No. Do you have some reason to think I did?"

Lauren looked at her perfect Kewpie doll face, but wasn't fooled into thinking there wasn't a razor-sharp mind behind the blond curls and perfectly applied lip liner. Lauren was a pretty good read on people and, as far as she could tell, Ruby Jean had no idea what she was talking about. "Well, someone has been calling my office and asking questions about me. As I said, I understand, I just—"

"It wasn't me, but . . . you know it was someone from Cedar Springs?"

Lauren nodded. "The phone number is local."

"Do you have the number? I mean, maybe I recognize it."

"I don't want to put you in any kind of awkward situation."

"I can't see how it would. By the way, I was the one who bugged Jake to take you out on a date. I already knew what I needed to know from what Arlen and your mother told me about you before you got here. Although, I have to say, you're a bit different than I expected."

Now it was Lauren's turn to lift an eyebrow. "Really? How?"

"Don't worry. Different in a good way. It's just, Arlen told me who you worked for and your mom told me how dedicated you were to your job, and I guess I sensed that she worried you didn't take much time off."

Lauren fought a smile. "And you knew my mom and I were having problems and thought your brother might be able to smooth out a few of my uptight, Washington woman, workaholic tendencies?"

Ruby Jean flushed a little, but her smile was undaunted. "Something like that."

Lauren grinned. "Good call."

Ruby Jean's rich laughter filled the room and Lauren couldn't help but join in. "Well, maybe it was the glasses and the tight ponytail, but I thought you might be a bit . . ."

"Prudish? Stiff?"

"Washington D.C.-ish," she said. "Which is a lot different than Colorado."

"That is true." Lauren leaned in closer. "Can I ask you all what the secret is?"

"Secret?"

"There is enough vitality and energy in this town alone to single-handedly fix the energy crisis if we could find a way to channel it. It's like you're all—"

"High?" she said on a laugh.

"No. Well, not loopy high."

They both laughed again. "I don't know," Ruby Jean said. "We have stresses and things we worry about, just like the next person, but the air is cleaner up here, and when you look out on that view every day . . ."

Lauren sighed a little. "Yeah, I know. It's already grown on me. And my mother is acting like she's found the fountain of youth." She glanced out the big picture window looking out the back of her motel room toward the river and peaks that loomed beyond. "Maybe she has," she added, more to herself than Ruby Jean.

"I like your mom. She's really so accomplished and just so . . . well, graceful and elegant. But down to earth, too. I'm not sure what she sees in Arlen," she added with a laugh, "but I'm sure glad she did, because we all love her a lot. We're all glad you came out."

Lauren turned back to Ruby Jean, wondering if she'd meant that comment about Arlen as the kind of toss-off thing that someone says, being self-deprecating, or if she really meant it. She knew Ruby Jean worked for him, so she had to think before she spoke out of turn. It was one thing for her to be honest with her mother about her feelings, but she didn't have to make things awkward or difficult for her mother, either, by allowing word to get back to Arlen about her continued concerns.

"What did I say?" Ruby Jean asked, her tone sincere.

Good thing Lauren didn't have plans on a new future playing poker. "No, it was nothing."

"Just . . . you really don't know what your mother sees in Arlen?" she asked gently. "It's okay, you can be honest with me. I'm loyal as the sky is blue, but I choose my loyalties wisely. I work for Arlen and I do a good job. But I have a much stronger duty to my brother, and by extension to those he cares for. He cares a great deal for you."

Lauren glanced up at her then, unable to hide her curiosity, wondering what Jake had said to his only family member about her. He'd made it clear, as had Ruby Jean in their short acquaintance, that he wasn't apparently the settling kind.

Ruby Jean smiled quickly and reached out once again to squeeze Lauren's arm. "Don't worry, it's all good. He's totally head over heels. I'm loving every minute of it. Heck, the whole town is. We've all waited a long time to finally see him fall. And it's turning out to be well worth the wait."

"I'm relieved you all feel that way." And she was. Instead of feeling pressured or trapped, she was truly thankful. It was a nice thing to know. "I'm not sure how I'd hold up otherwise. You're a pretty formidable lot."

"We take care of our own. Your mom is one of our own now. Not just because she's the mayor's wife, but because we've all genuinely come to like her. I don't think I've heard a single soul say an unkind thing. That's not to say we didn't do our share of gossiping and wondering when word came back that our long-divorced mayor was coming back from the conference with a wife. I mean, you can imagine."

"I'm not sure I want to," Lauren said wryly.

Ruby Jean laughed. "Oh, we did our research and quick. And naturally, when we found out she was all but East Coast political blue blood, we were . . . even more curious."

"You're being polite."

"Yes," she said bluntly, but smiling, "I am. As I said, we can be pretty awful, but we hadn't met her yet. We honestly didn't know what to expect. But given Arlen's past two wives—" She immediately stopped.

"It's okay," Lauren told her, then leaned in again. "I'm from Washington. We dig dirt better than anybody. I did my homework, too."

Ruby Jean sighed in relief. "Good. And he's been widowed and divorced a long, long time. In fact, we all sort of thought he'd kind of put himself out to pasture, more or less. Either that or he was having a very discreet relationship with someone in some other town. And there aren't any around here, so that would take some doing. Still, it circled the rumor mills more than once."

"Was it? Just a rumor?"

"I know the schedule the man keeps because I'm the one who books it. Trust me, if he was having a relationship of any kind with anyone, anywhere, no way would I not know about it. Or at least suspect it."

"I didn't think that, either." Lauren looked away, certain she wasn't doing any better a job in hiding her real feelings now than before.

"Hey, don't worry. If you did your homework then you know that Arlen is from the West Coast, originally, and while his pedigree isn't quite like yours or your mother's, it's not country bumpkin politics, either."

"Oh, I never meant to infer—"

"No, I know. But, I'm just saying, Arlen married the bluest of blue bloods Cedar Springs could claim with his first marriage, and his second . . . well, no one knew Paula all that well from what I've gathered, but she did come from a privileged background, as well. So your mother and Arlen might have more in common than you think. We certainly weren't surprised to learn that was who he'd fallen for. We just weren't sure what to expect. According to the older members of our community, Cindy, his first wife, was very social, very outgoing, and though a bit of a princess, she truly enjoyed her role as the mayor's wife, and not just for the luncheons. She was a good volunteer and had her causes, as well. But she was raised here and had the core, small town values we'd all been raised with, so it made it hard for her to be too high and mighty."

"And Paula?"

"Total opposite on that score. More what you'd probably expect from someone with wealth. And she wasn't from here, either, and kept to herself rather than try to connect with the townspeople, so that didn't help her cause. She was a lot younger than the mayor, but smart, independent in her own right from what I know."

"I read she had several degrees and sat on a national board or two, which was impressive at her age."

"Family related, I think, but yes. She was reputed to be very . . . focused. But the word was what she was focused on was having a baby."

"I heard. Which never happened. It led to their divorce?"

"I'm sure it was part of it. I was too young to remember it directly, but Arlen marrying your mom brought all the old stories to the surface, so I've heard my fair share recently and that's pretty much the general conclusion. The divorce was quick and quiet. She left the area, he stayed, and that was the end of that."

She smiled. "Until he runs off umpty-ump years later and elopes with your mom. Pretty romantic is how I see it."

"Do you?" Lauren heard herself ask before thinking better of it.

"Well, maybe not in the traditional "swept off her feet" kind of way, but they are an older generation and it's clear they have great respect for one another."

"Having seen them together over time now, would you say you can see them as the eloping kind of couple?" Ruby Jean got a sort of deer in headlights kind of look on her face and Lauren felt instantly contrite. "I'm sorry, I shouldn't put you in the middle like that. Forget I said that."

"No, you just caught me off guard." She gave Lauren a considering look. "You want an honest answer?"

"Not if you'll feel awkward or uncomfortable giving it."

"No, but this is just between you and me."

"Agreed."

"For most of my adult life, Arlen has been a bachelor. He definitely appreciates a pretty face, as do most men as far as I can tell, but he's never been what you'd call a ladies' man. Hard to do in a small town."

"A small town with a large tourism base."

"True. And, to be honest, though I do control his schedule, it's hard to say what he does—or did—with his personal time. He might very well have enjoyed the company of women passing through. But if he did, he was very, very discreet about it because I've never once heard about it. All I'm saying is that while he's definitely a man's man, he doesn't strike me as the kind of man who puts that as a high priority."

"That meaning romance, or sex?"

"However you want to define it, yes. He has always been pretty focused on his work, on getting things done. That seems to be where he derives most of his satisfaction. Some men are like that. Workaholics to the extent where the personal life is always secondary."

Lauren smiled. "I don't mean this to sound denigrating, as I know he's been the mayor here for a very long time and has been credited with doing a lot of good work for your town. But is being mayor here such an all consuming thing? Especially for a man who has been doing it as long as he has?"

"He has other interests. His ranch, state politics, and other business interests in Denver and still back in California. I'm just saying that that seems to be more what drives him. We were surprised when he up and eloped, because, no, he doesn't seem the eloping type, despite being married twice."

"But he did."

"And so did your mother, who I get the impression didn't seem the eloping type, either. Who knows why they did? They might not be the traditional newlyweds, but they do make a handsome couple and they do have common interests, and they both seem to be happy. I'm just happy for them that they found that much. It seems to work for them."

"Yes, yes it does," Lauren said, thinking maybe Ruby Jean had hit on it after all. That Arlen derived his satisfaction from work. Maybe her mother was the woman best suited to understand that and still provide the kind of companionship he needed. And maybe that level of companionship was all her mother wanted as she embarked on a search that was more about self-discovery. "Thank you."

"For?"

"The clarity I desperately needed. I think I finally get it. And I really, really wanted to get it."

Ruby Jean smiled, clearly not understanding all the undercurrents, but not having to. "You're welcome. Glad I could help. Now . . . how about that phone number? Maybe we can find some clarity there, too."

She smiled that Kewpie doll smile with her pinup girl face and Lauren sort of stared.

"What?" Ruby Jean asked good-naturedly at Lauren's staring.

"It's just . . . did you seriously used to walk on the wings of airplanes?"

"Seriously," she deadpanned, then laughed her delightful laugh. "But then, it's not the kind of thing you do jokingly."

Lauren laughed with her. "I'm really glad you dropped by today. Seriously." She went over and grabbed her computer bag. "You know, if it wasn't you making the call to my old co-worker, I don't know who it would be." She slid out her laptop and propped it up on the dresser to boot it up. "Okay, here it is." She rattled off the number and turned to find Ruby Jean standing there looking rather dumbfounded.

Lauren's relief at thinking maybe she'd finally come to terms with Arlen did a rapid fade. "That's not a good expression right there."

"That's my phone number."

"What?"

"My personal office number. Only I didn't make any calls about you to anyone. Well, other than the one I made to my brother to ask him to fly you in from the airport."

"Does anyone share your office?"

"I have my own office, but it's not a big operation, so we're all in and out of each other's areas all the time. But generally don't use each other's phones as a rule."

"How many numbers does your office have?"

"Three. The main office line, which goes to Melissa's desk and connects to all of our offices; my office line is the secondary one, and Arlen has a private line."

"Is your number advertised along with the main number, or just—"

"No, just the main one."

"Would anyone other than Melissa or Arlen use your phone?"

"Meaning was it definitely one of them? I guess it would be highly likely, but then why not just use their own?"

"So it tracks back to you?"

Ruby Jean smiled. "How paranoid should we be about this?"

Lauren smiled briefly. "I just want to know who's been asking questions about me. It was a woman who called, so I'm
guessing Melissa, then. But why would she do that, unless—"

"Arlen asked her to? If he's been concerned about your
mom—"

"The call was made after I got here and met with them. My
mom and I patched things up pretty quickly. So . . . I'm not sure
why he'd be following up at that point. I hadn't told my mother
I'd left my job yet—"

"You left your job?" Ruby Jean's mouth fell open, then quickly
snapped shut. "Was it because of your mom?"

"Yes, I did, and no, it wasn't about her moving out here. Apparently Arlen found out from whatever contacts he has in D.C.
and told my mom before I could. But he's had opportunity to
ask me directly—privately or openly—whatever he wanted to
know. If he was concerned about my future prospects, I'm not
sure why he'd use such a convoluted path and not just ask outright. So . . . something isn't adding up."

But what else is new, Lauren thought. Every time she took a
step forward with coming to terms with all the various ele-
ments, something else would pop up. "Playing devil's advocate
and assuming he did initiate the call, why the call from his office? Even if he put Melissa up to it, it seems, I don't know . . .
sloppy. If you're going to go to all the trouble to be stealthy
about it, why do something so obvious? It's not making sense."

"I agree." Ruby Jean looked at Lauren. "So . . . are you back
to wondering if it was me?"

"What? No. We might have only just met, but no, I believe
you." And Lauren did. Not just because she was Jake's sister
and therefore somehow automatically trustworthy. But standing here in front of her, looking at her, listening to her . . . no,
she didn't think Ruby Jean McKenna was a flat-out liar.

"So . . . ?"

"So, I don't know. I'm not sure it matters; it was harmless, I
guess, but—"

"But if someone was calling around, digging into my business on some kind of pretense, I'd want to know. Regardless of the motivation."

"I agree. You know your boss far better than I do, so, speaking strictly between us, is this behind-the-scenes maneuvering the kind of thing he would be involved in?"

"Let me ask you first . . . what is your take on him? I'm a little behind the curve here with where things stand in your family and—none of my business there, so I'm not asking—but it would help if I knew a little of your mind-set before talking out of school."

"Understood, and I admire the integrity. And the loyalty. So, my thinking is, he keeps tabs on the goings-on in Washington, which says to me that despite being out of the faster moving political circles of San Francisco for a significant period of time, and never moving up into the ranks in Colorado, he still has a very keen interest in the political world beyond his small town. Whether that means he still has ambitions, I couldn't say. But he keeps close enough tabs to know about the change in my employment situation, which, trust me, was not news, even back in D.C. Staffers, even highly placed ones, come and go all the time. Unless there's scandal attached, no one really pays attention other than those directly affected by the change. But Arlen knew. And he told my mother before I could, whatever his real reasons."

Lauren held Ruby Jean's gaze, wanting to gauge her reaction as closely as she could as she continued. "He also strikes me as a man who, as you say, is very dedicated to his work, and from what I've read about him—and when your mom runs off with a total stranger, you can dig up an enormous amount of stuff to read if you really want to—I get the sense that he's all about getting the job done, whatever that may be. And he's perfectly willing to use whatever means it takes, or whomever he needs to use or step over, to get the job done."

Ruby Jean would make a great poker player. Which, with her face, said a surprising lot. After an extended pause, she said, "So, I take that as a yes, then."

Lauren bit back a surprised laugh. "Um, yes. No offense to you, his loyal adviser and assistant. But my gut tells me that he would have no trouble making such decisions if he felt the ends justified the means."

Ruby Jean tilted her head. "You've been around politicians for a long time. I'm much newer to the game. How often are you wrong in your gut assessments?"

"At your stage in the game, often enough. In recent years? Rarely."

Ruby Jean nodded. "Then I'd go with your gut on this one."

Not exactly an open slam against her boss, which was to her credit. But the point had been made, tacitly nonetheless. Lauren nodded. "Thank you. I appreciate your candor."

Ruby Jean shrugged. "I'm not really good with subterfuge. Ask Jake." She grinned then. "Perhaps my future in politics will be limited a bit by that fact."

"Are you hoping for a future in politics? Personally, or in an adjunct role, like I had?"

"I don't know," she said, sounding sincere but not exactly uncertain. "I think I mostly want to find some kind of direction, and I'm good at what I do, so why not follow that path to wherever it might lead?"

Lauren thought about that . . . and wondered where Ruby Jean saw her path as the personal executive assistant to a small town mayor could take her. Unless she planned to parlay that in some way to one of the larger cities on the front range or beyond.

"Have you thought about leaving Cedar Springs, moving on to a bigger pond, bigger fish?"

"More lately than ever before. I'm torn on that, though. My preference is to stay here. I'm not particularly driven to be a city girl. But I'm not sure I can fulfill whatever potential I might have if I stay here. I'm not even sure what's out there for me. But I do know what's here . . . and so far it hasn't been challenging enough for me."

Lauren thought again about whatever it was that had put

Jake in an awkward place between her and Ruby Jean. And wondered if they'd shared enough, bonded enough, for her to just come out and ask. Her gut said yes. And Ruby Jean had been the one to tell her to go with that. So she did. "There's something else I need to ask you. And I'll understand if you don't want to discuss it, but it's created something of an issue between me and Jake. And so I thought, now that we've met, maybe we can just bring it out in the open and deal with it together."

Ruby Jean frowned at first, but that quickly cleared and Lauren knew she was very aware of what Lauren was referring to. No poker face this time.

Just then Lauren's phone rang. It was Jake. "Hey there, I was—"

"Hey, yourself," he said, his voice doing to her all the good things it always did. "Think you can head up this way? I have some interesting information for you. I was trying to track down Ruby Jean, but—"

"She's standing right here. Want to talk to her?"

"She's—really?"

Lauren laughed. The Jake she was coming to know was rarely caught speechless. "Yes. She dropped by to say hi and introduce herself. It's turning out the McKenna family is a pretty spectacular bunch."

Ruby Jean grinned as Jake laughed. "I'm very glad you think so. Why don't you both come up? Three heads might be better than one."

He sounded jovial enough, but Lauren had already come to know him well enough to hear the underpinnings of tension. "Everything okay?"

"Yep. Interesting, but okay."

She frowned. "Okay. We'll be right there." Ruby Jean was also frowning now as Lauren closed her phone. "Your brother wants us both up at the school. Can you go?"

"Sure. Want me to drive?"

"I've got Jake's Jeep. I can give you a lift."

Ruby Jean smiled again. "Why don't I follow you up." She walked to the door. "Then you won't have to be giving me a lift back into town. You know, if you wanted to hang out up at the school. Or something."

Lauren scooped up her laptop and bag and grabbed the Jeep keys. "Did I mention how smart the McKennas arc?" She was smiling as she followed Ruby Jean out the door.

Chapter 23

Jake paced to the open door of the hangar housing *Betty Sue*, then back to the plane.

"You expecting Santa Claus or something, son?" This was from Freddy. He was one of Paddy's old pals. He and four of the other guys had driven in earlier to start work on *Betty Sue*.

Jake threw him a grin. "Better, really." He'd been caught off guard by the news that his sister and Lauren had been becoming fast friends while he was struggling, trying to figure out if the puzzle pieces he was collecting amounted to a bigger picture worth assembling, or if he was just wasting his valuable time on nothing. He was glad they'd already met. Relieved, really. If they hadn't already broached the whole "Arlen running for governor" thing, he hoped there would be no reason to hedge on it now.

"What's she look like?" This from Ace, who was even older than Freddy, who'd hit eighty-five earlier that month.

"What makes you think it's a woman?" Jake asked.

"Man smiles like that . . . it's always a woman." All four men had finished that last part in unison. They all chuckled and Jake joined them.

"You'll meet her in a few minutes. She's coming up with RJ. I'll need to take a short break, go talk with them about something. But I'll be back. Scooter radioed that he'd be flying in sometime after seven with the parts from Fort Collins."

"Good job."

"I've got rooms for you guys down the hill at Rosie's—"

"We brought our cots. We're bunking out here with *Betty Sue.*"

"Guys, no need. We're well funded enough that you shouldn't have to rough it like that. I can—"

"You go spend time with the woman of your dreams," Ace said, then glanced up at *Betty Sue,* whose propellers he was currently working on. "I'll spend time with mine." He gave a little burnish to one of the blades.

The other men chuckled and Jake grinned. "Okay, but we're catering in meals. And if you change your mind, or your back and knees change it for you, just let me know."

There was a bathroom and full shower facilities in the big hangar, which Paddy had put in back when he bunked at the school while building it into a functioning business. Had it been any other time of year, Jake would have insisted they take the rooms. "Just make sure to roll the doors shut and start the space heaters when the sun dips." Jake heard his Jeep crunching gravel in the lot outside and walked to the door. "I don't need any of you guys kicking the bucket this close to race time."

They all good-naturedly handed it right back to him. "Whaddya mean? We're living forever, don't you know?"

"I'll be the one delivering your eulogy, son," Oscar chimed in, and they all laughed.

"Keep an eye on them, Hank," Jake said, still chuckling.

The hound managed a single tail thump, then went back to sleep underneath Ace's camp chair.

Jake strolled outside, feeling a lot better about things on the race end now that the guys had started showing up. He'd be right alongside them tonight, working well toward the wee hours. But first, he needed to take care of this so he could get his focus back. And so he could get things fully back on track with Lauren.

He hadn't known what to expect from the Lauren–Ruby

Jean summit meeting he'd missed, but RJ pulled in right behind
Lauren and by the time he got across the tarmac to the parking
area, they were already shoulder to shoulder, laughing and in
deep conversation. He'd wanted them to hit it off, but seeing
them like that had his steps slowing. And his heart filling. It
had been important to him, but he hadn't any idea how much it
meant. Or would mean. To have the woman he wanted to spend
his life with bond so truly to the only other love in his life. Between the funding for the *Betty Sue,* and now this, life was
pretty damn sweet. "You are one very lucky man," he murmured to himself, picking up the pace again as they spotted
him and headed his way.

He got possibly the two best hugs of his life, then slung his
arms around their shoulders and guided them toward the front
school office.

"So . . . what's shaking, big brother?" RJ asked.

"Let's get inside," he said, then turned toward Lauren and
dropped a quick kiss on the side of her neck below her ear.
"Damn, I've missed you," he whispered in her ear.

She turned and smiled directly into his gaze and, in that crys-
tallized moment, there wasn't a single doubt in his mind. He
was in love with Lauren Matthews.

"All right, you two," RJ said, nudging him in the ribs with
her girl weapon elbow.

"Seriously, that thing is so pointy," he said, ducking out of
the way of another jab and bumping hips with Lauren.

They stumbled together into the office, laughing and joking
and he seriously debated whether or not to just chuck the
whole Arlen issue out the window. Only he was RJ's boss and
Lauren's stepfather . . . and the subject was just going to come
up again and again until it was deliberated and discussed and
finally put to rest. Might as well get it all out on the table now.
Then he could focus on the race. He glanced at Lauren. And to
do whatever he had to in order to convince this woman to stick
around for, oh, the next sixty or seventy years.

"So, I've been doing a little digging," he said, motioning

them toward the other office chairs as he spun his around and took a seat. He glanced at his sister. "Have you two talked about . . . you know?"

She glanced at Lauren. "We were just about to when you called."

"You okay if we just proceed with everything on the table?"

"Yeah," she said, then smiled at Lauren. "I'm okay with it."

"Thank you," Lauren said. "You can trust me."

RJ nodded, then looked back to Jake. "What have you been digging up? Anything having to do with that phone call to Lauren's old coworker, by any chance?"

Jake frowned. "No. Why, did you two find out anything?"

"I talked to Daphne again," Lauren said. "She back-tracked the number of the person who called about me. The number is local here."

"It's my office number, Jake. But I didn't make the call."

Jake looked between them. "Who do you think, then?"

They both shrugged. "That's what we were talking about."

"Daphne said it was a woman. So, could be his secretary."

"Melissa? I don't know why she'd—"

"If Arlen asked her to," Ruby Jean said with a shrug.

Jake leaned back. "Sure, okay, but why?"

"We don't know," RJ said. "What did you find out?"

"I took those papers back to the library," he said to Lauren, "but before I did, I found a little blurb in one of the older ones about the fire that burned down Arlen's house."

"That's a very old issue. Why did you have old newspapers out?" Ruby Jean asked.

"Part of that 'researching the total stranger my mom married' thing."

"Ah," Ruby Jean said, clearly completely understanding.

Jake looked between them and realized they'd bonded even more tightly, more swiftly than he'd realized. And while this made him very happy, he was also quickly realizing that this could give RJ an ally at times when he'd have liked to keep things more even. Ah well, the price one paid he supposed. And was quite willing to make the sacrifice. But that didn't mean he wouldn't whine a little about it.

"What about the fire?" Lauren asked. "I'm assuming you mean the one that burned his house down forcing the rebuild?"

"Yes, it was just a little blurb saying that the fire marshal couldn't determine—conclusively—what had been the cause of the fire."

"I thought he said it was lightning."

"I know. Maybe that's hard to prove, I don't know. But when I took the papers back, I went ahead and dug a little farther back and found the original article about the fire. No mention there, either, about any storm or lightning strikes in the area. There was a mention that this fire took place just as he was finalizing his divorce from Paula."

RJ glanced at Lauren, who was looking at him. "Meaning?"

Jake shrugged. "I'm not sure. I don't even know why it caught my attention; it just did. I have the issue with me if you want to look at it."

"Do you think he was burning down the house as a way of keeping his soon-to-be ex from getting her hands on it?" RJ asked.

"I have no idea. I was trying to reach you to see what you might know of that time. I know you were way too young to remember, but—"

"Given my penchant for town gossip, you mean?" she said pointedly but with a laugh. "I prefer to think of it as collecting town lore and history, but yes, that kind of thing does interest me. However, if you'd asked me more than six months ago, I'd have said I got nothing. But since Arlen's recent marriage—" she nodded with a smile toward Lauren—"the older citizens here have been replaying his first two marriages, and in some pretty great detail, given the way they both ended."

"And? Anything that might shed some light?"

"Well . . . hmm, let me think. Paula was pretty well off, an heiress in her own right, if not actually in possession of her inheritance at the time of their marriage. She was due to inherit after her father passed, and she was a very late-in-life baby for him, so it wasn't a distant future kind of thing. So I don't know how badly she'd have wanted their house or property. She wasn't from here and cut out of town before the ink was dry on the divorce documents. Doesn't sound like someone after amassing assets here."

"Could have just been for spite. Was it an acrimonious split?"

RJ shrugged. "Not as far as I've heard. From the stories being rehashed, it was more about their inability to procreate."

"Did Arlen want a family, too?" Lauren asked.

"He never said he didn't—wouldn't play well to the voters, for one—but the consensus seems to indicate she was far more dedicated to the idea than he was."

"Why not adopt?"

"I think it had something to do with her inheritance passing down only to blood relatives. I don't know, but that was the rumor. Anyway, the split was fast and she was gone, never heard from again."

"The article said she'd been staying out at the house prior to the fire, but they didn't know for sure if she was still living there when it burned or if she'd already left," Jake told them. "There was no one at home at the time, and only Arlen stepped forward afterward. When asked, he said his ex had moved to an undisclosed location and wished to have her privacy respected. The divorce was final days later."

Neither RJ nor Lauren said anything for a few moments.

"Like I said, I don't know why the story mattered, but . . ."

"His first wife died in a car crash, driving drunk, right?" Lauren asked.

Ruby Jean nodded.

"And he didn't stand to get anything from her family, did he?"

"Other than their goodwill and what he'd already gotten as

their son-in-law, no. Not if you mean specific assets or anything."

"There was talk that he'd hoped her family would help him gain a more visible role in Denver politics and perhaps make a run for higher office. Then Cindy died, and that was that." Jake looked at his sister, and she gave a little nod. "Until now," he added.

"Yes, until now," RJ said. "Has your mother said anything to you about Arlen having political plans that might involve him making a run for a different office?"

Lauren's mouth dropped open, then snapped shut. "No. What office?"

RJ leaned in. "This is strictly, strictly in confidence. He let it slip to me. No one, and I mean no one, knows. If this gets out, he'll know it was me and I'll lose my job. I don't want to put you in an awkward spot with your mother, but—"

"It's okay. I'll respect your privacy."

RJ glanced again at Jake, then looked at Lauren and said, "He's supposedly putting together a team, and the financial backing, to make a push to get on the ticket for governor of Colorado next year."

If Lauren's mouth had dropped open a moment ago, she appeared truly shocked this time.

"That's the complication," Jake said, leaning forward and putting his hand on her knees. "I hope you understand why I had to—"

"I do," Lauren said. She covered his hand with her own. "I totally do." She looked at RJ. "He just let this slip? No offense, but he doesn't strike me as the type to let something as major as that slip by accident. Could he have 'slipped' it to you on purpose? And if so, any ideas why?"

RJ wasn't offended by the question. "Trust me, I've thought about that. It could have been a loyalty test. To see if I was trustworthy enough to be asked along on the ride. That's the most logical."

"Do you think maybe that's behind the calls about me to Washington? Just fact-finding to make sure he's bulletproof from any surprises? Make sure I wasn't fired for some unreported scandal?"

"Could be, I suppose. He's . . . well, he's not paranoid by nature, but he's a very cautious, very meticulous planner. He hates mistakes and hates things going wrong that he could have otherwise controlled."

"Micromanager?" Lauren asked.

"In some ways. More a microplanner. Once he's set on a path, he doesn't mind delegating."

"So, if the call tied into his campaign prep in some way, and the call came from a woman in your office and that woman wasn't you . . . the finger points toward Melissa," Lauren said. "Do you think he's let it 'slip' to her, too? That maybe she's his secret campaign worker bee here on site?"

That sat RJ back in her seat. "I'd have said no, but, you know . . . I guess it's possible. I'm definitely his right hand and Melissa is kept pretty much to her secretarial role, but . . ." She trailed off.

"But, what?" Jake asked. "Does she seem hungry for advancement? Do you think she has her sights set bigger?"

RJ lifted a shoulder. "I'd have said she had her sights set on finding a man and getting out of the workforce altogether. She's not a traditional, white picket fence and babies type, but I never got the sense she was in her job with an eye toward a long-term career. More just biding her time and enjoying the elevated awareness that being the mayor's secretary brought to her, in terms of impressing her dates."

"Who does she date? Anyone special?"

RJ smirked. "You mean after Jake dissed her?"

"I didn't diss her, I politely declined your attempts to match us up."

"She mostly dates out-of-towners," RJ said. "Resort guests, especially the ones with deeper pockets."

"What's her background?" Lauren asked. "She's not from around here, is she?"

RJ shook her head. "Came to town following her ski bum boyfriend, liked the resort town life. They broke up, she started seeing another instructor, got her own place, and they didn't last—big shock; I could have told her never to cast her lot in that direction, confirmed bachelors and playboys, all—and she took the job with Arlen, and . . . here she still is."

"Is there any way that perhaps Arlen is positioning her for the transition team given she has no ties here?"

Jake looked to his sister, who was clearly giving the question serious thought. "I've never thought about it that way," he said. "Have you?"

"No. He treats her, well, very stereotypically. She gets the coffee, runs errands, gets the phone, deals with the mail, coordinates his schedule with me. I've never seen him really treat her as a career woman, if you know what I mean. He's very much a man of his generation. He stops short of calling her honey, but I'm pretty sure he thinks it."

Both the girls smiled at that and Jake was glad that he didn't have to face half the crap they did in the workplace. He only had to put up with Hank. He looked to Lauren. "Do you think he's talked to your mom?"

Lauren's smile faded and she lifted a shoulder and sighed. "I really don't know. Given our talk yesterday, talking about my future and how much she loves it here . . . I'd have to say no."

"I can't believe he'd be even considering something as huge as this without discussing it with his wife," RJ said. "But . . . who knows?" She looked to Lauren. "I know this puts you in a very, very difficult position."

Lauren lifted her hand to stall her apologies. "I understand. And thank you," she told Jake, "for trying to resolve this without putting me there. I do appreciate it. But I appreciate more being given the chance to help solve the problem."

They all sat there and stared at each other for a few long moments. Lauren finally broke the silence. "My mom knew, about my job. And she opted to wait until I was ready to tell her. I think, in this case, with nothing being imminent, or even certain—"

"It's certain," Jake said. He looked ruefully at Lauren, feeling badly for piling on. "I put in some calls to the guys who are funding the sponsorship for the race. I knew they were also pretty politically active and thought they might know if there was any talk. I got a call back from Roger a little while ago. It's no rumor. He's definitely making inroads."

"With what?" Lauren asked, then lifted a hand. "I don't mean that to sound so insulting, but he's been tucked away a long time here. Has he really maintained, or fostered, the kind of connections he needs to be seriously considered? And where's his war chest? That kind of campaign takes significant donors. Beyond even the Covingtons or the assorted business interests here. I know he has interests with some of the resort owners, but they're partly Swiss-owned—I checked—so that's not helping him out in any huge way. Do the Covingtons have the kind of pull that can sway other big pocket donors to get behind him?"

Jake glanced at RJ, then ducked his gaze for a moment. This was the part he'd been dreading.

"Jake?" Lauren asked. "What is it?"

RJ leaned forward and put her hand on his knee, but spoke to Lauren. "I have no idea what he might have cooking with the Covingtons. I do know that he stays in contact with people in San Francisco, still has some business there though I'm not really involved in any of that. But I know he communicates out there regularly. He has connections in Denver and in Washington. He's also formed some bonds with other town mayors, most of them mayors of much larger towns than ours. He's politically very savvy for a man who has been buried in the wilds of the Rockies for so long. So, while it's not probable that he's got the kind of deep pockets he needs, it's not impossible, either."

Both women turned to him expectantly. "What else do you know?" Lauren finally asked.

He swore silently. "Remember, we don't know what the situation is between your mother and Arlen, as far as running in this race goes, and we've already jumped to enough conclusions."

Lauren's expression fell. "It's my mother," she said quietly, resignedly. "That's his connection, isn't it? My mother's name, her father's name, my dad's name, all of her lifelong contacts." She held his gaze. "I'm guessing her money, along with whoever she can get on his bandwagon?"

"Your mom, yes. And . . . you."

Lauren's eyes widened, clearly surprised. "Me? Seriously?"

"Maybe that was the reason behind the calls to D.C.," Ruby Jean said. "To confirm that you were really gone, and possibly to confirm that you hadn't already accepted another position, or if you had, what the position was. Would make sense then, to use the headhunter guise. Determine you really are a free agent with no attachments, then your name can be casually dropped with those to whom it would matter, without risking having egg on your face later if it came to light that you were already dedicated to some other campaign or politician."

"What is being said, regarding me?" Lauren wanted to know.

"Just that he has not only Charlene's widespread and very well connected support, but that you would be throwing your significant weight, given your very dedicated reputation, and very direct contacts, behind him as well."

Lauren sank back in her chair. "I . . . don't know what to say to that. Other than I know my mother wouldn't have sanctioned that, not without making sure I was really on board. And she knows, given our conversations as recently as yesterday, that while I am far more at peace now than I was before I got here . . . that I still have some major reservations about Arlen. She'd have to know that I wouldn't vocally throw any support in his direction, when I haven't even done it privately as yet."

"You don't think she knows about any of it," Ruby Jean said.

Lauren stood abruptly and paced, saying nothing, and both Jake and Ruby Jean let her have a few moments to think. She finally stopped by the office door and looked at them both. "But there is one way to find out." She looked at Ruby Jean. "I could just ask her."

Chapter 24

Lauren steered Jake's Jeep into the parking lot of the motel. Jake was pulling an all-nighter working with Paddy's cronies on *Betty Sue,* so she'd opted to come back to her motel room. She had wanted to go out and meet the guys, but after the conversation in the office, she'd been pretty scattered emotionally and wanted some time to sort things out. Another time would make for a better hello.

But another time was not what she'd wanted with Jake. It wasn't just about wanting to spend the night with him, but needing to. Not for the physical intimacy, in this case, but because she was so scattered and uncertain about what to do next. And she knew that he'd have helped her regain her focus and sort things out. They'd have figured it out together, she knew that. It surprised her how definitively she already knew that. She also completely understood his need to focus on the race, so she wasn't upset. He'd even asked her if she'd rather stay up at his house. But she'd ended up deciding that maybe she needed to completely step away from all of it in order to figure out how to handle the next step.

Ruby Jean had offered to drop her off, but Jake had told her to take the Jeep. His sister left first, but Lauren had ended up with only a few scant minutes alone with Jake before someone named Scooter was touching down on the runway and Jake had to go off and oversee the off loading of the parts and pieces that would help get *Betty Sue* race-worthy.

Lauren turned off the ignition, but didn't go right up to her room. They hadn't made any decisions on whether she should talk to her mom, and had finally decided to think on the whole mess for a bit before making any moves at all. After all, the race for governor hadn't even been declared yet. There was no hurry. And better to approach things in a way that wouldn't damage future fragile bridges being built in her family, and with the McKennas, by making hasty accusations or causing strife in her mother's new marriage where none might actually exist.

But Lauren knew. She knew in her heart that it did exist. Jake had confirmed it with that call from Roger. Confirmed it enough for her. For the first time, that knot in her gut felt like it was there for a reason. Instead of wondering if it was just her, if she was overreacting, she finally felt like she'd figured it out. Or started to.

Which so entirely sucked. Because while the puzzle pieces were starting to line up right, the resultant picture was oh so very wrong.

She climbed out of the Jeep, wishing the door was made of something more substantial than tarp and plastic so she could snap it shut. She was in her room, shutting the door, when she remembered that she'd never followed up to see if Debbie was back. The whole bicycle mystery seemed so very distant and unimportant at that moment. She slung her computer bag on the bed, then paused. "Or, is it . . ."

She started to pick up the room phone, then decided it would be better done in person, and left her room to head to the little front registration office. She pushed through the doors to find Jennifer there, not Debbie.

"Hey, good evening," Jennifer said, bright smile and welcome expression.

"Hey, Jennifer. By any chance did Debbie get back in town?"

"Her son made the finals, so they won't be back for a few days, but she called me from the hotel phone where they're staying. And I did remember to ask her about the bicycle." Her smile fell. "I'm really sorry to tell you this, too, but she has no idea about it."

That had Lauren pausing. She'd been so sure she was going to get some answers. "Really? Nothing?"

Jennifer shook her head. "She said that other than Melissa stopping by earlier that afternoon to drop those papers off for you, there wasn't any activity that she knew about regarding you or your room. I asked the other guys on the maintenance staff, but no go there, either. I really don't know what to tell you."

"Well, if it was left outside my room, I'd just cross it off to someone being a Good Samaritan, finding it and knowing it was mine, dropping it off. But it was in my room. Wait—" Lauren straightened. "What did she say about Melissa?" Her mind had been so discombobulated by the bombs dropped this afternoon that at first, when Jennifer had mentioned Melissa dropping by, Lauren had mentally checked it off as the welcome basket visit. But that had happened earlier in her stay. "What papers did Melissa deliver? I didn't get anything from her that day."

Jennifer looked completely defeated. "I'm sorry, I didn't think to ask Debbie that. I just assumed it wasn't related. I really am sorry about this. If you'd like to move to another room, I'd be glad to comp you an upgrade, or . . . whatever you feel is right. We've never had anything like this happen before."

Lauren started to take her up on the room change, then thought better of it. "No, that won't be necessary. I'm going to be checking out soon, anyway."

"Oh, I hope it's not because—"

"No, no, that's not it," Lauren assured her, though it certainly made changing her plans a bit easier. "If you do hear from Debbie again, ask her for more details on the Melissa visit. And if anyone escorted her to my room, or . . . just ask her to tell you everything she remembers."

"I sure will. And I'm really, really sorry about the trouble."

"Don't worry about it." She smiled and left a sad looking

Jennifer at the desk. For all that she had privately had her fun with the town's overwhelmingly upbeat attitude, as it turned out, there was no fun at all in seeing one of the happy, shiny people get her balloon pierced.

She climbed the stairs to her room . . . and thought about Jake's invitation. He'd asked her to think about staying up at his place. He was going to be really tied to *Betty Sue* and keeping his lessons going, and if she was up there, they'd be able to at least spend some time together. She'd begged off for tonight, wanting some time to think through all the revelations. But now that she was back in her motel room, she realized this was the last place she wanted to be.

She grabbed her computer bag, then put it down again. And packed up all of her stuff instead. She hadn't been particularly fearful of staying in her room since the bike incident, but then she hadn't spent the night alone since then, either. "And I don't plan to tonight, either." At the very least, Hank would keep her company. And Jake would only be a shout away. She stowed her suitcase and computer bag in the back of the Jeep, but didn't officially check out. Jennifer felt low enough at the moment and she just couldn't bring herself to make her feel any worse.

As Lauren drove back out to the school, she worked at this latest piece in the puzzle. Melissa had come to see her at some point on the same day her bike was taken. But Lauren had been with Jake at the barbecue, then later, up at his house. She had no idea exactly when her bike was taken, or when it was put in her room, so there was no way to establish a specific timeline. "For God's sake," she muttered. "I sound like I'm on some cop show now. Timelines." But as she rolled through town, her thoughts turned to the facts, and the facts were that, according to Jake's sources, who had no stake in the matter one way or the other, Arlen was using her mother, and her, as props to get himself positioned for a serious run at the governor's office. How could that be going on and no one in Cedar Springs knew about it?

Lauren could only assume that the flipside of living somewhere where everyone knew everything about you is they also assumed they knew everything about you. It probably had never occurred to anyone in Cedar Springs that their mayor was still dreaming of a bigger political future, much less taking action about it. It's hard to see what you don't even suspect. Which possibly extended all the way to her mother.

The all-too-familiar knot tugged more tightly in her gut. She wanted—badly—to call her mom, not just to tell her, but to talk it out with her, too. It had been a very long, difficult six months, losing not only a mom, but one of her closest confidantes. Now things were supposedly better, but she still couldn't go to her. Not yet. Lauren honestly had no idea what her mom would do with the information, or how she would react. Lauren couldn't risk Ruby Jean's career by blurting things out before they'd thought them through very carefully.

Of course, looking at both sides, she supposed it was possible that her mother did know but was keeping mum, even from her own daughter, because it suited Arlen's needs best at the moment for the word not to get out. Lauren seriously doubted her mother had gone along with both their names being used to further his chances, but he might have taken a little license there. And Lauren honestly couldn't see her mother giving up her newfound bliss in Cedar Springs to step back into the spotlight, either. Especially a far more glaring one than she'd ever had before, even given her old life, as the First Lady of the state. Prior to coming out here, Lauren might have believed it. If Arlen had been more her type, and it had been a more traditional courtship, she could have seen her mother—the one from the East Coast—making that decision.

But not now. Not the woman she'd spent the past few days with. Then another lightbulb went off. Maybe her mother did know, and maybe she was fine with it because she planned to stay right here in Cedar Springs while Arlen ran things from the capital. Business was a little different out here in the West, and so perhaps it would be less controversial if the governor's wife wasn't largely present in the capital, but spending the majority of her time back in their hometown. It would explain why her mother was so at peace with her less-than-passionate marriage. Maybe it was more a marriage of convenience than her mother was prepared to admit, whether to Lauren or possibly even herself. But if it got her a ticket to a new, more fulfilling life and Arlen a ticket to the governor's mansion, then . . . people had united for stranger reasons.

So much to process, so much to think about. And Lauren hadn't even begun to think about what she wanted for herself in all this. Where she saw herself after the dust settled regarding everything swirling around her mom and Arlen. It was one thing to acknowledge that she wanted Jake. Another entirely to figure out what in the hell she was going to do with herself if she decided to stick around Cedar Springs and keep him.

Her mind was spinning with all the possibilities, with the decisions that needed to be made, the talk she'd eventually have to have with her mother.

Which was probably why she didn't see the car pull out of a side street directly into her path—until it was too late.

Chapter 25

Jake stretched, arched his back, then rubbed his hand over his face. The combination of the stress of the past few weeks, nailing down funding for the race, and the sudden new relationship in his life, combined with the attendant drama there, had all apparently caught up with him. It wasn't even that late, but he was fighting the fatigue already.

"It's bad when the old farts are perkier than the young buck," Oscar commented off-handedly as he continued to work on modifications to the manifold Jake had spent the better part of two days earlier in the week trying to repair. In fact, it's what he'd been working on when he'd left to go pick up Lauren for the first time. It was almost impossible to believe everything that had happened since. It had all evolved so quickly. If anyone had told him he'd not only be willingly involving himself with someone this close to race time, not to mention her family drama, too, but actually looking forward and excitedly anticipating whatever came next, he'd have never believed it. And yet, here he was.

"Earth to Jake."

He looked up to find Ace staring at him, holding a diagram he'd just finished on a proposed engine modification. Everyone else chuckled as he pulled his head out of the clouds.

"You want to take a look at this? Then go call your girlfriend. Better yet, have her come up here, go take a break for about an hour, then come back when you can use the head on your shoulders again."

He smiled a bit sheepishly and endured the good-natured ribbing that followed. He'd earned that and more. "Might not be a bad idea." He checked over Ace's schematic, then ducked out of the hangar and pulled his cell phone out as he strolled toward the parking lot, looking up at the full moon. It was crazy how much he missed her, and she'd only been gone an hour or two. He grinned as he punched her number. But it was a crazy he didn't want a cure for.

Her phone rang a few times and his grin started to fade when she didn't pick up. Maybe she was in the shower. He doubted she'd gone to bed. Then another thought hit him, but he immediately rejected it. Or tried to. She wouldn't have gone out to talk to Charlene. They'd agreed to sleep on it and get together again in the morning to discuss the smartest way to proceed. Her voice mail picked up and he left a quick message telling her he missed her and to call him whenever she got his message.

He flipped his phone shut, but wasn't ready to head back inside just yet. He thought about going to the front office and looking through the articles again. Lauren had printed off everything she'd scanned and made copies of the rest, so he had the same file she did now. So did RJ. He smiled again, briefly, thinking about how happy it had made him, seeing the two of them hit it off so naturally. He couldn't have asked for more.

There was a siren in the distance, down in town, and it drew his attention from his thoughts. He'd been walking toward the front office door but detoured around the building to where the road leading to the school cut in toward the parking lot. The vantage point there was a good one, and he could see all the way down into town. Sirens weren't a common sound in Cedar Springs, so he was curious to see what was up. The flashing lights belonged to a police car, judging by the color, and an ambulance. Car accident, he was guessing. He hoped it was nothing serious. He stood there and watched for a few minutes, but his thoughts were already straying back to Lauren and the situation with Arlen.

His cell phone rang and he grinned, popping it open without even looking at the incoming number. He loved the little rush he got whenever they made contact. He hoped it took a long, long time before that little thrill faded. "Please tell me you were naked in the shower when—"

"Jake? Jake McKenna? This is Sergeant O'Hara—"

"What's going on, Darryl?" he asked, surprised, then froze, his gaze tracking back to the flashing light below. A sick dread filled his gut.

"Well, it looks like your Jeep was involved in some kind of accident. Where are you?"

He had brief flashbacks to the day they'd come to tell him about his parents, but he shoved those brutal memories ruthlessly aside. "What happened? Is Lauren okay?"

"Lauren? You mean Lauren Matthews?"

"Yes," he said, fighting down the wave of abject panic that threatened to engulf him. "She had my Jeep. She would have been driving. Is she okay?" He tore his gaze away from the flashing lights below and started trotting back toward the back hangar.

"I don't know," Sergeant O'Hara said. "There was no one on the scene when we arrived."

Surprise momentarily slowed Jake's steps. "What? Maybe she's dazed, wandered away from the scene. Have you looked?"

"We're doing that now. I'd appreciate it if you could come down here." He gave Jake the address of the intersection. Right where the flashing lights were.

"On my way." He broke out into a run and knew he looked a little bit wild when he swung through the door into the hangar. Xavier had flown Jake's plane back from Holden earlier in the day and picked up his truck, so Jake had no available ride. "Oscar, I need the keys to your truck. Lauren's been in an accident."

He'd never seen men that old move that fast. And was eternally grateful. He caught Oscar's keys when he tossed them and waved. "I'll call you as soon as I know anything. Thanks!"

It took every bit of focus he had to keep his imagination from running wild as he navigated the winding road into town. The accident was at the intersection just after the road bottomed out. It was the last crossroad before climbing upward toward the school. Jake pulled Oscar's truck over behind one of the two police cars blocking off the end of the street. A small crowd had gathered, but it was late enough that all the shops and restaurants were closed, and they weren't close to any houses, so thankfully it hadn't become a full-blown spectacle.

Jake wove his way toward the ambulance, but it wasn't until he skirted around the side of it that he saw his Jeep. His heart stopped as he saw how it had slid sideways and slammed into a small tree. The driver's side tarp door hung drunkenly on one hook, allowing him to see that the air bag had deployed.

"Jake?"

He turned to find Sergeant O'Hara standing next to him. He knew Darryl because the officer's younger brother had been a student of Jake's a few years back, but that was their only connection. "Did you find her?"

The officer's face was expressionless, but Jake didn't miss the bleak look in his eyes. "We're still looking. There isn't any blood, so it doesn't look like the impact caused any extreme external injuries."

External. Jake hadn't missed his use of that word. "Any idea how it happened?" In the winter months, accidents like this were unfortunately all too common. But it was a clear summer night.

"There are skid marks, which leads us to believe she swerved to miss hitting something and lost control of the vehicle."

Jake nodded, but was already walking over toward the Jeep.

O'Hara shadowed him. "Don't touch anything. We're still investigating."

"Did you check to see if it hit anything other than the tree?"

"They're doing that now."

There were two officers with flashlights in addition to the larger klieg lights the emergency medical crew had set up. The whole area was bathed in an ethereal blue-white glow.

O'Hara held Jake back. "We need to let them do their job."

"Who's looking for her?" He should be looking for her. He needed to get a grip here and focus, but it was just a swirl of light and sound and—

"Jake?"

He turned then to find Ruby Jean pushing her way past two of the emergency personnel. She ran to him and hugged him tight, and it was only then, when he saw the fear and concern on her face, that his own focus snapped into place.

"What happened? Where is she? Is she okay?"

"Apparently she hit a tree, we're not sure why, but it looks like she swerved to miss hitting something."

Ruby Jean twisted to look over her shoulder in the direction of the ambulance. "She's okay?"

"We don't know. We can't find her."

Ruby Jean swung back, mouth half open, then finally blinked. "What? What the hell do you mean you can't find her?"

He repeated what O'Hara had told him.

"Well, are they looking for her? Do you think she tried to walk up the road toward the school? She was probably on her way to see you."

RJ was right. If she'd gone to see Charlene, she'd have been headed in a different direction entirely. He turned and found O'Hara in the growing crowd. "Is anyone looking up the road, toward the school?"

"Yes," he said. "No tracks, nothing yet."

"We need to be doing something, dammit," Ruby Jean said. "Where the hell would she have gone?"

"She might be dazed," Jake said. "The air bags came out. I don't know." He looked at the Jeep, at all the people who were trying to figure things out, and tried like hell to focus, to figure it out. She hadn't simply vanished.

Chapter 26

Lauren squeezed her eyes against the stab of pain throbbing in her head. It felt like someone had clubbed her with a bat. Her body felt like lead and her thoughts were fuzzy, like she'd been asleep too long. It took a few moments before she became lucid enough to sort through a few things. Her head hurt like hell. So did her face. And her chest. What the hell had happened?

She didn't try to open her eyes, but she tried to move her hands, intending to probe a little, more out of an instinct than forethought. But her hands wouldn't budge; they seemed pinned, or trapped.

"Don't bother struggling."

She stilled, her awareness of her current situation abruptly slammed into fast-forward as she scrambled to figure things out a hell of a lot faster. Where was she? What had happened? And who the hell had just said that? She opened her eyes into slits, then winced a little at the increased pain. It was dark, but even the little bit of light emitted by the dashboard stung her vision. Dashboard. She was in a vehicle. A moving vehicle, she realized a moment later. She'd been driving . . .

She closed her eyes again to keep the pain from spiraling and tried like hell to think. Driving. Jake's Jeep. She'd been going up to the school, thinking about her mom, about Jake, about her future. That was all she could remember. She carefully rolled her head to the side and tried again to open her eyes. The shadow next to her slowly morphed into the shape of a woman as her vision began to correct and focus. "Who—"

Then the woman turned to look at her. And two things hit Lauren at the same time. Arlen's secretary, Melissa, was the driver . . . and she was holding a rather large gun.

"Why?" Lauren croaked.

Melissa snorted and turned her attention back to the road. "Because you are presenting a growing obstacle to me achieving my goals. I've worked too hard to let you just waltz into town and ruin everything."

Lauren closed her eyes and tried to think past the pain. Her hands were tied in her lap and strapped beneath the seat belt. She moved her feet slightly and was thankful to discover they weren't otherwise bound. For whatever good that was going to do her. But at least she could run. If that ever became an option. "What . . . obstacle?"

Melissa laughed, but it was an ugly, hateful sound. Lauren didn't open her eyes again, but she could see in her mind the image of Melissa and that gun. She remembered how she'd thought Arlen's secretary was so pretty and perky when they'd first met. It was amazing what anger and hatred could do to that. "You . . . came to my room," she said, wincing again against the pain. "Again." She had no idea the extent of her injuries, but her head was pounding like a pipe against an anvil, and her face didn't feel so hot, either. She tried not to think about that, and focus instead on Melissa, and why they were in this vehicle.

"I had to know what you were up to. I'd heard you'd been snooping around. At the library, in Arlen's very own personal office. I thought the crushed bike would make you rethink things, but you didn't stop."

Lauren tried to focus on what Melissa was revealing. She knew about the library and was responsible for the bike. Okay. But she also knew about Arlen catching Lauren in his office. And the only person who knew she'd been "caught" was Arlen. Which meant . . . "You . . . and Arlen?"

"Bright girl, but then all we've heard from Charlene for the past six months is how brilliant and talented you are. My God, I was sick of you before I even met you."

"I liked you," Lauren said, her thoughts becoming words before she could censor them.

She barked a laugh. "I was surprised by you. I expected an uptight, workaholic snob. Of course, your mother wasn't anything like I expected, so maybe I shouldn't have been surprised. I could almost like her. If she hadn't married Arlen."

Lauren scrambled to process the nuances of what she was hearing. And figure out just how far over the edge Melissa had plunged. The gun in her lap didn't bode well on the crazy scale.

"Does my . . . mother . . . know?" Lauren shifted her head, trying to find a position that stopped the clanging pain. "About . . . governor . . . you?"

The car swung in a slow swerve as Melissa hit the brakes, rocking Lauren, who couldn't brace herself without her hands. She groaned a little as her head swayed, then jerked back when Melissa regained control of the car. She felt them slow down, but even when she opened her eyes again, it was too dark beyond the windows to tell where they were.

"What do you know about the governor?"

Lauren hadn't meant to reveal anything, but she could barely string her thoughts together. If the damn throbbing would just stop, for just a second, so she could think. At this point, they were probably well past worrying about Ruby Jean's job, but she still did her best to protect her new friend. "I have . . . contacts. There's been . . . talk. That's why . . . digging."

The car swerved to a complete stop, forcing another grunt of pain from Lauren as the seat belt tightened automatically to hold her in place.

"Contacts. I know your contact. Did Ruby Jean tell you? Of course she did, now that you're banging her brother. I knew she couldn't be trusted! I told him to let it slip to her, to prove to him that she couldn't be trusted. Who else knows?" Melissa demanded, sounding dangerously more crazed than she had up to that point. She wasn't shrieking, but her demand held an edge of hysteria. "Does Charlene know?"

Well, that answered one question. Her mother had no idea. Lauren's throat tightened as it hit her what this was going to do to her. "No," she rasped. "Not from me. You and Arlen . . . are you . . . ?"

"I am the woman behind the man. Not Charlene, and certainly not ridiculous Ruby Jean. I mean, come on, have you seen her? And that name? No way is he taking her to Denver. And no way would she ever be able to do for him what I do. I was the one he turned to. I was the one who encouraged him to dream again. We're partners. Real partners."

"He married—"

"Yes. It threw me when he came back from Florida married. Married!" She almost shrieked that last word, then seemed to regain her grip. "But I realized, right away, that he'd just done that for us."

And that answered the crazy scale question. Not in a good way. Lauren wondered if Arlen knew how insane his secretary was, or if her dreams of grandeur were the result of private loony tunes fantasies. Was she actually involved with Arlen? But Arlen had told Melissa about finding her in his office out at the house. Why else would he tell her that if they weren't otherwise involved. Or maybe Arlen was simply using her and she just hoped it would lead to more.

Lauren closed her eyes again, against the throbbing and the tumble of thoughts battling each other inside her head. She needed to think, dammit.

"And just when I have it all lined up, you waltz into town. Snooping around and immediately hooking up with Jake McKenna."

Melissa spat this last part out, and if she hadn't just been talking about Arlen like he was her dream man, Lauren would have sworn she was jealous about Jake. Or maybe she was the kind of crazy that just hated anyone who had something she couldn't have. Jake had mentioned that Ruby Jean had tried to set them up and he'd turned her down.

"Everyone is talking like you're the second coming. Charlene is all smiles and happy, and now Arlen's having second thoughts—"

"About running for governor?"

Melissa laughed, and this time the sound made Lauren's flesh crawl. "No, you stupid bitch. About making her disappear the same way he made his last two wives disappear. Arlen is brilliant, you know. He knows exactly how to get what he wants from people. I've watched him, and I've learned. It's how I figured out how to get what I wanted from him. I was taught by the best." She looked smugly at Lauren. "You're not the only one who knows how to dig up the dirt."

Lauren's mouth dropped open and she couldn't seem to close it back up.

"What, you don't think just because I'm a little younger than you and live out here in the middle of nowhere that I can be smart and powerful? You Capitol Hill bitches don't have the corner on being power players you know. And I haven't always lived out here."

"Arlen . . . killed . . . his wives?" Was Melissa just spewing more crazy talk . . . or did she really know something?

"Arlen finds the people who can do the most good for him, for his vision, his work, and when he's done with them, he moves on. In business, you can fire people, or simply cease to do business with them, but in marriage, when your spouse ceases to be profitable to your long-term goals . . ."

"Divorce," Lauren said.

"Looks bad. Widower is much more sympathetic."

"He is . . . divorced."

"Only because he didn't think of the fire sooner."

Lauren felt her body parts start to turn cold. Very, very cold.

"I have waited to meet someone like Arlen my whole life. I've been used, mistreated, abused, lied to, cheated on, all by men who told me they love me. Arlen is different. He's honest and straight with me and I always know exactly where I stand. He's made me see what's important in the world, and that's being in control of your universe. With you at the core and your goals like satellites, orbiting around you. Everything is merely a vessel you use to keep your goals orbiting smoothly."

Lauren wanted to point out that this honest man was presently lying to everyone else, and if she was telling the truth about his past wives, he'd been lying for a very, very long time. She could also point out that, by its very nature, the whole "me at the center of my universe" theory kind of precluded Melissa from being anything other than a satellite. There could only be one center.

"Why . . . this?" Lauren asked. "You'll get caught."

Her laugh made Lauren's skin crawl. "No, I won't. I learned, remember? From the best. I've been watching you. And Jake. Charlene says everything is fine, but you're still digging. The bike was my first attempt to discourage you. But you just wouldn't stop, you wouldn't leave. And Charlene was saying you might stick around because of Jake." She spat his name like it was snake venom. "Then I saw him go to the library, so I followed him. That stupid old bat who works there blabbed all about how he'd been upsetting her precious filing system by taking out old newspapers. After he left I ducked back there to see if he'd put them all back, the ones you'd scanned into your computer . . . but I saw he'd taken more out. And I knew it was about the fire." She gunned the engine, but they remained where they were. "You were getting too close to figuring things out. I couldn't let you do anything to ruin Arlen's dream. My dream. We're so close."

"You used . . . Charlene. Me. We'd find out . . . eventually."

"Not necessarily," she said, her voice so dead, so . . . emotionless.

And for the first time, Lauren truly began to fear that she wasn't going to get out of this alive. Not that her prospects had been great up to that point, but she was good at talking people around a point, good at strategy, good at figuring out how to work things to the advantage of her side. What she needed right now was an exit strategy. Preferably a bulletproof one. It would help if she knew where they were headed. "Where are you . . . taking me?"

"My plan was to convince you to leave, to go back to Washington. I was going to promise you anything you wanted. Run Arlen's campaign, a high-level position on his staff. At first when Charlene said you'd come around, I thought we could use to you our advantage, get you on our side. But you wouldn't quit snooping!" She smacked the steering wheel with the hand that was holding the gun, making Lauren flinch. She looked over at Lauren. "We can't trust you. You can't be trusted."

"You should have . . . told me. I'd have understood."

Melissa screamed and Lauren felt the bile of abject terror rise in her throat. "Liar!" she screeched. "You, Jake, Ruby fucking Jean, all of you!"

"They'll know something happened to me," Lauren said, forcing the words past the ball of fear in her throat. "I can't just disappear. The election is too far away. You can't cover it up for that long. They'll keep digging."

Melissa started rocking in her seat as she floored the gas and drove them like a bat out of hell with God only knew her destination. Lauren looked out the window and the front windshield, but one rural road surrounded by mountain peaks looked like the rest of them to her.

"You can't go back," Melissa said. "You'll ruin everything."

Lauren switched tactics. "Take me to the airport. Take me to Holden. I'll fly back to Washington."

Melissa's mad bark made it clear what she thought of Lauren's offer.

"I want to make a deal," Lauren said. "I can help you."

"What deal could you possibly make now?" She waved the gun around, making Lauren shrink back against the seat, setting off fresh waves of pain. "You have no deal to offer."

"I do."

"What?" Melissa shrieked, only this time it sounded like it cracked on a sob. She was breaking down.

Which meant Lauren was toast, or it meant Melissa was realizing that her sudden plans to do away with Lauren weren't going to get her the result she'd hoped for. Lauren prayed it was the latter. "My mom . . ."

"What about her?" Melissa growled.

"I don't want her hurt."

"You don't get a vote."

"I could get Arlen votes, though. Lots and lots of them. And money," she croaked, forcing out the words past the pain. "All the money he'd need to mount the campaign of his life."

"We'll get that from Charlene."

"Not if she's grieving my loss. She'll be lost to you both, completely. And you need her alive at least through the campaign. I have clout, Melissa. I can get you what you want."

"Why should we trust you? Why should I believe you? You'd say anything right now."

"I'll get you want you want, because you have something I want."

Melissa slowed the truck and looked over at her. "What are you saying?"

"You don't have to trust me; you know I'll do whatever you want me to because you have my mother. I'll get Arlen the election, and when it's over, you give me my mother. I'll take care of making sure it works out so Arlen doesn't look bad. I don't want her dead. I'll do whatever you want."

Melissa slowed the truck until it was just coasting.

Lauren pushed, knowing she was close. "Do we have a deal?"

Chapter 27

"Okay, I will. No, there's no need for you or Arlen to come down here. The Jeep has been towed over to Billy's auto shop. We're all still searching, but Charlene—" Jake broke off, hating the fear and heartbreak he heard in her voice. It made it that much harder for him to hold his own act together. It had been over an hour now. He and RJ had gone to Lauren's motel room, but it looked like she'd checked out. He had no idea what to make of that. Mabry said she hadn't checked out at the desk. So, all Jake knew was that she'd been heading toward the school, toward him, when the Jeep left the road. If, for whatever reason, she'd been taking off, she'd have headed out toward Holden, or Denver.

He'd finally gotten ahold of Charlene, after leaving a dozen messages for her. She'd been out in her greenhouse, potting new seedlings. He and Ruby Jean had been taking turns calling Charlene and Lauren's cell phones. He wished it had been better news when one of them had finally called back. "Yes, I promise I will call you the second we know anything." He hung up just as Ruby Jean walked up. "News?"

She shook her head. "You got a hold of Charlene?"

"She hasn't heard from her. She wants to come down and help us look, but I persuaded her not to. I don't know, though, she sounded more frantic the longer we talked. She could show up. Arlen, too."

"We really don't need the mayor down here; it will just get everyone buzzing all over again. Darryl finally has most people going back home again, other than the ones volunteering to help us look."

Jake nodded, but he was only half listening. Where in the hell was she? If she wasn't answering, and she hadn't called him back, or stumbled to a nearby house . . . then where the hell was she? The only alternative was simply not something he could bear to think about.

"We're going to find her, Jake. It's going to be okay."

"I wish like hell I could believe that."

She shook him. "You have to. And I know this is going to sound crazy, but something tells me she's not here."

"What are you talking about?"

"The accident with the Jeep was bad, but it wasn't that bad. I don't know. I have a really bad feeling, but it has nothing to do with us finding her in a ditch somewhere a hundred yards away."

"Don't say that; don't even think that."

"I'm just saying, Jake, this has something else written on it."

"I'm not following."

"All the snooping she's done, you've done, the weird things that have happened. Now she's suddenly packed up and left the motel. None of her things are in the Jeep. Think about it."

"Are you saying that you think she's hitched a ride? Or that someone caused her to wreck on purpose? And . . . what? Took her? But who? And where?"

Ruby Jean lifted a shoulder, but her expression said it all.

"I—I can't even—I don't know where to go with that. Who would do that? Charlene said Arlen was home with her, working from his home office, had been all evening. Who else would—"

"It was a woman who called Lauren's coworker, from my office phone. It wasn't me, so that leaves—"

"Melissa? Why on earth would she—" He broke off, thinking back earlier when he'd run into her at the library. She'd been there dropping off donations, but could she have known anything about what he was doing there? And, furthermore, would she have even cared? Cared enough to do something to Lauren? "No, it doesn't make any sense. She has no motivation to do anything like that."

"She's very dedicated to Arlen. She makes no secret that she admires him."

"What are you saying? Do you think they're . . . involved?"

"No, not like that. I'm just saying, she really looks up to him. Maybe she'd be willing to do him a . . . favor if he asked."

"A favor that includes kidnapping or hurting someone? Have you lost your mind?"

"Jake, calm down. I'm just trying to follow any lead we might have."

Just then Jake's phone buzzed again. He yanked it out of his pocket so fast it almost went flying from his hands. The screen showed Lauren's name. His heart rate tripled. "Thank God!" He flipped open the phone. "Lauren, where are you? Are you all right?"

But there was only static and white noise.

"Lauren," he shouted. "Can you hear me? Tell me where you are."

All he heard was something that sounded like a droning noise. He tried to calm his breathing so his heart wasn't pounding in his ears.

"What's going on?" Ruby Jean demanded. "Is she okay?"

Jake put his hand up and focused on what he was listening to. He walked a little farther away from the cluster of emergency vehicles, but was careful not to lose signal. It was just droning, on and on, like . . . the sound of a car engine. So she was in a car! But why wasn't she calling him then? He looked at Ruby Jean, the sick ball of dread that had been his constant companion since O'Hara had called, now turned to an icy knot of terror. If she was in a car, and couldn't contact him . . .

"What's going on, Jake?"

He started to tell her, but then there was some new noise on the line. And he realized it was muffled speech. Someone was talking. He ducked away and cupped his hand over his hear to funnel the sound.

There was static, then droning again, then ". . . longer."

"Shut up!"

Jake's throat closed over. Two separate voices. He couldn't hear them well enough to know whose was whose, much less who was the owner of the second one.

". . . Denver."

They were heading to Denver? That was over four hours away by car, but he could fly—but then how in the hell would he find them?

". . . closer to get . . . Holden."

That had to be Lauren. She was trying to get the driver, whoever it was, to take them to Holden instead. Shit, which way did he head out? They were in opposite directions with completely different flight paths.

". . . drop me . . . no one . . . see you."

There was just droning again, for what felt like an eternity. "Come on, come on," he muttered under his breath. "Give me a clue, baby, give me another clue."

"Denver . . . you'll . . . gone too long."

Back to droning, then a louder, "Okay. Holden. But you . . . clean up . . . know who you are. You can't let on . . . is wrong."

". . . Mom safe . . . won't . . . betray. Don't hurt her."

Jake looked up to find Ruby Jean standing in front of him, literally bouncing on her feet but remaining silent as he'd instructed. "Tell me," she mouthed.

He lifted a finger to stall her, but then the line went dead. "Dammit!" he erupted, and immediately tried to dial back, but it went straight to her voice mail. He turned to RJ and told her everything he remembered about the call.

"Protect . . . Charlene?" she said. "What in the hell—"

"I'm flying to Holden. You call Charlene; get her out of the house, away from Arlen, away from everyone, until we know more about what's going on. Tell her we haven't heard anything, but that you'd feel better if she was here with you. I don't care what you tell her, just get her out, then you two head up to the school." He'd already called the guys and told them what was going on. They'd offered to come down and help with the search, but the last thing he needed was one of them falling and breaking a hip. He'd told them to just keep at it with *Betty Sue* and he'd call with updates. "Better yet, go to my house, stay there. Get Hank."

"Jake, let me come with—"

"No," he all but shouted. "Get Charlene; go to my house. I'll call you when I land in Holden."

She grabbed him in a tight hug. "Stay safe. Or I'll kill you myself."

"Do not leave my house. Make sure Charlene stays with you until we figure this out."

"Can I tell her what we know?"

Jake paused for a split second, then just shrugged helplessly. "At this point, I don't think it matters any longer. Talk to her; maybe she'll have some insight. Call my phone, leave whatever messages you need to. I'll get them as soon as I land."

He didn't see O'Hara and was glad of it. He'd just as soon they continued on doing what they were doing. He knew now it was a waste of time, but he didn't have time to explain to them what he knew, nor did he really want them to know just yet. He didn't want any more information in the hands of anyone else until he knew what the hell was going on. He'd call in as soon as he had Lauren safely with him.

He ducked around the back of one of the police cars, then slid into Oscar's truck. No one standing around would recognize it anyway. He backed slowly out, turned quietly around, and drove sedately all the way to the end of the street. Then drove like hell on fire straight up the mountain to the school. With the help of the guys, he was in the air less than fifteen minutes later.

Chapter 28

Once Lauren had convinced Melissa to take her to Holden and dump her there, she stopped talking and started focusing on assessing her injuries as best she could. Melissa had said she needed to clean up, so clearly she didn't look much better than she felt.

She'd felt her cell phone hum in her jacket pocket numerous times since she'd come to and each time it stopped it was like another little piece of her confidence dissolved. It had to be Jake. So close, so very close, and yet nothing she could do. She'd tried squirming a little, very little, so Melissa, who had the eyes of a hawk and the peripheral vision of an eagle, wouldn't notice, hoping maybe she could press the face of the phone against something, anything, that might answer one of the incoming calls. But she had no idea if she'd ever been successful. Or what good it might have done if she had been.

She turned her thoughts away from Jake because it made her throat tighten and tears threaten. Her mom was in that same category. The only positive part was that it reassured her that her decision to stay and figure things out with Jake, with making a life for herself in Cedar Springs, had been the right one. Confronted with the reality of losing him had been as terrifying and gut wrenching as the prospect of losing her own mother. It definitely clarified any doubts she might have had.

Which was only a good thing if she managed to pull this off and keep Melissa from thinking too much or scraping enough of her sanity back together to realize she couldn't trust Lauren as far as she could toss her. Something Lauren might unfortunately learn about up close depending on how Melissa actually intended to drop her off.

She had to figure out what to do when she was abandoned out there. It was late by now and she doubted a little airport like Holden ran flights all night long. Would Melissa trust her to leave her there until someone showed up in the morning? Or, worse, would she insist on keeping Lauren trapped in the car with her until then? Lauren felt like she was holding it together fairly well, all things considered, but she wasn't sure how much longer she could keep it together. Her nerves were shot; her head was splitting; her body was starting to feel like it had been the target in a batting cage. At this point, she could only focus on getting away from Melissa. The rest would work itself out. Somehow.

She must have dozed off, which was alarming in and of itself since she didn't remember dropping off, but the vehicle coming to a stop woke her up. "Where . . ." was all she managed to croak. Her head was still throbbing, but it wasn't the clanging chaos it had been before. Any relief was welcomed at this point. Her body ached, from the accident, from having her wrists bound in an awkward position, and from sitting in this SUV for who knew how long. But the rest had helped a little. She didn't feel quite as groggy and out of it.

Lauren squinted her eyes open and immediately shut them as overhead parking lot lights cast a bright blue glow into the interior of the car. But she'd seen enough in that brief glimpse to know they were at Holden.

"I'm going to check on flights."

"No," Lauren blurted, then dipped her chin as the pain in her head throbbed anew. "What I mean is, right now no one can connect you with me." She felt slightly pumped by the return of her ability to speak in full sentences without wincing. "My Jeep—"

"Jake's Jeep," Melissa corrected somewhat acidly, though she seemed distracted, probably trying to sort out how to handle the next part.

Lauren hoped she could take advantage of that. "They'll find the Jeep. Know I was in an accident. I had all my stuff packed—"

"I know; it's in the back; I grabbed it." She slid a disgusted look at Lauren. "Shacking up already? You just met him, what—"

"No one knew I'd packed," Lauren said, opting not to respond to that. Melissa was in some sort of committed situation with Arlen, but she was clearly pissed about Lauren being with Jake. And to think Lauren had thought everyone in Cedar Springs was so perky and happy. "If I go solo, I can come up with any story about why I left. I can play on the problems with my mom. Let me go in, go into the bathroom and clean up, then I'll get the next flight to Denver. If I look a little rough—"

Melissa snorted and Lauren tensed her jaw.

"All I'm saying is, they'll find my Jeep. They'll know I was in an accident, so reports about me looking like I do won't be a surprise if and when they follow up on my flying home in the middle of the night."

Melissa drummed her fingers on the wheel, still clutching the gun in her other hand, which she was tapping nervously against her thigh.

Lauren kept her gaze, at least peripherally, on both actions. Her captor was agitated, definitely not in command of her emotions and struggling to think things through clearly. Not much different from how Lauren was feeling at the moment, actually. "Untie me so I can go in. I'll get my bags, walk in there, and you'll never have to see me again."

"How can I be sure you're not going to call anyone? What guarantee do I have that you won't screw me over?"

"How can I be sure you won't hurt my mother? That you have enough clout with Arlen to make sure he doesn't hurt her?

You're counting on my help with the election. An election in which he has other supporters and benefactors. I'm counting on my mother staying alive. And my only security there is doing what I can to keep you and Arlen happy. I think I have the bigger stakes here. I'm not going to take chances, especially given your account of Arlen's past actions." Lauren really didn't want to think about that at the moment. If she let her mind go down that path before she extricated herself from this situation, she'd lose any hope of pulling it off.

Melissa tapped faster and jiggled the gun, making Lauren supremely nervous. She felt her phone buzz again in her side pocket, currently trapped beneath her wrist, which was pinned by the lap part of the seat belt. She tried to shift slightly to press whatever part of the face of the phone against the stiff surface of the strap, but had no idea if she was accomplishing anything.

"I don't want you sitting in there all night. Too much time. Things could happen." She was talking more to herself at this point.

"I could rent a car then. Be on the road to Denver." She knew it was about a four-hour drive, give or take. "You'd be back in Cedar Springs well before I leave the state, so that would help cover your tracks."

She seemed to think about that. "I want you to contact me, tell me when you're leaving. Your flight numbers. I can check that."

Lauren didn't bother to tell her that a flight number wouldn't necessarily mean she'd bought a ticket on that flight. "That would link us. My call to you."

"I'm his secretary. I could just say that you tried to reach them and couldn't, to let them know you'd left, so you left a message with me."

Lauren didn't have a response for that. Still, she could figure out a flight number. Could probably get them to find that information right inside the Holden hangar. There may not be any flights, but the lights were on inside and there were cars parked in various slots. Someone was working. And she had every intention of renting a car. How the hell else was she going to get back to Cedar Springs? She just had to make sure that Melissa didn't decide to hang back and follow her. Maybe she'd head toward Denver, then when she was sure she wasn't being followed, duck over somewhere and hide out for a few hours before heading back. To make certain she didn't come across Melissa at any point. There were very few roads that connected anything to anywhere out there, so there wasn't going to be much, if any, room for subterfuge.

"Okay," Lauren said. "I'll call you with the flight information."

"Then I want a phone call, from a Washington-based land line, when you get in. Proof that you're back on the East Coast."

Well, that made things a little trickier. So, her time frame was going to be a bit tighter. Worst case is she could conference call Daphne, have her patch a call through back to Cedar Springs. Or just get Daphne to pretend to be Lauren, with a fuzzy connection. Or something. She'd worry about that part later.

Then Melissa abruptly slid the gun between her thighs and leaned over to untape Lauren's wrists. Lauren desperately wished she was like some super cool movie heroine who could masterfully head butt her captor, then take her in a quick, decisive battle for control. But one head butt was likely to land her in a coma. At least that's what it felt like. And Melissa was a lot closer to the firepower than Lauren was.

So she sat still—very still—while Melissa used a penknife to free her wrists. As soon as they were free, Melissa snatched the gun again and waved it an inch from Lauren's nose.

If Lauren thought she'd tasted fear already, she'd been pathetically wrong. The bile rose so swiftly she had to fight the nausea and pray she didn't puke right there in the truck.

"Straight in, clean up, rent a car, straight out. I'm going to be sitting right here. If you take too long, I'm going to come in, and damn the consequences." She shoved the muzzle of the gun against Lauren's temple.

Lauren could feel it vibrate against her skin, proving how badly Melissa was shaking. That was not a good combination. "Okay."

"I'm keeping your bags out here. And your phone." She leaned back, the gun still trained on Lauren. "Put it on the center console."

"I need that back," Lauren warned her. "All my contact info is in there. Private numbers. Potentially big donors. If Arlen wants my help, then I have to have that phone." She saw a considering look enter Melissa's expression. "Those numbers and names won't mean anything to you. And they won't give you the same attention they'll give to me. I have to keep the phone."

"Fine. Just as soon as you come out with a set of rental keys."

Lauren groaned silently, but nodded. She'd just have to contact Jake . . . and her mother, as soon as she was on the road. And somewhere where there was cell reception. She flexed her wrists and felt tears sting her eyes as the blood rushed back into her fingertips.

"Phone," Melissa barked, smacking the top of the console that separated the backs of their seats.

Lauren slid off her seat belt and fished her phone out of her pocket. The screen was dark, and there was no way of secretly checking her call history to see if she'd been successful in "answering" any of the calls. "Here," she said, laying it between them.

She could always make a call from inside the airport building.

"Ten minutes. Any longer, I'll be coming in after you." She waved the gun. "Don't test me."

Lauren's hands were shaking as she reached for the door handle. Was she actually going to walk away from this? *Don't get ahead of yourself.*

"Ten minutes."

Lauren nodded and slid out of the truck. Her knees buckled the second she put her weight on them, but it was more due to the overwhelming, almost crippling wave of emotion that coursed through her than her actual physical condition. In fact, she didn't think she was as bad off as she'd initially thought, injury-wise. It mostly felt like her head and chest. But once she got her sea legs under her, she realized the rest of her felt mostly okay. She ached everywhere, but that might have been as much the lock-jaw tension she'd been under the past several hours than the accident. That tension didn't leave her as she walked directly, if not exactly confidently yet, toward the hangar. She wasn't bobbing and weaving, so there was that.

She tried to force her thoughts to what best to do next, how to handle those ten minutes to the very best of her ability, but all she could think about, all she could feel, was that big-ass gun aimed directly at her back. She felt it as keenly as if it had laser traction. Her thoughts didn't free up until she stepped into the building and had the door shut behind her. She immediately stepped to one side, to have a solid wall at her back.

She glanced at the bathroom and thought how ironic it was that she couldn't seem to enter this airport looking like anything other than roadkill. Only this time that description was a little too close to reality to be all that amusing. She dismissed the cleaning-up part of the deal. No time to waste and she frankly didn't care how scary she looked. These people here probably knew Jake. Someone here knew Jake. She just had to find that person and make them listen to what she had to say.

But the moment she started toward the desk, another man came sprinting across the small waiting area.

"Lauren Matthews?" he asked, looking at her then beyond her as if expecting to see someone else. "Are you alone?"

"Not really. Who are you?"

The young Hispanic man grinned, showing off an impressive set of very white teeth. "I am Xavier. And I am very, very happy to see you."

It was one too many things to process. Was this a trap? Should she run? But her instincts were apparently still too shaken up to inform her, because all she could do was stand there and stare at the man. "Why?" It wasn't, perhaps, the most lucid question, but it seemed the best way to figure out what side he was on.

"You borrowed my truck. When you flew in. I work here. I am a friend of Jake's."

Xavier. She wasn't sure she'd caught his name the first time, but she'd been a little discombobulated having just met Jake. Wow, she thought a bit abstractedly, that seemed like a long, long time ago at that moment. So much had happened since then. But the little ache that sprang alive inside of her told her all she needed to know about what she wanted where Jake McKenna was concerned. "How did you—" She wasn't sure anymore what was going on. "Is he—did you speak to him?"

Xavier nodded, then looked beyond her again. "We need to get out of here. Come, follow me."

Lauren looked back now, too. Half expecting to see Melissa come through the doors, guns blazing. "I—I'm not sure that's a good idea."

"Who is out there?"

"She has a gun," was all Lauren said. "A big one. I have ten minutes to rent a car. She has my phone. And all my stuff."

"I have a phone. Jake is flying in. He'll be here any minute."

Lauren just stared at him. Had he really just said— "Flying in? Now?" How had he known? It was one too many things to figure out.

"He called," Xavier said, looking more than a little anxious now. "Told me you were in trouble, that you might come here. I've been looking out for you. Come, we have to go."

"Where?"

He took Lauren's arm and she didn't fight him, but she looked over her shoulder the entire time that she half-walked, half-tripped along behind him.

"You okay?" he called back to her. "You don't look so good."

"I'm . . ." She didn't try to finish the thought. It was taking massive effort just to concentrate on keeping up with him and trying to figure out what to do next. "Accident," she said. "I'm fine."

She was huffing a little, and her vision was a tiny bit blurred, her head swimming a little as they pushed through another set of doors and found themselves back outside again. She looked back one last time, but most of her view of the interior of the airport lounge was blocked now. She had no idea where Melissa was. She swung her gaze around, then closed her eyes as her vision swam. She really needed to just sit down. Five minutes. Collect herself, take a quick stock of herself and this quickly changing situation.

"This way," Xavier said, pulling her farther away from the main building.

Lauren wasn't sure if she should just blindly follow the guy, but he didn't have a gun. Which, at the moment, made him one of the good guys.

She heard a whine and a rumble. Xavier slowed and pulled her closer to the side of the hangar building they had just gotten to. "Sounds like he's coming in."

Jake? Here? Could it be true? She felt both intense relief and heightened fear. She didn't need him anywhere in the vicinity of Melissa and her big gun. "Where is the—"

Xavier turned her just then and she saw the lit runway and the lights flashing up in the sky, just beyond the end of it. *Jake*.

She was keenly aware that her ten minutes were close to expiring. And anyone with eyes could tell Melissa what direction the crazy, banged-up woman had gone. She felt like any second it was all going to go terribly wrong. Jake landing, Melissa and her gun out there somewhere, Xavier with his hopeful, happy face, glad to play Good Samaritan. It was all too surreal . . . and too terrifyingly real.

"Just get on the ground," she murmured under her breath. "Can we get any closer to where he's going to end up? How soon can we take off again?" Once she was in the air, away from crazy Melissa, then she could breathe, then she'd be able to think straight.

"Not right away, but it's okay, he'll make things okay. Jake is good at fixing things."

Can he make us all bulletproof, she wanted to say, but forced her thoughts in a more positive direction. With another quick glance over her shoulder, she urged Xavier to keep moving.

They rounded the front of one of the hangars just as the small plane touched down.

"This way," Xavier said. "He'll come to find me as soon as he taxis over."

Lauren saw Jake's plane rolling toward another hangar about three down from where they were and picked up her pace until she left Xavier behind. She was running now, wanting nothing more than for that door to open and to see him step out of the hatch, but all she could think was "Melissa-gun, Melissa-gun," and wanted him out of harm's way as fast as was possible.

She had no idea how far behind her Xavier was now. Her gaze was fixed on that door. The plane had rolled to a stop long before she got there, and the hatch was opening just as she half-stumbled, half-ran across the final stretch of tarmac. The stairs took a lifetime and a half to lower, but when they did, she was already on the steps when Jake appeared in the open doorway.

"Oh, thank God," he said, and a split second later, she was pulled tightly into his arms.

And that was when she burst into tears.

"I don't know why I'm crying," she said, her face muffled against his chest. "I was fine. Handling it. Under control."

Jake hugged her tightly. "I know you did. What happened? What in the hell happened?" He leaned back just enough to tip her face up to his. "Oh, baby, who did this?"

"That bad?" she asked.

"You're the most beautiful thing I've ever seen," he said, so heartfelt it made her tear up all over again. "Whoever hurt you is going to feel the wrath of hell—"

"It's Melissa, Jake. It's—a long story." Reality came crashing back in and she struggled in his arms until she could look behind her, across the tarmac, toward the airport buildings.

Xavier was standing by the open hangar door, waving. Jake

lifted a hand in a salute back at him. "Melissa," he said, not sounding entirely shocked. "Why the hell is she doing this?"

"We can't be standing here like this, Jake," Lauren said, the tension springing right back and making her feel sick all over again. "She'll come after me. She has a gun, Jake." She shuddered involuntarily. "A really big gun."

Jake pulled her up the last step and they ducked down into the body of the plane.

"When can we take off? When can we leave? We shouldn't just sit here like this. How in the world did you know where I was?"

He sat and pulled her down into his lap, stroking her hair. "Your phone. Ruby Jean and I alternated calling every other minute and at some point, your line opened up. I overheard you talking. I didn't know who it was. Did she run the Jeep off the road?"

"Jake, I want to tell you everything, but we really need to get out of here." Her heart was still pounding so hard it made it hard to breathe, to think. She wanted them as far away from crazy Melissa and her lethal bullets as she could get."

"We will, we will, but—"

"So, everyone knows? About the Jeep?" She let her chin drop, then raised it again as more reality slammed into her still scrambled brain. "My mother! We have to—"

"She knows about the accident, and I had Ruby Jean call her and tell her I was flying out here. We didn't know much more than that, but she knows, she's fine, she—"

"No, she's in danger, Jake. From Arlen. Melissa said they were just using her, using me now, too, for political gain, but then he was planning to make my mom vanish like he did his two other wives."

"*What?*"

"I know, she's like, totally insane. I don't even know if that's true, but we can't take any chances. I want my mom as far away from Arlen as possible until all this is settled."

"I heard you say your mom was in danger, on the phone. Ruby Jean is getting her away from the house, from Arlen. But . . . you really think that Arlen—"

"I don't know what the hell I think. My head feels like it's split half in two."

"We should get you checked out, we—"

"We need to get the hell out of here and away from Melissa. I can tell you everything I know while we fly back to Cedar Springs. We can fly back, right? I mean, is the school equipped for night landings?"

"Yes, the strip is lit and the guys know I'm coming back. They'll handle what needs handling, but—"

She climbed out of his lap. "I'll feel better when we get in the air."

Jake shifted his weight to the armrest and turned Lauren toward him, rubbing his hands up her arms. "You're safe now. We'll get back to Cedar Springs, call over to the clinic, see who's on call tonight and get you looked at."

"I'll be okay." She touched his face. The past few hours had been so surreal, it was hard to reckon all she'd just been through with where she was now. With Jake, in his plane, safe. Not tied up in the front of a car with some crazy person pointing a gun at her head. "I just need to get away from this, from here, make sure my mother is okay. Jake, this is serious, dead serious; we have to stop them."

"We will. I'll put a call in to O'Hara—he's the police officer who responded to the scene of your accident—"

"I'm so sorry about your Jeep, I never even saw—"

"Shhh," he said, pulling her close, between his legs so he could slide his hands around to her back. "Please. I was terrified, Lauren, when we couldn't find you. Then we found out you'd packed everything and left your room but hadn't checked out. I didn't know what to think or where to look. Scared the ever-loving shit out of me. I couldn't think straight—"

"I was coming to you," she said, feeling immensely warmed by his concern, hating that he'd been put in that position. "I couldn't stay in that room. It was giving me the creeps that someone had been there. That someone was Melissa, by the way."

Jake stood and they crouched a little inside the small confines of the plane as he pulled her into his arms. "I thought I'd lost you," he said, his gaze boring into hers. "I've never felt so—the thought of losing you—"

"You didn't," she said. "And I'm not going anywhere." She framed his face with her hands and told him the one thing she was absolutely clear about. "I'm here, Jake. I'm staying here. I'm in. You were right. This is more. And I want it. I want you."

His hands shook as he covered hers with his own, then pulled her into his arms and kissed her like a man taking his last breath. She knew just how he felt. Only here, in his arms, in this moment, did the terror subside. But for now, that moment had to end, and it did, all too soon. She pulled from his arms, tugging on his hands. "Come on, get me back home. There's unfinished business. And I'm worried—really worried—about my mom."

"I'll put a call in to RJ. She and your mom should be up at my house. They're okay, Lauren. But we'll call; we'll make sure. You can talk to her."

Lauren finally started to feel like maybe they were really going to turn this around, figure it out, take action. And be safe. "I feel like I'm in the middle of some kind of nightmare."

Jake smiled and gently pulled her bruised face in for another kiss. This one gentler, but no less profound in what it did to her. "We'll get through it together," he murmured, kissing the corners of her mouth, then her lips, so softly, then the corners of her eyes. So reverently, it made her eyes sting with tears.

He pushed the hair from her face. "We're a team, you and me. Nothing is taking us down. We'll take care of our loved ones. It's all going to be okay. Better than okay. We're going to get this resolved, then go back to being bloody amazing."

"Okay," she said, feeling stupidly shaky, but she'd hit the wall. "Can we go home now?"

"Home. I really like the sound of that."

Unfortunately, the sound that immediately followed that pronouncement was the one made by the cocking of a gun.

Chapter 29

Jake immediately pulled Lauren behind him as he spun to face the intruder. "Melissa, hey," he said, striving for conversational ease, but he was having a really hard time getting past the gun she was holding. "Let's talk and get this worked out, okay? Why don't you put the gun down—"

"Why don't you all come down here," a voice called from outside the plane.

Melissa turned, the gun waving dangerously in her hand. Jake started to make his move, but then she said, "Arlen! How did you know—"

"All of you," he said, causing Melissa to frown and Jake to hold off. At least for the moment.

"But . . . I did this for you. For us. Don't be upset with me."

"Now," he repeated, his voice cold and hard. "Don't try my patience."

Jake crouched down to spy out of one of the side porthole windows. Arlen stood on the tarmac, not too far from what appeared to be one of the resort's private helicopters. But Jake was too busy looking at the sleek black gun in Arlen's hand to spend much time wondering who had flown him in on the chopper.

He looked back to Melissa, who had all but forgotten about the two of them. Lauren tugged his hand and jerked her head toward Melissa, clearly thinking the same thing he was. He wasn't sure what value Melissa was to Arlen, but if he could get to her, that was at least one less gun pointed in their direction. He squeezed Lauren's hand back, gave her a brief nod, then started to make his move, only to have Melissa trot on down the stairs in that exact same instant. Dammit.

Jake steered clear of the open doorway, but both he and Lauren crouched down out of direct view but still able to witness the reunion through the side windows. There was no hug, no display of real affection. Melissa stopped a few feet short of Arlen, gun by her side. Arlen's however, was not.

"She was figuring it out," Melissa said. "They had the papers. About the fire. She was never going to stop digging. I just wanted her to go back and leave us alone."

"Hand me the gun, Melissa," Arlen said calmly, coldly.

"But—aren't we going to do something about them? We're a team. I've done everything for you. I even got Lauren to promise to help you with your campaign when she gets back to Washington."

Arlen looked at her, his expression one of barely concealed disgust. "Now, why in the world would she be inclined to do that?"

"So we don't hurt Charlene."

Jake flashed a look at Lauren, whose poor, banged up face had gone pale again. "It's okay," he said quietly to her, even though, at that moment, things were far from okay. Every time Arlen or Melissa spoke, he had more questions and fewer answers.

"Why in the hell would I hurt Charlene?"

Melissa looked incredulous. "Because that's the only way—"

She didn't get a chance to finish her statement. Arlen reached out, snagged her elbow, and bodily yanked her next to his side. He didn't threaten her directly with the gun, but he was holding her quite close, too close to hear what was being said unfortunately. But from the steely cold look in Arlen's eyes, to the almost bug-eyed fear that was on Melissa's, he didn't imagine it was a welcome home, honey kind of thing.

When he was finished with his short, but apparently very effective, lecture, he took Melissa's gun and directed her to stand off to one side. Then he looked back at the plane. "I ask the both of you to exit the plane now, if you would. There has been a terrible misunderstanding. I'm certain we can work everything out." He lowered both hands, each holding a gun. "She's of no harm to you, Lauren. And Jake, neither Lauren nor her mother are in any kind of jeopardy from me."

"You'll have to excuse me, Arlen," Jake called out, "if I don't take your word for that. You're still packing some serious firepower there. Put the guns down, and we might be able to have a conversation. Lauren has been terrorized for the past several hours by your less-than-stable secretary. You both have a lot to answer for. I'm—we're—more than willing to have a discussion, but it will have to take place back in Cedar Springs. Lauren needs her injuries attended to. So, if you'll be so kind as to back away from the plane, we'll be leaving now."

Arlen lifted the guns. "Perhaps I didn't make myself clear. I can't allow these misunderstandings to compound themselves. We need to come to an understanding here and now. If you don't mind."

Jake turned to Lauren. "I want you to get in the far seat there," he said, nodding to the seat behind her. "Strap in. I'm going to work my way closer to the hatch—"

"Jake—"

"—and try to crank the stairs up. If I can't do that, then we'll have to create some kind of diversion so I can get to the cockpit and get this bird moving."

"With the stairs down?"

"We don't have to take off, we just have to move. In a game of chicken, Arlen and Melissa are going to lose."

"But what if they start shooting? What will keep him from just running toward the stairs and boarding?"

Jake could see she was holding it together at this point with a slim thread, and he couldn't blame her. He had no idea what had gone on the past several hours, but none of it had been good, that much he knew. He banked the fury that had been simmering since he'd discovered who her captor was. Just looking at Lauren, normally so direct and in control, looking so beaten and scared . . . it made him want to do more than play chicken with a Cessna. "We're going to get out of here."

Lauren nodded but didn't immediately move to take a seat. Jake started to move closer to the door.

"I'm losing my patience here, Mr. McKenna," Arlen said.

"Wait," Lauren whispered. "I'll distract them; you get into the cockpit and start this baby up while I crank up the stairs. Just show me where the thingie is and how to pull them up."

"The thingie? Lauren, we can't risk—"

"I'm risking everything here tonight. My own safety and those of the people I care most for. My mother." She captured his face in her hands. "And you. I can't stand that you're in this, that you're in danger, because of me."

"We're in this together," he told her, never more serious.

"Then prepare to run to the cockpit. On the count of three."

"Lauren, wait, what are you—"

She pushed past him and moved directly into their line of vision—and target range. She motioned behind her back for him to move past her into the cockpit. "Arlen, I have no idea what has been going on. I assure you, my concern was, and is, only for the well-being of my mother. Melissa has some sort of delusional fixation on you. I get that; you get that. But I need to get back to Cedar Springs. We'll talk there."

Jake smacked the wheel next to the door and dove for the cockpit. Lauren immediately stepped clear of the door and began cranking it.

"He's coming at us," Lauren called as Jake rapidly went through the steps necessary to start the engines. He desperately wanted to look over his shoulder, but they hadn't a second to spare if they wanted to pull this off. He couldn't believe how strong Lauren was, how mentally tough. Well, that wasn't true. He knew she was tough, but this . . . He did look over his shoulder then, in a quick glance, and saw her cranking the wheel with all her might to pull those stairs up, and allowed himself a brief smile. That was his woman, right there.

"He's getting closer and the damn stairs are only a few feet up—"

"Hold it right there!" came yet another voice—a woman's voice—from somewhere beyond Arlen. This was followed, not by the sound of a gun being cocked . . . but by a shotgun being ratcheted into firing position.

Lauren's hands froze momentarily on the wheel as Jake spun around to see what was going on now.

"Mom?" Lauren said, a moment later.

"I have no idea how to use this thing," Charlene yelled, "so that makes me plenty dangerous."

"I do." Ruby Jean stepped forward, took the hunting rifle from Charlene's hands, and quite capably shouldered it. "You might want to drop the firepower, Mayor. And, by the way, I quit."

Jake abandoned his seat and moved quickly to lower the steps again as Arlen shoved one gun into his pocket, grabbed Melissa by the hair, and pulled her in front of him, arm around her throat, pushing the other gun against her temple. "Not so quickly there, Ms. McKenna."

"This is so not good," Jake murmured.

"How in the hell did they get here?" Lauren asked.

"I'm not the only one in the family who can fly a plane," Jake said, looking at his sister with a mixture of pride and abject terror. Now the whole family was in the line of fire. Great. Just great.

"The police have been summoned, Arlen," Charlene informed him. "Sergeant O'Hara contacted the Holden office before we took off. They'll be here any moment. In fact—"

Just then sirens sounded in the distance. Ruby Jean stepped forward and Jake's heart leaped in his throat.

"Seriously. Put the gun down," RJ demanded. "Both of them.

You're outnumbered. And, frankly, at this particular moment, given what she did to Lauren, none of us will be too heartbroken if you put a bullet in Melissa's head."

"RJ—" he warned, just as Lauren said, "Maybe not a bullet, but if he roughs her up a little . . ." She looked at Jake and he knew right then he was never letting her go. "I'm just saying."

"Marry me," he said.

She smiled at him as the police cars rolled in. He didn't know how big the department was in Holden, but it looked like they'd sent pretty much the entire force. Police swarmed; guns were put down. Arlen's hands went up in the air, and Melissa tried to claim she was a victim. Ruby Jean handed over the shotgun, and she and Charlene made sure Melissa was taken into custody, as well.

Jake turned back to Lauren. "Not exactly the way I'd intended to propose."

Her eyes widened a little. "You intended to propose?"

"Eventually. When you'd gotten used to the idea of me being around forever."

"I might be able to get used to that."

Ruby Jean and Charlene stormed up the stairs just then and everything became a series of hugs, kisses, apologies, and revelations. The whole story came out later at the Holden police station. Not from Arlen, who'd called for his lawyer immediately and been close-mouthed since. Charlene contacted hers, too. To seek an annulment. Ruby Jean, Lauren, and Jake provided what little they knew. Melissa filled in most of the gaps, when she wasn't alternately screaming invectives at Arlen and sobbing to the police about how horribly she'd been used.

"And to think, I used to avoid family drama," Jake said as he and Lauren were dropped off, close to daybreak, back at the airstrip. Ruby Jean and Charlene were flying back in the other school plane. They weren't really sure, as yet, what parts of Melissa's claims were true, and what might be part of the delusional fantasy she'd constructed about her future life together with Arlen.

Whether or not Arlen had actually had a hand in his first wife's death or his apparent ex-wife's disappearance—Melissa had tried to hunt her down only to discover she didn't apparently still exist—one thing had emerged from his personal secretary's furious rants, and that was that Arlen had made a career out of choosing women for his own personal gain. Which generally translated into political gain, as that was how he gauged himself as a success. According to Melissa, he'd targeted Charlene the moment he'd met her in Florida, quite pleased when everything had fallen in line so swiftly. Lauren had been a side benefit he'd been happy to exploit, as well.

Arlen wasn't corroborating any of that, of course; that would take months in court and some very expensive lawyers to sort out. But Melissa had known enough damning facts and truths from how he'd initially romanced Charlene that Charlene could corroborate, to make it pretty clear she at least had that much correct.

Charlene and Lauren had spent a long time sequestered in a room alone together at the police station, talking and coming to terms with what had happened. Jake didn't know what exactly had been said, but when they emerged, the two were holding each other tightly and were very clearly a united front.

Jake reached across the space between the pilot's and copilot's seats, taking Lauren's hand before revving up the engines, when it would be harder to talk. She'd cleaned up a little at the police station, more than a little alarmed upon first seeing herself and just how banged up she was. Jake still thought she was the most beautiful thing he'd ever seen.

"So . . . you give my heart-stoppingly romantic proposal any additional thought?" he asked. "Given as how we've had so much free time to consider it." He'd been teasing, trying to lighten the bit of despondency he sensed after she and Charlene parted so RJ would have someone with her on the flight back. Lauren hated that her mom was suffering from the pain of betrayal. She was humiliated and embarrassed, too, and it would take some time before she worked her way through that, but

Jake had promised Lauren they'd all be there for her. He suspected with the way the town had taken to Charlene, they'd be behind her, too, especially once the whole story came out. If it hadn't already reached home already.

"Actually," Lauren responded quite seriously, though she was smiling that crooked smile while she said it, "thinking about that proposal—and it was very romantic to me, by the way—is what's getting me through this endlessly long night. Morning," she added, noting that the sun was starting to come up.

"Lauren, don't feel you have to—"

She leaned over and grabbed his sleeve, pulling him toward her for a kiss. Even despite the burn marks on her face from the air bag explosion, and the rapidly discoloring contusion on her temple, she kissed him passionately and fully, pouring more into that single connection than he'd felt from her ever before. Which was saying a hell of a damn lot.

"I am feeling so many things right now, and it's going to take a long while for all of us to sort through this." She framed his face with her hand. "But one thing I'm very, very clear on, is that I want to be beside you while I figure it out. So . . . if you'll have me, dramatic family issues, no future prospects, and looking like roadkill, then I want a shot at being with you, too. How we do it, I don't care. However long it takes for us to take whatever the next steps are . . . I want to figure all of that out with you."

Jake's smile was so wide it hurt. But nothing had ever felt as good as what he saw in Lauren's eyes. "You're it for me," he said.

She grinned. "Sometimes you just know."

Then she shifted back to her seat and put her headphones on as she studied the console in front of her. "Okay, so . . . tell me, what do these buttons do?"

Jake frowned. "Maybe we should save the lessons for another time."

"As long as I get lessons."

He grinned, then. "I might be able to work out a special package deal rate."

"What would that package deal include?"

"A lot of hands-on instruction."

"Mmm," she said, strapping herself in as he began to taxi down the runway. "I always do much better with showing instead of telling."

"Hold on," Jake said, grinning, watching as Ruby Jean took off in front of them while he taxied into position. "We're about to embark on one hell of a ride."

Epilogue

"I can't even look." Charlene covered her eyes as Ruby Jean stepped out on the wing.

"Holy mother of—" Lauren couldn't even finish the sentence. Mostly because her heart was lodged squarely in her throat. "I know she used to do this, but holy heaven, I never really imagined . . ." She closed her eyes, then opened them again, fixated on Ruby Jean's flight suit–clad figure, performing a little routine on the wing of the ancient-looking biplane, like she was dancing down the sidewalk. "In a million years, and for a million dollars, you could never make me do that."

Lauren was very proud of herself for how well she was doing with her flight lessons. But there were never going to be any wing-walking lessons. Not in this lifetime.

Her mother turned to her only after Ruby Jean had completed the stunt and was safely back in the plane. The crowds cheered and roared as the pilot continued on with the air show. Lauren had thought watching Jake race *Betty Sue* in the preliminary heats had been terrifying enough.

"I'm not sure I'm going to make it through this," she told her mother.

"Of course you are," Charlene responded, taking Lauren's arm as they wove their way through the throngs that had amassed for the air race in Reno. "Someone has to revive me when I faint dead away, and I want that someone to be you."

"Oh, well, then. When you put it like that."

"Snow cones. We need snow cones."

"I'll buy," Lauren said as they pushed their way toward the string of vendors. They had a little over an hour before heading over to the field where Jake would race in the final, championship heat. It was a perfect day, with a brilliant blue sky, the temperature a comfortable seventy-five. Lauren and Charlene had passes that allowed them over where *Betty Sue* was being maintained. Paddy's crew, as she'd come to affectionately think of them, along with the pit crew working the race, and occasionally Roger and his gang, were all there in between races and events.

They started to head that way, nibbling at the sweet crushed ice. "I was kind of surprised when Ruby Jean said she wanted to go back to working air shows," Lauren said. "But she's clearly a natural up there." She looked at her mother. "Have you given any more thought to the town council's proposition?"

It had been just shy of two months since the big showdown with Arlen and Melissa. Things hadn't progressed that far with their respective trials, as both were pleading not guilty, so it was going to drag out. But the townspeople had been far more swiftly decisive, almost universally condemning both Arlen and Melissa for their alleged activities. Well, some more alleged than others. Charlene had been welcomed back with open arms and, by proxy, so had Lauren. Those arms only spread more widely when she announced she was staying.

The town had been united when it came to Charlene, whom they'd circled around like soldiers protecting their fort. With Charlene solidly on the inside of that circle. The town wanted to find someone to run for mayor to replace Arlen. The wanted to reunify everyone and get the town back on a positive, forward-thinking track, which was a challenge given the scandal was the biggest thing to ever hit their small resort town. To that end, they'd approached Charlene about running to fill her soon-to-be-annulled husband's now vacant office. It had been a tremendous vote of support and respect, which both Lauren and Charlene had been vocally thankful for. To embrace them both was one thing, but to accept them so fully was as humbling as it was heartening.

"I am," Charlene said, "but . . ."

Lauren paused a few dozen yards shy of joining the *Betty Sue* crew and pulled her mother to one side. "Mom, please don't feel you have to say yes just because they were generous enough to ask. It's very, very flattering, but it's not a good reason to take a job like this if you don't really want it."

"I don't think I do," Charlene said, finally speaking out loud what Lauren had felt from her all along.

"Then don't. They'll be disappointed, but they'll accept your decision."

"I have found my home in Cedar Springs. That's not going to change." Though her address had. She'd spent a little time looking, then had paid for a small but beautiful cabin-style home, much like Jake's, on the opposite side of town. It was perched up in the hills with a view that was beyond spectacular. She was happy, if still smarting from the dissolution of her marriage. Her friends and former acquaintances had been far more supportive and less judgmental than she'd feared. Of course, being two thousand miles away didn't hurt. And Charlene had discovered that what mattered to her in her old life didn't amount to as much in the new one. It had helped her move far more swiftly through the healing process . . . and, Lauren thought, had been a significant part of why she'd so clearly won over the citizens of Cedar Springs.

"However," Charlene said, covering Lauren's hand with her own. "I think perhaps you should consider running."

Lauren stopped, turned. "What? Me? For mayor?" She laughed. "No. I'd run your campaign, and do my best to run your office if you decided to give it a shot, but you know I'm a behind the scenes type."

Charlene laughed and shook her head. "All this personal growth and you still can't see the forest." She tossed her empty snow cone cup in the trash can, then walked up to Lauren and cupped her face with both hands. "You were miserable behind the scenes. You always felt hamstrung on making any real progress. And, yes, Washington can be a very cynic-inducing, jaded-viewpoint world. Cedar Springs isn't like that. Sure, you have the resort and all of the very real concerns that come with balancing such a huge elephant in the room with the needs of the local, everyday citizen. But, Lauren, you could make a difference here. See, feel, touch, and be a part of the successes you create. For you, and for them. I think they'd be damn lucky to have you. And if they're as savvy as I think they are, they'll jump at the chance." She smiled and leaned up to kiss her daughter on the cheek. "I'd even be your right-hand man. Or woman, as the case may be."

Lauren stood there, speechless. She'd never even considered it. She'd spent the past month relocating her life from Washington to Cedar Springs. She'd intended to be smart, invest in her own place, allow things to move along slowly with Jake . . . but after a few weeks where they both acknowledged that where they wanted Lauren to be was under the same roof, preferably Jake's roof . . . so they'd just gone with what worked.

Sometimes, you just knew.

And it had been spectacularly good so far.

"What do you think Jake will say?"

"About what?"

She whirled around to find him right behind her, looking ridiculously sexy in his flight suit and pilot-style sunglasses. "Mom thinks I should run for mayor. Please tell her—"

Jake picked her up and spun her around. "About time you figured that out. Half the town council has been chomping at the bit, waiting for Charlene to politely decline—sorry, Charlene," he said to her, "—but everyone knows you don't want the job." He looked back to Lauren. "They'll go for it, for you." He kissed her hard on the mouth, then the nose. Put her down, then picked her up and spun her around again. "Are you going to go for it?"

Lauren laughed, completely at a loss on how to handle this

sudden turn of events. "I—I don't know. I guess I have to think about it."

He put her down and winked at Charlene. "She's going to be great."

Charlene beamed proudly. "I know it."

"The race," Lauren said. "The finals are less than—" she looked at her watch and blanched. "Shouldn't you be over there doing . . . whatever it is you have to do?"

"I am heading that way. Did you see RJ? I told you she was a natural."

"My stomach is still in my throat, which is convenient since that's where it's going to be as soon as you take off in that death rocket. Thank God you don't do this routinely," she said.

"No closing your eyes. We're taking the trophy today and I want you right there with me when they hand it over."

She smiled. "I'm pretty sure that's going to be Roger's spot."

"You can be on my other side." He bussed her cheek. "I have to run."

"Okay." She kissed and let him go.

Only to have him turn back and pull her into his arms and lay a kiss on her that drew whistles and more than a few cat calls. She blushed but discovered she didn't mind it in the least. "You know, if I decide to run for mayor, you can't do things like that in public."

"Really?" He grinned and tossed her a salute as he started trotting over to his crew, who were now calling for him. "Watch me!" he called back, then disappeared into the throng.

Lauren wasn't sure if he meant the race . . . or her future public life. And decided she didn't care. She and her mother met up with Ruby Jean, then went and watched Jake McKenna bring home the trophy in a heart-stopping race that was as exhilarating as it was terrifying to watch.

And at the press conference afterward, where the trophy was presented . . . it was Lauren who pulled him into her arms and laid one on him. Much to the delight of the gathered press corps . . . and everyone back in Cedar Springs, who enjoyed the snapshot of that kiss—with Jake clutching the trophy—when it graced the front page of their newspaper the following Sunday.

Two Sundays later, the front page declared Lauren had officially tossed her hat in the ring.

And two months of Sundays after that . . . showed a picture of an entirely different ring. The one gracing the left hand of their soon-to-be newly elected mayor and her new husband.

She was wearing a flight suit at the time, one that matched her husband's, which was appropriate given they celebrated their vows by Lauren taking her first solo takeoff just after the I dos were swapped.

She then proceeded to fly them to a destination known only to the brand-new pilot. She'd been thrilled to pull off such a well-held secret.

And Jake made sure he showed his appreciation to his new wife for her ingenuity and confident flying prowess with some ingenious prowess of his own. "Fly me," he challenged, laughing as he stripped off her jumpsuit and pulled her down on the wide sea of bed . . . barely hearing the waves crashing on the shore of their own private island getaway.

She grinned. Rolled him over on his back. And did just that.

Try Dianne Castell's newest book, HOT AND IRRESISTIBLE, in stores now from Brava . . .

"Who the hell was that?" McCabe said from behind her. "And this day just keeps getting better and better." Bebe turned to face Donovan. "Dara's none of your business, so forget her."

"Dara who?" He had his cop stare firmly in place. She hated being on the receiving end of cop stares, because it meant the cop wasn't budging till he got an answer.

"Dara is my mother-of-the-year. Make that stepmother. There, now you know. Happy? And what are you doing here anyway? Thought we were meeting at the station?"

Donovan's eyes widened and he let out a soft whistle, his gaze on Dara retreating down the street. "How the hell did that happen?"

"You're not letting this go, are you?"

"What do you think?"

"I think you're a pain in the ass." But the crack wasn't as sarcastic as she intended because he wasn't all pain and he certainly had a nice ass. And right now he was all yummy with his black hair damp from a recent shower and a soft navy shirt and worn jeans hugging lean hips. "I'll give you the ten-cent version to shut you up. Best I can figure Dara was paid to take me and, no, I don't know why, and, no, I don't intend to find out because my real parents must be total scum to sell a kid. And, yes, I did change my name and don't you dare go feeling sorry for me because I sure as hell don't need a pity party and now you want to tell me what you're doing on my front stoop at this hour?"

Her gaze met his and she braced herself for the *Oh, you poor thing* look, but instead Donovan bent his head and kissed her. She started to protest, but her lips were busy and suddenly her tongue was, too, and then her arms got into the act and then her insides melted into hot goo, which had acid beat all to hell and back. This kiss was all wrong on every level except one . . . Donovan McCabe felt so darn good when she was feeling crappy as hell.

And don't miss Terri Brisbin's first book for Brava,
A STORM OF PASSION, coming next month!

Whatever the Seer wanted, the Seer got, be it for his comfort or his whim or his pleasure.

She stood staring at the chair on the raised dais at one end of the chamber, the chair where he sat when the visions came. From the expression that filled her green eyes, she knew it as well.

Had she witnessed his power? Had she watched as the magic within him exploded into a vision of what was or what would yet be? As he influenced the high and the mighty of the surrounding lands and clans with the truth of his gift? Walking over to stand behind her, he placed his hands on her shoulders and drew her back to his body.

"I have not seen you before, sweetling," he whispered into her ear. Leaning down, he smoothed the hair from the side of her face with his own and then touched his tongue to the edge of her ear. "What is your name?"

He felt the shivers travel through her as his mouth tickled her ear. Smiling, he bent down and kissed her neck, tracing the muscle there down to her shoulder with the tip of his tongue. Connor bit the spot gently, teasing it with his teeth and soothing it with his tongue. "Your name?" he asked again.

She arched then, clearly enjoying his touch and ready for more. Her head fell back against his shoulder and he moved his mouth to the soft skin there, kissing and licking his way down and back to her ear. Still she had not spoken.

"When I call out my pleasure, sweetling, what name will I speak?"

He released her shoulders and slid his hands down her arms and then over her stomach to hold her in complete contact with him. Covering her stomach and pressing her to him, he rubbed against her back, letting her feel the extent of his erection—hard and large and ready to pleasure her. Connor moved his hands up to take her breasts in his grasp. Rubbing his thumbs over their tips and teasing them to tightness, he no longer asked, he demanded.

"Tell me your name."

He felt her breasts swell in his hands and he tugged now on the distended nipples, enjoying the feel and imagining them in his mouth, as he suckled hard on them and as she screamed out her pleasure. But nothing could have pleased him more in that moment than the way she gasped at each stroke he made, over and over until she moaned out her name to him.

"Moira."

"Moira," he repeated slowly, drawing her name out until it was a wish in the air around them. "Moira," he said again as he untied the laces on her bodice and slid it down her shoulders until he could touch her skin. "Moira," he now moaned as the heat and the scent of her enticed him as much as his own scent was pulling her under his control.

Connor paused for a moment, releasing her long enough to drag his tunic over his head and then turning her into his embrace. He inhaled sharply as her skin touched his, the heat of it seared into his soul as the tightened peaks of her breasts pressed against his chest. Her added height brought her hips level almost to his and he rubbed his hardened cock against her stomach, letting her feel the extent of his arousal.

As he pushed her hair back off her shoulders, he realized that in addition to the raging lust in his blood, there was something else there, teasing him with its presence.

Anticipation.

For the first time in years, this felt like more than the mindless rutting that happened between him and the countless, nameless women there for his needs. For the first time in too long, this was not simply scratching an itch, for the hint of something more seemed to stand off in the distance, something tantalizing and unknown and something somehow tied to this woman.

He lifted her chin with his finger, forcing her gaze off the blasted chair and onto his face. Instead of the compliant gaze that usually met him, the clarity of her gold-flecked green eyes startled him. Connor did something he'd not done before, something he never needed to do—he asked her permission.

"I want you, Moira," he whispered, dipping to touch and taste her lips for the first time. Connor slid his hand down to gather up her skirts, baring her legs and the treasure between them to his touch and his sight. "Let me?"

Be on the lookout for
THE MANE SQUEEZE from Shelly Laurenston,
out now from Brava . . .

The salmon were everywhere, leaping from the water and right into the open maws of bears. But he ruled this piece of territory and those salmon were for him and him alone. He opened his mouth and a ten-pound one leaped right into it. Closing his jaws, he sighed in pleasure. Honey-covered. He loved honey-covered salmon!

This was his perfect world. A cold river, happy-to-die-for-his-survival salmon, and honey. Lots and lots of honey . . .

What could ever be better? What could ever live up to this? Nothing. Absolutely nothing.

A salmon swam up to him. He had no interest, he was still working on the honey-covered one. The salmon stared at him intently . . . almost glaring.

"Hey!" it called out. "Hey! Can you hear me?"

Why was this salmon ruining his meal? He should kill it and save it for later. Or toss it to one of the females with cubs. Anything to get this obviously Philadelphia salmon to shut the hell up!

"Answer me!" the salmon ordered loudly. "Open your eyes and answer me! *Now!*"

His eyes were open, weren't they?

Apparently not because someone pried his lids apart and stared into his face. And wow, was she gorgeous!

"Can you hear me? He didn't answer, he was too busy staring at her. So pretty!

"Come on, Paddington. Answer me."

He instinctively snarled at the nickname and she smiled in relief. "What's the matter?" she teased. "You don't like Paddington? Such a cute, cuddily, widdle bear."

"Nothing's wrong with cute pet names . . . Mr. Mittens."

She straightened, her hands on her hips and those long, expertly manicured nails drumming restlessly against those narrow hips.

"Mister?" she snapped.

"Paddington?" he shot back.

She gave a little snort. "Okay. Fair enough. But call me Gwen. I never did get a chance to tell you my name at the wedding."

Oh! He remembered her now. The feline he'd found himself daydreaming about on more than one occasion in the two months since Jess's wedding. And . . . wow. She was naked. She looked really good naked . . .

He blinked, knowing that he was staring at that beautiful, strong body. *Focus on something else! Anything else! You're going to creep her out!*

"You have tattoos," he blurted. Bracelet tatts surrounded both her biceps. A combination of black shamrocks and a dark-green Chinese symbol he didn't know the meaning of. And on her right hip she had a black Chinese dragon holding a Celtic cross in its mouth. It was beautiful work. Intricate. "Are they new?"

"Nah. I just covered up the ones on my arms with makeup, for the wedding. With my mother, I'd be noticed enough. Didn't want to add to that." She gestured at him with her hand. "Now we know I'm Gwen and I have tattoos . . . so do you have a name?"

"Yeah, sure. I'm . . ." He glanced off, racking his brain.

"You don't remember your name?" she asked, her eyes wide.

"I know it has something to do with security." He stared at her thoughtfully, then snapped his fingers. "Lock."

"Lock? Your name is Lock?"

"I think. Lock. Lock . . . Lachlan! MacRyrie!" He glanced off again. "I think."

"Christ."

"No need to get snippy. It's *my* name I can't remember." He nodded. "I'm pretty positive it's Lock . . . something."

"MacRyrie."

"Okay."

She gave a small, frustrated growl and placed the palms of her hands against her eyes. He stared at her painted nails. "Are those the team colors of the Philadelphia Flyers?"

"Don't start," she snapped.

"Again with the snippy? I was only asking."

Lock slowly pushed himself up a bit, noticing for the first time that they'd traveled to a much more shallow part of the river. The water barely came to his waist. She started to say something, but shook her head and looked away. He didn't mind. He didn't need conversation at the moment, he needed to figure out where he was.

A river, that's where he was. Unfortunately, not his dream river. The one with the honey-covered salmon that willingly leaped into his mouth. A disappointing realization—it always felt so real until he woke up—but he was still happy that he'd survived the fall.

Lock used his arms to push himself up all the way so he could sit.

"Be careful," she finally said. "We fell from up there."

He looked at where she pointed, ignoring how much pain the slight move caused, and flinched when he saw how far down they were.

"Although we were farther up river, I think."

"Damn," he muttered, rubbing the back of his neck.

"How bad is it?"

"It'll be fine." Closing his eyes, Lock bent his head to one side, then the other. The sound of cracking bones echoed and when he opened his eyes, he saw that pretty face cringing.

"See?" he said. "Better already."

"If you say so."

She took several awkward steps back so she could sit down on a large boulder.

"You're hurt," he informed her.

"Yeah. I am." She extended her leg, resting it on a small boulder in front of her and let out a breath, her eyes shutting. "I know it's healing, but, fuck, it hurts."

"Let me see." Lock got to his feet, ignoring the aches and pains he felt throughout his body. By the time he made it over to her, she opened her eyes and blinked wide, leaning back.

"Hey, hey! Get that thing out of my face!"

His cock was right *there*, now wasn't it? He knelt down on one knee in front of her and said, "This is the best I can manage at the moment. I don't exactly have the time to run off and kill an animal for its hide."

"Fine," she muttered. "Just watch where you're swinging that thing. You're liable to break my nose."

Focusing on her leg to keep from appearing way too proud at that statement, he grasped her foot and lifted, keeping his movements slow and his fingers gentle. He didn't allow himself to wince when he saw the damage. It was bad, and she was losing blood. Probably more blood than she realized. "I didn't do this did I?"

"No. I got this from that She-bitch." She leaned over, trying to get a better look. "Do I have any calf muscle left?"

He wasn't going to answer that. At least not honestly. Instead he gave her his best "reassuring" expression and calmly said, "Let's get you to a hospital."

Her body jerked straight and those pretty eyes blinked rapidly. "No."

That wasn't the response he expected. Panic, perhaps. Or, "My

God. Is it that bad?" But instead she said "no." And she said it with some serious finality. In the same way he'd imagine she would respond to the suggestion of cutting off her leg with a steak knife.

"It's not a big deal. But you don't want an infection. I'll take you up the embankment, get us some clothes—" if she didn't pass out from blood loss first "—and then get you to the Macon River Health Center. It's equipped for us."

"No."

"I've had to go there a couple of times. It's really clean, the staff is great, and the doctors are always the best."

"No."

She wasn't being difficult to simply be difficult, was she?

Resting his forearm on his knee, Lock stared at her. "You're not kidding, are you?"

"No."

"Is there a reason you don't want to go to the hospital?" And he really hoped it wasn't something ridiculous like she used to date one of the doctors and didn't want to see him, or something equally as lame.

"Of course there is. People go there to die."

Oh, boy. Ridiculous but hardly lame. "Or . . . people go there to get better."

"No."

"Look, Mr. Mittens—"

"Don't call me that."

"—I'm trying to help you here. So you can do this the easy way, or you can do this the hard way. Your choice."

She shrugged and brought her good foot down right on his nuts.